From the Depths

From the Depths

Based on a True Story

Julie A. Barnes

Writers Club Press
New York San Jose Lincoln Shanghai

From the Depths
Based on a True Story

Writers Club Press
an imprint of iUniverse, Inc.

For information address:
iUniverse, Inc.
5220 S. 16th St., Suite 200
Lincoln, NE 68512
www.iuniverse.com

ISBN: 0-595-12225-6

Printed in the United States of America

For Beatrice Steele, the strongest woman I know
Shae, my angel girl
Noah, my miracle

"Let your father and your mother be glad,
and let her rejoice who gave birth to you."
Proverbs 23:25

The adventure of life is a learning process that often seems without purpose when difficulties continually arise. In childhood we adapt to whatever situation we must, because humans are very resilient in their youth. It is usually not until adulthood that the traumatic events of the past take on significance.

The choice to live in the present is a conscious, on-going decision that few perfect. Without the ability to forgive, it is impossible. Reliving bad experiences intensifies anger, which leads to the destruction of the spirit. The world has not learned to forgive, though history continues to prove that it is necessary for peace.

There is a perfect plan for each of us, although the way may not always be pleasant or clear. Faith is believing in that which we cannot see, as we bravely carry on in this imperfect world.

Everyone has a story to tell. Mine may be shocking because of the spiritual issues, but these incidents are true, as well as most of this story, and can be substantiated. Some names have been changed to protect privacy.

CHAPTER 1

The thin girl finished her after-school snack of saltine crackers and milk, put her cup by the sink and went to find her mother. Usually, Andie's mother was upstairs in her bedroom watching soap operas. Andie could not understand why a person would watch a show filled with arguments. "As sand runs through the hour glass, so do the days of our lives," the theme's slow, baritone words were followed by a crescendo of melancholy music that made her feel as if she had just missed out on a wonderful moment which would never return. Sometimes her mom took a nap, even with the TV blaring loudly.

The pervasive smell of stale cigarette smoke lingered in the spacious bedroom. Andie looked out the window to the backyard, drawn by the expanse of new green framed in the window. It had been a long winter. She was surprised to see her mom standing by the rock garden. Andie had never seen her just strolling around outside, and she felt a burst of excitement at the chance to spend time outdoors with her mother. Hurrying down the stairs, she tried to think of topics that might hold her mom's attention.

The back of her mother's perfect beehive hairdo did not move in the Iowa spring breeze. Andie paused, imagining her mom turning to sweep her up into a big hug, but she could not remember it happening once in her eight years and knew that it would not occur today.

"Hi, Mom. Are you thinking of planting something?" she asked.

"Oh, hi." Her mother's monotone words and expressionless face did not lessen Andie's hope.

She watched as her mother smacked a new pack of Lucky Strike cigarettes against the palm of her left hand, making a snapping sound. Andie had tried to imitate this brisk sound using one of her mom's packs, but had never achieved the succinct, commanding "pop!" Her mother deftly peeled off the seal and extracted a cigarette, her long, red nails brilliant against the white paper.

"I um...I did really well on my spelling test. I got all of them right—even the extra words! Miss Henry told me that the principal wants me to be the first in a special class. I'd be able to go to the library when I finish my work, without even raising my hand, to do independent study. That just means I can choose a subject and do a report on it." Andie took a deep breath and scanned her mother's face for a reaction.

"That's nice." Her mother tried to turn away from the wind, the cigarette clenched tightly between her lips. She cupped a hand around the end of the cigarette, her brow furrowing more severely with each attempt on the lighter. Her grimace intensified as she inhaled, and her face seemed to draw itself in around the cigarette, pulling at it as if for sustenance.

So much care and tending seemed to be required for smoking, Andie thought. The pinched, mad look that her mom's mouth made around the cigarette when she lit it always startled her, no matter how many times she observed it.

A thick cloud of gray filled the air as her mother exhaled her first drag. Andie wondered how she could hold that much smoke in her lungs. Often when her mom was speaking, each word came out on a puff of smoke, and sometimes three whole sentences would be floating in smoke—burned words, Andie thought.

Her mother appeared to be assessing the rock garden, which was nestled in the center of their lush backyard. Last summer, a huge deck had been built on the third floor, creating a wide cover for the colorful patio furniture below. Andie shifted from one foot to the other, the same awkwardnesssetting in whenever her mother was unresponsive. It was something that Andie felt she had to battle, trying to conquer the loaded silence.

"Mom, do you have a green thumb?" she asked, proud to know such an adult expression. She was learning about plants in science class and intended to deliver a compliment about the plants in the house.

"What?" Her mother's face contorted with anger as she turned, the cigarette in her hand veering close to Andie's face. "Don't you ever, ever say that again!" her mother shouted, glaring at her. "Do you hear me? How dare you!" She abruptly strode past Andie, walking briskly into the house.

Andie was stunned. Tears welled up in her eyes as she tried to make sense of the exchange. Obviously her mother thought that "having a green thumb" was something horrible or perverted. Andie wanted a chance to explain that she was referring to plant growing, but knew that the matter was closed. She could not imagine being able to break through the barrier of such emotion.

She sat on one of the large rocks that framed the garden and sighed. Another chance to be with her mother was ruined. Andie scooted over to get away from where the smoke had been. The rough edges of the rocks caused a distant kind of satisfaction as they pressed against the back of her legs.

She crawled behind the group of evergreen trees that bordered the garden. She had spent hours in this fragrant green fortress. Occasionally, she would bury an item that she happened to have—a candy wrapper, a nickel, a button—so that one day after she had forgotten it, she would discover the item and recall the moment when it had been stashed away.

Andie pulled a pink, rectangular eraser from her pocket and with the point of a sharp stone gouged a tiny letter "A" into the smooth surface. The scraped area was a lighter pink. She dropped to her knees and began to dig a hole near the middle tree, enjoying the cool brown earth against the palms of her hands. She carefully placed the eraser in the hole and then slowly covered it up. Smoothing down the loose dirt, she felt that a piece of her was safe for now. Hidden from the element's eroding effects, the eraser would be put out of her mind. She knew that one day she would dig around and see it, relieved to rescue a part of her past, holding it firmly in her hands.

* * *

Andie walked home from her friend's house, thinking about what to eat to tide her over until her parents came home for dinner. The rumbling of her stomach made her walk more quickly. Hunger was so powerful that it was audible! It made her think of her stomach as a baby crying to be fed. She patted it.

She saw her ten-year-old brother, Scott, marching toward her as she entered their yard. His exaggerated movements could only mean one thing—he was as mad as a hornet, and she was about to be attacked. She considered running back to Judy's house because her mother was home, but decided to somehow make her way past Scott into her own house. She could not think of anything that she had done to make him upset, so she continued on her path across the yard.

"Give it back!" he said. "Right now! I told you that you couldn't touch it!" His brown hair, freshly chopped into a butch, made him appear younger. He was tall for his age, but rounded with a doughy plumpness. His thick, black eyebrows accentuated his close-set, dark eyes which had no distinguishable color nor held any peace.

"I don't know what you're talking about," Andie said slowly and carefully. "I haven't touched any of your stuff, Scott." She looked beyond him as if that would end the discussion and walked toward their house.

"I'll give you one minute to get my rifle and give it back to me! I saw you looking at it yesterday, so don't even try to lie!"

A sense of dread caused her to pick up her pace. Yesterday she had merely watched as Scott and his shifty friend, Kirk, walked out of the garage with the new air rifle. Even though she had wanted to test it out, she knew better than to mess with anything of Scott's.

"Maybe Kirk took it yesterday after you went inside. He was still playing with it. I saw him," Andie declared.

When Kirk had spent the night a few weeks ago, her parents had gone out for dinner. Andie had been in the kitchen making a peanut butter and jelly sandwich when Kirk walked in, loose-jointed and lanky, hovering behind her as she finished spreading the jelly. He opened a drawer and pulled out a large knife. At first, Andie thought that he meant to make his own sandwich, so she turned to offer him the loaf of bread. His eyes narrowed and locked on her face as he brought the knife up to her throat, then he laughed as she began blubbering like a baby. He appeared to enjoy watching her mounting fear. She had peed her pants. He dropped the knife onto the counter, snickering as he walked away. All evening she had sat in her room listening for him to come after her again, but he never did. Scott had to see that it must have been Kirk who had misplaced the rifle.

Scott's chubby face moved closer. "Are you calling my friend a thief?" His lips were pressed tightly together, pale around the edges.

He shoved her hard, and she wind-milled her arms to keep from falling backward. He sprang forward, swinging one leg behind her ankles and pushing her again. Andie's head slammed on the ground, and she experienced the familiar sickening feeling of the air being knocked out of her. She tried to cry out, but felt an aching pressure in her chest and stomach.

"You stupid brat! I'll teach you to take my things and lie about it!" He kicked at her back and sides, making grunting sounds and yelling "there" with each connection.

Andie thought that she was going to vomit. The pain in her ribs, especially along her back, was excruciating. As she rolled to avoid the blows, she willed herself to stand and run. She knew that he would not stop kicking her once he had reached this state of rage. It usually happened in the house where she had a better chance to run and lock a door behind her, climbing out of a window if he tried to pick the lock. Once, she had wiggled down the laundry tunnel when he had trapped her in the bathroom, but this year she would be too big to fit through the narrow space. He was selective in choosing the places for his assaults, so that they would not be seen by anyone else. He must have really lost it this time to be doing it in broad daylight right in front of their house.

She was trying to shield her stomach from him as he jumped over her body, and she wondered fleetingly if he would finally kick her in the face. Usually he would not hit her face, because it would leave obvious marks of his abuse. It would be better for him to leave evidence, she knew, so she could prove to her parents that he really did beat her up.

Whenever she tried to explain to them what he did, her father said, “It’s just sibling rivalry. You shouldn’t antagonize him, Andrea. I don’t want to hear about this anymore. You two just need to get along!” Scott was not reprimanded because they never saw him hurt her; in their presence, he was civil.

She rolled over and looked up at him. His chest was heaving as he zeroed in on her sudden attentiveness. Instead of kicking her face, he put his tennis shoe flat against her nose and pressed down. Fiery pain spread up behind her eyes. She felt him step down harder, so she grabbed his foot and twisted it sideways. He yelled in surprise as he fell next to her. Leaping up from the ground, she felt a rush of dizziness as she scrambled to right herself.

Stumbling, she ran toward the back door of their house. She felt a keen stab of terror as she tried to turn the knob. It was locked. She dashed to the next door leading to the laundry room—the one that was always left open during the day. He was up and running toward her now. She threw her shoulder against the door as she grabbed the knob, trying to turn it. It was locked. The sliding patio door was a few feet away. The handle did not move when she yanked on it, and she realized then that he had locked all of the back doors. He had probably planned this! Running around the corner of the house to get to the front door, she felt his hand grab the back of her shirt.

"You're dead now, you brat! No one will save you!" He laughed in a queer, high-pitched way.

She turned toward him and rammed her arm up against his wrist, making him lose his grip on her shirt, and then she was off, up the slight incline to the Johnsons' backyard. Andie was a natural athlete, her slim, muscular body well-developed from daily, vigorous activity. She kept running through other backyards, winding her way along a path that the neighborhood kids used as a short cut.

She did not hear him coming after her, so she slowed down and looked behind her. He was not there. Continuing to walk rapidly, she caught her breath, poised to run if she heard the slightest sound of footfalls.

When he did not appear, she figured that he had given up due to their parents' imminent arrival. She circled back a different way to view the driveway, but could only see the end of it. After a few cautious steps, no movement came her way. Exhaling slowly, she walked onto the driveway and saw that the garage door was still closed. Her parents were not home yet.

She was walking to the front door when the muffled slap of shoes on concrete caused her to freeze. As she glanced behind her, a glint of metal flashed toward her with a soft whisper. She ducked down just before a cracking sound exploded near her face. She looked up and saw, imbedded in the garage door directly above her head, a golf club. It was one of her father's irons. Scott's wild eyes darted from the hole in the door to her, then back again. He was holding the golf club like a batter, amazed at having struck out. Andie sprinted into the house through the front door and flipped the latch to lock him out.

The enormity of what happened shot through her, sending a spike of adrenaline coursing through her system. Her heart raced and her arms were quivering. If she had not turned in time to see him, he would have buried the wedge of metal in her skull. The double garage door was heavy and strong; her head would have been split like a dropped watermelon.

She heard pounding on the front door as she hurried upstairs to her bedroom. After locking her door and pushing her dresser in front of it, she made sure that her windows were locked in case he climbed up the trellis to the overhang in front of the two windows. Sitting on her bed, she tried to stifle the sobs that were straining to come out of her mouth. She could not break down. She needed to be alert.

The banging soon stopped, so she walked over and looked out the window to see her parents' car in the driveway. Relief soared through her. She hopped up and down, laughing, while tears wet her cheeks. She moved the dresser back into place and opened her door.

There was no vibrating rumble of the garage door opening, so she knew that her parents must have seen the hole before they pushed the remote control opener. They would finally know the truth about him and she would be safe! He would be in so much trouble.

She took the stairs two at a time down to the front door and hurried outside to see Scott and her parents standing near the hole. Scott was crying. The golf club lay by his feet.

"Andrea! What kind of idea was it to lock your brother out of the house all afternoon?" her father demanded, while her mother stood scowling at her.

"I had to go to the bathroom so bad," Scott wailed. "But I couldn't get in! She even looked out the window, laughing at me a bunch of times. I didn't mean to bust the door!" he bellowed. "I just tried knocking as loud as I could!" He cried harder, covering his face.

"I'm sorry, Son, but you really should have thought about what might happen to the door, hitting it so hard." Her father patted Scott's shoulder and bent down to pick up the golf club. He ran his hand along its shiny length, noticing that it was apparently unharmed.

"You, young lady," he yelled, pointing at her, "need to apologize to your brother! What you did was uncalled for! I don't know what's wrong with you sometimes!"

Scott glanced at her, a triumphant smirk lifting one side of his mouth.

"He tried to kill me, Dad!" she yelled. "He's lying! He pushed me down, chased me, then swung the golf club at my head when I wasn't looking. I could be dead!" She looked from her father to her mother as they stared at her appraisingly.

"Is that what happened, Scott?" asked her father.

"No! She just doesn't want to get in trouble! She always lies," Scott replied, no longer crying.

"Dad, I swear I'm not lying! Why would I do something stupid like that?" Andie asked, stamping her foot. "He wasn't trying to knock on the garage. He was trying to break my head open because he was mad that I got away from him! I could be dead right now and you don't even care!" she shouted.

"Andrea, you tell him that you're sorry!" her father ordered. "Then go up to your room. You're grounded!"

She put her hands on her hips. "You can ground me for the rest of my life, but I have nothing to be sorry for!" Running into the house, she heard her father angrily yelling at her to come back.

Later that night, after she had mumbled "sorry" to all three of them, just so they would leave her alone, she burrowed down in her covers and thought about running away. She knew that she never would, but wished that there was some way to disappear from her life. She doubted that they would miss her if she were gone. Runaways always ended up dead in a ditch, and she wanted to live, so she had no choice but to stay. Now that she knew that Scott was capable of killing her, she would need to be on guard. Her parents considered them old enough to be home alone, so there would be no security in a baby sitter.

Hugging her pillow, she started sucking her thumb. She reserved sucking her thumb for bedtime and moments of extreme stress, realizing that at eight she was much too old for it. She never did it at school or in front of her friends. Her parents sometimes painted nasty tasting liquid on her thumb before bed. In the middle of the night, she would go into her bathroom and scrub until only a trace of bitterness remained. Back in bed, her thumb still tasted foul, yet the comfort it gave made the acrid flavor worth enduring.

Chapter 2

Andie was relieved when school began that fall because it seemed a safe, comfortable place. The teachers noticed her efforts to be helpful and studious. She received positive reinforcement with an unquenchable thirst, causing some of her classmates to label her a teacher's pet. Andie did not care about the rudeness that some kids doled out; nothing compared to the wrath of Scott. She attracted friends by being kind, humorous, and defending those who were picked on by the bullies. One boy was always the target of ridicule.

Wayne was born with a bright mind, hidden by physical deformities. Half of his body was normal, but his entire right side was misshapen. His face was dominated by an enormous, bulging upper eyelid that draped over his right eye. The pink tissue of the inner eyelid protruded grossly and oozed a yellow fluid that adhered to his sparse eyelashes in gooey strings. Half of his nose was bulbous and sloped lower than the left side. The right side of his mouth was enlarged and twisted, impeding regular speech. He loped along in an awkward, jerking gait because the right side of his body was larger and uncoordinated.

All of the students were asked to bring in a baby picture for the big bulletin board in the main hallway. By the end of the week, everyone would have a turn guessing the identity of each baby. The board was filled with plump-cheeked, smiling babies. Among them, Baby Wayne gazed out of one eye, his toothless mouth half open in what resembled a surprised snarl. The swollen eyelid was even more pronounced on his thin face.

A number of kids had speculated about whether he was born deformed or if he had developed these features. The picture confirmed he had come into the world that way. Andie wondered how his parents had felt when they had first seen him. He was an only child. There was a rumor that in his eyelid was a tumor connected to his brain that the doctors could not remove or else he would die. He had undergone numerous corrective surgeries.

Wayne was tormented daily. He loved airplanes and often hurried down the echoing school hallway with his arms extended, his little brown briefcase dangling from one hand. He made an airplane sound that caused his meaty lip to quiver as he vroomed, serpentining close to the walls. Some kids called him names, mocked his garbled speech, and pushed or poked him.

One day Benjamin Grunden, a poor student who was always getting in trouble for talking during class, walked by Wayne during study time and rammed the end of his wooden ruler into Wayne's right eye. Wayne's shriek of pain was the most inhuman sound Andie had ever heard. He fell onto the floor, screaming and writhing. The teacher ran to him and helped him into a sitting position.

Wayne was crying and bellowing, "Nooo!" Drool trickled onto his shirt front, and there was a smear of blood on his cheek. He kept one hand over his eye. The teacher escorted Wayne to the nurse's office where his mother was notified. He would not return to school until the following week. Benjamin was taken to the principal's office, undoubtedly to feel the sting of Mr. Murlinger's renowned paddle.

The day after the incident, Andie approached Benjamin at recess, where he stood against the red brick wall watching a basketball game, and told him that she would beat him up if he ever touched Wayne again. Benjamin looked smugly at her through his perpetually half-closed eyes and shrugged his shoulders. Andie grabbed the front of his shirt, twisting it and pulling him quickly forward. "If you think I'm kidding, I'll be glad to show you how serious I am!" She yanked him around the corner of the building, out of the playground teacher's sight.

Shoving him to the ground, she sat on his chest and pinned his arms above his head with her knees. She flicked her middle finger firmly on the bridge of his nose, hoping to rouse him from his irritating somnolent state. "Pay attention because you won't have another chance. If I ever find out that you even look at Wayne the wrong way," she said, flicking his nose harder. "I won't have any problem finding you after school and making sure that you can't walk straight on your way home. Got it?"

Benjamin sneered at her and struggled to get free. "Maybe I'll leave the retard alone."

She dug her knees into his outstretched arms, then pressed upward on his chin with both hands. "Wayne is ten times smarter than you! You're the retard, you stupid jerk!" She tensed her body and began to bounce all of her weight up and down on his chest. Some students had noticed them and were coming over to watch.

Benjamin started crying for her to stop.

"Look at how tough you are, Benjy! Do you like to pick on people? Is it fun? Does it make you feel big?" Andie had entered a vicious part of herself, created by countless episodes with her brother. "How would you like a stick jammed in your eye?"

"Hey, hey, hey! What's going on over here?" The playground teacher, a heavy woman with blond braids hanging to her waist, had seen the crowd gathering. She pulled Andie off Benjamin and began walking her to the principal's office, calling out to the unusually quiet children that she would return in a moment. Once inside, she slowed down and asked Andie what had happened, but Andie just shook her head and studied her feet as she moved through the long hallway.

In his office, Mr. Murlinger sat with his hands folded in front of him, pausing a long while before he finally spoke. "Fighting is not allowed at school, Andie. I know that you're aware of the rules. You've never had a behavior problem before," he said, his penetrating eyes searching Andie's face. "On the contrary, you're an outstanding student, and you usually set a good example for the other kids. I'm disappointed that you've resorted to violence—it never solves anything." He stood up.

"However," he continued, "Benjamin is someone who has been causing quite a bit of difficulty for the teachers and some of the students. I know that you were in class yesterday when Wayne was injured." He paused. "Did this have anything to do with Wayne?"

"Yes, sir," Andie replied. "It had everything to do with Wayne." She suddenly started crying, overwhelmed by the powerful emotions of the last fifteen minutes and embarrassed to be in trouble. "I'm s-sorry, Mr. Murlinger. It won't happen again." Andie attempted to compose herself, wiping at her tears.

He waited a few moments until she had calmed down. Once again seated, he leaned forward and said, "Andie, I have a favor to ask you."

She looked up, surprised by his statement.

"Would you be willing to sit next to Wayne at lunch?"

Her eyes widened. She sat up straighter in the chair. "Yes, sir. I certainly would be."

"Good," he replied with a slight smile. "I'm going to let the teachers know of this arrangement. I expect you to continue setting a good example for the others. I'm counting on you, Andie." He stood and opened the door for her.

She walked by the infamous paddle that hung on a hook next to the door. Everyone feared towering Mr. Murlinger, who limped menacingly down the hallways, one arm lamely swinging by his side due to a childhood bout with polio.

Andie sat next to Wayne as he smacked and chomped his way through lunch each day. Wayne often asked her to find out if a pretty girl named Kelly liked him. He wanted to be her boyfriend. She did not have the heart to tell him that Kelly had said, "Oh, dear" and laughed gently when she had asked her about Wayne. She told Wayne that Kelly was too shy to admit that she liked him.

On the way home from school, Andie walked Wayne across the vast field to their neighborhood. She kept the marauding groups of after-schoolers away from him. On a few occasions she had to use force to keep him safe, but even the tough kids noticed a fierce look on her face when they started taunting Wayne. She would immediately go after anyone and she never backed down. It became well known that it was not worth the turmoil of confronting her to bother Wayne.

Nearing her yard she turned and called out to Wayne as he continued on his way, "See ya later, alligator!"

He gleefully responded, "After a while, crocodile!" Giggling and snorting, he flew down the street with his arms out to the wind, free to glide home.

Chapter 3

Andie and Scott were called into the den for a talk. Their parents had never done this before, and Andie noticed how nervous they seemed as they sat across the room from one another. Her mother was staring at the brown shag carpet and her dad was wringing his hands. No one spoke for what seemed like a long time. Her mom gave her dad a beseeching look as he cleared his throat.

"Kids," he began. "Your mother and I have waited until you were old enough to tell you this. We feel that you'll understand it now." He put his fist in front of his mouth as if he might cough, then looked up at the ceiling for a moment.

"After we were married," he continued, "we wanted to start a family, but we were not able to have our own children. We decided to do what is called "adopting." That means we chose you to be ours when you were babies. You were both born in Des Moines, but to different parents. They were college students who could not afford to keep you because they wanted to finish school first. So, they gave you to us to keep. We have given you a good home and raised you like our own." He hesitated, glancing over at Andie's mother, who was anxiously frowning at a lamp.

Andie's mind reeled with the words: "chose you"..."different parents"..."could not afford to keep you." She sat up tensely in her chair, looking from her mother to her father. The strained atmosphere in the room was increasing. Between absorbing this information and witnessing her parents' awkwardness, she did not know how to react. It was exciting, like nearing the top of a rollercoaster ride and checking to see if you were strapped in right because the guy who loaded you was missing teeth and dirty.

"Well, what do you think about this?" her father asked, glancing at Scott, who slouched in his chair.

"What did our parents look like?" Andie asked. As she said the words, she almost expected her father to answer, "What do you mean? We're your parents."

Her mother put her face in her hands. Andie looked from person to person in the hushed room.

Finally her dad responded, "We never met them. We were only given a brief description. Scott's were both tall with dark hair. Yours were blond and of average height."

More questions occurred to her, and she was about to ask if they had been chosen from a room full of babies. The first image of her birth mother appeared in her mind—a young woman hiding behind a door, watching to see if her baby would be picked from a room full of cribs.

"Scott, what do you think about this?" her dad asked. Scott slumped lower in his chair. "Son, this is just a detail that we wanted you to know, all right? This doesn't change anything." Her dad's voice sounded strange. Her mom was openly weeping now, shaking her head slightly from side to side.

"Talk to us, Scotter! We want to know what you're thinking. Please!" her father begged.

Andie could no longer tolerate the tension, so she stood and loudly announced, "It's okay, Mom and Dad! It's okay that we're adopted! I think it's neat!" She turned to Scott and said, "Say something, Scott! Tell them that it doesn't matter! What's wrong with you?" Andie stood rigidly in the middle of the room, waiting for her parents to relax.

"Andie, sit down," her father instructed. "Scott needs to talk to us about what he thinks."

Slowly, Scott stopped digging at the carpet with the toe of his shoe. "I don't care," he mumbled petulantly.

Her dad went to kneel by Scott's chair and placed a hand on his shoulder, but Scott averted his eyes.

Her mom spoke up in a wavering voice, "Scott, Mom needs to know that you're not upset. Can you tell me that? Can you, please?" She was trying hard not to cry again.

"All right!" Scott blurted out. "It's fine, okay? I just want to go watch TV."

Her parents seemed to be digesting this as they stared at him. Moments went by while no one spoke. Her dad stood, and then her mom lifted herself out of her chair.

"Okay, guys," her dad said, trying to smile. "Thank you for listening. Go on and play or whatever. We're here if you need us."

He was trying, with forced casualness, to make a cheerful outcome of the meeting. Andie sat glaring at Scott, angry at his obstinate behavior and miffed that her feelings had not merited any regard. They waited for Scott to get up and walk past them before they left the room.

Andie went upstairs to her bedroom. Brand new thoughts and feelings were forming and taking hold of her imagination. She sat harvesting this bounty of information. Different parents, who were they? Did they wonder about her? Where were they? If she saw them, would she recognize them? What if she walked right by them? Would they slow down and stare at her, or would they rush up to her, knowing that she was obviously their long lost daughter? She imagined them hugging her, crying because they wished that they had never given her away.

It had happened that when people met her family, someone would often ask, "So, where did you get this tall blond one?" Scott and her parents had brown hair, dark eyes, and large noses. Her parents were both short. Though the question was rhetorically posed, her parents would respond, chuckling with forced lightheartedness, as they mentioned a blond-haired aunt. Andie used to wonder who the aunt was, as she had never seen her. Her father was an only child and her mother had one brother. Her parents must have felt like a window to their bedroom was inadvertently left open while they undressed—uncertain if anyone outside had caught a glimpse of their bareness.

Scott had a different set of parents. He was not even a blood relative. This fact relieved Andie, somehow making his cruelty easier to understand. A blood brother would never try to kill her. A blood mother would be loving and affectionate, like her friend Judy's mom. Thoughts of her birth mother were foremost on her mind. Her real mom must be sweet and loving. The realization that this person existed seemed incredible.

Andie would wake up in the morning, remembering her new secret, wondering for a second if it was all a dream. Now she had a different life to imagine, one that was always pleasant, never bleak and lonely. Fantasies proliferated as the months went by. She made one attempt to question her mother about her biological parents, but her mom had burst into tears, fleeing up to her bedroom. She tried to get answers from her father, who said that he did not know their names or where they lived. He curtly told her to never bring up the issue again with her mother. Andie knew that it would remain a taboo subject. She also knew that talking to Scott would be futile. They never played together or conversed, and he was more volatile as each week passed, so she went to greater lengths to avoid him.

At dinner Andie studied all of their faces for a sign of emotion or change. They carried on watching the TV screen while they chewed. Her mother's somber face and long silences conveyed sadness, but no one else seemed to notice. Her parents usually ended up talking about problems related to their restaurant.

They owned a cafe that was popular because of its affordable prices and large servings of home-cooked food. Breakfast, lunch, and dinner were available six days a week. With the business came a slew of ongoing problems—pregnant waitresses calling in sick, dishwashers caught stealing, prices changing on meat supplies, the "hippies" in the park across the street trying to come in barefoot and asking to use the bathroom, a deep fat fryer needing to be replaced. There was usually one waitress or another that her mother complained about. Her father would start out defending the waitress, but end up saying, "All right, Joan! I'll see what I can do about it."

Scenes of the war in Vietnam were shown nightly on the news. Andie knew that fighting and killing were everywhere. The secret was to be smarter than your enemy.

CHAPTER 4

Andie was certain that she was more intelligent than Scott. Her parents offered him one dollar for every B grade on his report card. Andie stood by listening to them cajole him, saying that they just knew that he could do it.

"What will you give me for an "A," Dad?" she asked hopefully.

"Andie, be quiet," her mother said impatiently. "We're talking to Scott right now!"

She could tell that Scott was mad at her for asking because he glowered at her. She gave him a brief happy smile, knowing that she would pay for it later, but it felt good to rile him. Besides, she wondered, why shouldn't she be rewarded for her grades?

On weekends her parents would often go out for the evening to parties or nightclubs. They also had cocktail parties where everyone dressed up, talking and laughing in the spacious living room, drinking and smoking at the dining room table. Andie would sneak to her bedroom doorway to observe the guests. Sometimes she was allowed to stay up late and mingle with them.

Her dad showed her how to mix drinks. She was eight years old, taking orders for highballs of V.O. and water, scotch and soda, gin and tonic. Her mother preferred Black Velvet whiskey and water. Never had Andie seen her mom so lively and animated as when she was in this setting. She laughed and gestured boldly as she talked to everyone, looking pretty in her high heels and jewelry.

Andie experimented, mixing an extra strong drink for someone when it was ordered. The person would often start coughing and sputtering, saying something like, "Honey, this is a little too stiff for my taste." Some did not request a different drink, but continued sipping away at the fancy glass. On the rims of the women's glasses were varied shades of lipstick kisses. Andie sniffed the tops of the bottles, certain that they should smell enticing for all of the interest and desire they created, but they reminded her of cleaning spray. Only the peppermint schnapps smelled remotely palatable; it would taste like Christmas.

Each week her mother drove to the liquor store on the other side of town by the railroad tracks, where the houses were run down and some of the yards strewn with junk. While she waited in the car, Andie watched the people hanging around the area. They looked bedraggled and menacing, as if they were up to something sneaky. She worried that one of them might try to steal her, and so she was always relieved when she saw her mom at the checkout counter. Her mother would finally walk out of the store with a large cardboard box. The bottles were snugly tucked into individual slots like well cared for babies. Andie thought that going to the liquor store was like going to the grocery store—all moms must make this trip each week.

One of her parents' favorite nightclubs was the Purple Parrot. While Scott stayed at a friend's house, unable to be in charge of Andie, she went along to the club. She preferred going anywhere to being trapped in the house with him, so she sat quietly in the backseat of the car as her dad drove to the club.

The music blared in the smoke-filled room, pounding in Andie's chest. Her mom gave her a handful of quarters for the jukebox and a Shirley Temple to drink, then her parents disappeared into the dimly lit, murky room. She sat on a stiff vinyl booth seat listening to "Green Eyed Lady" and other songs, wondering why all of the people wanted to stand so close together. Though they were so close, they had to practically scream to hear each other over the music.

By the end of the evening, the smoke was thick in the crowded room, so Andie stood next to the sink in the bathroom with a gooey glob of toilet paper in her hand. She soaked it in cold water, then pressed it against her burning eyes. Ladies came in to drain their bladders and put on fresh lipstick. A few of them noticed her and asked why she was crying. When a pretty woman was sympathetic, Andie imagined her real mother acting as kind and concerned.

Her mom finally pulled her from the bathroom, and they went out into the wonderfully clean night air. Her parents smoked in the car on the way home, so she cracked her window and kept her face close to it. She was so tired that after climbing into bed, she fell right to sleep without even sucking her thumb.

* * *

Andie was becoming more troubled by her father's behavior. When she was younger, he used to make up bedtime stories about jungle animals. Her mom never told stories or read books to her. If her dad had the energy, he would play bear cubs, wrestling with her on the living room floor. His liveliness and intelligence stood out in sharp contrast to her mother's solemn ways. Andie looked forward to his coming home, although he was away long hours. Even if he was unfair at times, he exuded a love for living. He was outgoing and witty, which made him popular with his peers and well known because of the amount of people he encountered on a daily basis at the cafe. She thought that her dad was famous because everyone in town seemed to know him.

He would call out jovially to each patron as they walked in the door of the cafe. His angular face and dark complexion were accentuated by the sweat from the heat of cooking. He wore a tall, white chef's hat when he stood by the large grill in the front of the restaurant, flipping hamburgers and frying onion rings and shrimp. The hats had mushroom-shaped tops that Andie would punch down and then puff up again. There was a whole box of them in the cafe's basement office. He also had calendars of naked women on the office walls.

Her mom often took them to the cafe at night to eat dinner. When they finished their meal, her mom would sit up front by her dad or talk with other people who came in to eat. She and Scott were left to roam around for an hour or more until their mother was ready to go home.

Andie would sometimes go into the office and turn the pages of the calendars. A few women had on cowboy boots or other apparel that she thought was silly on a naked person. Their lips were parted in a sly, hungry way. In his desk were magazines of naked women—Playboy, and sometimes a Penthouse, which really shocked her. Women were sprawled out, making sure that their private parts were exposed in plain view for anyone to see. Andie did not even realize that a woman's parts looked like this down there. To know that her father enjoyed looking at these pictures! She did not feel comfortable being a female around him. Some of the pictures even showed naked men and women wrapped together in strange positions. She no longer wanted to play bear cubs or be physically close to him. The pictures of naked women would flash through her mind when he came near her.

The young waitresses in other restaurants were her father's favorite prey. Her family often went out to eat when her father was not working. He was boisterously cheerful to these women and so commanded a friendly response. The waitresses wanted a good tip, so few were rude. And he was a fabulous tipper. He usually managed a hand-sliding-casually-around-the-hip maneuver on one of them by the time the main course was served. When any decent looking woman walked by, his eyes trailed her, devouring the curves of her body. If one was well-endowed in the chest, he was nearly beside himself. Andie became even more distressed when he started making his comments. "Has she ever got a nice pair of knockers!" he'd say, smiling and straining to get the next glimpse. "What a body!"

Her mother would sit silently, looking the other way as she drank her cocktail. Andie could tell that it upset her, but she never tried to stop him, or else had tried long ago without success.

Sometimes when Andie was speaking to him, he would suddenly get a wide-eyed, slack look on his face, oblivious to the conversation as a woman passed by. She watched his eyes dart from the woman's chest to her hips, up and down, down and up again. If her face was attractive it might get a glance, but it was the bulging parts of the torso that he relished.

Her parents were going out for the night. Andie paced in her bedroom, then decided to do what she had been putting off for weeks. She knocked on their door, then entered as her dad finished getting dressed. "Dad," she asked, summoning her courage, "why do you look at those magazines with naked women in them?"

He stopped buttoning his shirt. After a short pause, he answered, "Well, they have good articles, and I appreciate the beauty of a woman's body. Men just like to look at them."

"So, why don't you just look at Mom's body instead? She's beautiful," Andie countered.

He laughed and said, "Yes, she is. But...well, I happen to like all of the different types of beauty that many women make up." He looked in the mirror and ran a hand through his thick hair, thrusting his chin out and narrowing his eyes for a second. He turned and left the room, ending the discussion.

Her mom came out of the bathroom and went to her wide closet to select her shoes. Andie could not tell if she had overheard the conversation. She continued to dress for the evening, ignoring Andie's presence. Andie walked to her own bedroom, locking the door in preparation for the long night ahead with Scott.

Chapter 5

During the summer when Andie was twelve, she noticed that her mother had started sneaking a liquor bottle from the high cabinet and pouring a quick splash of it into a glass that was kept in the front of the dishwasher. She could hear the slight squeak of the cabinet door and soon the clinking of the glass against the dishwasher rack as it was put back until the next time. Her mom would begin drinking in the early afternoon and continue until her dad came home, then she would make both of them a drink. Andie thought that it must be a relief for her mom to finally have one or two drinks without hiding them.

Her mom's words would become slurred as the day wore on. She reeked of whiskey, becoming friendlier with each drink. Sometimes Andie wanted her to start drinking because she would be in such a rotten mood until she could get to that cabinet, so Andie would conveniently leave the kitchen for periods of time until she heard the final clinking of the glass as it was put away.

If Andie rushed into the house through the back kitchen door coming home from Judy's, her mom would often have a startled, guilty expression on her face and be standing awkwardly somewhere in between the cabinet and the dishwasher. Andie would feel bad for causing her discomfort, so she would act as if nothing was amiss and go up to her room.

In the morning, she did not like to be around while her mother sat grimly at the kitchen table staring at her ashtray and drinking Tab diet soda. She would often postpone breakfast until she could be alone in the kitchen, away from the gloomy woman living in her mother's body.

Her father was gone most of the time, even though he worked fewer hours. He played golf at the country club, bridge and poker at the Elk's Club, and had many friends. Her mom no longer had friends coming over. She had quit the bowling league, her only interest, years before. She never went to the country club because she said that the people were rude and snobbish. A cleaning lady had been coming weekly since Andie was four years old, so her mom never had to do heavy cleaning.

Their three-story house with a recreation room in the basement allowed the family to avoid each other with ease. Andie's friends told her that she was rich. She had a large bedroom with light blue carpet and a blue canopy bed covered with stuffed animals. In the basement were a ping pong table, a pool table, and a mini air hockey table. There was one wall of shelves filled with board games and craft kits. If she asked for something, she could usually get it. Her mom would wordlessly give her money, or pick up the item and solemnly pay for it. She could eat anything whenever she wanted, without even asking first. When she went out to play at night, Andie would ask her mom what time she should come home. Her mom always said, "Oh, whenever the other kids go in."

When friends came over, her mother would be cheerful to them, offering snacks and drinks. If it was later in the day, she would become garrulous, embarrassing Andie. She would carry on and on, repeating herself, slurring words. Andie would nervously watch her friends as her mom bumped into the corner of a table or couch, swaying and losing her balance.

Scott also went to the country club to play golf. The previous year, at thirteen, he had won the state golf tournament and showed great promise in the sport. Her father had always been an avid golf fan and was thrilled that his son had the potential to become a professional golfer. Trophies covered all of the surfaces in his room, so a special shelf was built. Unfortunately, Scott had a terrible temper on the golf course. Even during tournaments he had been known to furiously throw his clubs, sometimes smashing them into tree trunks if he missed a shot. Her parents soothingly talked to him about controlling it.

Andie was glad that Scott was away most of the time. His attacks did not occur as often, but when they did it was worse because he was so much bigger and stronger now. She spent most of her summer playing with their new dog, King.

Scott had decided that he wanted a dog, so her parents bought an expensive, registered Golden Retriever puppy that had a champion lineage. They told Andie that because she was allowed to collect toads, rabbits, and gerbils, Scott deserved to have his own pet. On the drive home from picking up the plump soft pup, Andie sat in the back of the station wagon. If she tried to pet the puppy as it nosed close to her, Scott cried out, "Dad, Andie's taking him from me!"

Her dad told her to leave King alone and lectured her about how it was Scott's dog, so only Scott would get to take care of it. She was somehow assigned the "master" of their ten-year-old, cranky Schnauzer, Buffy. She was forbidden to play with, feed, or call out to the new dog.

Andie had always been a passionate animal lover—bringing home stray dogs and cats until their owners were found, rescuing abandoned wild bunnies, which usually died after a few days of licking a formula of sugar milk from the end of an eye dropper. Puppies were her all-time favorite. She would try hard not to go up to King and pet him, but he was so cute that she would end up touching him. It did not help that he seemed to prefer her to Scott if they were both nearby. He would run straight to her anytime he saw her, licking her face and arms, leaving traces of sweet puppy breath. Scott would shove her, yelling at her to get out of his way. A huge kennel and dog house were put up in the back yard.

After one month, Scott stopped feeding and playing with King. He told Andie that the dog was stupid and that he had no time for it because he was so busy playing golf. She happily took over caring for King. They became great friends, walking and running in the field across the street, sitting together in the musty smelling dog house as she stroked his fur, speaking softly to him. Her father let her take him to obedience class to be trained. Andie would walk King around, holding his lead just right, following the instructions of the trainer. She worked with him for extra hours just before the last day of class. He did so well in the mock dog show that he won a shiny trophy for being the most improved. She hugged him all the way home in the car that night.

The end of summer was weeks away, with junior high looming too soon in the future for her. She was anxious because she would miss her elementary school with the supportive teachers and kids who knew and respected her. Her best friend, Judy, was not around as much because she had met new friends during the last year. Judy had always gone to the Catholic school, while Andie went to public school, so she spent nearly all of her free time with King.

* * *

Andie ended up missing the first month of junior high school because of illness. She had been feeling a gnawing, deep ache on her right side for a few days, and then one night after dinner it hurt enough to make her cry as she lay on the couch. Her mom looked at her blankly when she complained about how she felt, then told her to take an aspirin and go to bed. Three hours later, still on the couch, Andie looked up deliriously at her father, who had just arrived home, as he placed his hand on her forehead.

"Joan? Joan, she's burning up!" he exclaimed.

Andie was taken to the emergency room and admitted with a one hundred and five degree temperature. While a woman in a short, white coat asked her father questions, Andie tried to hold still so the lab technician could draw her blood. For each question regarding family history, her dad said that they did not know anything because she was adopted. Finally the woman skipped over the rest of the questions, made a broad sweeping "X" across the section on the medical information form, and wrote "ADOPTED" at the top. Her dad mumbled something about believing that a history of diabetes and heart disease had been mentioned, but that he was not certain. The woman ignored this and went on to ask about previous surgeries or hospitalizations.

One week and many tests later, the symptoms of a kidney infection subsided. Andie was eager to get out of the hospital. She hated needles and had undergone a blood test three times daily. Her parents had dropped by and stayed for a short time before dinner. She kept trying to feel comforted by their presence, but when they left she realized that what she missed was being home in her own bed without pain. Her parents brought her magazines and a stuffed animal, but they did not touch her. Finally, she was ordered home on bed rest until she regained her weight and energy.

Andie would sit downstairs in the den with King, who stayed right next to her as if he knew that she needed him. Her mother had begun working more at the cafe during the day, so Andie watched TV and helped herself to snacks. Three weeks later, she was well enough to start school.

She became shy during the school year. Almost everyone seemed to have already made friends during the first month while she was absent. She quietly went to all of the classes, missing her old school and its familiarity. The ninth grade students seemed so much more mature and adult-like. Many of the girls had bodies like women, and some of the boys had big muscles and deep voices.

Scott was in ninth grade and famous for winning every city golf meet, and especially for winning the state tournament while representing the school. People heard her name and immediately asked if she was his sister. Girls would seem reverent when they found out, usually giggling and mentioning that he was so good looking. When Andie walked by Scott and his group of popular jock friends in the hall, he would call out to her in a friendly way, "Hey, Andie! There's my little sister!"

She thought that he was like Jekyll and Hyde, because he never behaved this way once they were out of school. Apparently he knew the correct way a brother ought to behave, but chose instead to be malicious.

Andie walked into the house after school on a Friday and ran to the kitchen to answer the phone. It was for her mom, whose cigarette in the ashtray had burned all the way down through its non-filtered end.

"Mom! The phone is for you!" Andie said loudly.

When there was no response, she set the phone down and walked into the living room, calling upstairs toward the bedrooms. Then she checked the bedrooms, the den, and the basement. Her mom's car was in the garage, so Andie knew that she must be somewhere in the house.

"Mom!" Andie yelled. She had not looked in the formal dining room because it was only used for special occasions. Walking around the corner into the dining room, Andie gasped. Her mom was sprawled out, lying on her stomach next to the long walnut table.

"Mom!" Andie screamed as she crouched down, shaking her mom's shoulder. Her upper body flopped lifelessly as Andie shook it harder. She looked at her mom's slack face and began to panic as she realized that her mother might be dead. She had rarely touched her mom's body in any capacity, and felt that she was violating it somehow as she vigorously shook it, screaming as loudly as she could next to her ear. Andie was checking for signs of breathing when she heard the front door open. Scott had come home. She quickly ran to the top of the stairs to meet him.

"Scott, Mom's in the dining room and won't get up!" she said frantically.

Andie waited by the stairs, afraid to look at her mom again as Scott went into the dining room. She imagined that this would be the moment when Scott would reach out to her, because of their mutual concern for their mother. It occurred to her that her mom may have drunk a lot of whiskey, but she did not know if alcohol could kill someone.

Andie heard mumbling and the rustle of clothing. Scott came back around the corner toward her. He looked at her and said with disdain, "What's your problem? She's fine." Then he walked out of the house.

She could hear her mom in the kitchen picking up the receiver of the phone and putting it back onto the cradle. Scott had not even cared that their mother had been flat on the floor with drool on her cheek, looking like a corpse.

Andie peeked around the corner to see her mother sitting in her usual spot at the kitchen table, lighting a cigarette. Andie could not face her. She decided to go outside and see King, who danced in his cage when he saw her approaching. She laughed at his eagerness as she attached the leash to his collar. They ran across the wide field, his leash taut as he pulled her along behind him. At times, she thought her feet might leave the ground and she would fly up into the air like a kite just launched.

The following week, Andie came home from school to find both of her parents home, which was strange because her dad was never there in the afternoon. A large paper bag sat on the kitchen table.

Her dad sat at the kitchen table. "They'll be here pretty soon, Joan, so you'd better tell her."

Nonchalantly, her mother turned from the sink and said, "King's new owners are coming to pick him up."

"What? What do you mean new owners?" Andie asked incredulously. She quickly went over to the bag on the table and saw cans of dog food, his leash, his extra collar, and the small folder with his shot record. "No!" she yelled. "What are you doing? You can't give him away!"

"Andrea, Scott didn't live up to his obligation of caring for King. He's a big dog and takes a lot of work, which Scott's not willing to do now. So, King is going," her father explained.

"No, no! I'll keep taking care of him like I've been doing! He's my dog! He's a good dog! He's no problem!" Andie started to cry. She grabbed the bag from the table and carried it downstairs to the basement.

She left the bag in a closet and quickly ran back up to the kitchen. "He's not going anywhere!" she yelled. "How can you even think about it? You know that I've been taking good care of him! Saying that King has to go because Scott won't do it is not a good reason! It's not fair at all! I will not let him go!"

"The good reason is that we say so, young lady! You watch your mouth!" her father retorted. "They'll be here shortly, so you go get that bag and bring it up here right now!"

Andie ran from the room. She went outside and into King's pen, tightly wrapping her arms around his thick chest and breathing in his familiar smell. Then she placed her hands on the sides of his soft mouth, looking into his friendly eyes. She caressed his sleek forehead, trying to stroke her memory into his canine mind. She knew that he was about to be gone forever no matter how much she protested.

Soon, voices were heard approaching from the side of the house. An older couple walked along beside her father. Andie buried her face in King's coat, realizing that she would not be able to endure watching him go off with them.

"Okay, Andrea, you've had your good-bye. Go get his things!" her father ordered.

She did not want these people staring at her. Getting up quickly, she hurried past them into the house and down to the basement. She tossed the bag up the basement steps and slammed the door. Soon, she heard them come in and then finally leave. Andie sat in a chair crying, feeling more forlorn than she could ever remember.

She believed with absolute certainty that she would have been happier with her real parents, dirt poor or not. She longed for someone to care for her. Didn't her feelings even matter to her parents? She felt as if she lived in a house with strangers who gave her wonderful material things, but had no real compassion for her. They went through the motions of being a family for the public eye. Her mom was nice to her when she had drunk enough whiskey.

Nothing was ever secure. It was a daily challenge to remain safe in her own home. She cried for the loss of King, but it turned into cries for the loss of a mother who might hold her and love her, one who would be interested in her and not find a bottle of whiskey more appealing.

Bitterness was becoming a frequent visitor.

Chapter 6

Andie and her best friend, Karin, were up in her bedroom getting ready to leave. Andie was excited because she had just gotten a moped like Karin's and they were going on their first ride. At fourteen, they were exhilarated by the freedom that they would have cruising around town. She and Karin had been inseparable since the end of seventh grade. Karin's parents were in the midst of a nasty divorce, so Karin took refuge in Andie, and Andie adored Karin's sweet, humorous nature. They knew that they would end up together all of their lives, maybe even marry brothers so that they could be related.

Heading out the front door, Andie saw Scott pulling into the driveway in his red Camero. He thought he was such a hotshot, she mused. She went over to her shiny new moped and twisted the lever to the "on" position. She wanted to get a neat key chain for her key.

"Whoa there!" Scott said loudly as he walked over. At sixteen, he was bigger than most men, his chubbiness turned to solid muscle.

"Hey, Scott! If you see Mom, tell her I'll call her from Karin's, will you please?" Andie was trying to hurry and leave.

"Tell her yourself!" he said. "What am I, your secretary? Let me take that nice new moped of yours over to Jeff's for a minute." He proceeded to grab the handle bars, waiting for her to get off.

"No, we have to leave now. Maybe when I get home you can," Andie said.

"Get off! I'll be back in an hour or so. You can wait!" He pushed her, and she fell sideways onto the driveway.

"Stop it, Scott! I told you we have to leave now. Why do you do this?" Andie demanded.

He stepped back from the moped. "I'll tell you why! Because a certain little spoiled brat gets everything and she doesn't deserve it!" He brought his leg up and rammed his foot into the moped's seat. It fell over onto Andie, who was still sprawled on the ground.

Before she could contain herself she screamed, "You stupid idiot!"

Karin watched in fear and amazement as Scott shoved the moped aside and yanked Andie up, putting a lock hold around her neck with one arm, her back against the front of him. He swung his other arm around and into her, punching her hard in the face and chest.

Andie struggled to get away and managed to connect her heel with his shin. He cried out in pain, becoming more enraged. In a frenzy now, he hit her harder and tightened his arm around her throat. He happened to notice Karin still standing there, unable to move. Karin shrank back at the ugly expression on his face as he dragged Andie backwards into the house and shut the door.

Scott let go of Andie, spinning her around to face him. Then he charged into her with his hands on her neck, forcing her to step back quickly until she bumped into the wall. He squeezed her throat with both hands, then began punching her stomach with one fist. He pulled her hair and slapped her face. He would stop and wait until she opened her eyes, acting as if he were about to quit, then quickly swing at her again.

Andie tried to draw away from him, but his arms kept flying at her. His face was red and sweaty, only inches from hers as he roared about his hatred of her and what he was going to do to her. Her face was wet with his spit. He lifted her up off the floor by the neck with both of his hands and pushed in as he squeezed. She was aware that he would kill her if he did not stop soon. She could not breathe. Waves of pain and numbing fear filled her with a desire to be dead so that she could finally rest.

The doorbell rang.

Scott froze for a moment. Andie could sense that he was deciding that it was Karin, and that her friend would be his next victim. He let go of her neck and she slid down the wall to the floor, gagging and struggling for breath. Her throat burned and her head throbbed. She blinked to clear the tears from her eyes so that she might see straight. If it was Karin, she had to warn her.

Scott dramatically flung open the heavy front door to see a short, skinny man standing there.

"I don't know what you're doing," said the man, who had been unloading his moving van across the street, "but you'd better stop it before I call the police!"

Andie could not see him, but she heard his words and hoped that she was about to be saved.

"I'll handle this brat!" Scott shouted, slamming the door as he yelled.

She cowered down as Scott walked toward her with an evil smile on his face. She still had not recovered her breath and her aching throat felt like something was blocking it.

"Now where were we?" he said, rubbing his hands together.

Andie hung her head in defeat, knowing that she was about to die.

"No one is calling the police to help you, Andie!" Fury was building rapidly as he picked her up and heaved her against the wall, reaching for her neck again. She arched her back and tried to escape from his death grip. She could feel the same panic and tightness in her chest as when she had gone too far under water, not knowing if she would get to the surface. He made a horrible, growling moan as he continued to choke her.

She went limp. Going against all natural instinct, Andie stopped struggling and let her body completely relax. After a few seconds, Scott stopped squeezing and let her drop to the ground where she landed in a wilted heap. She could hear him huffing to catch his breath as she remained still.

She looked up and yelled, "Scott!" startling him. "Go upstairs and get the knife! Get it! Right now!" she screeched hoarsely, her throat burning. "Get it, then bring it here and stick it in me! It'll be fun for you!" She coughed violently. "You'll be so happy watching my blood fall on the floor! Mom and Dad won't even make you clean it up!"

Scott was breathing heavily, looking at her as if he did not understand.

"Killing me will be a lot faster with a knife! Think about it! Get the knife and kill me!" Andie had reached a state of mania; she could feel it taking over, but she did not care. It felt good in a way.

Scott slowly lowered his hands to his sides. He glanced around the room as if he had just realized where he was. Frowning, he looked behind him at the front door, then back to Andie. "I'm leaving," he announced. "You…you just better stay out of my way from now on! And I have a promise for you," he said, leaning down and poking his finger hard into her breastbone. "If you tell Dad or Mom about this, I will kill you!" He turned and left the house.

On the way to his car, Scott looked over to see Karin stepping backwards away from him. "Hey, Karin!" he said, pointing a stiff finger at her. "Just to let you know, if you tell anyone about this, I will find you and I will kill you." He got into his car, then sped off up the street.

Inside the house, Andie waited on the floor to see if he was coming back, amazed that she was still alive. Everything had a dreamlike quality about it. She wiped her face and saw blood on the side of her hand. Wincing, she stood and leaned back against the wall. She thought she heard the deep rumble of Scott's car. She slowly walked toward the front door, just as Karin opened it.

"Andie! Oh my gosh, are you all right? Your face!" Karin exclaimed, holding the door open.

"I don't know. I need to sit down." Andie stepped outside and dropped onto the patio chair. "He almost killed me, Karin. He almost killed me."

"Your face is bleeding! Maybe you should go to the hospital," Karin said worriedly.

"He told me he would kill me if I tell my parents. He will," she rasped painfully. "Next time, he will." Andie felt a numbness settling over her as she stared at the mailbox. The numbers on it seemed so normal.

"Let's go inside and I'll clean your face. The blood looks like it's from your nose." Karin stood. "I'd rather get out of here in case he comes back. Come on, Andie." She gently helped Andie to her feet.

She let Karin take over because she did not feel capable of making decisions. After gently washing her face, they packed an overnight bag and left a note for her mom. Karin's parents were upset when they heard that Andie had fallen off her moped, and they warned the girls to be more careful. Andie was too embarrassed to tell them the truth.

The next afternoon, Andie knew that she had to go home. Her face was reddish purple, swollen in some spots and excruciatingly tender. A faintly darkened area was appearing on her throat. There was a deep cut on her swollen lower lip, and one eye was puffed halfway shut. A purple imprint resembling a row of knuckles graced her cheekbone. She knew that there was no hiding her appearance. Karin persuaded her to tell her parents the truth. Once they saw the extent of her injuries, Scott's severe brutality would be an undeniable fact. Her parents would come down so hard on him that she would be protected from any further assaults.

Andie saw that her mother's car was the only one in the driveway. Her mom was in the kitchen with the TV on. Andie walked in and stood in the doorway. She was about to take a giant leap into a frightening reality. Once unleashed, the truth could kill her. Her mom looked up.

She squinted at Andie and asked, "What happened to your face?"

"Mom," Andie said. "Scott did this. He attacked me yesterday in front of Karin!" She recounted the entire incident, while her mother sat stiffly in the chair, a cigarette burning in the full ashtray.

"So, now you can see that I was telling the truth all the other times when I told you that he hurt me. And this time, I was really scared to tell you because he swore that he would kill me if I told you! I'm afraid he's going to try!" she exclaimed, exhausted from reliving the scene. She sat on a chair and watched her mom slowly crush out the butt of the cigarette.

"Mom?" Andie asked. "What are we going to do?"

"I'll have to talk to your father when he gets home," she replied. She shook another cigarette out of the pack and lit it. Her eyes glanced to the TV. "I can't believe that Scott would do that to you."

"Well, believe it! He would've killed me if I hadn't played dead. Karin was here. You can ask her!"

"I don't need to ask Karin, Andrea! I just said that it's hard to believe that he would do such a thing," her mother replied impatiently, seemingly engrossed in a TV show. "Dad will be home and then you can talk to him."

Andie waited, observing her mom taking long drags of her cigarette while she watched Laurel and Hardy on the screen. She realized that this was the end of the discussion and her mom was apparently unfazed. Andie felt the fine claws of fear working their way into her stomach.

She stood and waited for a moment to see if her mom would do anything else, but she did not even look her way. Andie went upstairs to her bedroom, wondering if she would live through another day. She looked around the room and decided to listen to music on her new eight track tape player, turning the volume up as loud as it would go after putting on the headphones.

She chided herself because she shouldn't have been surprised at her mom's lackadaisical reaction. When had she ever taken a stand for her? Andie would wait until her father came home. He would not allow Scott's vicious behavior. He would protect her.

While on the phone with Karin, she heard Scott come in and her mom greeting him. She waited to see if he would get in trouble, but her mom carried on in her usual way. Scott went into his room, which was right next to hers.

Finally, her father came home. She could vaguely hear him talking in his loud voice to her mother. It was a short conversation. He knocked on her door and came in. "Mom tells me that you and Scott got in fight," he began as his eyes flickered across her bruised face. He looked as if he had just taken a bite of something rancid.

"Dad, look at my face. We didn't get in a fight—he beat the crap out of me and almost killed me. Didn't Mom tell you what happened?"

"She told me enough to know that there's a problem here. Scott wouldn't kill you, Andrea. You can be so melodramatic!"

Andie made rapid pointing gestures at her face while he spoke. "Does this look like I'm exaggerating, Dad?" she said loudly. "Aren't you even worried about me?"

"Well, yes, of course I'm concerned! That's why I'm in here talking to you. We need to remedy this situation," he replied, rubbing a hand across his chin.

"Okay, listen. Scott told me that he would kill me if I told on him. So now he's going to be after me until he gets me. You have to stop him...I can't live like this! All the times when I told you, you never believed me." She started crying. "Now that I'm all banged up you finally notice!"

"All right, all right, Andrea. I'm going to talk to him tonight and set everything straight. You get some rest and don't worry." He stood looking at her as she cried, his face strained. He went back down to the kitchen.

Her mom knocked on her door for dinner, but Andie said that she was not feeling well and wanted to rest. She listened as Scott and her parents ate dinner with no discussion of his attack. She waited as the evening wore on and they all went about their separate activities in different parts of the house. Andie stayed in her room, expecting the moment to come when Scott would be confronted. At the end of the night, she heard Scott finish up in the bathroom and go into his bedroom. Andie went to her door and listened as her parents knocked on Scott's door and he told them to come in.

"We've got something to talk to you about, Scott. I think you might know what it is," her dad said. "You know better than to hit your sister."

Loud cries filled the hallway. Scott was wailing as if someone were stabbing him. He was trying to talk, but it was unintelligible to Andie.

"Easy there. Why don't you tell us what's going on," her dad said.

Scott continued crying, then finally spoke more clearly. Andie could hear certain phrases: "Called me an idiot"..."kicked me"..."wanted to borrow"..."so much pressure with golf"..."always antagonizes me"..."didn't mean to hurt."

Her parents were quiet. Andie tensely stood by her door, but could no longer wait. She carefully opened her door and peeked around the corner into Scott's room, where he was in bed with the blanket pulled over his legs. He was covering his face and sobbing away. Her parents sat on the side of his bed, her father closest to him with a hand on Scott's arm. Her mom had reached over to rub his shoulder. Andie, stunned and disbelieving, stepped back into her room and quietly closed her door.

He had completely fooled them. She felt nauseated and drained of energy. She had been ready to feel safe and free of the constant fear that she lived with. It would never happen! He would always come out ahead, no matter what. Now, he would kill her. She could not even summon tears to purge her distress. A detached hopelessness dominated her spirit. She had made a terrible mistake.

She heard her parents finally go into their own room after Scott had been gently consoled back to tranquility. She did not sleep well that night. Her door stayed locked with her dresser pushed in front of it. The next morning, her dad left for work early and her mom was getting ready to leave. They drove separate cars because they never came home together. Andie planned to hurry out of the house and go over to

Karin's. She had not heard Scott leave, but she did not want to wait because her mom would be leaving soon and then she would be alone with him. She was walking to the bathroom that she shared with Scott when his door opened. Andie tried to dart ahead into the bathroom, but he blocked her way, leaned over next to her ear and whispered, "You're dead."

CHAPTER 7

Andie tried to be at home only when she knew that her parents would be there. Scott had shoved her and pinched her a few times in passing, but he had not had an opportunity to be alone with her yet. He kept telling her that he was going to get her soon. She realized that even though he did not get reprimanded, her parents had seen the truth. A modicum of protection was provided by the fact that he knew they were aware of his behavior. Still, she was cautious all of the time.

Near the end of the summer before Andie would begin high school, Scott was in a car accident. She was at the country club swimming with Karin, when a friend ran up to tell her. Her first reaction was that she hoped he was dead. She was disappointed when she learned that he was fine, except for some bruises. Then she felt a pang of guilt—no one should wish a family member dead, but she kept wrestling with the thought that she could have been free.

Scott had tried to cross a highway, pulling out in front of an oncoming car, trying to speed across in his fast car. The side of the front of his car had been hit, spinning the Camero around and into a shallow ditch. It was considered the other driver's fault. Scott's car was damaged beyond repair, so her father was preparing to replace it.

A few days later, her dad asked her to help him find the title to Scott's car. A large square safe was kept locked in the basement. She watched as her dad got the key out of a box in a kitchen cupboard and then went down to the basement and opened the safe. It was loaded with thick folders and papers.

"Just grab some papers and look for the title. It'll have a border around the edge and be on thick paper," he instructed as he snatched a file.

Andie grabbed a black plastic file that had a zipper at the top. She opened it and pulled out various sizes of official looking papers. One fell onto her lap. She picked it up and scanned the front. It said "Baby Girl Woodson" and had her birthday on the next line. It took her a moment to realize that it was her original birth certificate that she held in her hand. She glanced surreptitiously at her father, who was sifting through a stack of papers, but he had not noticed her hesitation. There was another identical paper with "Keith Lee Dobbins" and Scott's birthday on it. Andie wanted to study the papers longer, but did not want her dad to see what she had discovered, so she put them back and carried on with the search for the title.

The next day she took the key to the safe and helped herself to the black file. She knew that she had been born in Des Moines. Her last name was really Woodson! Her dad had lied to her years ago when he said that he did not know her parents' names. He must have felt that she did not have a right to know and that it was his choice to decide. She wondered why Scott was given a full name, but she was not. Her fantasies and questions had grown during the years. Lately, she felt a growing desire to find out about her birth mother, but considered it impossible. Now this information had literally landed in her lap.

Scott was going to play in another golf tournament in two weeks—a golf tournament in Des Moines. Andie had not planned on going with her family, but she would now.

During the tournament, Andie sat in the pro shop while her parents followed Scott around the course. She took the phone book from the pay phone cubicle and flipped to the "Ws." Five Woodsons were listed in Des Moines. She copied them down on a napkin using a short pencil from a box on the counter. She was keyed up with excitement and anxiety. The paper was safely folded in her pocket on the way home.

After two weeks of pondering how to proceed, she decided to write a letter. There were three Woodsons with a man's first name listed, one with the initial "J", and one with "Meredith."

She wrote, "I am writing this letter with the hope of locating my birth parents. I do not wish to intrude into anyone's life, but I would appreciate some information about my beginning. I was born November 18, 1963, in Des Moines. My original birth certificate lists Woodson as my name. Please forward this letter if you know one of them. The return address is my friend's, as I do not wish to upset my parents. Thank you very much."

She did not give her name. She couldn't decide where to send it to first. Should she mail a copy to each address? Maybe this was not a good idea. What if her birth parents didn't want anyone to know about her? She was torn. Finally, she decided to mail only one letter to one address. She would let fate decide if she was supposed to find them. She chose Meredith, whimsically picturing her birth mom living alone, never having recovered from the trauma of missing her long lost baby. She kept the napkin with the other names on it and waited.

* * *

High school started that fall, and Andie was enjoying her classes with all of her new friends. In November she would get her driver's license, which meant having an even better way to escape from her home. She and Karin often talked about boys they liked and basketball. They had joined the girl's basketball team, but did not strive to be the "starters." Attending practice and playing in scrimmages was enough to make it worthwhile. It was intimidating to think of being the ones who had to take on the role of star players.

Scott was already being recruited by college golf teams. Andie was counting the weeks until he would graduate and move away. It was hard to imagine him truly out of her life.

She tried not to dwell on the fact that after four months there had been no response to her letter. She figured that Meredith was probably no relation to her birth parents. The other possibility was that she had caused havoc in some family and was cursed from afar for disrupting their lives.

When Karin called to tell her that a letter had arrived for her in a large envelope, Andie hurried to her house, her mind full of questions about what the letter might contain. She asked Karin if she could be alone as she read it.

The letter was postmarked "Biloxi, Mississippi." Andie's hands trembled as she tore open the envelope and read the neatly handwritten words, "You have probably given up on receiving a response to your letter you sent to a Woodson in July. Indeed, I've spent many nights wondering if I should write. You see, the letter you wrote was sent to my mother. And I am your mother. My hesitation in writing is the very same as yours: not to hurt your loved ones. But, I have spent nearly sixteen years now wondering whatever happened to you and praying that you were being raised by parents who really loved you. I feel you have a right to know how you came to be given up for adoption. If your parents knew your history, they might already have told you.

I was a young, insecure, and shy teenager desperately needing "someone." My home life was not close, affectionate, or strengthening to me in any way at all. As a matter of fact, I couldn't wait to grow up and be on my own. When I was sixteen, I met a boy and we became friends. He was from a broken home, was living with his father and stepmother, and was having as difficult a time at home as I was, more so really. He was eighteen and finishing high school. It is said that love is blind, and I know what that means. I saw in him only what I wanted to see—good looks, lots of jokes and humor, affection. I ignored his possessiveness, jealousy, temper tantrums, and violence. I ignored it, thinking he would change into just what I wanted him to be. And oh, I loved him! Our relationship closed out my girlfriends, my other activities which didn't seem to matter to me anymore, and we were in our own world. Then, my world came crashing down: by then I was seventeen, and pregnant! He was my first true boyfriend and through the months, we had become totally each others in the only way we knew how; a sort of haphazard, clumsy love that left me feeling nervous and guilty, but still giving in.

What we wanted to do was to get married. But my parents would not consent. They insisted that I go stay at a home for unwed mothers and give the baby up for adoption. Being a minor, I had no choice in the matter. So, I finished classes at "the home" and on November 18, 1963, a very frightened little girl gave birth to another tiny girl. I saw you only once: when I snuck into the nursery full of sleeping babies and found your bed. My heart went out to you, and I knew that I would never see you again. It was very painful giving you up. But, I was assured you would be given to parents who really deserved you. And I felt so unworthy.

Many years have gone by, but not a day passes that I don't pray for you and your loved ones. I am married now and have four children. We are a close, affectionate family; something I always wanted and never had. I try to treat my children the way I always wanted to be treated.

My husband knows about my past and has left it entirely up to me as to whether I would write you or not. My children do not know. Perhaps some day when they are older, we will tell them.

Let me say this; if this information quiets your quest about your identity, then I am glad that I wrote you. The love you have for your parents, and they for you, is far more than I could have given sixteen years ago. I gave you birth; she has given her whole heart. She is your mother! She diapered you, saw your first smile, saw your first step, rocked you to sleep. She has given you her life. Be thankful for her and your father. Respect them, love them, obey them, trust them with your future.

About boys; if you have a boyfriend, please remember what I have written. I pray that you already love yourself enough to have confidence and security in your life and what the future holds for you. Take time to evaluate just where you are right now, where you have been, and especially where you are going. Have you any goals or ideals? Will you go to college or plan a career? Think about your young life and all that the world has to offer you...and all that you have to offer others. You are a precious person in many peoples' eyes. You are precious in God's eyes.

I did not know the Lord as a teenager. In fact, we've only come to know His overwhelming love in the past couple of years. Take this letter to Him in prayer. And if you don't yet know Him, seek a minister full of His spirit and share this with him. He can offer counsel if you need to talk to someone.

God bless you now and forever, dear one, and may you find peace about who you are...Someone who loves you."

Andie was lying on the floor as she read the letter, crying near the end when she realized that this was the first but final connection to her mother. Placing the letter next to her, she put her head down on the floor and wept bitterly. She slapped the floor with her hand, feeling too many emotions at once, knowing that she had missed out on a better life.

What a wonderful person her mother was! She was truly concerned and loving, and she thought about her every day! With this knowledge also came the awareness that she would never be the recipient of this love and compassion. But she was supposed to have been! Andie was devastated that there was no name or return address on the letter. Her mother was far away in Mississippi with her four other children, loving them and hugging them, not wanting any further contact with her.

She cried until Karin finally came in. Andie held the letter out to her. Karin read it and began crying. She sat next to Andie and put her arm around her. "Now you know, Andie. You finally know."

She spent the night with Karin and they reread the letter many times, sorting through the messages. Andie now knew that her parents had used the scenario of "college students who wanted to finish school so they decided not to keep you," to probably try to convey the importance of getting an education and give the impression that the young couple was upstanding. But it was unfair to have led her to believe that she was disposable, telling her that her birth parents had chosen attending classes instead of keeping her. Her real mother and father had wanted to keep her!

She knew that her dad had made this explanation up; it sounded just like something he would say. College was the only road to riches. He believed that having a lot of money and nice possessions was the epitome of success and the key to happiness. She had been told that she must go to college. Andie remembered driving home in the car with her family when she was young. As they approached their wide lawn, her father often said in a pride-filled voice, "I wonder what the poor people are doing!"

Andie pictured her real mother and her family living in a clean, modest home filled with comfortably worn furniture. They would eat breakfast and dinner together, talking happily as they reached for the bowls of warm food. Her old friend, Judy, came to mind with the four sisters in their pleasantly small house. Andie had loved to be with them because it was where she had first learned the way a family should be. Sure, the girls argued—they were all one year apart, yet their parents supervised with fairness and love. Andie enjoyed spending the night with the four girls, who shared two bedrooms. Their parents would come in at night to talk about the day, then they would kneel down by the bed and all say their prayers. Everyone got a hug and kiss before the lights were turned out. Andie imagined that this was how her real mom would live with her family.

Andie's four half siblings were probably much younger. Her mother had been seventeen when she was born. If she remarried, perhaps at twenty-five and had children one year later, the oldest would be nine. She might even have a little baby half-sibling. There was such an intense desire to see their faces. Andie always wished that she had a sister. Somewhere there were four children and each one of them was linked to her.

Even though she hid the letter far under her mattress, it worried her that it might be found. She could not imagine how her parents would react if they found it. First, she had gone into the safe when she was not supposed to, then she had searched out her real mother. They would view her as a traitor. The subject had remained strictly off-limits. Her mom would break down at the mere mention of adoption, but there was no way that she was going to throw the letter away, and she did not want to leave it anywhere else. If the house caught on fire, it would be the one thing she would be sure to save.

It was good to know how she had been brought into the world and why she was given away. Every day Andie would look in the mirror and try to imagine what her mother looked like and wonder if she were thinking about her at that moment. She was not able to stop hoping that she could meet her one day, though it seemed impossible. She would daydream and become lost in thoughts of reuniting with her real mother, then always remember that her mother did not want any further contact with her. It left an ache inside of her that she could not relieve.

At night she often got the letter out, slowly rubbing her hand across it, knowing that her mother had touched the same surface. If only she could extract a trace of love from the ink, from the hand that had been up against the paper, see the face that had stared at the sentences as they formed on each line. She had almost memorized it word for word and would try to picture her parents, the two young lovers meeting in odd places, kissing and hugging. She wondered about the terrible home life and loneliness that her mother had experienced, hoping that it had not been as bad as her own was now. How she longed to know this woman who had formed her inside of her young body. If only her mother had been allowed to marry her boyfriend and keep her—what would her life be like now? It would be wonderful to have two parents who looked like her and loved her as a part of them. It was so magical to be blood related.

Andie realized that blood families had their share of problems. No one was guaranteed a perfect life. It seemed that there would have been a better chance for love where God had put her in the first place. Didn't adoption unnaturally go against His intended plan? He had put her inside of her mother, so didn't that mean that she should have stayed with her mother? Could circumstances have disrupted His plan, or had He planned her life to be with other parents? Then did God want her life to be filled with fear, pain, and loneliness?

Andie had not been raised with any religious teaching, but the experience of watching Judy's family praying had sparked a curiosity long ago. Her Grandma Reeves had talked about God and Jesus and told her to say a prayer before bed each night. Andie prayed the short prayer at night and would add, "and please help my Mom to stop drinking, and me to meet my real mother, and for me to be able to have my own children, amen."

She was not too sure that the prayer did any good, because God should not have allowed Scott to hurt her or her parents to let him. God should have let her stay with her real family in the first place if He knew all that was to come in her life. Still, praying was a habit that she got into which helped her relax at night, and she did not want to give up on the hope that someone might be there for her. Enough people seemed to believe in God, or there would not be so many churches. Now that she knew her real mother believed, Andie wanted to understand.

She asked her dad about God and going to heaven, and he told her that you just had to be a good person, that you didn't have to be one of those "religious fanatics" to get into heaven. He was raised as a Catholic, but had turned away from it because of its "rigidity." Her parents used to take them to a Protestant church, usually on Christmas and Easter, where they would arrive all dressed up in their finest clothes. Andie remembered wearing tight, white gloves that made her feel grown-up and carrying a vinyl purse with a metal snap that had pinched her fingers when she was not careful. No mention of the service took place afterward, but they always stopped for doughnuts. They quit going when Andie was six.

Some of Andie's friends attended confirmation classes at the same church where her family used to go. She got the youth minister's name and the next week called the secretary to set up a meeting. Andie took the letter with her as she drove over to the huge, white church, knowing she was about to experience what her real mother would want for her. She entered the quiet building and found the youth minister's office, knocking softly on the door.

"Come in!" said a brisk male voice. Andie walked in and stood awkwardly as the middle-aged man studied her with hard eyes.

"So, Andrea, what brings you here? Sit down," he instructed.

"Well, I wanted to talk to someone about something..." she began, feeling stupid for sounding so vague, but he made her uncomfortable.

"And what might that be?" he asked, unsmiling.

"I, um, I found my birth mother. I was adopted, and I have a letter from my birth mother. I don't know who to talk to," she replied as she held the letter out to him.

He looked at the letter and then stared at her. Finally he said, "So, you came here to talk to me? I don't even know you. I haven't seen you or your family at church and you aren't going to be confirmed. What do you think I can do for you?"

She had not expected this kind of response. Where was the minister full of spirit that her mother wrote about finding, if not at her church? Her parents had always told people that this was their church.

"Why don't your parents come to church? They claim membership on a minimal commitment, but have nothing to do with the church. Now you come here expecting to be counseled when I don't even know you. I think you need to go home and ask your parents why they never go to church," he stated.

Andie, not wanting him to see her cry, hurried from the room, leaving the church through the front door. She looked up at the white peak with the shiny cross at the top. It shimmered through her tears, distorting and shrinking. There was no comfort here.

Chapter 8

Andie found rinsed out peanut butter jars full of whiskey in the cabinet under her mom's bathroom sink and underneath the side of her bed. She searched the entire house and found stashes of whiskey in many places, in the laundry room behind the detergent, sitting in the middle of the canned goods on a top shelf of the pantry, even in emptied pill bottles tucked into the bottom of her purse. Now she understood why her mother was drunk more often. Andie was always anxious when she had to ride in the car with her. Amazingly, her mom had not been in an accident, even though she often walked to the car swaying, rummaging in her leather purse for the keys, missing the ignition a few times as the keys jangled noisily.

She got up the nerve to confront her father about her mom's problem. Andie believed that he must not be aware of it, or he would have done something about it by now. Her father told her that he knew her mom drank quite often, but said he did not know about the hidden containers. He admitted that he could not do anything to stop her and that he had already told her to "take it easy on the booze." Apparently, it would be too expensive to put her in a rehabilitation facility, which he said did not guarantee a cure anyway. Andie pleaded with him to find somewhere for her mom to get treatment, but he said that he simply could not do anything because her mom was a depressed person. She had never been truly happy, primarily because she could not have her own children. Her father told her how she cried because her body could not make children, a fact that pierced through Andie, knowing that she was not really wanted. It felt like a worse abandonment than the one by her birth mother because she was here in the flesh to be loved, but would never be enough to fulfill her mother's desire for a family. She knew that Scott seemed to liven her mom up with his presence, but she herself must have somehow fallen below the expectations of what a daughter should be.

Her dad confided to her that he really did not enjoy being around her mom anymore, but a divorce would be too expensive. He made sure that he had a lot of activities to occupy him. Andie wanted to ask him what he expected his children to do if he was not around and his wife was not fully capable of functioning, except she did not want to be disrespectful. She knew that it probably wasn't easy for him to have an alcoholic wife. While thinking of his own needs, he was bailing out. She supposed that he figured the household was running smoothly enough without him, as it always had. He was rarely home at dinnertime, so her mom had Scott run up to one of the fast food restaurants to pick up dinner. Her dad said that her mother believed that he had affairs, but he swore he never cheated. Even though he was lecherous, Andie believed him. He was the only sober authority in her life.

She would go from feeling angry at her mother, to feeling sorry for her, and then she tried to ignore any feelings because it was all so painful. She wanted her mom to be happy, but knew that the secret of her whiskey kept her from thinking of anyone else while she plotted to meet with one of her stashes like a lover stealing one more kiss. Andie wanted to help her, to be let into the world of this continual thirst where she could lead her out onto dry, firm ground.

Waiting until her dad and Scott were gone, she asked her mom to go into the living room, its new cream colored carpet already stained by careless shoes. The request came off in a kind of formal way, and her mom just looked at her for a moment, then slowly walked ahead. Andie had never asked her to have a talk before. Her mom sat quietly in the love seat across the room, while Andie deliberated, still uncertain how to bring up the subject tactfully. Her mom picked at her cuticles, looking worried like a child about to be reprimanded.

"Mom?" Andie asked. "Are you...happy?"

Her mom stopped picking her finger and looked over at an end table. "Well, sure I'm happy," she answered with condescension, her tone implying that it was a ridiculous question.

"No, Mom. I mean really happy. In your life."

"Of course I am!" She peered directly at Andie, almost causing her to back down. She sounded like she was about to get angry. "Why are you asking?"

"Mom," Andie had to force the words out. "I know that you drink." There had been so much secrecy for too long, that admitting this fact was embarrassing, and she felt the heat of deep shame rising to her cheeks.

Her mom gazed at her. Her mouth was open as if she were about to speak, eyes suddenly without any trace of annoyance. She looked down at her hands and sat as still as glass.

"I want to help you, Mom. I'm worried about you," Andie said. She saw that her mother's bottom lip was quivering.

"Mom?" Andie went over and carefully placed a hand on her shoulder. "It's all right. I want to help you. I want you to be happy. Please, Mom, I just want you to be happy."

Her mom began crying heartily, then leaned sideways, fished a tissue out of her pocket and blew her nose loudly. She could not look up at her daughter. "I've tried to quit for you. I don't know! I just can't! I don't want to be this way, but I don't know what to do!"

"Mom, don't worry. I'm going to help you, okay? Whatever you need me to do, I'll do. Whenever you feel like taking a drink, come and tell me and I'll help you. Just try with me. I know you can do it! You'll feel so much better." Andie was relieved to be consoling her mother instead of ignoring her problem, and the conversation was going as she had hoped because her mother was admitting her problem and wanting to quit. She realized how many years had gone by without anyone offering to help. Andie had looked up information in the library about alcoholism and knew that alcoholics must decide that they wanted to quit, then after deciding to quit they would need support the rest of their lives.

"I will, Andie. I'll try for you." She blew her nose again. "From now on I'm going to be different, you'll see. I don't know why I'm not happy. It's just so hard sometimes!"

She was not sure what her mom was referring to—life in general, or living without a drink. She gave her mom's shoulder a slight squeeze. "I'll go dump out the liquor bottles," she said, standing.

"No! Don't do that! We might have people over and…it's too expensive! I won't touch it, I promise," her mother said emphatically.

Andie looked at her mom's pink nose, which was riddled with thin red veins, as her mom dabbed at it again. "Well, I guess we don't need to. Just be sure that you come and tell me if you want a drink, all right? If I'm not home, Mom, just go out of the house. Take a walk, or go shopping. Just get away from it."

She waited until her mom got up from the chair, then awkwardly tried to give her a hug. Her mother stood stiffly, arms at her sides, until Andie let go of her. It seemed as if her mom wanted to hug her, but was too embarrassed to do it. Her mom walked into the kitchen and poured a diet soda as Andie followed and watched.

"Okay, I'll be up in my room if you need me. And I'm going to stay home all weekend, so maybe we could watch a movie or something." They never watched TV together, and Andie imagined them eating popcorn and talking while they sat together on the couch.

"Oh, you don't need to change your plans for me. I'm going to be fine. You go ahead and do what you've planned," her mom said.

"I want to stay home with you. We'll have fun."

"Well, we'll see," her mom replied dismissively, lighting a cigarette.

This was one of her mother's most popular sayings. It meant that the discussion was over and whatever the matter, it was pending on her later decision. But her mom often forgot whole conversations from the day before, so Andie was used to repeating herself.

Two days passed with no signs of drinking. There was no obvious aroma, no slurred words, no sleeping slumped over on the kitchen table, no creak of the cabinet. Andie checked the stashes, but the level of whiskey was the same everywhere. Her mom seemed cheerful until the end of the second day when she became increasingly moody and tense, so Andie stayed in her room listening for the liquor cabinet, hoping that she would not hear it.

On Saturday morning, her mom left for work. Andie stayed home until her mom returned mid-afternoon. Scott was at a friend's house for the night, and she and her parents were going out to eat Chinese food. Her mom told her that she wanted to take a nap until it was time to leave.

When her dad arrived home from the Elk's Club, Andie put her homework away, feeling pleased with herself and looking forward to proving to her dad that her mom could be helped. Her mom would soon be grateful to her, and they would be close like real mothers and daughters. This bad mood of hers would pass when she got over the tough part of quitting. Andie got dressed and heard her parents in the kitchen, so she went downstairs.

Long before the three of them sat down in the booth at the restaurant, Andie was aware that her mother was intoxicated. She had never told her father about their discussion or agreement. He seemed oblivious to her mom's clumsy movements and slurred speech. Her mom ordered a Black Velvet and water.

Andie could not eat her plate of sesame chicken. She kept looking at her mom, who was on her second drink and chewing sloppily on an eggroll. Her mom abruptly announced that she had to go to the bathroom. She pushed herself up, leaning on the edge of the table to steady herself, then slowly turned to walk toward the back of the restaurant. As she swayed and lurched, she had to reach out to tables and chairs to maintain her balance. Andie tensely watched, and then she noticed a large stain on the back of her mom's skirt. A wet area, the size of a salad plate, stood out plainly on the light colored material. Andie was revolted and embarrassed, for herself and her mom. She felt like crying and screaming at the same time, wanting to run out of the restaurant so no one would know that the ridiculous drunk woman was her mother. Along with her humiliation was an undercurrent of intense sorrow and a desire to save her mom from this liquid culprit that robbed her of all dignity.

"Dad!" Andie whispered. "Look at Mom's skirt."

Her father turned to see her mom making her way slowly through the crowded restaurant. "Oh, no," he said.

"She's really drunk, Dad."

"I know, I know. Finish up, because we're leaving as soon as she gets back here," he drained his martini and then ate the two olives that were lanced on a tiny sword.

Andie waited, not touching her food, certain that everyone in the restaurant had turned to stare at her mom's ambling procession to the bathroom and her wet skirt. Her mother finally appeared after much too long in the bathroom, attempting to look regal and proper as she bobbed around the tables, new lipstick applied heavily on her parted lips.

They were all quiet on the drive home. She figured that her mom had decided to drink, had felt bad for not alerting her, then drowned herself in whiskey to ease the guilt. Andie went right up to her bedroom, knowing that her mom was going to really "tie one on" before the night was through. She could not bear to look at her mom's dopey countenance during her pursuit of oblivion.

* * *

It was a difficult decision, but Andie decided to show her mom the letter. She reasoned that her mom had such a problem confronting the fact of the adoption, that the part in the letter where her birth mother professes that her mom is her real mother would offer a sense of solace. Her mom was keeping her distance and drinking even more heavily. Neither of them had mentioned their failed agreement. Andie thought that she should reassure her that she loved her and wanted only her as a mother. There seemed no way to reach her. The rift continued to increase since the night at the Chinese restaurant.

No one in her family ever said the words "I love you," but Andie believed her mom needed to hear it. Maybe it would give her some peace so that she would stop drinking. Andie had told her mom only once before that she loved her. She had heard her mom crying to her dad in their bedroom one night, after the two of them had returned from a two week vacation in Acapulco. Andie, ten at the time, tiptoed to her door to find out why her mom was crying. She heard her saying something about not being a real mother and that no one treated her like one or loved her like one. She was upset because no one had bought her a Mother's Day present. Andie listened to this, becoming sad and anxious. Bursting into their bedroom, she yelled, "I do love you, Mom! I do. I love you!" She had stood there, anxiously looking at their surprised faces. It was Mother's Day, but the baby-sitter had not informed Andie or Scott.

Andie wanted her mom to hear that she was loved and thought of, even by her birth mother, as a real mother. It would be something that they could share. Maybe her mom would feel included in the discovery if she was honest.

She watched her mom read it while they sat at the kitchen table. When she finished reading, she laid her head down on her arms and sobbed pitifully. Andie was distressed to see that her plan had backfired. "Mom, did you read the part about you being my real mother? It's true! I...love you, Mom," Andie pleaded.

"How could you?" her mother exclaimed, pushing herself awkwardly from her chair and then rushing out of the kitchen.

Her father later confronted Andie about what she had "done" to her mom. He said how disappointed he was in her and how glad they were that at least Scott was satisfied with them. Scott had never done such a thing, nor tried to ask any questions. Her dad asked why she was not satisfied with them, didn't they give her everything a girl could want? Andie knew he was referring to material possessions. She tried to explain that she was only curious, that it was not due to a lack of love for them that she had searched, but he remained distant.

She had now set herself apart from them by the ultimate betrayal. After everything that they had done for her—not even their own child, but one unwanted and destined to be poor—she had sought out the people who had not even cared enough to keep her.

Chapter 9

During his senior year, Scott was offered a full scholarship to the University of Tennessee and the opportunity to join the varsity golf team as a freshman. It was a great honor and source of pride for her parents. Her mom was drinking more now, even in the early morning, but at least it made her easier to deal with. Andie just kept to herself and waited for the time to pass.

She and her boyfriend, John, had been dating for a year. He was often at her house, so she was safe around Scott because of his presence. Scott's latest girlfriend, Leah, was in Andie's class and known to be a big flirt. She had lost her virginity on New Year's Eve in Andie's parents' bed. Her mom and dad had gone away for the weekend, knowing that they would be having friends over. Scott had asked Andie to wash the bloody sheets, but Andie told him she was not touching them and that John was waiting downstairs for her.

The fall could not come quickly enough. Andie had never been able to live without anxiety and fear, and she imagined that her life would become better, finally, when he was gone.

* * *

The day he left, Andie reflected on the fact that she had survived through all the years of his tyranny. Scott was sent off to Tennessee with a new car, her mom's tears, and their repeated promises to visit him soon. Andie woke up each morning and felt a smile spread across her face. She had not even realized the extent of her oppression until he was gone. She did not have to sneak around carefully avoiding him, worried that she might get killed, or feel sickened listening to her parents sweetly praising him about his latest golf score. He was gone!

He called often and talked about how the university was so impersonal. "I'm just a number here!" he would complain. He no longer enjoyed the notoriety of being well known in town. Apparently the classes were "way too hard" and he missed Leah, writing letters to her daily. Andie had seen Leah going around with a handsome football player.

Weeks later, her dad showed her Scott's most recent letter. He wrote to say that he was going to quit college because he missed and wanted to marry Leah.

"So, he'll be driving back this weekend," her father said.

Andie was stunned. This couldn't be the end of her freedom! He'd only been gone for a little over one month. "What! Where's he going to live?" she asked frantically.

"Well, here, of course! Mom and I would like to make the basement into a sort of apartment for him. He's older now and needs more space until he gets married."

"You've got to be kidding! That's where I always bring my friends! Why should he get this treatment when he's nothing but a failure!" Andie was livid. Not only would he be back in her life, he would also be taking over the area that had always been her retreat.

"Don't ever let me hear you say a thing like that again!" her father bellowed. "You have no room to talk! Scott at least tried to go, but he misses it here at home! So you just shut your mouth!"

His anger seemed too great for the moment. Andie figured that he was disappointed in Scott, but did not want to admit it. Her dad would not be able to brag about Scott's scholarship anymore.

She walked away from him saying nothing more. This was a nightmare. After she had counted the weeks until he left, he was now coming back. She decided to make herself extremely scarce for the next year and a half until she could leave.

* * *

During the end of her senior year, a hypnotist came to her school to put on a demonstration for the students. Andie was eager to get to the auditorium. She wanted to find a seat close to the aisle, so that when he called for volunteers she could dash up onto the stage. The other students were talking about what they had seen other hypnotists do on TV.

She was disappointed when she was seated in the middle of a row, but at least she was only eight rows away from the stage. The ten lucky students, seated in chairs on the stage, were squirming and whispering. The man called for silence and began speaking. He had them watch a spinning wheel, their backs to the audience. He spoke in a soothing voice, telling them that they were feeling heavy and tired. He continued this until a number of them did appear to be relaxed. He then dismissed the kids who were unaffected and asked them to take their seats.

Andie was vaguely aware of being in a sitting position, but she was dreaming at the same time. She was playing basketball. She heard a distant, familiar voice calling her name, but she was not able to reach it.

The hypnotist turned to the audience and told them that sometimes people in the audience were susceptible to the suggestions and might be affected even while sitting far from the stage. He commanded anyone who had "gone under" to listen to his voice. He told them to wake up at the count of three. On three, Andie looked around to see John quizzically staring at her from the seat next to her. She thought that she had been about to catch a pass from a basketball teammate and was making rapid movements with her arms. John told her what the hypnotist had said and then asked her how it felt to be hypnotized. So much time had seemed to pass, but John told her that it was only a few minutes. He laughed and teased her about waving her arms around.

It felt pleasant and relaxing to be hypnotized, as if she had been in a dream that was much more real than any she had ever had during sleep. She wished that she could be on the stage to feel it for a longer time as she settled down to watch the performance.

Kids she knew to be shy were made to imitate chickens and crying babies and to sing as if they were in the shower. One girl was even "soaping up" her private area as she sang off key. A skinny ninth-grader was told to make his arms into steel rods, then his legs, and then his entire body. He was lifted with the help of two big kids and stretched out onto the tops of two chair backs with only his neck and ankles resting on them. His body remained rigid and straight as he was lifted and positioned. The hypnotist patted the kid's belly and tried to tickle him, but the boy did not move until he was finally lifted from the chairs and told to sit.

Kids danced and sang with no inhibition. At his command, they would immediately cease what they were doing and become silent and still, like dangling marionettes waiting for the next order. When he had released all but one boy, he began the grand finale. He told the boy that when he awoke, he would walk down the wooden steps to take his seat, but on the third step his shoe would become stuck to the step. He would not be able to lift it off of the step until he heard the words "free yourself."

Chris was a trouble maker, who was in detention on a regular basis. He was told to "wake up." Chris looked surprised to be on stage with everyone looking at him, but he recovered quickly, bouncing slightly as he stood, waving to his friends in the audience. He asked the hypnotist if he had been hypnotized, not believing that anything had occurred. When he began walking down the steps, obviously enjoying himself, he suddenly faltered to a stop. His tennis shoe was stuck on the third step.

Chris looked down at his leg, then tried to pull his foot free. He leaned against the wall and tried to pull sideways. He finally reached down to yank on his tennis shoe. He looked up at everyone, panic on his face. He said, "What the heck?" and pulled frantically. Everyone began laughing, which only added to his fear. He sat down and tried to use his other foot to push the stuck foot free. He glanced at the hundreds of people laughing at his predicament as he scratched and tore at the base of his shoe. He stood again and tried to jump into the air to pull himself free. His foot anchored him securely to the step as his body jerked to a halt with each upward lunge.

"Free yourself!" the hypnotist commanded.

Chris had been leaning too far forward when he was released, so he fell down the rest of the few steps, landing on his stomach while everyone continued laughing. Andie was now glad that she had not been on the stage. Chris threaded his way between the knees of students as he found his seat, a bewildered expression on his sweaty face.

Andie thought for a long time about what she had seen in the auditorium. The powers of the mind were incredible! She remembered when her dad had tried to quit smoking by being hypnotized. He had gone for a single session and it had worked for a month, but then he had started right back again.

She wondered how a person could become a hypnotist. After doing some research, she learned that there were courses which people could take, so virtually anyone could learn to do it. She imagined hypnotizing Scott to be kind and her mom to stop drinking—the possibilities seemed endless.

Chapter 10

Andie arrived at Iowa State University ready to begin a new life. Scott had lived at home in the basement until the end of the summer before she left for school. He worked part-time at a drug store after flunking out of the nearby city college. He still entered every local and state golf tournament, but usually placed third or fourth, having lost his special touch. He had been served with a paternity suit by the sheriff. Leah had broken up with him a few weeks after he returned from Tennessee, so he dated many girls at once and often bragged to his dad about getting some "snuss." This was his slang term that was supposed to refer to sex. Her dad would ask if he was getting any snuss and which girl was the best. Even though her father had hired an attorney to prove that the mother was a tramp, the baby boy came out resembling Scott and the blood test confirmed it, so Scott was in for eighteen years of child support. He wanted nothing to do with the boy and did not request any visitation.

Andie thought it was terrible that Scott had sired a child, because she had come to the conclusion that there was something inherently wrong with him, and now his progeny would be carrying on his psychotic traits. She had read a lot about the "nature versus nurture" debate and had the opinion that nature played a dominant role in deciding the outcome of a person. Environment could guide and mold behavior and very likely obliterate negative characteristics, but left to flourish freely, natural tendencies would take over and become solidified. You could spin a blob of fresh wet clay on a potter's wheel, but it would never take on a refined graceful shape if it was left alone. It would only slope and shift randomly into a distorted mass that would harden to become unchangeable. Scott had not been raised with violence, yet his rage was apparent at an early age. Andie had been raised in the same house with the same parents, yet she was a pacifist.

She had managed to live through the remaining time at home with the help of her ever-present friends. Scott had gotten a hold of her on two occasions, but she had survived. She believed that he was insane, psychotic like a person who appeared normal, then chopped up cats in the basement for fun.

Karin had recently moved to Arizona with her mother after her parents' long-awaited divorce. Andie wrote pages of encouraging letters to her, and they spoke often on the phone. She missed her humor and compassion. Karin had been the closest thing to family that she had known. Her new friends were mainly her partying buddies.

Andie began drinking alcohol at college parties. Everything recreational seemed to be centered around drinking. There were "kegger parties," which were the least expensive way for the most people to get drunk. Huge silver kegs of beer were put on ice inside of a garbage can and tapped early in the afternoon. There were drink specials every night at the bars, and always a "ladies night" when females could drink for free all evening. At first, she had hesitantly tried rum and coke, still not liking the taste of anything else, but soon graduated to margaritas and gin and tonics. She had been drunk a few times, even vomiting in a sticky bathroom of a bar. She was miserable the next day, her head throbbing and her stomach rolling with nausea.

Many of the students smoked marijuana regularly. Andie tried it and enjoyed the feeling more than that of alcohol. Her mind became free when she smoked. Everything was more interesting when she was stoned, her senses heightened, fresh meaning extrapolated from the most ordinary events and situations. She and her friends would go to the mall, sharing a joint on the way, then walking around and laughing hysterically. Food was more appealing and seemed to taste better after smoking, so they would gorge on plates of nachos heaped with meat and cheese, hot fudge brownie sundaes, or stop at a fast food restaurant and order sandwiches and french fries. Andie gained twenty pounds during the first semester, her face puffy and her clothes no longer fitting. She felt bloated and unattractive, but most of her friends were chubby, so she did not dwell on it.

Andie knew that she could have gotten good grades, but there was so much she had never been able to do under the constraints of her home life. What seemed important now was to enjoy her independence and freedom from fear. There was no one to boss her around or depress her, drawing her into their misery. For the first time in her life she did not have to live with daily anxiety, hiding from Scott, tiptoeing around her mom, keeping her emotions repressed. She wanted to finally have a good time, and she felt that she deserved it.

Her parents expected her to call them each week, which she always tried to do. She became annoyed with their constant questions about what she should "major in." They had suddenly become interested in her life, but it seemed they wanted to control her. She would remain as cheerful to them as she could, but she resented their condescending interference in her new life. Usually, she tried to call around dinner time, so that her mom would remember the phone call. If she waited more than seven days to call, her mom would say, "I thought that you'd forgotten about us" in a belligerent tone. She was not always a happy drunk now. The cafe was not doing as well, so they were forced to sell the house and move to an apartment. Scott was living with friends and continued working at the drug store.

Her parents had been involved, up to a point, in her activities in high school. They would often go to her basketball games and made the appearance of being supportive. When she went out, they told her to "have a good time" and gave her plenty of money to spend. They were the parents who gave her groups of friends rides to activities and events. It seemed that they enjoyed having a lot of kids in the house, so Andie often had parties and sleep overs. When she was young, she had elaborate birthday parties with loads of presents.

She knew that they cared on some level, but the dominant memories were negative ones. She was usually sociable and enjoyed people, yet she knew that almost everyone would let her down, except Karin. Andie's boyfriend, John, had followed her to the same college, but had joined a fraternity and found that he preferred sorority girls. Andie was deeply hurt by his rejection. He had been someone she relied upon and trusted, but he had shrugged her off for the opportunity to date other girls. Andie was asked to join a number of sororities during "rush week" when all of the interviewing and recruiting took place, but she did not like the idea of having to conform to anyone's rules or ideals.

* * *

During the end of the second semester of Andie's freshman year, she went to Des Moines, which was half an hour from her school, to a party at Drake University with a group of friends. They planned to spend the night and then return to school the following afternoon.

Andie was stoned, sitting on an old couch next to a guy who was snoring even though he was upright. She picked up a tattered phonebook from the cluttered end table. Flipping through it, she stopped at "W" and found the name Woodson. There, at the same address, was Meredith. Andie had never thought to contact her again, because she had never heard directly from her in the first place. The idea to call her came and went quickly—she would not know what to say. But it seemed that she should do something now that she was in Des Moines again. Andie wanted to locate the house and drive by it in the morning. She checked the map in the front of the phone book and saw that she was only a short distance from Meredith's address.

When morning came, Andie had changed her mind. She had decided, instead, to go right up to the home of her grandmother and knock on the door. She wanted to meet her and hoped that she would tell her more about her real mother.

The dull haze from the previous night was split clean through by her first look at the house where her mother had grown up. Andie was nervous, wide-eyed and starting to perspire, as she parked in front of the small, white house. There was a "W" woven into the metal grate on the front door.

Maybe the woman would not be friendly, Andie worried. Meredith was the one who had wanted to give her up for adoption. Her birth mother had written of the poor home life that she had experienced here. Andie walked up two cement steps. It was only eight o'clock in the morning, so Meredith might be sleeping. She thought of leaving. This was all too spontaneous in the first place, so maybe she should do it another time. She stood on the last step for a moment, ready to turn and go. Then she remembered the kind words her mother had written years before.

She knocked quietly on the door and waited. There was movement behind the sheer curtain. A tall, gray-haired woman opened the door, smiling and obviously long awake.

"Can I help you?" she asked, raising her eyebrows.

Andie immediately noticed the almond shape of the woman's blue eyes. They were her own, but surrounded by fine wrinkles. Andie's expertise at discerning family resemblances had been perfected by years of study.

"I wrote you a letter a long time ago," Andie began awkwardly.

"Letter? Hmm. And what is your name?"

"Andrea Reeves. But I didn't sign my name. It's just that, I uh…I think you're my grandmother," Andie said, bracing herself for rejection.

The woman put her hand up to her mouth. Her eyes filled with tears. "I knew you would come one day. I just knew it."

Andie gazed at her in astonishment. Her grandmother came toward her and wrapped her arms around her, gathering her into a gentle embrace. They both cried as they stood in the doorway. Drawing back to look at one another, they started laughing, then hugged again.

"Here! Come in, come in! We have so much to catch up on!" She guided Andie into the house and pointed to a row of pictures on top of a piano. "And there is your mother," she said, pointing to a large photograph in a silver frame.

Everything seemed to come to a standstill as her eyes fixed on the face that she had always longed to see. Her mother. Her beautiful, smiling mother! She had long, blond hair and the very same eyes and shape of face as her own. Her round, apple cheeks were shiny, just as Andie's always appeared in photographs. The lines around her mouth were exactly like hers when she smiled. Andie had never had the experience that most people took for granted. She now saw where she came from. It was so clearly apparent that she was a part of someone. Andie felt connected to the world in the most elemental way for the first time in her life. A profound shift took place in her spirit.

"What's her name?" she whispered.

"Her name is Sarah," her grandmother replied. "And your sisters names are Laura and Lisa. They're twins. You also have half brothers who are twins, Tim and Eric. They're eleven years younger than you."

Andie tried to take everything in, but it was happening so quickly that she was overwhelmed.

"Your sisters are only one year younger than you, and they're your full-blooded sisters. Her grandmother directed her over to the kitchen table. "Please sit down. I don't mean to bombard you with all of this. I can't believe that you're really here!"

Full-blooded sisters, how was this possible, Andie wondered as her thoughts raced. "But, how?" Andie tried to speak, unable to believe that she had, upon entering the house, been handed all of this information so readily.

"You see, Sarah married your father six months after you were born, as soon as she turned eighteen. The girls were born eight months later. Here's a picture of them." She handed Andie an old photo in a small frame of two identical girls with blond hair and blue eyes. Andie, flabbergasted, was looking at herself at age ten. Not only did they resemble her, but if Andie were in the picture, they could easily be considered triplets.

"Oh, my gosh," Andie murmured as she sat staring incredulously at the uncanny image.

"You look just like them, you know," her grandmother said softly. "I knew it was you when I first opened the door."

Andie shook her head, trying to gather her thoughts.

"Let me get some more pictures." Meredith got up and rummaged through an end table cabinet in her small living room. "Here we are." She set the album down in front of Andie.

Andie opened the book. There were her sisters, grown up now and still just as similar to her.

"This is Laura and her husband, Tom, at the beach. The whole family lives in Florida now—your mother, all the kids and her second husband, John. They lived in Mississippi for two years. I believe that's where your mother was when I forwarded your letter to her. And here's Lisa and her boyfriend, Alex."

Her sisters had long, straight hair and wore the same types of clothes as Andie—jeans, T-shirts, even a baseball hat put on backwards, big comfortable clothes that gave Andie the impression that they were also athletic. Andie silently looked through the entire album. She saw her blond half-brothers, so young and wiry, with cute smiling faces and the almond shape to their eyes as well. More pictures of the whole family together left her aching to know them. She would have fit right in. It was as if she saw exactly where she would have naturally thrived and formed into what she was meant to be.

They lived in a modest home. Scenes of camping trips caught her eye. Andie's family had never camped and would have been horrified at the thought of not staying at posh hotels in Miami for their vacations. Andie had enjoyed the few camping trips she had taken with friends' families when she was young and had always wished to go more often.

Her birth mother smiled shyly in the photos. Seeing her face from different angles, Andie noticed how similar her mother's entire look and posture were to her own.

"My second husband, Ralph Woodson, did not want Sarah and Joe, your father, to get married. Everyone else, me, Joe's parents and other relatives, all wanted them to keep you. But Ralph was the one with the ultimate say. It was his house and he made the rules. He was very angry at Sarah for humiliating us. We sent her to the Salvation Army home for unwed mothers for five months. At least there was a place here in town for her to go, but it was so dismal there. Actually, we didn't see her much during that time. And finally she called us and asked to be picked up to come home. Ralph wanted no mention of the incident, but I had to ask Sarah about the baby's gender. When she told me it was a girl, I couldn't help crying at the loss of my first granddaughter." Meredith had tears on her cheeks as she reminisced. She looked over at Andie and smiled sadly. "But, now you're back. I knew you'd come back one day."

Andie was touched to realize that she had permanently affected the lives of these people, her family. She glanced again at the pictures of her sisters and knew that she must meet them.

"You know what? I'm going to call Sarah right now! She has to know about this. About you!" Meredith picked up the phone and began dialing.

Just like that, Andie thought, to be able to reach her mother that quickly and easily. An ordinary phone would connect her in seconds to her birth mother. This was suddenly going too fast. What would her mother say? She believed that Meredith must know her daughter well enough to know that this was an appropriate way to handle the situation.

Meredith greeted someone, then waited a moment. "Sarah? Yes, hi dear. I'm fine. How are you? Good, good. Listen, I have someone sitting here that you might like to speak with. You'll never guess! No. You've met her only once before a very, very long time ago…yes! Yes, indeed. That's right. I know, I know. Wait. But she's sitting right here in the kitchen with me. Here! Here she is!" Meredith extended the phone to her.

Andie looked at the phone. She had not thought that Meredith was going to do this. It seemed as if time had slowed down as she reached for the phone. She put it up to her ear, looking at Meredith's eager face. There was no sound on the other end. "Hello," she said softly.

There was only silence and the fuzzy, vacant hum of the open line. Andie wondered if anyone was really there, it seemed so impossible in the first place.

Then she heard an even softer voice than her own whisper, "Hello."

Andie had a quick moment of believing that she had heard the voice before. It sounded delicate and kind.

"I don't know what to say. I feel as if I'm talking to a ghost," the voice said.

Andie was thrown off, wanting to tell her that she had never died. She had never allowed her real mother to be extinguished in any way since learning she was adopted.

"I don't know what to say either. I hadn't planned on talking to you. I'm sorry if this is so sudden," Andie apologized.

"This is…very overwhelming."

"I just decided to come here this morning because I was in Des Moines. Your mom told me about your kids and showed me pictures of all of you. I hope you don't mind," Andie said, looking at Meredith, who was perched on the edge of her chair.

"My kids still don't know about you. I wouldn't know what to tell them," she said. "I really should be going soon. This is such a shock to me."

"Oh, I'm sorry, all right. Do you think it would be possible for me to write to you?" Andie asked hopefully. She felt that if she were to get off the phone without asking this, her mother would be forever out of her reach.

"Well, I suppose you could. Right now, I just don't know what to think. Have my mom give you my address."

"All right. Thank you. And I'm sorry if this was too much for you. I didn't know," Andie said, trying not to feel dejected.

"I'll be okay. I just need some time to take this all in. It's not your fault. I'll look forward to getting your letter. Good-bye."

Andie said good-bye, realizing that this had not been a fair way to have approached her mother. Apparently, Meredith did not know her daughter that well.

"Sarah takes things hard sometimes," Meredith said. "She'll be just fine. Would you like to stay for a while? Have some lunch with me?"

Andie agreed to stay for lunch. She would have to leave soon to pick up her friends and get back to school. Meredith chatted almost nonstop, mainly about herself once the preliminary "catching up on things" was supposedly done.

She learned that Ralph Woodson, the man whose last name was on her birth certificate, had killed himself seven years after Sarah had given her away. Meredith had found him hanging by the neck from a rope attached to a rafter in their garage. Andie found herself at a loss for words while Meredith rambled on about personal subjects, never asking Andie about her own life. When Andie left, she felt as if she had just been caught up in a whirlwind to be tossed back out into normal life, her mind reeling.

Meredith had given her Sarah's address in Orlando and two pictures to keep, one of her real mom and one of her sisters when they were young. Back at school, Andie lay on her bunk in her dorm room, studying every detail of their faces. Now that she had found them, she was never going to be content until she met them.

Chapter 11

With her freshman year behind her, Andie spent the summer months back home with her parents in their spacious two-bedroom apartment. She needed to figure out what she would do when fall came. She did not want to waste time in school, yet her father's message was repeated daily—she had better decide on a major and get her act together! Back home with them, she was dismayed by how quickly she fell into old patterns and emotions.

She did not want to tell them that she wanted to move to Phoenix to be with Karin. She and Karin had spent hours on the phone in the last few weeks, trying to plan Andie's escape. Andie worked as a waitress at the cafe, saving all of her money so that she could get out of Iowa.

Her parents now had to work seven days a week. Her dad had tried to launch a steak and lobster restaurant a few years back, but it had been bad timing. A recession had hit their city, causing massive layoffs in the meat packing plant, the John Deere factory, and had trickled into every other business in town. No one was spending much money on eating lobster and steak. Her dad was repaying an enormous amount on a business loan. The property was to be purchased by the city for land where a highway would be built, but that arrangement was still pending, so the restaurant was equipped as a lounge that Scott managed.

Andie tried to stay away from the apartment and her mom's increasingly erratic behavior. The lounge that Scott managed was frequented by people she knew from high school, so she went there almost every night. Drinks were free because the bar was owned by her parents. Scott attempted to be hospitable in front of the crowd when she came in, pouring a rum and coke or margarita. Andie would go outside with her friends and they would smoke a joint, then eat some of the free food that she would order for everyone.

She began smoking a joint before she went to work. It made the job more challenging to try to remember the orders and not laugh at the people who appeared strange to her. She would smoke in her bedroom, even when her mom was home. It was easier to deal with her mom when she was high. She was careful around her dad, but he was gone nearly all of the time. All of the warnings that she had heard about marijuana were quite alarmist; getting high was similar to having two or three strong drinks, except you did not become so full and woozy and sleepy. When she felt bored or upset, a joint would lighten her mood and refresh her interest. A drunk person might continue drinking until he passed out. She could smoke joint after joint and the high would eventually wear off without the day-long hangover that went with consuming alcohol. The next day she would just feel a bit forgetful and slightly tired until she lit up another joint.

Summer was passing by quickly, and Andie made the decision to move to Phoenix. She had saved enough money and would live with Karin and her mother until she and Karin eventually found their own place to rent. Andie figured she would work and then look into the schools when she decided what she wanted to study. Karin had said that the night life was excellent and there were many schools, so Andie was eager to be on her way.

Sarah's address and the photos were carefully hidden. Andie had written and thrown away many letters, never feeling as if any of them captured what she wanted to say. She knew that Sarah was deeply disturbed by the sudden introduction into her life. She thought it might be best to give her some time to adjust to the idea that she had been found.

She told her parents that she would be leaving in two weeks. They had believed that she would be going back to college to take the classes that she had signed up for before her freshman year had ended. Her father was furious with her and told her that she was "nothing but a pain in the ass." He suddenly acted as if he had the right to make decisions about her life when he had virtually ignored her for years. Andie was disgusted with his chauvinistic, hypocritical ways. She stayed at a friend's house, going home only to prepare her belongings.

The day of her departure, Andie packed her car and said good-bye to her parents. Her dad dismissed her with a wave of his hand and told her that she was making a big mistake. Her mom cried, for no reason that Andie could understand. She was just glad to hit the open highway on her way to a place far from a lifetime of misery. She smoked joints throughout the long drive, listening to loud music as she passed through cities and fields. She wondered about all of the people in the houses she saw. Did they have good lives, or were they suffering through some private hell as the days went by? When Andie was young, she would try to see into houses as they drove past them at night, catching glimpses of someone sitting at a kitchen table or walking across a room. It had made her feel better to see people living privately, unaware of her eyes, and she wanted to know what it was like to be someone else in a completely different life.

Andie stopped in small towns to eat and stretch her legs. She enjoyed hearing the conversations coming from the people around their tables and watching families eating together. No one knew her—she was a traveler passing by to a distant land, a notion that made her feel older, worldly. She took her time on the trip, staying overnight in wayward hotels, stopping at any tourist attraction advertised on road signs. She called Karin and told her that she would arrive a couple of days later than she had planned. At each meal and instead of driving late at night, she sat in various local establishments taking in the lives around her. Cafes like her parents' were the best places for getting the feel of a town.

It was reassuring to discover such a vast amount of people in the world carrying on with their routines, apparently content to be where they were, doing what they were doing. Andie wanted to try on their lives and determine what kept them functioning in each place, yet she did not ever want to be trapped in any one life.

Soon, the green fields became scarce, replaced by pale, parched ground with scraggly bushes and flat dusty land. Closing in on Arizona was like entering a time warp to the past, or some desolate future. Everything seemed dry and lifeless as the desert stretched on and on. Her throat was scratchy from the air, so she bought extra drinks at gas stations. Occasionally, there were dead armadillos on the side of the road, looking like deflated gray footballs with tails. Something about this land did not feel right. Maybe it was because she had come from the lush heartland where the soil was fertile and the greenery abundant. This was a ghost land compared to her home. But the red hills in the distance were pretty, and it was interesting to be in such an unusual place.

She drove into the valley of Phoenix near dusk. A red mountain range bordering the far east side of the valley caught her attention. If she looked just right, she thought that she could see the profile of a child's face gazing upward into the sky. Andie drove into Mesa, finding the roads that led to Karin. She had not realized what a good navigator she was.

CHAPTER 12

It was like coming home to be with Karin again, although Andie still had not gotten used to Phoenix in the late summer. The temperature would get up to one hundred ten degrees, with no wind to offer relief. Karin worked at a hospital in the dietary department, and Andie spent her days looking for a job. Unless she wanted to be a waitress, there was nothing that would pay her enough to live well. Without an education, she would never be able to make much money.

Andie soon found a school that she wanted to attend. The session started in two months, so she had time to arrange the financial aid. It was a broadcasting school, where she could learn to become part of the journalism world. In college she had contemplated studying journalism, but there were so many prerequisite classes to take first. Here, she would delve right into the meat of the subject. She would help run a radio station, writing news and commercials, being a disc jockey, and learning all facets of both radio and television operation. It was expensive for the one year program, but compared to four years of college she would not have as much to repay on her student loans. She had given up on her old dream of becoming a nurse.

Andie was biding her time until school would begin. She would eventually need to find a part-time job because her finances were becoming strained from all of the nights out and buying groceries. She and Karin would go out three or four nights a week to bars and night clubs. There were so many new things she was going to be able to do. Andie now had time to look around at her world. She had spent most of her life engrossed in survival, so she had missed the chance to evaluate society. She watched 20/20 and other news programs on television. She liked to read the newspaper and keep up on current events.

She had finally mailed a letter to Sarah just before she left Iowa. It was three weeks later, and she was waiting for a response. In her letter, Andie had written briefly about herself, leaving out family information. She included pictures from when she was six months old to the present time. Karin was amazed at their likenesses when she saw the pictures of Sarah, Laura, and Lisa. Andie hoped that Sarah would want to meet her one day soon, but knew that it might be impossible because of Sarah's children not knowing that she existed. She kept the pictures of them next to her bed.

One evening at a night club, Karin introduced Andie to a group of people. One guy was handsome and would glance over at her, but stood slightly back from the group. Andie was bold after three drinks, so she approached him and started a conversation. Her extra weight made her feel self-conscious, but he seemed interested. They were both surprised to learn that they were from the same home town in Iowa, but they had never met because he had gone to the Catholic high school that Judy attended. She thought that his name sounded familiar. He was her brother's age and even knew Scott. He said he was sorry, but he thought that Scott was an idiot. Andie liked him immediately. They talked for the rest of the night and planned to get together again. Steve was living with his mother temporarily, having just arrived, until he could find a place of his own.

It occurred to her that she and Karin needed to move out—maybe they could all share a big house. Karin had been hinting that her mom wanted her to start paying rent. When Andie asked Karin if they should move, Karin told her that she would feel guilty leaving her mom alone after so recently moving down from Iowa with her. Her mom was emotionally unstable, which was getting on Andie's nerves. She would rant and rave about her ex-husband, saying terrible things about him. She expected Andie to be her audience whenever she was home, but Andie had experienced enough living with a person in crisis for awhile. Karin finally admitted that she was not going to move out yet, but that she would as soon as the right time came.

Steve and Andie were together almost every day since their first meeting. He also liked to smoke marijuana, so they would go hiking and sight seeing, sharing a joint. They seemed to have so much in common, and he was carefree and exciting. They soon became lovers. John had been her first, but Steve seemed older and more experienced. She believed that she was falling in love with him. He was always cheerful and made her laugh, and his desire for her made her feel secure and appreciated. It was only one month later that they found an apartment and moved in together.

Karin seemed relieved that Andie had found a place to live. Her mom had begun to make comments to Andie about using the house as a landing pad. Steve had a good job, so he would pay most of the bills while Andie was in school. Andie knew that Karin was somewhat hurt that she was with Steve most of the time, but life went on. She still talked to her almost everyday. Karin had a part-time boyfriend that she would break up with every few weeks, so Andie did not feel guilty about her decision. Things seemed to move along so quickly now that she was an adult.

Andie was watching a news program on television one night. The report was about how the economy had changed during the last one hundred years. Andie had so many new thoughts about life and questions that she wanted answered. As she sat there, she decided to do an experiment. Since she would be investigating and reporting for school soon, she wanted to practice. While she smoked another joint, she formulated a plan.

The next morning she went to the nearest library where she hoped to interview an elderly man for his opinion on the economy and how he viewed the changes in America over the years. Mesa, a suburb of Phoenix, was loaded with retired people, so Andie believed that she could find a willing subject in the library. She would tell the person that it was a school project, which was somewhat true. It was her own practice project to prepare for school.

Andie carried her notebook and looked around the quiet library. She headed for the reference section by the card catalogues, noticing a few other young people. They were probably from the city college that was right down the street. One older man caught her eye immediately. He was tall with a distinguished air about him, wearing a light blue sweater that complimented his neatly groomed, white hair. Andie walked toward him, but he was turning and heading for the door to leave. She was disappointed, even though there were plenty of other elderly men in the building.

She walked over near the line of long tables in between the rows of shelves and saw a few men seated at them. One man was alone at a table, reading a book. She went right up to him with a feeling that he was the one. "Excuse me, sir. Would you have a few minutes to be interviewed for a school project?" Andie asked politely.

The man looked up at her slowly, a smile spreading across his weathered face. "I have all the time in the world."

"Great, thank you! This shouldn't take very long." Andie sat down, opened her notebook and uncapped her pen.

The man was intelligent and poised. Everything that Andie asked him, he had an answer for that was full of insight, almost as if he had prepared for all of her questions. Andie could not believe her luck—he was a wellspring of knowledge and ideas. They conversed for nearly two hours. He asked her about herself and she told him of her recent move to the area and the school she would attend. He wanted to know about her family and if she had many friends in the area. He was kind and gentle, like a concerned grandfather. Andie felt extemely drawn to him and believed it was because of her affinity for older people.

She had volunteered at a nursing home for two years when she was in elementary school. She used to sit and listen to her aging friends talk about the old days. Andie would hold their hands or fetch them a drink. They would often stare out of their windows at the warm sunshine that she was able to feel on her skin every day as she walked home. She had the utmost respect for the elderly.

The man began talking about religion, asking her about her background. She confessed that she had not been raised with any particular faith, but that she believed in God. He told her that he was a high priest in the Mormon church. Andie had heard of the Mormons, but knew nothing about their beliefs. Mr. Farley went on to tell her about his religion. He told her that the Mormons were the true chosen people of God. The church of Jesus Christ of the Latter-day Saints was the Lord's kingdom once again established on earth. Jesus Christ had appeared in ancient America to twelve Nephite disciples. Joseph Smith, the founder of the religion, was the prophet that saw the vision of a messenger in 1823, who told him of an ancient record engraved upon plates that were hidden in the ground in New York. A man named Mormon ended up reading and translating the messages from the plates, which contained a sacred record of the people in ancient America. The book of Mormon was first published in 1830.

Andie was fascinated by his story. She had respect for Christians and accepted the fact that Jesus was God's Son. Mr. Farley told her that the Mormon church was the fastest growing religion in the world. He told her that Mesa had one of the largest populations of Mormons, next to Salt Lake City and that there was a legend that part of the special golden plates might be hidden in the Superstition Mountains. Many people had tried to find the plates, but had never returned after going up into the mountains to look for them.

She was captivated by this charming man. When he invited her to come over to his house the next day for lunch, she eagerly accepted. Steve would be working and she still had weeks before school would begin.

The next day she followed his directions to an isolated area. His house was set back off of a long dirt road with no other homes nearby. It was not easy to find, but Andie finally arrived. His wife, a short, plump woman with a net over her gray hair, opened the door and greeted Andie. She said that she had lunch ready for them, and then sat quietly as her husband chatted with Andie.

Andie admitted that she was living with her new boyfriend, which she could tell was disturbing to Mr. Farley. Most older people frowned upon cohabitation outside of marriage, but she did not want him to think that she was a bad person. They went into the living room after lunch while his wife stayed in the kitchen and cleaned.

He asked her more about her family, so she told him of her recent discovery of her birth mother and family. He wanted to know where they lived and if she had plans to meet them. Andie felt pleased that someone was so interested in her. He listened attentively and asked many questions.

Bringing up the subject of religion again, he pulled out a book of Mormon from the bookshelf next to him. He said it was for her and that he knew she was going to be in the library the previous day. He told her that he was waiting for God to bring the right person to him for a special plan. Andie thought that he was exaggerating, but found him whimsically eccentric. Although, it would be great if there were a predestined path in this new life of hers. Maybe he was right—they were supposed to meet. After all, she had walked right up to him in the crowded library instead of finding someone else.

Andie was rising from a chair, getting ready to leave. She hesitated as she picked up her purse, feeling an odd sense of detachment. She tried to recall what they were just doing, but could not remember anything. Mr. Farley had his arm around her shoulder and was thanking her for the wonderful visit. She did not want to appear strange or rude by asking what they were doing a moment before.

He handed her the book of Mormon and told her that he looked forward to seeing her the next day. Andie nodded her head and thought, yes, of course I'll be back tomorrow, though she had no recollection of this being discussed. She opened the door and gasped at what she saw outside.

It was night! She had only been at his house for lunch and a short visit, hadn't she? The sun did not go down until nearly nine o'clock at this time of year. How had all of the time passed? Andie was disoriented as she said good-bye and got into her car. Sitting there a moment trying to gather her thoughts, she felt an unshakable dullness in her mind. She drove home with a sense that she had left something behind at Mr. Farley's house. The haze was similar to when she first woke up in the morning from a very short night of sleep, except that she was not tired. In fact, she was physically very wide awake.

She and Steve took a walk that night and then sat in the Jacuzzi by the pool, drinking White Russians, her mind settling down after the alcohol and marijuana took effect. She asked him if he knew anything about the Mormons and told him about the sweet man that she had met. He did not know much about the Mormons, having been raised in a Catholic home, but lately he had been exploring Buddhism. Andie told him that she had heard that people were not supposed to worship idols. He said that there were so many religions in the world and each was thought to be the only legitimate one by its believers. How could anyone know for sure?

Andie was determined to learn more about the Mormon history and their link to this area. She was going to be a reporter and this was a good story—mysterious hidden gold plates, the chosen people of America.

Late that night, Andie was still not tired. She stayed up reading the book of Mormon, which seemed to use the same kind of language and structure as the Bible. She did not understand what the premise of the book was, but knew that Mr. Farley would explain it to her soon.

The next morning, she was still alert. She drove over to his house and found him home alone. After eating their sandwiches, they sat and discussed religion again. He told Andie that the Mormons would lead the way into the future if they had strong members who were willing to spread the word. He said that it was fate that brought her, a journalist, to him. There was a lot of work in the future for her to do for the Mormons. Andie listened, intrigued by his words. He sat directly in front of her, speaking softly and looking into her eyes. It was flattering that he thought she had such a purpose. She relaxed and listened to his melodic voice as it soothed her.

When she left, it was once again night time and she felt even more perplexed. She remembered sitting down and talking right after lunch, but after that point she did not know what they had done to pass seven hours. She felt very confused when she tried to recall anything. Mr. Farley was telling her that he would see her the next day and she was agreeing with him. She had the feeling that something was just on the other side of her awareness, as when she tried to recall a name and it was on the tip of her tongue, but it eluded her. She drove home feeling troubled, yet determined to read her book of Mormon and eager to see Mr. Farley the next day.

It was incredible how he was so familiar to her, but she had only known him for three days. Now she had a real purpose in life, thanks to him. She believed that she was destined to be associated with the Mormons. He had left her feeling a strong conviction that she would be able to attain great heights and aspire to help many others if she listened to him and followed his direction. Andie had always wanted to be able to aid mankind through something that she did. She loved to help people and make them feel good. Now she could do it on a grand scale.

For the next two weeks, Andie spent all of her days at Mr. Farley's. She informed Steve that she was busy, so she would not be home much on the weekends. Steve noticed that she was not sleeping anymore and she had lost weight. When he mentioned this to her, she said that she did not have enough time to eat or sleep. She sat reading the book of Mormon and taking notes. If he offered food to her, she felt sick. She would rarely take a drink, even with the Arizona heat zapping the moisture from everything. She had lost her sense of humor and even appeared confused when doing simple tasks. Steve figured that she would snap out of it. She just needed to get some sleep.

Chapter 13

Mr. Farley was speaking to Andie. He told her that she needed to shed her past life before she could begin her new one. Her divine purpose would not be fulfilled unless she was willing to trust in him to guide her to her destiny. Andie listened as he told her that her family and friends would interfere with her work. It was imperative that she understood that she was not to speak of any of this information. If she did, she would be unable to go on to what she was supposed to be in life. Enemies were everywhere. The adversary had many tricks to deceive her into being weak and forever doomed. Now that she knew what her role was, she would be constantly bombarded by people who would try to stop her from fulfilling her work.

There would be a party held in her honor over the coming weekend. Farley said that some other Mormons were looking forward to meeting the person who would be an important part of their lives. Although, it was required that she first break away from everyone in her present life to move forward into her real life.

Steve told Karin about the way Andie was behaving, so Karin tried to call often only to find that Andie was always gone. Andie would come home late at night and sit up in bed while Steve slept, then she would walk around the apartment complex or write in her notebook. Her confusion had grown and she felt very sad at times, but then she would feel a burst of hope and purpose for her new life. She knew that she had to be careful not to speak to anyone about what Mr. Farley had said.

After her next visit to Farley's, she drove to a gas station and took her purse and the papers in her glove compartment and threw them into the dumpster. She cried as she did it, feeling confused and torn, but still following the prompting she did not understand. She went home knowing that the next day was the party at Farley's, the day when she was supposed to end all other relationships.

Steve was out with friends all evening, so Andie left early in the morning with a bag of clothes and drove around until the time of the party. She arrived to see a large canopy in Mr. Farley's backyard. She felt as if everything were a dream these days. Still, she was even more driven to carry out her purpose, then she would feel better and be able to think clearly.

People were seated at chairs and milling around under the canopy, but no one seemed to notice her. She did not understand why Farley had said that they all wanted to meet her. She was ignored. He introduced her to a few people and they barely acknowledged her. Andie was confused and hurt. She sat and watched everyone for the rest of the evening, noticing Farley glance over at her occasionally.

When everyone had left, he told her that the reason no one paid attention to her was because she had not totally broken away from her old life. Only when she did this would they accept her. He finished talking to her and then stood. Andie was to leave, go back to her apartment, pack all of her things, and never return to the suburb of Chandler where her apartment was located. If she did return to it, she would see hell on Earth. She listened fearfully, believing completely.

Andie packed everything from her apartment that she felt she would want to keep. She cried as she looked at the pictures of her sisters and Sarah. She had wanted to meet them, and now she was supposed to give them up forever. She figured that she would not even be allowed to write to them to explain. This did not seem fair.

She felt a bit of stubbornness in her soul. She knew that she was expected to return soon. Where would she sleep tonight—at his house? She did not like this idea, yet she felt powerless to go against it. Lately when she thought of him, she would feel anxious. He was the one who was in charge of her now.

Andie also packed a Bible that Steve had in a box on the floor of their closet. The Mormons believed in Jesus Christ, but she felt as if she were cheating when she grabbed it and stuffed it into her backpack. She locked the apartment behind her as she left.

She drove to a spot where she could look at the Superstition Mountains and stopped the car. She sat for a while and began crying. She pulled the Bible from the backpack and flipped through the New Testament. She had read bits of the Bible over the years and knew about certain passages from attending Catholic mass with Judy's family. She read for nearly half an hour until she unintentionally turned to the last page of Revelation. Chapter twenty-two verse eighteen and nineteen stated: "For I testify to everyone who hears the words of the prophecy of this book, if anyone adds to these things, God will add to him the plagues that are written in this book: and if anyone takes away from the words of the book of this prophecy, God shall take away his part from the Book of Life, from the holy city, and from the things which are written in this book."

Andie was stunned. Joseph Smith had seen a vision of a being that told him of some sacred plates in a grove in New York in 1823. He went on to establish "Christ's" church in its supposed original purity upon the Earth. On the cover of the book of Mormon it stated "Another testament of Jesus Christ."

This went against the Bible!

There were to be no other testaments. Jesus was to come again one day, and He was supposed to reveal Himself to everyone to let the truth be known, not just a small group of people in America. The book of Mormon had gone against what was laid out on the last page of the

Bible. They had added a whole book and professed that He had come back already. Then what was the book of Mormon? Who was right? Andie was very confused, but felt a building suspicion of Farley and his beliefs. She felt disobedient, but she had to think about all of this before she did anything else.

But wait, he had said that the adversary was strong and would try to trick her into disbelieving. The adversary was not the Bible though—it had the testament of Jesus in it. It was the word of God, so the Bible was true. Andie's mind jumped from one thought to the next. She was determined to sort through her jumbled mind and think clearly.

She drove to the Mormon temple, which was near Farley's house, deciding to take a tour through it to see what she could find there. The enormous lawn, the size of a few football fields, led up to a gigantic, white building with immense pillars. The first thing that Andie saw when she went in was a towering, white marble statue of Jesus Christ. She had to tilt her head back to see the top of it. The entrance to the temple reminded her of an art museum, everything hushed, very stately and grand in appearance. An ornate podium held the registration book for visitors to sign on their way in. A tour was just beginning, so Andie joined the group as they were escorted to a large theater. The cushioned chairs were fixed to the floor, with each row slightly elevated above the one before. A burgundy velvet curtain with shiny gold trim covered some kind of stage or screen. The lights dimmed and the curtain slowly swept open.

A spotlight illuminated a figure that frightened Andie at first because it was so realistic. Then the face began to move as it spoke. An image was being projected onto the face, making it appear to move. She watched the reenactment of Joseph Smith's vision and the messenger who told him of the hidden plates. Scene after scene followed, displaying the beginnings of the Mormon religion.

Andie could barely remain seated. She was filled with such incredulity. Farley had maintained that the Mormons believed in the simple life, not valuing material possessions. So far, Andie could see that they flaunted and used an enormous amount of money to win people over. Her upbringing in a wealthy home that was barren of love had ingrained in her a loathing of the greed for possessions. She had told Farley this, but he had obviously downplayed the Mormons true holdings and their ability to use it to persuade potential members.

Farley was a hypocrite.

The show ended and the group was ushered through a large room where pictures and artwork depicted the life of the early Mormon founders. They were then taken to one of five mini-theaters, where short films were shown. They were supposed to go from number one to number five in order, until the final film was completed. Families were shown happily interacting and loving one another, except the mother was always in the background tending to her duties, subservient to the husband. The father would speak, but the mother stayed removed from the scene unless she was performing a chore or supporting one of her needy family members. The subtle messages were cleverly woven into the blissful domestic scenes, but the gist of it was obvious to Andie—women were second-class citizens. She had heard jokes about Mormons having more than one wife, and now she could see that there might be something to it. Women were of no status in their community, except as child bearers and meek wives. The slick, polished films were not blatant in this message, but after seeing five of them, Andie was well aware of their intent. After growing up with a chauvinistic father, she could spot prejudice easily.

The last step of the visit took them to a room where each person individually met with two "recruiters." They tried to talk her into becoming a Mormon. She attempted to reason with the two young men about what she believed to be the truth of the church, but they seemed disturbed by her heated lecture. She gave up, turning and leaving the room while they called out for her to come back and listen. She knew who she really wanted to talk to, the liar, Farley. The whole temple and its "tour" was a glossy, persuasive production to gain more members into the church by offering a chance to be part of their wealth and have a family where the man was his own little god. In fact, she had read something about each man becoming godlike in the book of Mormon.

Andie drove directly to Farley's house and knocked on the door. His wife answered and Andie told her that she had been to the temple, seen the truth, and wanted to talk to her husband. Mrs. Farley told her to wait, that he was resting because Andie had taken so much of his energy recently. Andie waited in the living room. Farley came creeping slowly toward her from his bedroom, his eyes staring into hers accusingly.

"Sit down, Andie! Are you not able to fight off the attacks of the adversary? Didn't I tell you that he'd try to trick you? We need to discuss some things. Now. Listen to me. Hear my words. You will listen and hear me," he stated.

Andie's body lost its tense posture and she sank into a chair. She relaxed and looked half asleep.

She remained listening for nearly an hour, then she was told to get up. He stood next to her, watching every move that she made.

"Tonight you will be with some friends of mine, two girls your age, whom I've arranged for you to stay with for a few days until we can find a permanent place for you. You will enjoy their company."

"All right," Andie agreed. Her clothes hung off of her frail body and her skin was pale and dry. She had not eaten in the last few days, and since the previous day she was not able to drink anything. Her lips were chapped and tight. She could feel waves of fatigue and a stabbing pain in her belly. The girls soon came over to get her, and she followed them in her car to their apartment. They seemed odd to Andie, whispering and snickering and then becoming serious. Andie had never been this tired. It was early evening and all she wanted to do was lie down. The girls made up a bed on the couch for her before they went into their bedroom and left Andie to rest for the night.

She lay in the quiet room, but could not relax. She had images flashing through her mind of Farley. He had instilled in her the belief that he could see her no matter where she was. She must obey his rules. She was not to drink, or eat, or speak of anything he had said. Tomorrow she was supposed to go to the temple for a special Sunday ceremony. She was worried about being in front of a crowd. Trying not to think of anything, because she just wanted to rest and not be in this terrible new world, Andie closed her eyes.

Bizarre images appeared in her mind and swirled nonsensically. Her heart beat faster and she began to feel frightened. Something was not right. She curled up and covered her face as an image of a snake biting her continued to play out, even with her eyes open. She had a fear of snakes ever since she was bitten by a large King snake as a child. The adversary would use a snake to torment her if she allowed him near her.

Andie looked around the quiet apartment and saw that glasses of water had been set out everywhere. They were all full and all of transparent glass. Why had they done this to her, she wondered. This must be a test. Farley was obviously friends with these girls. Maybe they had been brought to him at one time for a "special plan." Her skepticism was coming out again, but with it came images of the adversary and a giant snake waiting to rip into her with sharp fangs. She was trying to block out the images, but then she would remember that Farley could see her. Not only that, she was told that he could read her mind. She wrestled with her mixed-up thoughts and emotions.

Hours later, overcome with a desire to escape her fear, she allowed herself to believe that she would be safe if she could get away from the apartment. Maybe he could read her mind because he knew where she was, but if she left and stayed moving, he might not find her.

She carefully gathered her belongings and crept out of the apartment to her car. She did not know where to go. Her apartment in Chandler would be hell, and Karin and her mom had to be sleeping. She would drive around and think about it. She just had to keep moving.

Andie drove for two hours, at times almost paralyzed by the certainty that something was after her. She could sense the approach of evil as she drove aimlessly. She needed a plan. She decided to take the lone highway all the way out to the Superstition Mountains. If she climbed up the mountain, she could sit and view the city and watch for anyone who might try to approach her. She should be safe there for a while, away from anywhere that had been classified as hell or off-limits.

The dusty highway was not lit by lights, only reflectors. She tensely gripped the steering wheel, checking the rear view mirror for any cars. While she drove, the thought occurred to her that she was not obeying Farley, so she would have to face the adversary. It was probably going to take place on the mountain. Many snakes, rattlesnakes and others, inhabited this area, so she knew that she would be contending with one of her worst fears. She was willing to undergo this final trial in her quest, rather than following Farley. She had just enough stamina to decide that she would not follow him.

After driving more than seven miles outside of the city limit, her car sputtered and came to a halt. She felt as if Farley had reached right into her car and stopped it. But then she looked at the gas gauge and saw that the needle was buried below the "E." She had run out of gas in the dark desert, miles from any building or light. She slowly stepped out of the car, looking at the still distant dark mountains and then at the glow of the city, debating which way to go. She could continue walking to the mountains, or she could go back to the city. Jumbled fears and images floated through her weakening mind.

This had probably happened because she was not obeying Farley. He could see her anywhere, after all, and he had stopped her escape. There would be no safety in the mountains, so she might as well go back to him and deal with whatever was in store for her. He would be very angry with her.

She shook off her sandals and tossed them onto the side of the road. She left her keys in the car and the door open. She would repent for her sin of trying to rebel by roughing it to the city barefoot. She did not look back at her car as she walked down the middle of the highway. The dark desert sounds were sibilant. She did not look to the side for fear of seeing snakes slithering toward her. During her walk, she stumbled and fell a few times as her body struggled to continue moving without having had water or nourishment in days. Her mind was beyond her control. All she could hold onto was that she must return, or she would die. She had failed and would certainly be punished. She would try to atone for her sins when she got to the temple. She walked for miles.

* * *

The sun was coming up behind her, changing the sound around her with its appearance. Birds flew overhead, chirping and diving, as if they were heralding her procession back to the city. Far ahead, a car was approaching rapidly. She squinted at it, determined to carry on with her journey in the middle of the road. The police car slowed and pulled up next to her. She continued walking, looking straight ahead. A man rolled down the window and called, "Hey…you! What are you doing? Stop for a minute. Stop!"

Andie resolutely kept her sore feet walking on the center line. She did not acknowledge his presence; who knew what side he was on? He called out a few more times, then suddenly did a U-turn and drove off. Andie nodded her head in satisfaction for having kept him away. She walked on and on.

Some broken glass lay in the road ahead of her, right in the middle, another test. She walked across it, cringing as a few shards pierced her feet, but trying to deny the pain. She deserved to be punished. Her heart fluttered in her chest as her body strained against the assault of constant motion. In the distance was the wall of a subdivision. She had finally neared the edge of the city. The sky was completely lit now as she tried to think of the best direction to take to the temple. The sign on the wall said Sunland Village. Of course, it was Karin and her mom's neighborhood! She decided that she would walk through it. It was right there in front of her, so she was probably supposed to.

After entering the subdivision, she soon located Karin's street. It was early in the morning, so no one was out yet. She went up to Karin's front door and rang the doorbell several times, but there was no answer. Walking to Karin's bedroom window to knock on it and wake her up, she saw a fresh red rose lying on the windowsill. She burst into tears, realizing that this meant that Farley was right—Karin was dead. The rose was proof that someone was mourning her. She hung her weary head and sobbed, but no tears came. She reached up to her mouth and felt her lips. They were hard and dry, like her tongue. She could not summon any saliva to moisten them. Turning, she shuffled across the sidewalk.

She heard a sound, a familiar sound. It was coming from a neighbor's house, whose front screen door allowed the sound out into the quiet morning. Andie walked up to the house and pulled open the door. She went into the house and looked to the left toward the sound, where she saw a preacher on TV giving an early Sunday morning sermon. The elderly couple eating their cereal at the kitchen table put their spoons down as Andie sank to the floor directly in front of their TV.

A voice said, "Can we help you?"

Andie slowly turned away from the preacher, whom she had hoped to receive a message from. Blinking was becoming an effort as her dry eyeballs hindered the closing of her eyelids. Her eyes burned as she noticed the elderly couple sitting at a table, staring at her. She ignored them and turned back to the sermon.

The husband stood up, "Look here…you don't appear to be feeling well. Where do you live?"

Andie gazed at the TV.

The man looked at his wife. He went over and turned off the television. He knelt down next to her. "Are you hurt? Can we help you?"

She had thought that she would get a message from the man on TV, but now this man was wanting her attention. She looked at him and shook her head. He might know Farley. This was Mesa, land of the Mormons, and he was about the same age as Farley. Maybe he was someone who would give her a message. She let the man and his wife help her to the couch. It felt good to lean back. Her feet were throbbing, but she tried to block out the pain that had been radiating from various parts of her body for a while now. They continued to ask her who she was and where she was from. She only shook her head and pointed to her mouth. Farley would like that she was not speaking of anything when they reported her to him.

The woman brought a phone book over and told her to locate her name. Andie flipped through the pages and came to "F." She felt fear creeping into her soul as she located Farley's name and pointed to it. The couple would find out anyway, and this was probably a test of her loyalty. Now they knew where she belonged. He would be coming for her soon.

She vaguely heard them talking to someone on the phone. The woman brought a basket of laundry over to Andie and asked her to help her fold some socks. Andie fumbled with the thin black material, unable to figure out how to do it, but the woman took the socks and told her not to worry. The gentle woman was so kind that she wanted to stay with her and listen to her soft voice.

Then the man said it was time to go, so they escorted her to their car. They drove to an Alpha Beta grocery store, driving slowly around the parking lot until a man waiting by the side of his vehicle waved to them. They helped Andie out of the car. Andie could not look at Farley, and she was suddenly terrified to go with him. Why hadn't she stayed with this nice couple?

Farley quickly took charge of the situation, having noticed Andie's reluctant behavior. He thanked the couple and told them that she needed some medical attention immediately, so he had to be going right away. He put Andie into the back seat, slamming the door. Once on the street, he turned to her and said, "You will pay for this! I will not allow such disrespect and ingratitude. You were warned! You're an evil, ignorant child. You're going to be taught a lesson!" He began speaking a garbled, bizarre language.

Andie cowered in the back seat, exhausted and trembling. Arriving at his house, he pulled her from the car and walked her far into the back yard. He stood her next to a rectangular, roughly hewn table that was waist high. He began talking to her using words like those found in the book of Mormon. Andie at first could not understand what he was trying to say until he switched to normal speech.

"You have failed to fulfill your destiny at this time. You have not reached the level where you need to be, as I thought you had. There's no way for you to continue, unless you die and are reborn to try again in another life to reach the level you need to attain. I don't want to do this, but I've been instructed by God to carry out this order. You must die. Your blood must spill onto the earth for you to receive atonement for your sinful ways." He pulled out a six-inch knife.

Andie was riveted by fear and shock. He was going to kill her, stab her or slit her throat. She was shaking and moaning as he brought the knife close to her face.

"Andrea, I regret that I was not able to assist you in this lifetime. I tried, but you were resistant to my best efforts. There is no other choice but for me to kill you. You can come back and try again to reach the level needed for you to be complete. Your disobedience has kept you from fulfilling your work." He seemed to be preparing himself for his next move as he held the knife high, pointing straight up to the sky.

Andie covered her face, too horrified to move or speak. This is where she would die. She deserved to die. She had always imagined that being stabbed to death would be one of the worst ways to die. She waited for his first strike, wishing that she could have lived to see her sisters, but they would never know her.

Andie silently pleaded, "Dear God, please help me."

Minutes passed. He was silent. Then he said how difficult it was for him to have to kill her. She waited to feel the knife cutting into her, so she kept her eyes closed, shaking uncontrollably. He remained quiet for minutes. Andie stole a quick look at him. His eyes were rolled back in his head and his mouth was moving. This seemed just as frightening and Andie moaned, thinking that no dream had ever been as bad as this. His eyes snapped straight and looked at her, gray eyes like marbles, cold and dead. He looked at her as if she were detestable.

"You do not deserve to live. Even though God ordered me to kill you, I will not do it right now. You are spared for the moment. Now come with me!" he said angrily.

He guided her into the house to the kitchen and placed her in a chair, then began making toast. He put three plates in front of her and told her to choose one and eat. One piece of toast was dry, one had butter, and one had jelly. Andie stared at the plates, then looked up at him, puzzled and leery. He was hovering over her, swaying slightly as he watched her. She could not remember when it was that she had last eaten. She knew that he was the only one to allow her to eat. He was offering food to her, so she assumed it would be all right. She picked up the toast with butter and took a bite. Her dry mouth was not able to mash the piece well enough to swallow, and she thought that she was going to choke. It hurt her cracked lips to move her mouth.

"You have eaten from the fattened calf!" he roared.

Andie dropped the toast and began coughing and gagging on the piece lodged in her tight throat.

"Your choices are greedy! You are lustful and corrupt. I should not let you live!" he bellowed.

Andie closed her eyes, finally swallowing the toast.

Farley was doing something on the kitchen counter with a glass. She looked up to see him finish pouring a glass of milk. In one hand he held a small, brown glass bottle, similar to the kind that vanilla extract came in. The liquid was clear that he poured into the milk from the little bottle. He brought it to her.

"Drink this! Do it now!" he commanded.

Andie was thirstier than she had ever been in her entire life. She recalled the glasses of water in the girls' apartment and how she had yearned to take a drink then. It was painful to be so thirsty. But after her walk in the desert she had reached a point beyond pain. She took the glass and drank half of the milk. She relished the cool wetness as it coursed down her throat, filling her belly. Her stomach immediately cramped. She leaned on the table, clutching at her dirty shirt. She nearly vomited, but the cramps slowly subsided as she took deep, shuddering breaths.

He walked her to a chair in the living room and began talking to her. She soon relaxed and listened. He said that he was God and his brother was the devil. He had been battling his brother since time began. He had the power to give and take away life. There was an order that must be followed or the world would not be a good place to live. He was in control of her, and she must never stray from him again or she would be killed. There was evil in her that had to be purged. She needed to be made clean. He was going to perform an exorcism to release the demons that lived in her body. He told her that she might not live through it. Satan would be nearby, ready to take her if all did not go as planned.

He led her to a small, plain room with a twin bed in the corner and told her to lie on it. He said that he was going into the other room because he did not want to be present when the demons appeared. He would be praying for her soul while she stayed in the room. She would either come out of the room clean and alive, or she would die a horrible death at the hands of Satan and his demons. He closed the door.

Andie lay in a fetal position, listening for the sounds of evil to come. Certainly she would see Satan and his demons; what a sinful life she had led. She doubted that she would be leaving the room. Her death had only been delayed for a short time. A presence seemed to be in the room with her. The air was suddenly cold. Her mind spun out of control as she entered a realm of fear unlike any she had ever experienced. The room seemed to be shaking and odd shadows passed by the window. She curled up as small as she could and whimpered as she squeezed her eyes tightly closed. She did not want to see any demons; it would be far too much for her spirit to bear.

Time shifted and lurched. She could not tell how long she lay in sheer terror anticipating her worst nightmares. It seemed to go on for hours. Her soul was stripped bare of all sense of normalcy and security. She was alone against the devil and his minions. She wondered why it had to end this way. All she ever wanted was to be loved. Grief for her short, unfulfilled life consumed her. She began crying out into the blanket, fearful of being heard, but unable to remain still and quiet any longer.

When nothing came for her, having overheard her vulnerable cries, she screamed loudly. If she was going to be tortured and die, she did not want to wait any longer. She wanted this nightmare to end, so she challenged the forces that were to kill her, to do it now. She pounded her fists on the bed, hysterically thrashing and yelling.

Nothing happened. She slowly stopped screaming and moving. As the minutes passed with no sign of an enemy, she began to calm down. She peeked out around the room and saw nothing unusual, trying to listen carefully for sounds in the house. Where was Farley—could he see her right now?

Andie suddenly felt the resilience of one who has lived through severe trauma to flirt with, and even mock death. She flipped her middle finger up into the air and waved it around.

"Damn you to hell," she whispered, then covered her face, expecting certain retaliation.

None came, so she opened her eyes again.

She lay blinking at the ceiling. Nothing was pursuing her and she was still alive. If Farley had been praying and exorcising the demons from her, yet she still felt this rebellion, then his plan must not have worked. And yet, she had not been attacked by Satan.

She decided that she had to get out of the house. The door was slightly ajar, so he must have looked in on her at some point. Her thoughts were still not lucid, but her instinct for self-preservation was increasing. She got up cautiously, expecting something to rush at her. No, there were no demons, they would have gotten her by now. Farley was the one she had to escape from! She remembered his silver knife and felt a pang of fresh fear as she inched toward the door.

Peeking around the corner into the living room, she heard his voice in another room. She needed to hurry to the front door and get far away from him.

He was suddenly standing in front of her.

"So, you're alive," he snarled at her. "Now, you've got a new problem. You will soon see the true depths of hell. Your friend, Karin, just called. She got my number from those meddling people you bothered. She's insisting that we deliver you to her or she'll do something rash. She doesn't realize that she's putting your life in danger by making you go there. She's really dead. What you'll see are ghosts who will speak as their former selves did. You must absolutely not speak to these ghosts. You're on a path to cleanliness, but Karin may interfere enough to throw you off your destined course. Sit down for a moment."

Andie sat and listened, taking in all of the words he spoke. His message was the most powerful of all. She was now programmed to literally see hell.

He was still angry as they walked to his car. His wife walked next to Andie and kept her arm around Andie's waist. He stopped before opening his car door and locked eyes with her.

Without moving away, he suddenly vomited a gush of thick liquid near her feet. Wiping his mouth with his sleeve, he scowled at her and said, "You're vile."

Andie stared at the puddle of yellow-brown on the ground. Bits of grass poked up, coated with slime. She looked at him and began shaking her head, trying to back away, but Mrs. Farley held her rooted to the spot.

"No, oh no," Andie moaned at the apparition that was Farley's face. His eyes had narrowed to slits and his face seemed to be changing shape. It was the face of a serpent, nostrils flaring, skin wizened to a point at the wide mouth, glaring at her with hatred. She closed her eyes and felt Mrs. Farley's hand stroking her shoulder. She was pushed into the back seat of the car. They drove slowly in the right hand lane to Karin's house.

During the drive, Farley was alternating between his nonsensical eerie speech, and warning her in English about all of the demons that she would see. He told her that a demon was living inside of her and was trying to get out. If she went to hell she might never leave because the demon would recognize his home and try to keep her there. Andie shook her head from side to side. Mrs. Farley whispered to her that everything would be all right if she obeyed.

They pulled into the driveway, where Karin stood waiting. She ran to the car and pulled open Andie's door. "What did you do to her?" she demanded.

Andie was still shaking her head and moaning. She saw Karin and felt sad that Karin was a ghost, dead to her now. The Farleys ignored Karin and called out to Andie, "We'll talk to you soon! Be careful!"

"Don't you ever come near her again! I'll call the police next time!" Karin watched the car drive away.

Andie stood motionless. Karin put her arm around her, noticing how thin and pale she had become and that her lips were cracked and bleeding. "Andie? Are you okay?"

Andie stood mutely gazing at Karin's familiar face. How she wished that Karin was not dead. Ghosts could live on earth appearing in their same form, but only certain people could see them if they ventured to the wrong area. Farley had left her in another world.

Karin led Andie into the house. Her mother stood in the kitchen cutting up meat for dinner. Andie saw her and began screaming. Karin's mother's face was the face of a hideous demon, leering at her and flicking its long, thin tongue out toward her. The eyes were red and evil, worse than in a horror movie. It had recognized Andie as it made a hissing sound. Holding the knife, it tilted its head back and sent the message to Andie that it had been waiting for her.

"No!" Andie cried, grabbing Karin's arm and pulling her into the back bedroom. She had to get both of them out of there. She tried to open the window and get the screen off, but could not manage the lock.

"Andie, what are you doing?"

Andie frantically pointed to Karin and then to herself, gesturing toward the door where her mom was knocking. She got the window open and then scratched and pounded at the screen, finally denting the frame, which allowed her to push it outward. She grabbed Karin's hand and pulled her to the window. Karin climbed out first, then Andie followed. She hurriedly led Karin down the street to the edge of the golf course. The grass felt soft and moist under Andie's feet. She and Karin would be safe for a while. They walked along the fairways, seeing a few golfers starting out.

Karin did not know what to do with Andie, she just knew that she had to keep her from running away. The people that Andie had been with had done something terrible to her. Karin tried to ask questions, but soon gave up, realizing that Andie was not going to speak. After walking a while, Karin noticed that Andie was faltering as if she could not go on any longer. It was obvious that she needed to go to a doctor. Her face was an unnatural white and her lips were coated with dried blood. Karin began going in the direction of her house again, trying to divert Andie's attention from their destination. As they neared the street, she saw Steve sitting in his parked truck. Her mom must have called him. Karin waved to him and tried to point him out to Andie.

Andie allowed Steve to put her in his truck. Karin and Steve were talking about going to the hospital, but Andie was frightened of hospitals and needles. She shook her head at Steve and tried to get out of the truck. He told her he would only take her home to rest and feel better.

Rest, home—Andie wanted to go home. The word meant everything that she had never had. She wanted to be in a place to feel safe and loved. Steve and Karin were ghosts, but they had known her and cared about her. They might know the way, and she was so tired of trying to find it. She leaned back against the seat and shut her eyes as Steve drove.

They entered the suburb of Chandler and Steve said, "We're almost home." Andie lazily opened her eyes and looked out the window at a field in front of some apartment buildings. There were demons in the fields attacking people. One was ripping the leg off of a child, savagely biting into and shaking it from side to side. It flung the child down and held the leg up high. A woman was running away from a group of gray toad-like demons who hopped along after her. A few of the demons stopped what they were doing and looked directly at the truck into Andie's eyes. They began leaping and twirling, running toward the street, pursuing the truck. She moaned and covered her face.

Steve entered their complex and pulled into a parking spot. Andie hurried out of the car and motioned for Steve to go quickly. She went up the stairs, surveying the area for the appearance of the demons that must be close by. Steve locked the door behind them and took Andie into the bedroom.

"Sit down. I'm going to run a bath for you, then I'll get you something to eat. When did you eat last?" he asked gently.

Andie shook her head. Soon she heard the water in the bathtub and became anxious; Steve might be planning to drown her. She was definitely in hell, and he had been living here. Farley had warned her that Steve was evil and wanted to harm her. She had not wanted to believe him, but as she watched Steve methodically tending to her, she thought that she noticed a menacing glance. He helped her up and tried to take off her clothes, but she resisted. He attempted to pull her shirt off and that was when Andie knew for certain that this was a trick from the adversary. She was in his territory and he was using the perfect weapon to get to her. She struggled and began screaming as he pushed her toward the bathroom.

"Come on, Andie, you're filthy! It'll make you feel better!"

She hung onto the doorway of the bathroom, trying to stay away from the water where he would drown her. She darted to the side, catching him off guard. She shoved him violently backward and hurried toward the front door, opening it and running down the stairs.

Let the demons try to catch her! She was going to run, with every last ounce of her strength, out of Chandler and hell. She heard Steve right behind her. He easily caught her and tried to pick her up. She spun around, dug her fingers into his eyes, and began screaming the Lord's Prayer. He yelled and tried to shake her hands off, but she dug in harder. He bit her arm near her wrist to save his eyes, but she did not stop. He finally had to drop her before she gouged his eyes out.

She took off running onto the field, her labored breathing burning her dry throat. She could not summon much strength to run, but pushed her body out of fear. The highway was just ahead. If she followed it, she would be out of Chandler soon. She ran out onto the busy road as cars honked and veered to the side. A large truck swerved, missing her by inches. She looked through the rushing stream of traffic to see Steve running across the field. She ran down the center of the highway, causing two cars to collide and others behind them to bump into each other. There was the crash of metal and sound of shattering glass as a pileup of cars formed on one side of the road.

Sirens were approaching in the distance. A neighbor had seen the couple struggling outside and believed that an act of domestic violence was occurring. On their way to the apartment, the police came upon the line of cars jammed on the highway. Vehicles were in every direction on the road, some intact, others with their fenders or hoods crumpled. People were getting out and yelling at one another. In the middle of the road they saw a young woman running and looking fearfully at a young man who was calling to her. It might be the couple from the nearby complex where they had been called to stop a domestic crisis.

The first officer drew his gun as he approached the dirty, hysterical female. She was gaunt and frightened. He told her to get down on the ground and she did so immediately. He knelt down next to her and saw her bloody cracked lips and sunken eyes. "Tell the paramedics to come over here first!" he called to his partner.

"Please help," Andie's mouth formed the words, but no sound accompanied them.

Andie was loaded onto a stretcher and taken to the nearest hospital. During the ride, she attempted to fight off the paramedics when they tried to start an IV. She thought that they were demons who were torturing her with needles. They pinned her arms down and found a vein.

In her hospital room, Andie kicked and slapped at the nurses who tried to keep the IV in her arm. They strapped her arms down, but she continued to fight, kicking and twisting, so they had to put her in a four point restraint. Her ankles and wrists were pulled up into the air by wide leather straps attached to chains suspended from the bars of the bed. Her gown fell open, exposing her nude lower body, so that anyone who walked in was greeted by the sight of her bare torso. Andie was humiliated. A few times she was able to slip her thin, sweaty wrist out of the strap, then pull the needle and tubing from her other arm. A nurse would eventually come in and strap her down again. Once, she managed to slip both wrists out and was trying to get her ankles free, when a male attendant came in and roughly secured the straps, tightening them as far as they would go. He called for the nurse to put the IV in again, as Andie screamed and struggled.

Steve was at the front desk answering questions from the police, then from the admissions receptionist. He did not know if Andie had insurance. He told the police how she had been behaving recently and that she had never acted this way before.

Later, the doctor came out and said that they would have to transfer her to the county psychiatric facility. He told Steve that upon arrival there, he would need to convince Andie to voluntarily sign herself into the facility. He said that this was the best way to handle things, but that if she would not do it, Steve could notify the hospital and they would order it.

Steve gathered her bag of dirty clothing and followed the ambulance to the Maricopa County facility. Andie was wheeled on a stretcher from the ambulance to the entrance, where they were buzzed through two sets of doors until they reached the holding room. The dirty linoleum floor offered old plastic chairs to people waiting to be called. In another room people were handcuffed, waiting with a policeman. Steve thought that it looked more like a prison than anything else.

Andie was taken away by some people. She looked up at them from the stretcher. They were talking to each other and looking down at her. Her eyes would lose focus and their faces would blur together. She could not tell whose side they were on—God or Satan.

One person shoved a clipboard in front of her and put a pen in her hand. "Sign this, right here," he ordered, pointing to a line.

Andie turned away, but the pen was shoved into her hand and her hand was grasped and directed to the paper.

"Write your name!" he demanded.

Andie moved her hand, wanting the voice to stop yelling at her.

She was placed in another bed where a doctor examined her and warned her that she would be punished if she lashed out in any way. Andie held still, relieved that she was out of the restraints and that no one was trying to put a needle in her arm. She had purple marks along both arms at the inner elbows and wrists. She wanted to stop feeling everything and just cease to exist. People were trying to make her answer questions, but she did not respond. She only wanted to sleep. She dozed off for a while, disoriented and frightened whenever she opened her eyes.

A man told her to get up and come with him. Her legs felt like lead as she plodded into a large room full of people, where he left her in a comfortable chair near a window that was covered with thick bars. Andie fell asleep again, her head hanging down and twitching occasionally.

A loud crash woke her up. She opened her eyes to see two men fighting in the crowded room. One had picked up a small, metal garbage can and was hitting the other over the head with it. A person in a guard uniform entered the fray, becoming a target for the crazed man. The guard was jumped on, then bitten and scratched on his face and arms. Two other people joined in attacking the guard, who was lying on the concrete floor with blood on his face, screaming for help. Another guard appeared, waving a gun. The instigator was hit on the side of the head with the gun before he would get off the bleeding guard. The other two had backed up immediately at the sight of the gun. Suddenly a group of other uniformed men came in, pushing and yelling at the crowd of clapping and howling people.

Andie knew that she had finally reached the pit of hell.

Chapter 14

Andie curled up in the chair and squinted at all of the people who circled around her. Some came rushing up, trying to frighten her by shouting and lunging at her. One man with a scraggly beard spit on his hand and smeared it on her cheek, "You are mine," he said.

She turned her head away to block out the group around her chair, which eventually thinned to only a few persistent ones. An older woman was drooling and chuckling, trying to stroke Andie's hair, her eyes hard and unblinking.

People babbled to themselves, shouting into the air at no one. Some rocked violently back and forth while sitting in chairs near a long table. Most of the others were walking in a circle around an adjoining U-shaped hallway that led, at either end, back into the large room. Around and around they shuffled and stepped, wearing paper slippers or pacing barefoot.

All of their eyes were like those of animals, devoid of kindness or peace, watching for attacks from the other creatures in the room. The woman who had tried to pet her head had joined the group of walkers. She would stare at Andie as she came around into the main room, snickering madly, drool hanging in long strings from her chin. Two men were briskly walking, bumping into some of the others as they raced each other around the hallway. One was intent on being in the lead, so he would try to push the other one back if he got ahead of him.

Andie sat in the chair for a few hours, afraid to get up or look around, thinking it was a bad dream that she would wake up from soon. Somehow her life had slipped out of her control and she had landed in a bizarre nightmare. But the fear never stopped. It only became worse as she realized that she could not leave this place and no one was going to help her.

The sky outside the large window was beginning to change color, dark purple and red, then fiery pink and lavender. The Arizona sky was out of her reach. Two big carts were wheeled in containing cardboard trays of food stacked on racks. Nearly everyone sat down at the three long tables and ate their dinner. An old man, hunched over and limping, stopped beside Andie and asked if he could have her food. Andie nodded her head and looked the other way. She could not feel hunger, though her stomach ached and felt hollow. Her lips and mouth hurt, and sharp pains shot through her head, making her squeeze her eyes closed. She had on light blue paper booties—one kept slipping off of her left foot.

A woman took some mats out of a closet that had been locked, and she had a man help her pass them out to everyone. The woman came over and helped Andie out of the chair to an area on the hard floor where she made her lie on the thin plastic mat, like the kind used in kindergarten. Some slow, relaxing music was started, and the woman began telling everyone that they were feeling tired and comfortable. She told them to raise each arm and then each leg as she counted to ten, then they were to relax that part of their body. Andie was frightened at first, but began to relax as she listened to the tranquil music.

The lights were dim as each person was quietly led to a bed for the night. Andie was handed a plastic tub with a toothbrush, small tube of toothpaste, bar of soap, a comb, and a small bottle of lotion. She was taken to a room with twin beds and told to put her tub in the bathroom.

In the other bed, a dark form could be seen under the blanket. The attendant left her sitting on the side of her bed and told her to go to sleep. She stared at the form in the other bed, with visions of Farley as a snake throwing back the covers and leaping on her.

Andie got up and slowly approached the bed. The moonlight outside of the barred window at the head of the beds offered enough light to see the dark, straggly hair of a woman who was softly snoring. Andie relaxed and stepped backward to her bed. She climbed in and pulled the sheet up to her neck. The stiff pillow under her head felt like luxury as she fell into a fitful sleep.

A loud voice called out, "Everybody up!" as someone banged on the door. Andie's eyes shot open and she felt panic set in as she realized that she was still in hell. The night of sleep was her first in many days, so her body had finally rested, but her mind was now in overdrive as she tried to figure out what was happening. She sat up and saw a woman in the open bathroom, sitting on the toilet. The young woman had messy, dark hair and creamy brown skin. She looked very tired and was moving slowly. She saw Andie and came over to her.

"Come on, baby, let's get you ready for the day," she said to Andie, reaching for her hand. She walked Andie into the bathroom and guided her through brushing her teeth and showering. She helped her comb her hair and put lotion on her dry skin. She was gentle and thorough, as if Andie were her young child. Andie became soothed by the caring attention.

"Let's go eat breakfast now, honey." Ernestine led Andie by the hand to the main room and they sat down at the table, waiting for breakfast. Andie had not eaten anything since the bite of toast at Farley's house. She stared at her plate of scrambled eggs and toast, but did not touch it.

"Here, baby, eat this toast. I'll put jelly on it for you." Ernestine spread grape jelly with a plastic spoon onto both pieces of toast. She held one up to Andie's mouth, and Andie took a bite.

The rich, sweet flavor filled Andie's dry mouth as she slowly and carefully chewed the piece. She was suddenly ravenous.

"There you go," Ernestine said. She handed her the slice of toast.

Andie ate both pieces of toast and a few bites of egg. She drank a container of orange juice and a carton of milk. Her stomach was so full that she felt as if she had eaten a five course meal. Ernestine ate all of her own food and finished Andie's eggs.

After the meal, everyone would spend the day sitting or walking around the room and hallway. All of the bedrooms were locked. The men had rooms on one side of the building, but the mens' area was kept locked during the day. The circle walkers had already begun their endless trek around the hallway. Andie saw the old drooling woman shuffling along.

The outer door to the intake area opened as a newcomer was brought into the room. She yelled at the guard who escorted her, then turned to brusquely greet someone in the room that she knew. She radiated intense anger and high energy. Her dark eyes surveyed the room and stopped on Andie. Andie tried to act as if she had not noticed. The woman was taller than Andie and built like a man, even walking with a masculine swagger over to Andie's table.

"Who the heck are you, girl?" she demanded.

Andie ignored her and looked to Ernestine, who had turned toward the woman.

"I'm talking to you, little blondy! You better learn to answer when I talk to you. What the heck you doing in my chair?" she shouted.

"Come on now, get on outta here away from us," Ernestine said firmly.

"Ho, ho! Do we have another little child now? I'm not talking to you, big and ugly!" the woman yelled.

A guard came over and told the woman to sit in another area.

"I'll be seeing you later!" she said, glaring at Andie.

Andie had forced herself to avoid contemplating her predicament, because her mind was playing tricks on her. She still thought at times that she could be seen by Farley, and then she would look around and realize that others had taken over his job of watching her. She would feel panic overtaking her and begin to shake uncontrollably. She was intent on just being able to function physically again.

Ernestine was a welcome presence, but the other people continually bothered her. Whether or not they noticed her, she was disturbed by their bizarre, violent behavior. She let Ernestine braid her hair and lead her around the room.

Late in the afternoon, Andie sat near the window to look outside at the palm trees bordering the parking lot. She watched people park their cars in the lot and walk into the building. How easy it was to take freedom for granted, she thought. This was the same as being in prison, except the people here were all insane. Her throat felt like it was closing up. An overwhelming need to be outside, away from this distorted world, made her pace in front of the window. She had found a door in the hallway that had an emergency bar on it, and she wondered if it would open. Everyone else just walked by it without a glance. Maybe it was some kind of test to see if she was smart enough to escape. All of the people seemed demented and without the ability to figure a way out. There might only be a little more time left until these people turned on her. They seemed capable of killing her. What if they were really demons? They certainly didn't act human. She would be imprisoned with them in this horrible place where they could tear her to shreds. They had the power to overtake the guards if they all joined together.

She felt panic rising in her chest as she looked over and saw the drooling woman pointing at her and snickering. Andie began walking toward the emergency door. Suddenly, she felt someone come up against her side, leaning into her.

"Where are you going so fast, blondy? I got some other plans for your skinny self." The woman grabbed her arm and dug her nails into her skin. Andie pushed her away and ran at the door, slamming her weight into it, setting off an alarm. The door did not open. She pounded on the door, yelling and jumping up to hit the small square window near the top as the loud ringing echoed in the white hallway. The woman punched Andie hard on the back. Andie whirled around and shoved the woman to the floor. She began hitting the door again until she was roughly grabbed from behind. Three orderlies pinned her to the ground, mashing her face into the tile, telling her that she had just made a mistake she would regret. Their voices were cruel and mocking as they hand-cuffed her and dragged her to a small, brightly lit room.

They put her arms into the sleeves of a straight jacket, which crossed her stretched arms in front of her and pulled them tightly around to either side, her palms flat against her shoulder blades. The pain in her joints was greatly increased when they laid her on a narrow, metal table that was high off of the ground.

"There you go! That ought to teach you not to act up. Enjoy the scenery!" one laughed as he locked the windowless door behind him.

The entire ceiling was covered with rows of extremely bright lights that could not be looked at directly without causing pain. If Andie struggled, she would fall off the high table to the hard floor below. She moaned and tried to keep her eyes closed as tightly as she could. She wanted Ernestine to rescue her, but she knew that she was on her own.

Hours later, they came in and sat her up. Andie did not resist or respond to their questions. She had been claustrophobic ever since Scott had locked her in a storage trunk in their basement. He had taken the quilts out of it, shoved her down and slammed it shut on her fingers. She had pulled in her sore hand, and then it was dark for what had felt like hours. The moth balls in the trunk had made her eyes water, and she had to breath through her mouth to keep from vomiting.

"So now you know what'll happen if you don't follow the rules! It'll be worse next time, so just remember that. You hear me, Goldilocks?" the man sneered at her.

Andie let them undo the straight jacket and slide it off. Her shoulders throbbed and her muscles spasmed from the change in position after so long. Her head hurt from lying on the metal table. She was dizzy as they took her to the main room and left her in a chair.

Ernestine came over to her. "Baby, where'd you go? I been looking for you. Come on over here and let me see if you're okay." She smoothed Andie's hair and looked into her eyes, gently holding Andie's chin up. "They didn't go hurtin' you, did they?" she asked, troubled. "My poor little baby, I won't let no one hurt you again."

Andie laid her head down on the table and tried to get the image of the bright lights out of her mind. Even with her eyes closed she could still see a yellow-orange glow. She had panicked in the room, her heart speeding, her breathing fast and irregular as she envisioned what might come into the room next. She was an easy kill for the demons that would soon be coming in to get her.

The men had laid her on another sacrificial table, just as Farley had planned to do when he stood her next to the one in his back yard. She would die after all, just as Farley had told her she must. She was in sheer terror for hours. The pain in her shoulders had become unbearable, but she knew it would never end. People in hell would live with eternal pain and suffering. For her, this was only the start.

Chapter 15

The counselors tried to interview her the next morning, but she still would not answer questions, only nodded or shook her head in response. Steve had supplied them with family information, which only added to their impression that Andie was mentally ill. A dysfunctional home and the recent discovery of her birth family seemed enough to cause a breakdown.

Karin was outraged when Steve told her where Andie ended up—she couldn't believe that he had allowed it. He said that it had all happened so quickly that he hadn't known what to do. Andie had signed herself in for a mandatory five-day period, during which she would be evaluated to determine if she should stay longer. The decision was up to the counselors as to how much longer she would stay if they decided she must. It could be anywhere up to a year, and a stay in another facility could be recommended.

Karin was determined to convince them of Andie's sanity. No one had believed her when she told them of the Farleys' involvement. She learned that the Farleys had already been in to see how Andie was doing. They had been interviewed by the counselors, but the counselors would not tell Karin what had been said. She wondered how they had even found out that Andie was there. She was told that she could visit Andie just before dinner was served.

Karin arrived at four-thirty and checked in at the desk. She was cleared through to the main area and began scanning the room for Andie. She did not see her right away because many of the people swarmed around her as soon as she entered the room, blocking her sight. Then she saw her. She was sitting on a couch in between Mr. and Mrs. Farley. Their arms were around her and they were whispering to her. Andie looked scared and pale.

"What are you doing here?" Karin exclaimed. She grabbed Andie's hand and pulled her from the couch.

"We're visiting our friend, if you don't mind," Mr. Farley answered. "You can sit down, Andie. Karin can't bother you."

Andie stood next to Karin, not wanting to sit back down. "Get up right now and leave, or I'll call the police!" Karin ordered.

"There's nothing you can do. Andie wants to be with us. You'll just have to accept that. Sit back down, Andie," he commanded.

"No!" Andie said abruptly, taking a step away from the couch.

The Farleys took in this new show of strength from her. They slowly stood. Mr. Farley said, "We'll be back in a few days. You'll feel better then. You're just not yourself because of this awful place. We love you, Andie." He tried to reach out and touch Andie's hand, but Karin pushed his hand away.

"Leave her alone! You've screwed her up enough! Get out of here!" She steered Andie away from them as they slowly walked out of the room.

"Andie, what were they doing here?" Karin asked. "Oh, my gosh! I've been trying to get these people to let you out of here. Do you know where you are?"

"No," Andie quietly answered.

"You're in the county psychiatric facility where derelicts and insane people are kept. You don't belong here at all!" Karin said.

Andie looked fearfully around her. Karin lowered her voice. "Hey, I'm sorry. I just can't stand to see you like this. The Farleys messed you up. Do you realize that? You've probably lost fifteen pounds, and you were so dehydrated that they said you would've died soon if they hadn't gotten those fluids into you at the hospital. You really should've stayed in the hospital, but you were getting unruly and they didn't think you had insurance. This should be a crime what they've done to you, sending you here!"

"Karin, are you a ghost?" Andie whispered.

Karin laughed heartily and said, "No, but the people in here are raving lunatics. I'd like to be a ghost, the way they keep looking at me!"

Andie's mind made the connection that this was her same friend from long ago. Karin was real and alive. She started crying and hugged Karin tightly.

"Oh, Andie. I'm so glad you're okay." Karin hugged her, then leaned back and looked at Andie's haggard face. "Now we've got to get you out of here."

A man called out, "Visiting time over in five minutes!"

"Andie, promise me that if the Farleys come here again that you'll tell them to leave. Don't listen to them or talk to them. They have some kind of hold over you, so don't let them near you! I'm going to get you out of here, but you also need to show the counselors that you're normal. You have to start talking to them. If you don't, they can make you stay here for as long as they want. When you get out of here, we're going to rent some movies and stuff our faces all weekend, okay?"

Karin could tell that Andie was losing focus. She had shown that she comprehended things, but then she would drift off, gazing around the room. "Andie, the guy is waving at me to leave now. I'll be back tomorrow and we'll have you out of here. Is there anything that I can bring you?" Karin asked.

"No. Just come back," Andie replied. She didn't want Karin to go. When she left, Andie was afraid that hell would reappear. Right now, she could understand that what Karin had said was true. They said good-bye, hugging as Karin told her again that everything would be all right. Andie watched her leave, wondering why she herself did not have the privilege to walk out the door.

Lying in bed that night, Andie heard tapping on her window. She was frightened as she turned and looked out through the glass. Steve stood in the moonlight holding a notebook. Andie squinted, then he pressed the paper against the window. "I'm sorry. I love you very much," the note said.

Andie put her hand up to the glass. Steve wrote again, then held the notebook up. "I had to work today, but I'll see you tomorrow. We're going to get you out of there. You'll be home soon. I miss your smile." Andie tried to see into his eyes. She pressed her upper body against the window, longing to be next to him, feeling instead the cool surface against her cheek. She could hear Ernestine snoring and smacking her lips.

He held up another page. It read, "Talk to the counselors. It's the only way to get out. Show them you're feeling better and want to go home. Karin and I will be back tomorrow. I have to go. There's a guard out front. I was looking in a lot of windows. I love you." He lingered for a moment when Andie put her hand to her eyes, then her chest, and then pointed to him. She smiled slightly for the first time in a long while. He kissed his hand and laid it on the window by her face, then he was gone into the night.

Chapter 16

In the morning, Andie responded to the questions from the counselors. She could not tell them about Farley, so she said that she had taken some acid and other drugs at a party and had gone off the deep end. She told them that she was feeling much better, but needed to go home to start school. They continued trying to probe her mind for signs of psychoses due to her upbringing.

Andie could tell that they were skeptical. She was feeling better after another full night of sleep and the meals she had eaten. She asked them why she could not leave, and they insisted that she had to wait the entire five days to be evaluated. Andie was frustrated and felt like crying, but did not want to allow any emotions to be seen. She told them that she was scared of some of the people and that she didn't belong there. They just nodded their heads and scribbled notes on their papers.

She went out to the "day room" and Ernestine came right over to her. Andie stood looking out the window, trying to see birds or any other animals. She longed for the familiar, and a sign of normal life. She would be so happy if she could just walk outside into the sunlight, but she was at the mercy of forces beyond her control.

After Karin had rebuffed the Farleys, Andie began to understand that Mr. Farley had done something to her. She felt betrayed, and she was angry at herself for being so gullible. She didn't know how it had all happened, but she had lost her mind in the process. Why did he want to control her? Andie didn't even want to remember all that had occurred in the last few days. Visions of frightening situations flashed through her mind when she tried to relax. She was still exhausted.

Ernestine was helping her get her lunch set up, opening the pack of plastic utensils and salt packet. Andie looked at her face and knew that luck had placed Ernestine with her in this hellhole. Andie imagined that Ernestine had grown up with a flock of younger brothers and sisters. Andie's own mother had never been as attentive in her whole life as this woman was in a few days. Andie wondered why Ernestine was there, but did not ask. Ernestine gave her the impression, by the way she referred to things, that she had been in a while and would continue to be for a long time.

Karin and Steve came just before dinner. They had spoken to the counselors and learned what Andie had told them. The three counselors all took turns with a patient, then each wrote an evaluation. By the leading questions regarding Andie's consumption of acid and other substances, Karin and Steve knew what Andie had told the counselors to explain away her odd behavior. They were both encouraged by her sudden change and ability to reason, and hoped that she would be back with them soon. They told Andie that they would return the next day and that they believed the counselors would be releasing her the day after that.

In bed that night, Andie was having trouble falling asleep. She could hear Ernestine snoring and almost envied her easy acceptance of the circumstances. She was thinking about how the pen had been thrust into her hand to "sign herself in." She was never told what she was signing. There was no way that she would have signed herself into this place. There must be some legal recourse for such an act; she would have to mention it to someone. She was anxious about the final decision that the counselors would be making. The way things were going, she wasn't too sure that luck would be on her side this time. If she could leave, she would never take her freedom for granted. She finally feel asleep.

She awakened with a start. Someone was standing over her bed, breathing heavily. Andie could see the shape of the person, suddenly fearing for her life. It was the woman who had yelled at her. She had come up to Andie a number of times and told her that she was going to kill her, but Andie had heard and seen so much wild behavior that she had not taken it too seriously. Now, she was about to make good on her threat.

"I told you that you should have listened to me," she said as she pulled Andie's covers off and grabbed her hair with both hands.

"No! Help!" Andie screamed. She slipped off the bed, pulled by her hair. She fell onto the hard floor on her side and tried to kick upward at the woman. Just then the woman was grabbed and slammed to the ground. Ernestine put her hands around the woman's head and began bashing it on the floor with a meaty smacking thud each time it hit the tile. The woman pushed Ernestine off and they were suddenly standing and punching one another.

The intense fury and viciousness were overwhelming to Andie as she sat on the floor watching. They yelled loudly as they hit and kicked one another. The lights came on and two guards pulled them apart. Ernestine's chest was heaving and her mouth was bleeding. Andie felt cowardly for not coming to her rescue. The mean woman was telling Ernestine that she was going to kill both of them next time. Ernestine looked confused and tired as she was taken out of the room. Andie hoped that they wouldn't put her in the straight jacket. They probably had a few of those rooms, and who knew what else, for the rule breakers. Andie never saw Ernestine again.

The fifth day came with bright sunshine in the Arizona fall. Andie sat in the counseling room and waited to hear her fate, but they were taking their time coming into the room. One man finally came in and told her that they had made a decision, as Andie held her breath. He said that she would be released on the condition that she get follow-up psychiatric treatment. They had determined that her behavior had been drug induced. She was free to leave after she signed some papers.

She was free! After carefully reading and then signing the papers, she called Karin, who would soon arrive to take her home.

Andie stood waiting for the man to open the security door to the outside entrance. "Take care of yourself," he said as he shut the door.

She thought that someone was bound to run at her and tell her that it was a mistake; she would be staying after all. She ran to the door that led to the parking lot and pushed it wide open. The fresh, clear air was all around her, no bars to stop her from walking forward into the warm sunshine as it caressed her skin. In the facility, she had worn a loose pajama-like top and pants. Now she had on the shorts and T-shirt that Steve had brought in, which hung loosely on her frail body. She wanted to rip her clothes off and let the sun reach every part of her. She held her face up to the sky and closed her eyes, taking a deep breath, overjoyed to walk out into the day and feel the warm goodness of freedom and life.

CHAPTER 17

Andie was sitting on the grass, hugging her knees to her chest, when Karin walked around the corner from the side parking lot. Karin ran to her, relieved at the coherent look in her eyes.

"Andie!" Karin exclaimed, helping her to her feet. "Let's get out of here."

"Oh, thank God! We'd better hurry," Andie said, looking behind her at the door.

Once in the car, Andie told Karin to hurry out of the parking lot, still anxious that someone might try to stop her from leaving. Relaxing when they reached the highway, Andie looked around at all of the familiar sights and felt as if she had been living in a barbaric country and was just returning for the first time in years. Karin stopped at a convenience store and told her to wait while she got them each a drink. Andie watched all of the cars pulling in and the people hurrying in and out of the store. She wished that she had just moved to Phoenix and could start over. Karin handed her a giant cup of soda, a bag of chips, and two of her favorite candy bars. "I'm going to have to fatten you up," she said.

Steve was waiting at their apartment in Chandler. Andie was nervous when they began driving on the highway where she had been picked up by the ambulance, but there were no demons in the field. Steve had left work early after Karin called with the news, and he had lunch waiting for them when they arrived. After sitting with Steve and Karin in the kitchen, Andie became tired. She was grateful to be home, but nothing could keep the exhaustion from setting in. Karin told her that she would see her tomorrow, and as she left, made Steve promise to call right away if Andie needed anything.

Andie continued to feel exhausted each day, even after sleeping ten hours at night. That week, she and Steve went to an animal shelter and picked out a fat, white puppy with amber eyes. She named the puppy Ashley and started training her to follow her everywhere. The puppy was intelligent and responded right away to commands. Ashley would follow her to the mailbox each day, sniffing the sidewalk, catching up quickly if she lagged behind. Caring for the puppy's needs helped Andie to begin functioning again, though she sometimes could feel darkness closing in on her.

She tried to ignore the feelings of panic and fear that would set in unexpectedly, causing her heart to race. A sense of impending doom would overtake her and she would not be able to shake it off for hours. Steve would light a joint and offer it to her, which relieved her slightly, but a few times had caused the panic to start. School would begin in a few weeks, so Andie needed to get control of her fear. Everything seemed overwhelming.

She would go into the grocery store and try to shop, but the aisles became too narrow and the colors on labels of cans and boxes lining the shelves were too brilliant under the bright lights. She would start to panic, breathing rapidly and looking for the nearest exit, leaving her half-filled cart in the middle of the store. Sometimes in the apartment the ceiling seemed too low, so she paced and tried to get her mind away from the keening distress that would rapidly build. Andie did not know who might have seen her the day that she had freaked out, and was embarrassed if she noticed anyone looking at her for too long. She and Steve would sit in the hot tub late at night, drinking Kahlua and vodka, sometimes smoking a joint. Andie would be so drunk and relaxed that she would finally fall asleep on their futon bed with Ashley by her side. Still, there was no peace to her days because the world could change at any moment and become a place that was unreal and dangerous. The people around her all seemed to have secret motives, so she closed herself off, knowing that it was safer to observe life as it happened around her. If someone tried to engage her in small talk, she would become fearful of their motives. She questioned her own sanity; how many people were committed to an insane asylum, unless they were insane?

Karin came over one morning with a letter from Florida for Andie. Andie tore open the letter from Sarah and saw a stack of pictures. She looked through them first before reading the letter. Sarah had put the pictures of herself and her kids in chronological order as Andie had done with her own pictures for Sarah. At every age, they were so remarkably similar to Andie that she felt as if she had found some unknown pictures of herself that were lost. The pictures of Sarah when she was younger looked like Andie dressed up in 1950s style clothing. Sarah said that she would like to meet her soon, and that she had slowly looked at each picture of Andie as the pictures showed her from an infant to an adult. She felt that it was important for them to know each other, and said that when the girls were born, she thought that God was replacing the daughter that she had given away. She wanted Andie to write again soon and find a time and place where they could meet. Sarah was not sure how she was going to tell her children about Andie, but said that she was praying about it.

When she felt the familiar panic, she was able to slow it down if she looked at the pictures. They made her feel grounded and safe. She wrote Sarah and suggested that she could fly to Orlando over Thanksgiving break, which was only a month and a half away.

Sarah called her when she got the letter and said that she would like to see her at Thanksgiving. She invited her to stay at their house over the long holiday weekend. Andie eagerly accepted the offer. Sarah mentioned that she was going to tell her daughters soon, but her sons were only ten, so she would wait to tell them when she knew how to explain it. Andie felt she had survived a journey through hell and was rewarded by her deepest desire being fulfilled. She would get to look at, talk to, and start a relationship with her mother, and maybe even her sisters and brothers.

She began attending night school every weekday in a class of eleven men. She kept to herself, still unsure how to behave in public when the panic would start. This no longer seemed the best choice for a career, but she wanted to follow through with it, hoping her normal outlook on life would return. She could control the panic better as the weeks went by, but she awoke frequently at night, sweating and moaning as something evil chased her through her dreams. She sometimes woke up as she was moving around the apartment, frantically scratching and hitting the walls. It always took her a while to get her bearings when she awoke. She did not even have a sense of who she was at first; there was only a primitive terror that permeated her whole being and made her feel as if she were suffocating and dying. She was often worn out in the morning, so she drank cups of strong espresso to wake up.

Steve was glad that she was going to meet her real mother, but seemed reluctant at the thought of being apart from her. He told her that he wished he could go with her, but Andie did not want any interference. Though she had been relying greatly on his presence for security, she wanted to have this all to herself.

Andie answered the phone one night and heard a vaguely familiar voice ask to speak with her.

"This is Andie," she replied.

"You sound just like Lisa! I can't believe it! Oh, I'm sorry Andie. This is Laura, your sister!"

"Laura? You know? Your mom told you!" Andie exclaimed. "It's so great to hear your voice!"

"This is all amazing, like a dream. I have another sister! An older sister!" Laura said excitedly.

"Hey, I'm only one year older than you! When did your mom tell you?" Andie asked, feeling a welcome, easy banter with her sister.

"She told us last weekend at my house. I just got married, as you probably know. Anyway, we couldn't believe what she was telling us! How could we not know about you for twenty years? You're our full-blooded sister! This is so cool!" Laura exclaimed.

"Did she tell you that I'd like to visit over Thanksgiving?"

"Yes! You'll be coming, won't you?"

"I will, but I don't want to disrupt your family. I imagine that your brothers don't know yet. I'd never want to cause problems for anyone," Andie replied.

"Problems? This is the greatest thing to happen in a long time. You've got to come!"

"Oh, I want to more than anything in the world. I just don't want to be the cause of problems. If I ever was, I'd have to leave all of you alone. I've made this vow that I'll always respect your family this way," Andie explained.

"All right, stop this serious business! You're my sister and you're forever welcome in my house! I can't even tell you how excited I am to meet you. Mom showed us your pictures and it blows me away how much you look like us. Lisa and I grew up with people always looking at us because we're twins, but we aren't even identical. Everyone just assumes we are because they can't tell us apart. I don't think we look identical. Lisa has a different shaped face, longer, and I'm a little shorter than she is. You'll see what I mean when you get here. Mom said that you'd be staying with them," Laura said.

"She asked me to, yes," Andie replied, wondering for the first time if her sisters would feel uncomfortable with her in any way.

"This is so excellent. I'll be meeting you in three weeks! What kinds of things do you like to do?" Laura asked.

Andie told her about herself and mentioned her love of animals. Laura said that it ran in the family; she and Lisa worked at a veterinary clinic and each had pets—Laura, four registered cats that she bred for profit, and Lisa, three dogs. Sarah and the boys had two dogs, two birds, and various hamsters and gerbils. They talked for an hour and discovered many other similarities. It was like talking with an old friend who had been away for a while.

The next week, Andie received a letter from Lisa. She was amazed to see that they had the same handwriting. Lisa wrote of her own preferences, which were also those of Andie's—favorite color blue, a fiendish desire for chocolate, love of animals, tending to be shy in front of strangers, writing poetry for fun, reading a novel each week, and having played sports in school. Andie's spirit lifted as she lost herself in thoughts of these two incredible people. She wanted the days to go quickly so that she would be on the airplane, landing in Orlando to meet all of them.

She received two more letters from Sarah and one from Laura, whose handwriting was also similar. It was arranged that Lisa and Laura would pick Andie up at the airport. Andie's flight would arrive mid-afternoon two days before Thanksgiving.

Twenty years ago she had been a part of her mother, and now she would be reunited with her after a difficult journey through the span of time in between.

Chapter 18

Andie looked out the oval window at the streaks and puffs of white clouds and the tiny building tops below, as the plane began making its descent into Orlando. Her nerves were frayed from the hours spent in the cramped, droning airplane. She had fought off claustrophobia during the entire flight. What kept her from running wildly to find an exit was her desire to live to see her family, and the fat man next to her who had prevented an escape with his enormous rolling belly and massive thighs.

Andie gathered her carry-on bag from under the seat before the wheels had even touched down on the runway. She combed her fingers through her hair and chewed more urgently on her gum. Finally, after what seemed a procession of lost snails, the passengers in the forward rows began moving toward the open door. The fat man twisted with a huge effort to throw his girth out into the aisle, and Andie stepped quickly behind him like an impatient driver.

She reached the door and nodded briskly at the smiling stewardess, then took a step onto the echoing walkway, following the other travelers. Looking up the tunneled path, she willed her body to relax a degree from its heightened state of anxiety. This was the moment she had never believed would become a reality. Her blood family was welcoming her into its midst. She was about to be with her sisters.

She neared the doorway leading into the main area and saw the tops of many heads as people peered down the walkway looking for their arriving parties. Entering the building, Andie looked quickly around, trying to spot Lisa and Laura. Then to her left, in a row of unfamiliar faces, she saw her sisters. Andie's first thought was that she was looking at two smaller versions of herself. She was quickly standing in front of them as others bumped past behind her.

"You're…so small," Andie said in awe. She was at a loss for words as she tried to take in every aspect of them.

"And you're so big!" Laura remarked, throwing an arm around her shoulder. Lisa stood gazing silently with a shy smile at Andie, then gave her a hug.

"Welcome to Florida, Andie! Look at you, you're exactly like us! Maybe three inches taller, but what the heck!" Laura said, ushering her sisters into the flow of people that had forced them from remaining where they had been standing.

"I hope you guys don't mind if I stare at you. This is so amazing! I can't believe it!" Andie said as Lisa and Laura laughed.

"Oh, we'll be staring at you too!" Laura replied

"Definitely," Lisa added.

Andie thought that it must be true what she had heard about twins; one was usually dominant. She had always been fascinated by twins, maybe because they were so very interlinked, which was what Andie had desired to be with someone.

They stood by the luggage conveyer belt regarding one another. Andie finally felt that she had caught up with her thoughts. When she had first seen them, her mind seemed unable to process thoughts quickly enough, but her body had continued moving her along as if she could manage. She did not notice anyone else around them. Both of her sisters were so remarkable, so fully present and alive as they made small talk.

Andie felt that if the world ended right then, she would have been fulfilled by this glimpse of her sisters. She watched in fascination as Lisa and

Laura stood with their hands on their hips, thumbs in front and fingers fanned along the hipbone, one knee bent slightly as they leaned to the left. Andie observed how she herself must look as she stood that way.

It was like looking in a mirror, but three-dimensional and in duplicate. Every move of theirs had a nuance of her own. Their laughter held the same sound and depth. Andie had always thought that her laughter was odd, but after hearing them she felt free to unleash it, reveling in its similarity. She wanted to be with them forever. She could not imagine being away from them now that she had met them. Laura was spunky and cheerful, with a quick wit and dry humor. Andie was immediately drawn to her, thinking that she herself had been self-assured and bold before living in Arizona. Lisa had not spoken much, but seemed sweet and shy. Andie was familiar with this quiet way and wanted to tell her that she was often even more withdrawn. Andie tried to encourage Lisa to talk, but Laura was quick to speak. They were all excited.

While getting into the car, Andie insisted that Lisa sit in the front next to Laura. "So, what kind of music do you like?" Laura asked, pushing a cassette tape into the player and exchanging a look with Lisa.

"Oh, lots of different types," Andie answered, just before the car was filled with loud rock and roll music. Andie watched Laura and Lisa laughing, but could not hear them. Laura was snapping her fingers and bobbing her head to the beat. Andie laughed along and thought how wonderful she felt. She had not been this happy in her entire life. Her sisters were so familiar and comfortable to be with. Each word that they said and gesture that they made was like a newly opened gift. Andie wished that she could capture everything on film, so that she could view it later and keep it forever.

They drove to their mother's house, where they were supposed to wait for Sarah to arrive home from work. Her husband, John, had taken the boys out for the afternoon, so that the women could have some time alone. The boys had been told that a second cousin they had never met would be visiting.

Once she had turned down the music, Laura explained to Andie that their father had not been heard from since Sarah had divorced him when they were seven years old. Sarah had married John one year later, and he had adopted them on the grounds of paternal abandonment, since their father could not be located. The boys were born two years later, surprising all of them when it was known that twins were expected again. Sarah had another set of twins to raise.

Andie thought about the odds of being the only single birth of Sarah's five children. A set of twins would have probably been split up if they had been born first.

Laura pulled into the driveway of a small yellow house. "Here we are, my dears, " she said, attempting an English accent.

"Geez, Laura," Lisa groaned, turning toward Andie and rolling her eyes.

An hour later, they were sitting on the couch talking when the front door opened and Sarah walked into the room. She wore a light gray skirt and jacket for her work as a secretary in a law firm. She looked elegant and professional, her dark blond, shoulder length hair tucked behind her ears. Her eyes were kind and full of emotion as they fixed on Andie.

"Hi," Andie said, standing and walking toward her.

"Hello," Sarah replied softly. She put her arms around her daughter for the first time. "It's so good to see you."

Andie felt the strength of her embrace and returned it. She squeezed her eyes tightly against the tears that threatened to come.

"You don't know how much this means to me. I never thought I would see you again," Sarah said into Andie's hair.

Andie whispered, "Me too, me too."

"Well, Mom, it looks like there's another one of us. Now you're in for it," Laura said.

Sarah and Andie drew apart and smiled. Sarah reached out to stroke Andie's cheek. "You're beautiful," she said.

Andie could see the face that her own was designed from. Even Sarah's voice seemed familiar, with its hushed soothing tone and gentle inflection. She looked too young to have grown children.

"I imagine you girls have had a chance to get to know one another. What do you think?" Sarah asked, looking at Lisa and Laura.

"She's definitely just like us, except her boobs are bigger," Laura said mischievously.

"Well, I guess that's because you two had to share everything!" Sarah said.

"At least you won't have to worry about any sagging in middle age," Andie joked. They all laughed loudly, and the tension of the moment fell away.

Sarah went into the kitchen and came back with a pitcher of lemonade on a tray. "I have to discuss this with you before John brings the boys home. Tell me how you feel about it. They think you're a cousin that they've never met. But I've been praying, and I don't believe that the Lord wants me to lie about any of this. So when they come home, I'd like to tell them who you really are." She handed each of them a glass of lemonade.

"That's fine with me, whatever you feel is best," Andie replied.

"Yeah, Mom, you should just tell them. They'll be okay," Lisa said.

"You should, Mom. They need to know the truth," Laura offered.

Andie wondered how someone would know what the Lord wanted them to do. She believed that Sarah had probably reached this conclusion on her own, but because she was religious, she said it was the Lord.

"All right then. They should be home soon, so we'll just pray that the Lord gives me the right words," Sarah said, bowing her head and beginning to pray.

Andie quickly looked over at Lisa and Laura. They had closed their eyes and bowed their heads. Andie closed her eyes and leaned forward. She was embarrassed. It seemed awkward to just pray like this. She had only seen people bow their heads in church, and some of them had been sleeping. When she was little, she had prayed in a whisper at night with her eyes open. It had been a long time since she last prayed, and it reminded her of the bad experience with Farley. She was glad when Sarah finished.

The boys soon came bursting in the door, one with a plaster arm cast. They had tousled blond hair and pink cheeks from some recent activity. Sarah had them sit in the living room next to their father, but neither one could sit completely still.

"Boys, this is Andie. She's the one I told you would be staying with us for a few days. Look at her and tell me what you see."

Eric quickly spoke up, "She looks just like the beanies. Exactly like them!"

"Yep!" added Tim.

"Who do you think she is?" Sarah asked.

Eric hesitated and looked at his father, then at each of the girl's faces. "I'd say she's our sister."

Andie was surprised by Eric's reply. Everyone paused and looked at her.

"Is she?" he asked.

"Yes, she is," Sarah answered. She opened her mouth to explain, but the boys interrupted.

"Cool! We've got another sister!" Tim exclaimed.

"She can be number three! Hey, Andie! You're beanie number three!" Eric announced as everyone joined in his laughter.

"Welcome to the family," John said, getting up to give Andie a hug. The boys hugged her waist, Tim's cast bumping into her ribs.

"Oops! Sorry, Andie," he said, smiling up at her. "I broke it three weeks ago when I fell out of a tree."

"That must have hurt," Andie said, enjoying his earnest expression. The boys were both sweet-natured and friendly to her, never asking a question about how she came to be.

They went out for pizza that evening, and Andie felt like a celebrity as the boys argued over who got to sit next to her in the car and at the restaurant. Lisa and Laura went home briefly and then met them at the restaurant.

Andie smelled something familiar and asked what kind of perfume they had on. Andie wore only two types: L'air du Temps and Ciara. Laura said that she had on Ciara, and Lisa was wearing L'air du Temps. Andie continued to be amazed throughout the evening at the similarities and mannerisms that she shared with her sisters and mother. Their sense of humor was just like her own. The only time Andie felt uncomfortable was when Sarah or John mentioned anything pertaining to religion. When the pizza came, they bowed their heads and prayed right in the restaurant in front of everyone, ending it again with "...in Jesus Christ's name we pray, amen."

Later that night, Andie heard Sarah read the boys a bedtime story while they lay in their bunk beds. Then she heard them praying together. She pictured them getting a hug and kiss good night, and wished that she had been able to get this treatment when she was younger.

Andie felt awkward as she went into the hallway to tell them all good night. Sarah gave her another hug.

"It's such a blessing to have you here, Andie. Goodnight," Sarah said.

Andie went into the small extra room and sat down on the bed. She was worried about the fact that Sarah was probably disappointed that she was living with Steve. It had not occurred to her when she had first told Sarah on the phone about them living together. Her parents in Iowa had accepted it, never mentioning anything wrong with it; even Scott was living with his new girlfriend. Andie wanted Sarah to be pleased with her and felt that this stood in the way. She doubted that Sarah would mention it because she was too polite. It meant so much that Sarah would believe she was a good person.

The religious behavior was uncomfortable. Andie would begin having the panicky feeling whenever she thought about praying and seeking answers from some "spiritual" being. She wanted no part in any religion. It wasn't that she didn't believe in God, she just wanted it to stop there;

with God having created the world and loving people. Anything else might lead her down the wrong path, with evil lurking behind.

Chapter 19

Andie got up early and dressed, then went into the kitchen. While in the short hallway, she heard them in their rooms, probably having just awakened as well. A cookie jar shaped like a goose sat on the kitchen counter. Sarah had told her to make herself at home and help herself to food and drinks. Taking a chocolate chip cookie, she bit into it, enjoying the homemade chewiness. She picked out another one and was going to get a glass of milk, when Tim and Eric walked into the room.

"Hey, that looks good! I think maybe I'll have some for breakfast, too," Eric said happily.

Sarah came into the kitchen and stopped when she saw Andie holding the cookie.

"Oh. No, boys, you know the rule about sweets in the morning," Sarah said.

"But, Mom, how come she's eating cookies for breakfast?" Tim asked.

Andie was embarrassed and could not say anything with the large bite of cookie still in her mouth. When she was young, she had always eaten sweets for breakfast. Her mom had known about it and never stopped her. Andie knew it was not the most nutritious, but it seemed to help her wake up more quickly and she loved cookies and cake. She used to bake a chocolate cake a few times a week when she was in junior high. She would eat some at breakfast and then more after school and dinner.

"Well, I don't know. You're growing boys and you need a good breakfast. Now, would you like a bowl of cereal?" Sarah asked them.

Andie swallowed the piece of cookie and wondered what to do. She could not put the other cookie back in the jar. Sarah was getting bowls and boxes of cereal out as Tim and Eric waited, glancing at Andie.

"I'm sorry. I have a terrible sweet tooth and the cookies looked so good. I should've waited until later." Andie attempted to laugh.

Sarah continued getting the boys their cereal. "They know that they aren't allowed to eat sweets in the morning. But you're an adult, and you can decide what's best for you."

Andie felt wounded by the comment, believing that she was guilty of not making good choices. Now she had two things against her in Sarah's eyes.

Thanksgiving was the following day, so Andie helped Sarah that afternoon in the kitchen with some of the preparations. It would just be the immediate family gathering there for the holiday. Andie watched for signs of displeasure from Sarah, but did not notice anything obvious. Sarah asked her about her family. Andie told her some of the truth about her dysfunctional home. She wished to evoke some sympathy from her and show her how similar their upbringings were. Sarah became quiet when Andie spoke of her alcoholic mother and abusive brother. When Andie was done, Sarah began talking about how everyone should thank the Lord for all of their blessings. Andie thought that she had missed something in the conversation. Having an abusive family was something to be thankful for? Shouldn't Sarah at least feel a little sorry for her, seeing that she had played a part in making Andie available to be adopted? Andie wasn't trying to make her feel guilty, she just wanted Sarah to show some regret for having given her away. Maybe even wish that she hadn't missed out on raising such a nice child.

It was a little frustrating trying to talk to her. Even though Sarah was polite, there was a wall between them, and it seemed to be religion. If

Andie asked her opinion on something to do with her life, like attending journalism school and where to find work afterward, Sarah just said that she should pray about it. Andie wanted her to say something like, "Finish school and move here! There are a lot of opportunities in Orlando, and I want you to live near us." For this is what Andie wanted to do.

Now that she had seen her intended home and family, this is where she wanted to stay. She especially wanted to be with her sisters. She looked forward to seeing them the next day on Thanksgiving. Sarah was reserved when it came to discussing her own opinion; it was always that the Lord knew best. Andie wanted to ask her if it had been the Lord's plan to have her grow up in a family that had not cared for her, but she didn't want to seem rude or say anything to upset her.

When Lisa and Laura arrived the next day, Andie got her camera out and asked John to take a few pictures. They stood on either side of Andie and put their arms around her waist.

"You look like triplets!" John said.

Laura pinched Lisa's arm. "Hey!" Lisa yelled, and the picture was snapped.

The day was wonderful as they feasted and joked. Andie kept looking around the table, thinking how perfectly she fit in with all of them. What most families took for granted in their togetherness, Andie beheld as most miraculous. She was firmly linked forever to them and they to her.

The boys chattered almost nonstop and begged Laura's husband to go outside and throw the football, but he was too full and wanted to watch TV. Andie took them outside and played with them. They were impressed with her spiral throw, which she had perfected helping John practice for the high school football games that he had quarter-backed. Lisa and Laura watched and said that Andie was the biggest tomboy of them all. Laura tried to match Andie's graceful throws, but the boys said that Andie's was better.

"Will you come and see us again?" Eric asked, his dark blue, almond-shaped eyes hinting to Andie what a son of hers might one day look like.

"I'd love to, Eric. I'll try to come again soon," Andie answered. He took her hand and they walked into the house.

The next day would be her last full day with them. Her plane would leave the following morning for Phoenix. Andie imagined dropping everything and staying with them. Yet, this was still new to all of them, and she knew that Sarah would not like such an impulsive decision. Maybe she wouldn't want Andie to live nearby; she hadn't said anything to give the impression of this desire. Andie tried to fight off what felt like a childish yearning for approval and love. She was an adult now and needed to get rid of the neediness that she felt. She believed that Sarah recognized it and chose to ignore it. Sarah had enough children to nurture, so Andie didn't want to burden her with her own orphan-like feelings.

Sarah, Andie, and the boys got up early the next morning and drove to Disney World. Tim and Eric prepared her with a detailed description of what each of the rides was like, interrupting one another frequently. Sarah had to keep asking them to calm down.

The crowds were thick, and in each line they had to wait at least twenty minutes. It was fun, but Andie felt that she was missing her last chance to bond with Sarah before she had to leave the next day. She would be eating dinner at Laura's house with Lisa that night, so her time with Sarah was almost gone.

They drove home in the late afternoon, the boys much more relaxed after the long day of excitement. Andie had made a point to get to know them as best she could. Eric appeared to be the dominate one. Tim laughed easily and let Eric lead the way. They were each what a brother should be. Scott, with his evil ways, was some kind of monster. She imagined how it would be to have these two boys to live with. There would be no constant threat of violence, only chatter and at the most, fervent competition to get attention. How her life could have been! She figured that she was one of the few adopted people able to explore what their original life might have been like. It was awesome, but at the same time left her with a deep sense of loss over what could have been.

Her fulfillment would be derived by maintaining a growing relationship with them. Her sisters were the brightest spot of all. They seemed eager to remain in touch with her and told her over dinner that they would visit her as soon as they could. Laura had made a pan of lasagna and some garlic bread. For dessert, they had chocolate cake and bore the jokes from Laura's husband about being piggish as they each had two thick slices. They sat on the back porch after dinner.

"So what do you think of Mom?" Laura asked.

"She's very nice. You guys are lucky to have her as your mother."

"I hope you don't mind me asking this, but are you angry at her for giving you away?" asked Lisa.

Andie explained that she had never felt angry at Sarah, before she knew her, or now. What she had felt when she was younger was a deep sadness and yearning for something out of her reach. It had given her fuel for imagining the family that she was supposed to have. As her unknown birth mother, Sarah had always been high on a pedestal, the one who would give her unconditional love and acceptance. She told them about Scott and her parents.

"How could your parents allow him to do that to you for so long?" Laura asked, frowning.

"I don't know. I guess they chose to believe that he wasn't capable of it, and that I was a liar. I can't imagine that they knew about it and didn't do anything to stop him," Andie replied.

"Well, that's child abuse!" Lisa said. "It's neglect. You should have him try to do something to you now and then have him arrested."

"You know, I've thought of that. But in the end, my parents would probably believe some ridiculous thing that I did to make him hurt me, and he could end up killing me. I just try to block it all out and go on.

That's why I had to move out of Iowa. It's too painful to be around all of them."

"And you really aren't angry at Mom for making you go through all that?" Laura asked.

"It's not her fault. She wanted to keep me, but her stepfather made her give me away. Even before I knew that though, I never was angry. Maybe disappointed and hurt because my adoptive family didn't seem to care about me, and she might have cared if she had kept me," Andie answered.

If Sarah had kept her, Laura and Lisa might not have been born. Two teenagers faced with tending to a baby would probably have been careful to avoid another pregnancy. This was a new thought that Andie rolled through her mind.

Laura showed her three photo albums and they took more pictures. At times, Andie wanted to tell them about what had happened to her with Farley, but it was still confusing to her and she didn't want them to think she was crazy. She couldn't understand it herself, and it bothered her to even think about it, though she wished that there was someone to help her find peace with it.

Andie wanted the night to go on forever, but it was late. They drove her back to Sarah's house after midnight. Andie felt as if she was about to lose her composure as they hugged her in front of Sarah's door, but Laura was quick to notice it.

"We'll see you again soon, okay? I'll miss you, Andie. Now that I have a big sister, and I mean big sister, I won't settle for an occasional letter. We must get together often. Funds permitting, of course," Laura said, smiling.

"Take care, Andie. Call us when you get home, so we know you made it safely," Lisa said, hugging her.

"I will. Please visit soon, okay?" Andie replied. "I had a great time. You'll never know how much this means to me."

"To us, too. Get a good night's rest. We'll see you later. It's so great to have another sister. Take care of yourself and don't sit by any more fat men on the plane!" Laura said as she and Lisa laughed. They walked to the car.

Andie watched them drive away. She waved and laughed as Laura stuck her hand out of the window and made a peace sign. She could faintly hear loud music as the car disappeared around the corner.

Chapter 20

Sarah, John, and the boys drove her to the airport. They had eaten homemade waffles and crispy bacon for breakfast. Sarah gave her a small box to take with her and told her not to open it until she was on the airplane. They made their way through the security check and found the gate where Andie would depart. When it was time to board, Andie was struck with the urge to cry, but did not want to upset them. She hugged each of them and thanked them again.

Sarah cupped Andie's face in her hands. "I remember saying good-bye to you once before, but this time I'll get to see you again." She hugged her tightly, and then Andie could no longer hold back her tears.

"It's all right, Andie," Sarah said quietly. "Don't be afraid to feel things. God gave you a heart and a good mind. I thank Him for allowing me to know you. You're such a caring person. Go on now, and I'll talk to you soon. And remember, I love you."

Andie embraced them all again and tried to walk backwards so she could see their faces for as long as possible. Sarah really loved her! She wasn't disappointed in her, and if she was, she still loved her. Andie bumped into a large man and had to turn around to follow the others onto the plane. She laughed through her tears and imagined what Laura would have said about the big man in front of her being her potential seat mate.

The plane slowly backed out as Andie scanned the huge window by the gate. She thought she saw a man and woman and two boys waving at the plane. She put her hand to the window and longed to reach them. The woman next to Andie glanced at her as Andie patted the window and cried. When the plane left the runway and tilted up into the sky, Andie remembered the box and dug it out of her carry-on bag. She opened it and saw a round wooden box with a lid, delicately painted with pink hearts and flowers. Inside she found small squares of thick paper, which turned out to be notes that each of them had written to her and folded up.

The boys had written notes to say how much fun they had with her and that they were glad to have another sister. Eric had written "I love you" eight times at the bottom of his paper. John wrote that he felt like he had another daughter and that she was welcome anytime to stay with them. Sarah's was the longest. Andie read, "It has been an incredible few days. I will always remember these moments with you. At times it has been sad, but mostly happy. What I mean by sad is that I have had to come to terms with a lot of painful memories that I have repressed for years. You were always there in the back of my mind through the years, but surrounded by sadness. I believe that the Lord has brought us together and allowed me to set my past in order. I feel comforted by the fact that you have grown up to be a fine, intelligent young woman.

You are always welcome here with us. I think you know that we all love you and have come to feel that you are a part of our family in this short time. I pray that you will know the Lord and trust Him with your life. He is the reason that I have been able to find peace and true love.

Thank you so much for coming and sharing your life with us. I hope we will see you again soon. God bless you. I love you very much...Sarah."

Andie kept the notes on her lap and reread them. She finally tucked them away when the snack was served. She did not become claustrophobic on the flight because her mind was so full of thoughts and feelings about her family. When the plane began descending into Phoenix, Andie looked out at the red hills and long stretches of barren land and knew that this was not her home. She pictured her family sitting around the table at Thanksgiving, passing the food to her and making sure that she had enough to eat. Sarah was not judgmental. Andie was so used to being criticized and admonished that she assumed others would do the same to her. Sarah's faith in God was strong, so she relied upon prayer to make decisions and wanted others to do the same. But it frightened Andie to think about spiritual matters. All of the graphic scary movies and books that she had enjoyed when she was young did not compare to the horror she had experienced. People could get lost in religion. Unseen things were waiting in the spiritual realm that Andie did not care to meet again.

Andie knew that she needed to sift through the memories of her experience with Farley and try to eradicate its ill effects on her life. She had started to gain some of her weight back, but her mind was still fragile. She felt like a part of her being had been stolen by Farley and she could not recover it. He had raped her mind and spirit, but for what purpose? He had mentioned finding a good husband for her at one point when he had warned her of Steve's evilness. There was no way that she could turn him in to the police. What proof did she have, except her word against his? Karin and Steve would back her up, but the fact that she had said that she used drugs would ruin any chance of her story's plausibility. But what if he were doing this to other people? The odds were that she was not the only person to be chosen by Farley; he was so adept at what he did. She knew that she wanted to live near her family, but did not want to leave Karin or Steve. School would be over in August, so she had some time to figure out what to do.

Steve met her at the airport and listened quietly as Andie spoke of her family.

"So, when are you moving there?" he asked as he loaded her suitcase into the trunk of his car.

"Well...I'm not, yet. I'd like to be close to them one day, but I have school, and you and Karin here. Maybe you could go there with me sometime and see what you think," Andie replied.

"I'd follow you anywhere, Andie," Steve said, smiling with relief.

Andie went back to school the next week and began thinking about how it would be to be married to Steve. He had been so supportive during her dilemma, and he was cheerful most of the time. It was probably not right to just live together. She yearned for a family of her own. To have a child would be the ultimate dream for her. It would be the first time that she would live with a blood relative. Sarah would approve, Andie was certain. Laura had gotten married, and Lisa and her boyfriend were talking about it. It would be great if she and Steve could move there and live near them. Their kids could grow up as cousins and Andie would be an aunt.

Her daydreams about having children continued as the days passed. She noticed mothers and babies everywhere. Staring at resemblances and the careful way mothers tended to their children, she hoped it would be possible for her to get pregnant. She finally talked to Steve about marriage, though she was hesitant because she did not want to seem desperate. A man was supposed to do the asking. To her surprise, he laughed and told her that he was waiting for enough time to pass, so that it would be right to ask her to marry him. They both smiled ecstatically at one another and he said, "Let's do it."

The next week, just before Christmas, they were married by a notary public with Karin and one of Steve's friends as witnesses. Andie wrote to Sarah and told her that she had gotten married. When Sarah called to congratulate her, she sounded happy for her, but Andie thought there was a reluctant manner in her way of speaking. Sarah probably thought it was too sudden, but at least Andie knew she was doing the right thing, not "living in sin."

Andie's parents were surprised, and her mom was upset that they had not been told about it before it happened. Andie knew that it was one more thing that, in their opinion, she had not done right, but it was her life and she was an adult. People eloped all of the time, and she and Steve did not have enough money to have a big wedding. Andie had heard about people planning big weddings and then wanting them to be over quickly because of all of the details and stress involved.

They ate at a fancy restaurant and stayed up late that night. Steve called in sick at work to the construction supervisor where he finished concrete, and Andie skipped school two nights. It felt good to be Mrs. Lewis, grown up and to be taken seriously. Andie had one more thing that she needed to take care of before she could go on with her life. She must confront Farley.

CHAPTER 21

Andie did not tell Steve what she planned to do. She asked Karin to go with her to Farley's house, which Karin tried to talk her out of doing, but Andie said that she needed to do it to be able to prove to herself that he could not control her. She wanted to threaten him and make him think that he was being watched, in case he tried to accost someone else. Andie said that she would go alone if she had to.

They were on their way to his house in Andie's car. She found the long dusty road that led to his driveway and parked in front of his house. Andie was anxious and did not want to see him, but knew that she had to confront her fear head-on. Hopefully he was home so she would not have to go through this turmoil again. She thought of Tim and Eric, with their pure minds, and knew that this man had to be stopped somehow. She knocked on the door.

Farley opened it immediately. His eyes narrowed as he looked at them. "So, you're back. It's good to see you, Andie," he said.

"Well, it's not good to see you! You lost, Farley! You couldn't control me no matter how hard you tried. I won! You and your religion are a joke. I've warned the police, so there will be people watching you. Don't try to do this to anyone else!" Andie exclaimed.

Farley seemed to draw himself up taller. "You think that you can come here and spew this garbage at me?"

"I can do whatever I want!" Andie shouted. "You're a pathetic old man with no life except for trying to ruin other peoples' lives. But I was stronger than you! You will not do this to anyone else. You'll be watched very closely, so don't even try it!"

Farley's nostrils flared and his eyes became more narrowed. He breathed heavily, shifting from one foot to the other. "You are evil. You are not worthy of life!" he whispered angrily.

"Shut your mouth, you stupid man! You're the evil one, except you have no power!" Andie was tensely clenching her fists.

"Andie, let's go!" Karin said urgently. "Come on!"

"Just a minute," Andie replied. "I'm not done with him. Pershing Lamar Farley, you can just sit here and rot in your nasty hole until you die. And when you die, no one will miss you!"

Farley's face was contorting as if he wanted to exercise every muscle under his weathered skin. His mouth was partially open, and his eyes radiated malice. Suddenly, Andie saw her nightmare. His face pinched together as if he had sucked on a lemon, and then a serpent glared at her. The eyes were not human. She was stunned, but recognized her adversary for what he was.

"You can't scare me, you ugly creep!" Andie shouted.

"Andie? Andie! He…he looks like a snake! Oh, my gosh, he looks like a snake! Let's go! Come on, let's go!" Karin cried, pulling Andie's hand to lead her to the car.

"You can burn in hell, Farley," Andie said over her shoulder as they began stepping away.

Karin was moaning, "No, no, no, no."

"You'll be back," Farley hissed.

"Never!" Andie yelled. Karin slapped her arm.

Karin's face had gone white, her eyes rimmed with red. She would not look toward the house.

They quickly got into the car. Andie floored the gas pedal, leaving a cloud of dust from the sandy gravel driveway. When they reached the main road, Andie looked over at Karin, who was pale and listless as she stared out the window. Andie was worried that she might be in shock.

"Hey, Karin! Remember when we ran over that snake with my car? Just picture Farley with his guts blasted out of his mouth from being run over," Andie said.

Andie was still highly agitated and felt the same adrenaline rush as she had when she was younger after fighting Scott. She was away from both of them now, and they could no longer hurt her. Because Karin had seen the image of the snake, she was more certain of her sanity. The knowledge that she had ended up in the psychiatric place still bothered her.

"Andie? Did you see his face? It was a snake, wasn't it?" Karin asked.

"Yeah, I saw it. He did that before. He's pure evil, Karin, there's no doubt about it. Don't worry, okay? He can't hurt you. I know it's scary, but he's just a sick old man who gets mad enough to look like a snake," Andie said as she pulled into an ice cream store parking lot. "Come on, let's go in and have something to eat. My treat."

Andie knew from her own experience that Karin needed to be in a normal setting, and the children inside the busy store would distract her. "I guess, but I'm not hungry," Karin replied. Ice cream was her favorite dessert. She followed Andie inside and they waited in line, ordering double dip waffle cones when their turn came.

"Thanks for going with me, Karin. I'm sorry you had to see that. At least I know I wasn't imagining things when I saw him do it before," Andie said.

"I'll never go there again and you'd better not either! Promise me, Andie. No more contact with him. What a crazy thing! I still can't believe he looked like a snake. How is that possible?" Karin licked all around her cone to keep the ice cream from dripping onto her hand.

"I promise I won't contact him. I just had to let him know that he'd be watched. He looked like a snake because that's what he really is," Andie answered.

She watched a couple trying to control their two young children, who were running back and forth, jumping up to see the tubs of ice cream inside the long glass display counter. They kept changing their minds each time one of them called out a different flavor.

Farley seemed to think that she would be back. What nerve he had—as if she missed him. She wasn't so gullible. She was still glad that she had gone to confront him, and Karin appeared to be livening up.

"You kill me, Andie. You probably would've gone up to him and body slammed him if I hadn't stopped you," Karin said, starting to laugh.

"Well, I was about to!" They went into a fit of hysterical laughter. Andie dropped her cone, which caused them both to guffaw wildly. A few children pointed at them, giggling along.

"We'd better get out of here!" Andie said, still laughing and trying to clean up her mess with a wad of thin napkins. "Let's go home. I think we need to relax."

They tossed the rest of their cones into the trash container and went outside to the car.

"Does he have your address?" Karin asked. She shuddered from the recollection of Farley in his doorway.

"I suppose he does, he found out everything else. Why? Do you think I should move?"

"I would. Start fresh somewhere else. I'm sure Steve would understand," Karin replied.

Andie thought about it that night and brought it up to Steve. Karin had gone home shortly after they had confessed to Steve what they had done, and he had told Andie never to go near Farley again. What if there was a word he could say to put her into a trance? Andie assured him that it was all over. Farley knew that she had beaten him and that he would be watched.

Steve agreed that they should move, so they began looking for a new apartment and found one closer to her school. They moved in New Year's Day, after a night of partying. Andie was beginning to dislike the floating feeling of being high from smoking marijuana, so she drank more alcohol to alleviate the anxiety that the pot caused. Steve wanted to get high daily and usually had a number of beers after work. Andie often joined him because it was easier to get through the day without having to think straight, and it was difficult to relate to him unless she was in the same state of mind.

They spent time together on the weekday afternoons lying beside the large community pool. Steve loved to get high after work and then lie out in the sun. Andie would leave an hour later to go to school, so she never smoked that close to school hours.

On the weekends, the pool area was crowded with college students from nearby Arizona State University. Pretty young women in bathing suits walked by with their tan, lithe bodies. Andie felt self-conscious when she looked down at her pale, slightly flabby body. She had gained weight, but had not exercised and so the fat hung in little pockets from her hips and thighs. Even her belly was pouching out. She often noticed Steve watching women.

One day she could not remain quiet as his head turned, following a petite brunette. "Hey! You're a married man now. None of this wandering eye stuff, if you know what's good for you." She tried to keep her tone light, but she was deeply hurt.

"Just working my eyes a little, honey. You're the only one for me, you know that," he casually replied.

Andie wanted to believe him, but he didn't make it easy. Were all men like this, she wondered. It brought back the memories of how disturbing it was when her father looked at women. It was now her husband who did it, and here she was drinking and getting high. But she wasn't doing it to escape from his voyeurism. She only had a few drinks occasionally, and certainly no sneaky reliance upon it to survive. Anyway, marijuana was not addictive. She thought of taking some to her mom in Iowa and telling her to smoke it instead of drinking whiskey. That would go over like a ton of bricks, she thought. They believed that any drug was the same as LSD or heroin. And there her mom was drinking herself into a partial coma every day. Andie wondered what her liver looked like now.

She vowed to get herself in shape. She sunbathed and rode around on a second-hand bicycle. Ashley would run beside her as they went up and down the least crowded streets. Unfortunately, her toned body did not stop him. His head would turn whenever an attractive female was in sight, although he seemed to make an attempt to hide it from her. She had never felt that she was enough for anyone to love unconditionally, so even though it made her intensely jealous, she accepted that it would continue.

Andie had received cards and pictures at Christmas from her sisters and Sarah, and they wrote long letters to one another as the months passed. She called each of them every two weeks to hear their voices. Sarah often sent religious tracts and articles with her letters. Andie had read them at first, but they all said the same thing: look for the Lord, give your life to Him; He died for your sins so that you could go to heaven. She would briefly flip through them and then stash them away in a box full of photos and letters. Sarah was not pushy about it, but she always had something to send or mention about God.

Andie remembered what a Jewish friend had told her in high school: most Christians were trying to purge some major guilt from something in their lives. Sarah probably felt guilty about giving her away, so she had turned to Jesus because of her supposed sins. It must be the way that she coped with her feelings. To each his own, Andie thought. Sarah was certainly entitled to her own beliefs, but that didn't mean that she herself had to subscribe to them just because Sarah sent her religious information. Even though Andie wanted to please Sarah and have a relationship with her, her mind would shut down at the prospect of delving into the spiritual realm. I will find my own way, Andie decided.

Chapter 22

In March, Andie's menstrual period was late. When she realized that she might be pregnant, she was filled with a secret excitement. Steve was worried because he thought that it was too soon to have a child, and they had to struggle, living week to week on his paychecks. A child would be a burden right now that they did not need, he told her.

She went to a pharmacy and bought a home pregnancy test. After telling Steve to wait, she locked herself in the bathroom. With a dropper, she put urine onto the absorbent square and watched the "result window." The instructions said that it would take five minutes to see a plus or minus sign. The window area was already filling in, and a blue line turned into a plus sign. Andie fell to her knees and pressed her hands against her mouth, stifling a cry. Yes, she thought. A baby, her baby! She was pregnant!

"Thank you, thank you, thank you," she whispered.

"Andie? What happened? Are you done?" Steve asked in a strained voice.

She opened the door. "I'm pregnant."

"Oh...my...gosh," he said haltingly.

"It'll be all right, Steve. I'll be graduating from school and working before it's born. It'll all work out!" Andie pleaded.

"Well, I guess. It's just so sudden and all. Don't twins run in your family?"

"What a thought! I guess they do, but the odds are against it."

She was looking closely at him, trying to imagine what a child of theirs might look like. He had wavy, dark hair and brown eyes and a dark complexion. They both had wide cheek bones, but his face was angular around the jaw.

"Maybe you should go to the doctor to be sure. Those tests are probably wrong sometimes," Steve said.

"I'm never late, and the test is supposed to be accurate for a positive result. You're going to be a daddy!" Andie laughed as Steve smiled halfheartedly.

She made a special dinner that evening to celebrate the news. Steve could not hide the fact that he was troubled. Andie thought that it was still new to him, but he would eventually come to look forward to a child. She was greatly relieved to know that her body could produce children.

Pregnancy was a foreign world to her. Since she had never heard stories from her mom about the birth process, as most kids do at some point, she gathered information at the library and tried to keep her obstetrician in the exam room for as long as possible while she asked questions. She was frightened as she read about all of the possible complications for herself and the baby. She was anxious about needing an episiotomy or a Caesarean section.

Life was suddenly so risky and fragile. She avoided standing in front of the microwave for fear that it would cook her baby if it leaked; it was an old model after all. She gave up every drug, including caffeine, not even drinking soda or eating anything with artificial colors or flavors. She was plagued with guilt because of the pot she had smoked before she knew that she was pregnant. She took her prenatal vitamins daily and made sure that she ate enough protein and calcium. She caught a cold and worried about the Tylenol she had to finally take to get rid of a pounding headache.

Steve began working all of the overtime that he could. He often went out on weekend nights with his friends, even though Andie was home.

She was tired anyway, so did not mind because she would get to snuggle in her bed and fall asleep reading books about birth and baby care.

The baby was due in early December, so by August when Andie graduated from broadcasting school, she was very obviously pregnant. The instructor bluntly told her that it would be virtually impossible to find a job in "her condition." And he proved to be right. No matter that her resume and demonstration tapes received attention, once she showed up in person for an interview, she never heard from the people again. Andie looked for any kind of paying job, but she could not even get one at a fast food restaurant. Steve's overtime pay was just enough to make the doctor and hospital prepayment amount each month, but if there were any unforeseen expenses, such as a C-section or an intensive care stay, they would be heavily in debt. Steve had some unpaid credit card bills from the past two years that he had ignored, so his credit history was terrible, and they were unable to get any other credit cards or loans.

Andie's family was eagerly waiting to hear the news of the baby's arrival. Her parents in Iowa told her to call them twice a week when October came, which she dutifully did. Her mom had wanted to know the nursery theme and continued to send every imaginable jungle theme item that she came across. Her sisters and Sarah asked if she would call them when she went into labor. They still wrote often and spoke on the phone monthly.

Sarah sent an ornately painted ceramic cross to hang in the baby's room. Andie put it up next to the crib and stared at it. She wanted her baby to be safe. The world seemed so full of danger now.

She uttered a quiet prayer, "If you're there God, please protect this little baby. In Jesus name, amen."

Now that she had time to think without the effects of drugs hindering her abilities, she read through the information that Sarah continued to send. If only it were definitely true, she thought. If only God's Son, who was sent to save the world, heard everyone's prayers. How could anyone know for sure, she wondered. She had lived in fear of Scott for years and had prayed for help, but it had never come. Then Farley had gotten hold of her. None of the times she had prayed had ever helped her. The level of cruelty she endured actually seemed to be stepping up as she got older.

But, her baby—a girl, she hoped—would need every available measure taken to ensure her well-being, so Andie began praying again at night and sometimes during the day. She would notice Steve's red-rimmed, glassy eyes and fail to find a common ground with him. He would alternately be giddy, then become morose and distant. She tried reading aloud medical articles pertaining to the birthing process, but he only feigned interest. At least he wasn't mean to her, she thought. It was better than being in Iowa with her family. He still told her he loved her and tried to act happy about the baby when he was in a good mood.

Early one morning, she woke up feeling an ache in her lower back and tightening band across her belly. She sat up and smiled as another wave came fifteen minutes later. By four o'clock, the contractions were five minutes apart and strengthening, so they drove to the hospital. Andie was surprised that the contractions were not more painful, but by midnight she knew that she had been premature in her judgment. Steve fell asleep in the reclining chair next to the bed, but Andie could not sleep because of the intense pain that consumed her torso.

She thought of how incredible it was that every person on earth was brought into the world by a woman's extreme pain. Men should have the utmost respect for females after all that they had to endure, Andie realized, as she looked at Steve snoring in the chair. Lusting after women's bodies was shallow and demeaning. She braced herself as another strong contraction began.

Thirty-six hours after her labor began, Andie, near exhaustion, gave one final push and into the world came her daughter, Rylee Elizabeth. The agony had rendered her speechless and the room was spinning, but when the doctor placed Rylee on her abdomen, Andie forgot all of the pain.

The baby was so warm and soft and alive! Her little face was red and crumpled as she began whimpering like a dove. Andie felt the most intense desire to comfort and protect her. When the nurse took Rylee to be weighed and cleaned, Andie wanted to get up and follow her to make sure that no one would hurt her baby.

Steve leaned over and kissed her. "She's beautiful, Andie," he said, stroking her damp forehead.

Finally, a nurse brought Rylee back as the doctor finished stitching Andie up from the episiotomy. Andie waited for them to change the birthing bed back into a regular bed and then took Rylee from Steve.

"Look at her! She's so perfect," Andie said as she unwrapped and examined every part of her baby.

"She looks like you." Steve leaned down and kissed the small rectangle of forehead on Rylee.

"It's a miracle. This is truly a miracle," Andie said softly, looking at her daughter. "Hi, sweet girl. I've been waiting forever to meet you. Oh, don't cry! Here. You must be hungry," Andie said as she opened her gown, preparing to breast feed.

Rylee latched on hungrily, and Andie laughed at how much the baby seemed to know already. Andie knew that Rylee was getting the colostrum that God intended for her, with its high quality of infection-preventing nutrients and purity. She had read many articles on the optimum nourishment for infants and found that God had planned way ahead in this department. She was going to make certain that Rylee had the best of everything in life.

Chapter 23

The first few months seemed like a blur of feedings, diaper changes, and getting the baby to sleep. Andie devoted all of her energy to Rylee's care. Rylee had weighed nearly ten pounds at birth and had filled out in three months to look like a fat-cheeked cherub. She was born with a head of fluffy, dark hair and Andie's blue almond-shaped eyes. Her full lips were deep pink and had what a nurse had called "angel kisses" on both the upper and lower lips. The indentations did make her look as if she were waiting to be kissed, Andie mused. Andie had never seen such a beautiful baby. Rylee had a creamy, darker complexion from Steve, and the shape of her face was like a heart. Andie prayed every morning, thanking God for the gift he had given her.

Andie could not look at Rylee often enough. She marveled at her perfect, tiny feet and adored her curved pinkie fingers which were shaped just like her own. She would watch Rylee sleeping and wonder what baby dreams were about. There was no feeling in the world like having Rylee against her and kissing her soft cheeks. She thought about how it must have been for her mom to receive a phone call and then drive two hours to pick up her new baby. Andie, that baby, was the flesh of someone else. Had it seemed foreign to regard the characteristics of two unknown people in her new daughter's face? Andie had been one month old when they had picked her up from a Salvation Army orphanage. Sarah had told her about the place, and it did not sound like somewhere to thrive. She apparently had not. Her parents always joked about how Andie had looked like a sack of bones when they had gotten her. They said that everyone had wanted to feed her because they had never seen a baby eat so eagerly and quickly. Andie always imagined herself crying in the orphanage, but not being fed for hours.

Had the lack of a birth experience prevented her mom from being nurturing? Was that why her mom had been unable to love her like a mother should? Had her mom stared at her while she slept in her crib and smiled at her sighs and whimpers? When they had gotten Scott, they had been trying for three years to have their own baby, even driving to Chicago for experimental, expensive treatments. They waited two more years until their name came up on a list of adoptive parents wanting a girl. Scott had been the center of their world for two years. Andie had been a completion of the family unit, but had probably burdened her mother with the additional, draining care of a newborn.

Joan's mother had favored Joan's older brother and was a stern, gruff woman. Andie realized that her mom had fallen onto a path that was somewhat predestined. She began to feel sorry for her mom for not having been able to experience the wonder of birth and for missing out on a close relationship with her own mother.

Steve quickly became infatuated with his daughter. He carried her around the small apartment, singing to her. Rylee still woke frequently at night, so Andie and Steve took turns getting her back to sleep. Usually if nothing else worked, Andie would lay the baby next to her on the bed and nurse her again for comfort. Andie awoke at the slightest sound and often fed Rylee when she heard her stirring with hunger, before she had even begun to cry.

One morning Andie woke up with tiny red marks all over her breast where Rylee had continued sucking, having missed the nipple while Andie had fallen back to sleep. Steve joked and said that at least somebody was getting a hickey. Andie tried to ignore the comment, knowing that he was directing it at her lack of interest in making love. Steve was growing more insistent that she try, but Andie was consumed physically with the care of the baby and had no sexual desire. Even three months later, she was still tender from the delivery. She told him that she had read that it took a while to recover after the birth and that he should be patient. She was so tired anyway that if she reclined on the bed, she wanted nothing else but to close her eyes and relax. She had not had an uninterrupted nights sleep in months, and it was taking its toll on her. She was forgetful and would become easily frustrated with Steve when he did something that she thought was not proper with Rylee. He had dabbed ice cream on Rylee's lips one day and laughed about it. Andie told him not to do it again—Rylee was months away from solid foods and the ice cream had chopped nuts in it. He told her that she was obsessive and overprotective, but Andie did not care what he thought. Rylee was going to be safe, and that was all that mattered to her.

She was often happier when Steve was away, which he was more frequently now. As Rylee closed in on the milestone that Andie eagerly waited for, Steve was usually going out somewhere at night. Finally, Rylee was six months old and beyond the peak age for crib death. Andie had kept her own diet pure and healthy, so the breast milk would be as ideal as possible. She had lost most of the forty-five pounds that she had gained during the pregnancy, but still did not fit into her old clothes. She wore loose fitting shorts and some of Steve's big T-shirts. She rarely doted on her own looks now, instead she would tie her hair up in a ponytail and leave her face free of even mascara. She enjoyed the luxury of long hot showers and occasional naps. It amused her to think about how different she was now that Rylee was here. How had she lived without her? Rylee was shy of strangers from the beginning of her awareness of others. She would cry if Andie tried to hand her to anyone else but Steve and Karin. Karin came over often, and they would sit and watch Rylee fumbling with her toys and babbling. Every new thing that Rylee did delighted Andie. Karin's boyfriend had proposed to her, but Karin informed him that she was not ready yet, so he was constantly trying to win her over. Her parents had shown her the joys of marriage, and Karin was not in a hurry to experience it.

Andie felt as if Karin were the other parent lately. Steve had some new friend that he had met at a sports bar and said that they liked to go hiking and jogging together. He still enjoyed Rylee, but said that he had to get out of the apartment and have a life. He could not understand how Andie was content to sit home and do nothing else. But Andie knew that she was doing everything that she had always wanted to do. She was safe from fear, with her baby girl, and had a relationship with her blood family. Even her parents in Iowa had become interested in her life now, without being patronizing. They asked for pictures and bought her a video camera so she could send them tapes each month. They mailed her a check to buy anything that Rylee did not have, which Andie stashed away for an emergency.

Everyone had sent wonderful gifts for Rylee, and the apartment was full of baby equipment everywhere she turned. Andie thought it was amazing that such small people could require such big things. Sarah, Lisa and Laura wanted to come and see Rylee, so they were trying to get time off from work. Sarah always told Andie that she was praying for her, and now Andie could say that she was also praying for all of them. It was nice to have this in common with Sarah. Andie's prayers were usually for protection and thanks for Rylee, but she really did not feel that there was a response from God, although she knew that He had blessed her with Rylee, so He must be there.

Money was tight, so Steve wanted Andie to go to work. She told him that there was no way she would put Rylee in daycare. She would somehow make money from home, because she could not imagine handing Rylee over to strangers who were paid five or six dollars an hour for tending to numerous babies in a small room.

Andie looked in the paper for work out of the home, but nothing ever seemed profitable. Steve was spending too much money on his nights out, and she told him so. A heated discussion ensued, turning into a fierce fight. He stormed out of the apartment and did not return until the following night. She tried to avoid him, not wanting Rylee to hear them fighting.

He began staying out all night and often did not come home after work. Andie was hurt and wanted him to help her with Rylee, but he was cold to her when she attempted to discuss anything serious. As long as she carried on in a pleasant, superficial way, he did the same. The one thing that they shared was a love for their daughter. They would sit and enjoy Rylee and her latest achievements, but fail to find other topics in common. He was often stoned on marijuana, so Andie tried to go along with his mood as best she could in her sober state of mind. He was annoyed that she would not smoke or drink, and told her that she used to be more fun when she did.

They had started to have physical relations again a few months before, when Rylee was four and a half months old. It had been painful at first, and Andie did it more for Steve than for her own desire. She tried to make herself available to him, but often had to turn him away due to fatigue. When they were at odds, he did not even approach her. She was relieved in a way, because it was not pleasurable. She was still tender from the episiotomy and her milk would start flowing too easily. She did not feel able to go from being a mother to a lover in ten minutes, and Steve no longer tried to romance her into the mood.

Three weeks after their big fight, he came home and asked her if she wanted to go out for dinner. They went to a barbecue house and got their money's worth from the all-you-can-eat special. Rylee sat in a high chair and watched everyone around them, banging her spoon on the tray and babbling happily. Andie was relieved that they were back to being a family. She wanted to leave the past disagreements behind and start fresh.

She even enjoyed it that night when they made love. He was gentler then usual, and she was filled with emotion because they were finally relating well again. She got up early with him before work and made him coffee and breakfast.

"Last night was really nice," Steve said as he gathered his lunch and work bag.

"I enjoyed it, too. I'll see you this afternoon. Maybe we can take Rylee to that new park."

He gave her a hug and kissed her. "Sounds good to me."

Andie closed the door after him and leaned against it for a moment. Life was challenging, but she had made it this far. They were a family now, and she wanted it to be a place where Rylee would see and feel love. She must try to be more sensitive to Steve's needs, realizing that she had been so immersed in caring for Rylee that she was neglecting her role as wife. If she tried to be close to him, maybe he would give up drinking and smoking. She was not going to nag him about it anymore. If they were completely happy together, he might have a reason to stop.

Chapter 24

A few days later, Andie thought that she might be coming down with some kind of illness. Her lower abdomen ached and pain spread to the kidney area under her ribcage. Even with double doses of pain reliever, it began to wake her up at night. She woke up one night in extreme pain and thought her period had started. But when she went into the bathroom, there was no blood. She called her obstetrician and went in for an exam the next morning. The doctor gave her a shot of penicillin, a prescription for antibiotic capsules, and told her that they would call her with the results of her tests.

When the nurse called to tell her that she had gonorrhea, Andie first thought that it must be a mistake. She looked up facts about the disease in a home medical book and learned that symptoms in women usually began two to three days after exposure. Then she knew: Steve had given it to her. She was disgusted and felt dirty. How could he have cheated on her and exposed her to every kind of disease? What if she had AIDS now? The thought caused a sick, cold dread to flow through her. She pictured him with some woman and knew that she could never be with him again. It hurt so much to imagine him being intimate with someone else that she was not certain if she could function. Rylee was crying and hungry, but Andie was in a daze after feeling rage, then sadness, and finally, fear of dying. She thought of calling him at work, but decided to wait for him to get home.

She began packing a bag for herself and Rylee, but put everything away—he would be the one to leave.

Andie finally got Rylee to sleep after feeding her lunch and walking her around the apartment. She was overcome with fear for Rylee because if Steve had given her AIDS, then she and Steve would die and Rylee would have no parents. Rylee was so dependent upon her that Andie could not bear to think of how her life would be if someone else had to raise her. She would call her doctor and arrange an AIDS test to be done in a few months. She knew from reading about the disease that it usually did not show up in blood until one month after exposure, but it could take six months for the virus to appear. It was going to be a long, anxious time of waiting. Steve would be home any minute, and Andie was primed for a confrontation.

When he walked in, Rylee was up from her nap, playing on the floor next to Andie's chair. He attempted to kiss them, but noticed Andie's grim expression.

"What's wrong, babe?" he asked.

"Tell me, Steve, is it just one woman you're sleeping with or a number of them?"

He made a strained sound and rubbed his nose. "What are you talking about? I'm not sleeping with anyone but you, sweetheart!"

"Look at this," she said, handing him the bottle of pills. "This is for treating the gonorrhea that I have."

"You have gonorrhea? How did you get it? You've been with someone; I don't have gonorrhea!" he exclaimed, tossing the pills onto her lap.

Andie jumped out of her chair and went up close to him. "You gave it to me the other night, Steve! As if I would go out to find a man when I'm with Rylee every minute. Think about it! The doctor told me that if I'd waited any longer, I might've gotten an infection throughout my entire blood stream and died! How could you have done this? You risked my life for some cheap thrill! What if you gave me AIDS, you idiot!" Andie yelled.

"Shut up! Don't you call me that! If you were a real woman, I wouldn't have to go out and look for it! You sit around here like a dried up old cow and expect me to wait until you're ready. Three times a month is not enough for any man. If you want me to stay here, then you're going to have to change!" he shouted.

"Here's a news flash, Steve: I don't want you to stay here! You'll never touch me again! I want you to pack your things and get out of here!" Andie screamed.

Rylee had started whimpering and then began crying heartily. Andie went to her and picked her up, rubbing her small back. "You'd better go to the doctor, unless you plan to spread this all around to your women. You're nothing but a male whore! I can't even stand to look at you. Get out of here right now!"

Steve smiled wickedly at her and said, "At least I'm not crazy."

Andie stared at him in surprise. She knew he was referring to her stay in the psychiatric place, and that he was aware of how much it upset her to have this on her record. In the past, he had tried to reassure her that it was not her fault.

"You're the most disgusting excuse for a man I've ever seen. I'm sorry that Rylee has you for a father. She deserves so much better."

"We'll see who's going to be getting Rylee! With your past, a judge will decide that you're an unfit mother. Enjoy these last few days of having her, because she'll be with me soon!"

"Over my dead body! You will never take her from me. Don't even threaten me like this!"

"I'll be back tomorrow to get my things. I've got somewhere to go where I'm appreciated! She knows a good lawyer, so plan on going to court soon. You don't have any money, Andie! How do you expect to take care of Rylee? My friend loves babies—she can't wait to see her. Have a lovely evening, you psycho!" he said as he walked out of the apartment, slamming the door.

Andie looked at the closed door. She was shaking and trying not to cry. How could she not have known how cruel he really was? So many things popped into her mind that she wished she had said to him. She walked around the apartment, hugging Rylee. What if he could get Rylee? How was she going to provide for both of them now that he was gone? What if he had given her AIDS?

She lowered Rylee into her playpen next to her toys and then went across the room to sit on the couch. She put her face on the pillow and cried, not wanting Rylee to witness her distress. Would her past be enough to ruin her chance to keep Rylee? She still felt that she was not completely free of its effects, but she had always made sure that Rylee was well cared for. She had not had any sleep walking incidents in months. But without money, how would she defend herself in court? For that matter, how would she buy groceries and pay the rent for the month? She had a two hundred dollar check from her parents and around three hundred dollars in their joint checking account.

She wiped her tears away and blew her nose. After lifting Rylee up out of her playpen, she grabbed a bottle of juice and the car keys. She drove to her bank and tried to use her ATM card to withdraw money from the cash machine. The account was emptied, only ten dollars remained.

She fell asleep that night after hours of deliberating her choices. She had tried to reach Karin, but she was out with her boyfriend. The first things that she would need were a job and a less expensive place to live. She knew from her previous job search when she was pregnant that her broadcasting degree would only allow her to make around seven dollars an hour because she had no experience or connections. How was she going to make it? Steve might one day have to give her child support, but until she had a court order, there would be no help. And what if he won custody of Rylee? The thought kept her awake all night long.

Chapter 25

Andie scoured the newspaper classified section each day for jobs. Karin would be moving in with her boyfriend soon, because her mother wanted to find a different place to live. Everything seemed to be happening at once. Rylee caught a chest cold and could not sleep well. Andie patted her back, trying to loosen the phlegm from her congested lungs while they sat in the bathroom with the shower running hot, misting slowly around them like a dream.

Steve had come over with one of his friends and packed his bags, taking Ashley, the stereo, TV, microwave, and kitchen table in his truck. Ashley was too much work, and the other things were his before they had gotten married, so Andie figured that he had the right to take them. He told her that she would be hearing from his lawyer soon and to be prepared to hand Rylee over to him. She believed that he was bluffing about the lawyer. He would not provide her with a name when she asked for it. Her anger at him had overshadowed the pain of losing him as her husband. She went into a mode of survival, focusing on keeping Rylee safe.

She decided to ask her parents if she could stay with them temporarily, until she could get on her feet. When her father told her that she could, Andie felt a huge sense of relief knowing that Rylee would have a comfortable place to live. She would stay with Rylee in their extra bedroom, and they even had an old crib from her childhood in storage. Andie imagined taking Rylee to their restaurant and eating all of the good food for free. How wonderful to have a hot meal! She had been eating bowls of oatmeal and peanut butter sandwiches, saving the money for Rylee's necessities. She had asked her dad if she could waitress at their restaurant, even though it meant being near Scott, who still worked there as some kind of "partner" now. She considered going back to college at the nearby University of Northern Iowa and getting a real degree. If she waitressed on weekends, she could attend night school while Rylee stayed with her parents or a sitter.

Andie called her parents a few days later to tell them that she had gotten out of her lease and planned to drive to Iowa within the next two weeks. She brought boxes home from a liquor store and began packing their belongings. With all of the miles in between Iowa and Phoenix, Andie knew Rylee would be out of Steve's reach. She was going to call him once she got there to let him know where they were. He would be angry about being far from Rylee, but after possibly exposing her to AIDS, she was not concerned about his emotions. He had only called a couple of times threatening her, but nothing had come of it so far.

She tried to keep from thinking about the chance that she had contracted AIDS, but the follow-up visit to her doctor was not reassuring. She had nagging pain in her lower abdominal region, and found out that her Fallopian tubes had been severely scarred by the infection. Andie was devastated when the doctor informed her that she was probably sterile and that the pain might always exist from the scar tissue. She would not be able to have more children! She had always hoped to have more, especially since Rylee was born and she experienced the joy and love that a child brought. When she inquired about AIDS, she also learned that it could be transmitted through breast milk. If she had it, then there was a good possibility that Rylee would also have it.

Andie fought off the depression that set in with a vengeance. She needed to take care of Rylee, but at times she felt so burdened and downtrodden that it was difficult to get out of bed. Packing and organizing for the move to Iowa was keeping her busy, but her mind was bombarded with despair and fear.

She was finally packed and ready to get out of Phoenix, so she called to let her parents know that she was leaving the next morning. She was speechless when her father told her that they had decided it was not a good idea to have her live there, and that Scott was not "comfortable" with the idea of her working at their restaurant. He was matter-of-fact and casual about it, as if they were talking about a failed plan for a stroll in the park. She hung up the phone, not even attempting to argue or beg.

They did not want her there. They were not going to help her. He should have told her right away so that she would not have broken her lease and sold nearly everything. She was supposed to be out of the apartment in three days. She looked around at all of the boxes that held her most important possessions. She had sold Rylee's crib and changing table, as well as all the furniture, so that everything would fit into her car. She sat down on the floor and went into a long bout of sobbing until Rylee woke up and needed her.

"We're going to make it somehow, little one. Your mama will make sure that you're okay, I promise," Andie said quietly, her face still wet with tears as she stroked Rylee's silky hair. Rylee patted Andie's cheek and looked into her eyes. This child was her whole life. Her first real family was right here in her arms and depending on her for life. Andie closed her eyes and said a prayer, asking for help and comfort.

She called Karin at work and told her what had happened. Karin had been planning to come over that evening to say good-bye to them before they left for Iowa, and said she would come over to help Andie figure out what to do.

Andie took Rylee outside for some fresh air. She could not stand to look at the boxes and disheveled apartment. Rylee wanted to get down and crawl all of the time now, so Andie went to a soft grassy area and sat next to her. She wondered how everything had come to this. Why was it so difficult to have the one thing that she had always wanted, a family? She was too embarrassed to call her sisters or Sarah. Her parents in Iowa had let Scott come back to live with them after he had thrown away his full scholarship to college, and they even let him take over part of the restaurant business. It hurt so much to know that they would not help her now when she needed it the most. If she was alone, she would not have asked to move in with them; she would have managed on her own. But their granddaughter needed security, and they were unwilling to help, even for a short time. All of the money and gifts that they had sent for Rylee did not make up for their lack of true compassion.

Andie watched Rylee drooling and intently trying to pinch blades of grass. She found a brown twig and began lifting it to her mouth. Andie grabbed the twig and brushed off Rylee's dimpled hands. She carried her back up to the apartment and sat down on the floor to nurse her. While she was feeding her, the phone rang.

"Hello," Andie said warily, hoping it was not Steve or her parents.

"Andie, guess what? I have some news that I think will make your day. A friend of mine here at the hospital knows a doctor who has a house for rent," Karin said excitedly.

"Karin, I don't have enough money for any doctor's house. I don't even have enough for a one-bedroom apartment," Andie replied.

"No, listen to this! When Greg and I were looking for a place to rent, I heard about it. My friend knows about your situation and talked to this doctor and it's still available. He and his wife want to rent their three bedroom house for six hundred dollars a month. And here's the good part, they have four kids who need a baby-sitter, their other one just quit out of the blue, so my friend said that they wanted to meet you and see if they could arrange a deal. A house in exchange for childcare! You could be home with Rylee during the day, all of the time. What do you think?"

"Are you serious? They don't even know me. How could they leave their kids with someone they don't know?" Andie began. "I mean, it sounds like a great deal. I just can't believe it could be true."

"Well, they're apparently desperate and need someone right away since the other sitter just quit. The house is supposed to be partially furnished. Greg and I never looked at it because we'd found our house already and didn't want to be that far from the hospital. The four kids are all close in age, so you'd have your hands full, but you're great with kids. Should I give them your phone number?" Karin asked.

"Yes! Oh, my gosh, that would save my life right now! Give them my number and tell them I'm very interested. And tell them that I have excellent references. Thank you so much, Karin!" Andie exclaimed.

"You're welcome! I hope it works out. I'll call you back soon!" Karin said.

Andie finished feeding Rylee, then lifted her high into the air and dipped her up and down as Rylee giggled and squealed. She might be able to stay home with Rylee and not leave her with anyone else! She could manage being poor and struggling, but to leave her baby somewhere else for most of the day was what she dreaded more than anything.

An hour later the phone rang, and Dr. Morgan asked for Andie. She agreed to meet him at the rental house. Andie chose her best outfit for herself and one for Rylee, and wrote down some references on a piece of paper. As she approached the address given to her, she thought that she must have written it down incorrectly. This house was beautiful and huge. There was an arched entryway that led to an ornate wooden front door. The landscaping was exquisitely planned and maintained, like a tropical paradise. In the circular driveway a Mercedes was parked in front of a white mini-van. A dark-haired man in a suit and tie waved to her as she pulled up to the curb. A woman got out of the mini-van and unloaded children.

Andie greeted them and introduced herself and Rylee. The four children stood next to their well-dressed mother. The older ones were instructed to shake hands with Andie. The youngest was the only girl, just a few months older than Rylee, but already walking.

"Andrea, my wife and I have been left without a sitter for our children. I've heard many good things about you from some people at the hospital. If we can come to an agreement, and you are interested, this will benefit us both," Dr. Morgan said. He appeared to be in his late thirties or early forties, with thinning hair and a pleasant, smooth face. His wife was perfectly coiffured, wearing a fine linen suit, but was failing to conceal her frustration with her boisterous children.

"Well, Dr. Morgan, I'm in the process of a divorce, and I need a house to rent. I have experience as a mother, and I also did some baby-sitting when I was younger. Here are some references," Andie said as she handed him the piece of paper.

"Great! Why don't we show you around the house first to see if you like it," he replied as he ushered his brood toward the front door. He tucked the paper into his pocket without looking at it.

The house had patterned ceramic tile floors in the main rooms, and new carpet in two of the three bedrooms, which were spacious and had ceiling fans. Two of the bedrooms were furnished with full-sized beds and a dresser. The living room had a L-shaped sofa and modern artwork on the walls. Healthy plants sat in decorative pots on two end tables, and a large television and a VCR were in an entertainment center. There was a ceramic-topped kitchen table and six chairs, a dishwasher, and the cupboards had dishes and pots and pans. There was even a full spice rack and coffee maker. Andie walked around taking in all that was there.

"I can't believe that no one has rented this house. It's worth far more than six hundred dollars a month. And you have such beautiful new furnishings. How long have you had it on the market?" Andie asked as the children darted through the rooms and around the adults. Rylee watched in fascination, kicking her legs excitedly.

"I must be honest with you, because you'd find out one day anyway. We used to live here before our youngest was born, but then we needed more room, so we rented it out to an acquaintance who was a veterinarian. He lived here until just four months ago, when he passed away. Actually he died in the house, in one of the bedrooms. He committed suicide one night," Dr. Morgan whispered the last sentence.

"Oh, no. How…how did he do it?" Andie asked.

"With a gun to his head. The painters had to strip and paint the wall a number of times to get rid of the stain. There's still a slight shadow, but it's not very noticeable unless you're looking for it. If this is too much for you, we understand. Most people don't want to live here because of it. And all of the ones who did were not acceptable to us. But it is a very nice house. We had many good years here," Dr. Morgan said.

Her interest had not lessened. Even though it was morbid and unfortunate, this was an opportunity that would never come again. She was desperate for stability, and this house was a dream home. Rylee would have the finest of everything here.

"Dr. Morgan, I have no problem with this, although I'm sorry that your friend passed away. I'm still very interested in living here and caring for your children. It would probably be like home for them since they were used to living here. If you'd like to call my references and get back to me, I will look forward, hopefully, to making plans with you and your family," Andie said.

Dr. Morgan looked at his wife, and she nodded at him. "Andrea, my wife and I would like to offer you the position and the house. We're good judges of character and your daughter seems to be quite a healthy child. We would need you to start as soon as possible, even tomorrow if you could. The hours would be from seven a.m. to five p.m., and we would end up paying you each month instead of you paying rent. For the hours of childcare, you would earn sixteen hundred dollars a month. Deducting the rent of six hundred dollars, we would pay you one thousand dollars a month to live here and care for them. Does that sound agreeable to you?"

Andie had to stop her mouth from dropping open. She was not able to respond right away.

"Andrea? Would you need more money?" Dr. Morgan asked. "We'll even pay the utility bill."

"Oh, I'm sorry. I was just thinking. Yes, that sounds very agreeable," Andie replied, trying to suppress an idiotic grin that she felt tugging at the corners of her mouth. The doctor was worried that the deal was not good enough.

"Wonderful! Can you start tomorrow, or is that too soon?" Mrs. Morgan asked.

It was arranged that Andie would move in that night and begin childcare in the morning. She sat in her car for a moment and looked at the house. As she attached the two house keys to her key chain, she felt such tremendous relief and excitement, as if she had just won a lottery: one thousand dollars a month and a gorgeous house to live in! God had just smiled upon her in a tremendous way. She said a prayer of thanks as she drove to her apartment.

It took her a while to pack the car and keep Rylee safe and out of the way. She had to put her in her playpen and lock the apartment door behind her each time she carried the boxes out to the parking lot. She also had to readjust the boxes to make them all fit in the car, not wanting to make more than one trip to move.

When she got back to the house it was very late, but the outside lights were left on for her. The refrigerator and cupboards were filled with at least a hundred dollars worth of food. In one bedroom were four packages of diapers, baby wipes, and a diaper pail. In the kitchen, a high chair was set up next to the table and a booster seat attached to one of the kitchen chairs. A note on the kitchen table told her what her new phone number was and listed the work numbers of Dr. and Mrs. Morgan. They had thought of everything.

Andie set up Rylee's playpen in the smaller bedroom, with sheets tucked around the thin mat and her blanket on top. It would have to do for now for a crib. Andie tried not to look at the walls; she did not want to know which bedroom the suicide had taken place in. She claimed the master bedroom as her own and stacked most of the boxes in the garage.

She got up early the next morning and had coffee before Mrs. Morgan dropped off the kids. She assumed that Mrs. Morgan would stay a while to let the children warm up to her, but they were dropped off quickly, with a heap of toys and bags of extra clothes and snacks. Stuart, the two-year-old boy, was the only one who cried when his mother left.

The older boys constantly bickered and often shoved Stuart aside when he tried to join them in play. Kara, the fourteen-month-old, ambled around sucking her thumb, following the activity of her brothers. Rylee clung to Andie at first, but then wanted to get down on the floor near the other children. Andie was worried that the older boys were going to trample over Rylee, so she had to keep reminding them to settle down as she followed them around the house.

When lunchtime finally arrived, Andie knew that her days would be very challenging. The kitchen was a disaster after the kids were fed. Rylee and Kara made the smallest amount of mess, though they were the most uncoordinated eaters. The oldest boys, Colin and Sam, tested Andie's authority and patience at every opportunity. They even told her that this was their house, and she had to listen to them about how to behave in it. Mrs. Morgan had not informed her how to discipline them or what to expect, so Andie made them sit in a designated "time-out" area until they obeyed.

By five o'clock, Andie yearned for the freedom of tending to only one child. Mrs. Morgan was twenty minutes late, but she apologized three times. Andie told her that they had all done well on their first day, but a few time-outs had been necessary. Mrs. Morgan nodded and attempted to corner Stuart and Kara. Colin and Sam started fist fighting as they were leaving, so Mrs. Morgan briskly hit them on their bottoms, which caused them both to start screaming and crying, with Kara and Stuart soon joining in.

Andie closed the door quickly behind them, shaking her head. If this was the price to pay, she would do it, but there had to be a way to manage the children better so that she would not turn into a nervous wreck. No wonder the other sitter had quit. Andie was curious to know how many sitters they had gone through. She was locked into the position because of the house, although she would not quit no matter how difficult the children were to care for. She was with Rylee all day, even if she was not able to give her as much attention. Rylee seemed to enjoy watching the kids, and soon she would be walking like Kara and able to interact with the others more. Andie knew that she would be earning every penny of her salary.

Chapter 26

Andie used part of her first paycheck to buy a secondhand crib, changing table, stroller, some garage sale toys, and more art supplies. It had been a long first month, but she believed that she had made progress with the children. She had learned what each of them was like and what appealed to them. While the girls took their afternoon naps, she played games and did artwork with the boys. They carried home crinkled papers of finger-painted designs, crayon drawings, and play dough statues. They made cards for their parents that said "I love you," and designed alphabet and number charts. She taught them songs and told them stories that she made up. While they had challenged her at first, they now begged for more attention and were eager to please her.

She was worn out at the end of each day, but she enjoyed adding something to their lives. The kids were starved for adult attention. Kara would reach her arms up, wanting to be held, and then bury her face in Andie's neck and play with her hair, making little humming sounds in her chest. She was content to be held for as long as Andie would hold her. Rylee, on the other hand, had blossomed into a social baby. She always wanted to be near the kids, crying in protest if Andie tried to pick her up when she was crawling after the boys or Kara.

Andie tried to call Steve to tell him where she was living, but he was no longer at the number he had left. A woman rudely informed her that he had moved, and gave her a number where he could be reached.

When she finally talked to him, he was polite and even apologized for his past behavior. Andie accepted his apology, but knew that he could never win her back. He must have broken up with his girlfriend. He asked to see Rylee, so Andie gave him their address and arranged for him to see her on Saturday morning.

When he came early on Saturday, Andie could tell that he was going to try to win her affection. He was impressed with the house, and tried to find out how much money she was making. Andie did not tell him the details, but said that she and Rylee would be fine without help from anyone. While she packed Rylee's diaper bag, Steve asked her to go along with them to the park. Andie declined, because she had cleaning and shopping to do, so he left with Rylee.

It was sad to watch Rylee become excited when she saw Steve. Andie wished that Rylee could have had a complete family, but there was no way that she could ever trust Steve again. She still felt angry, although she did not let him see any emotion. Andie was quite experienced at closing herself off from people who had hurt her. She would make the best life for Rylee on her own, and allow Rylee to be close to her father. She had no right to deprive Rylee of this relationship. After growing up without the knowledge of who her real parents were, Andie would not do this to her own daughter.

She felt as if she had not had a moment to herself in ages. Even at night when Rylee was asleep, she would clean up the day's mess from all of the children and then fall into bed exhausted. She decided to quickly clean the neglected bathrooms and floors before going grocery shopping.

Two hours later, as she unloaded the grocery bags from her car, she saw a woman walk out of the house next door. The woman waved, then grabbed the hands of her two young boys and came over.

"Hi!" she said in a loud, friendly voice. "I'm Emily Rasmussen, and this is David and Bobby." The boys nodded shyly at Andie.

"Hello!" Andie replied, setting down her bags. "Nice to meet you." She extended her hand to the stocky, blond-haired woman, who appeared to be close to her own age and had a firm, brisk handshake. "I'm Andrea Lewis, but my friends call me Andie."

"Nice to meet you, Andie. Don't you have a daughter? I've seen you with the Morgan kids, but that cute little girl is always with you."

"I do. Her name's Rylee. She's with her father for the afternoon. Have you lived here long?" Andie asked, smiling as the boys pulled at their mother's arms, glad to be unencumbered for the moment.

"Hold on, guys!" Emily said sternly. "It's too difficult for them to stand still for three minutes, but when I want them to hurry, they're like turtles in mud. We've been renting this house for almost two years now. My husband, Jay, was transferred here from Dallas. We've moved a lot, but I'm hoping we can stay in one place since the boys will be starting school soon. How do you like the house?"

"It's so beautiful! I can't believe I live here." Andie noticed that Emily was peering at her expectantly, as if waiting to hear more.

"So...you're comfortable with everything about it?"

Andie had to laugh at her obvious curiousity. "Well, I haven't had any problems falling asleep, if that's what you mean."

"I'm sorry!" Emily laughed, smoothing a hand through her short hair. "It was quite a scene when that happened right next door to us. Pretty creepy, you know?"

"I'll bet it was. Did you know the man?"

"Not really. He always seemed to be in a rush. I heard that he was acting weird near the end. A friend of mine knew someone who worked with him." Emily glanced at her kids to see if they were following the conversation.

"It's too bad he had to end it all that way. I try not to think about it. Well, I'd better get my groceries inside. The popsicles aren't going to make it too long in this heat."

"Here, we'll help." Emily gave a small bag to each boy. They quickly had the groceries in the house and put away. Andie offered to make coffee, and they sat at the kitchen table for an hour while the boys played on the swing set in the back yard.

Emily had a full-bodied, contagious laugh that Andie liked to hear. She was also very blunt and disclosed personal information as if she had known Andie for years. She was tired of her husband and looked forward to his frequent trips out of town on business. Andie shared her story about Steve. Emily said she was lucky to finally be rid of him and wished she could make it on her own without her husband, because all that they did was fight when he was home. He was seven years older than Emily, and he had become distant and crabby. Emily was home all day with her kids, so she said that she would come over and visit while they watched the children.

A few weeks later they began knocking on each other's doors and then walking in without waiting for a reply. Andie had been missing Karin, who was planning her wedding with Greg and often working overtime. Karin had come over a few times to visit, but now that she was living with Greg, she was usually busy. Andie knew now how Karin must have felt when she had moved in with Steve. She was happy for Karin, but she missed their camaraderie. Emily was a welcome friend.

Emily often came over in the evening, and they watched movies or listened to music. She sometimes brought along a six-pack of wine coolers, and they would sip them and eat popcorn or chips. Emily had a penchant for vulgarity, and Andie found herself laughing often at Emily's strong opinions and ideas. Andie asked if she thought the man who committed suicide had gone to hell when he died.

"Anyone who commits suicide goes to hell. Only God can decide when a life should end. A woman in my Bible study last year had a really hard time because her brother killed himself," Emily said.

Andie shuddered at the thought of hell and demons, remembering the ugly, wicked monsters in the field near her old apartment. She wanted to strip her memory of the scenes that waited just on the other side of her consciousness. She had been having bad dreams again lately that woke her up, but so far she had not been sleepwalking. The dreams always had the same theme; a form of evil would suddenly appear in a person or thing and pursue her for what seemed like hours.

One night, Emily closed her boys in the extra bedroom to play with toys, then pulled out a joint of marijuana. They were on their second wine cooler by that time, so Andie decided, with Emily's encouragement, to take a few puffs. Rylee had just begun to drink cow's milk, so Andie knew that it would be safe to have a little. They smoked half of the joint, drinking another wine cooler with it. Andie coughed and choked at first, then she remembered how to take a small amount and hold it in her lungs.

She told Emily about her sisters and mother in Florida, and Emily was intrigued. Andie had written to them and told them of the changes in her life. Sarah had called her twice since Andie had moved, but Andie had been reluctant to tell her about her break up with Steve. When she finally did, Sarah seemed concerned, asking if there was anything she could do for them. She had said that she would continue praying for them. Emily related that she was a Christian, though she did not get to church as often as she would like. Lighting up the rest of the joint, she explained that smoking marijuana was not sinful because it was just partaking in a natural creation that God had put on Earth for people to enjoy. And Andie was enjoying the feeling again as she looked around at her beautiful house and saw it in a different light. What good luck I've had, she thought. They ended up laughing and staying up late, telling stories about their pasts.

The days were easier now that she had someone to be with. Soon, Andie was smoking nightly, not as much as she used to, but enough to keep the high going. Emily would make lunch one day, and then Andie would prepare it on the next, giving them both a needed break. Steve came regularly to pick up Rylee on Saturdays, and if Emily's husband was home, she and Emily would go out together, free from children and men.

Andie finally called her parents and told them about her house and job. They carried on as if nothing had transpired between them, the rejection unmentioned. Andie felt a sense of satisfaction that she had made it without them, although it still bothered her that they were unwilling to help and had reneged on their offer for her to move in with them. It was apparent that Scott had been involved in their change of heart. She would have probably been depressed being around them again anyway, she thought, and it would have worried her to leave Rylee with her mom. Andie knew that being drunk was much worse than being high. She did not stagger around or wet her pants like her mom; she had control over her actions when she was high. She bought a bag of marijuana every other week from Emily's brother and would begin to feel anxious when her bag was running low. Emily would give her some from her own stash if she ran out, and she did the same for Emily.

Sarah called one day when Andie had just taken a few hits of marijuana. Andie was nervous and tried to keep the conversation going, not wanting Sarah to learn that she was high. It was a Saturday, and Rylee had just been picked up by Steve, so Andie had smoked more than usual. When she got off the phone, she went back over their conversation and reassured herself that she had handled it well. It was easier talking to her parents in Iowa when she was high, because they carried on in such a superficial way that she always knew what to expect. She still did not feel that she knew Sarah very well. Andie looked forward to calling her sisters. She missed them and pictured them often, trying to imagine how they would react in certain situations that she encountered.

Laura could not believe that Andie wanted to do daycare. She was not in a hurry to have children, remembering all too well the days after her brothers were born and how much work it was to raise them. Lisa thought that Andie's job sounded great—being home with Rylee and getting to eat and drink whenever she wanted, or watching TV and playing games with the kids. She wanted to see pictures of the house and

Rylee, so Andie took photographs and mailed some to all of them. She was proud to be living well and taking care of everything on her own.

Chapter 27

Rylee was finally asleep after many attempts to keep Andie with her in the bedroom. Three story books and five hugs later, Andie sat in the living room watching TV. A knocking sound began, steady and forceful. Turning down the volume of the TV, she listened for the source of the sound. It became louder and more insistent, apparently coming from an area near the bedrooms.

She hurried to Rylee's room to check on her. Before Andie reached the door, Rylee started screaming, not crying in her night time sleepy way, but screaming as if she was in terrible pain. Andie quickly opened the door, realizing as she did that the knocking was coming from inside the room. She turned on the light and the knocking stopped. Rylee sat in the corner of her crib, screaming hysterically. Andie picked her up and tried to soothe her, but Rylee continued screaming in a high-pitched, terrified wail. The only time Andie had ever heard Rylee scream this way was when she had received her shots, but she had calmed down much faster then.

She took Rylee into the living room and turned on soft music, cradling her on the couch. Rylee clung tightly to her, and then began searching for a breast as if she wanted to nurse. Pouring a bottle of milk was challenging with Rylee wrapped around her neck, but she managed, leaving behind two puddles of white on the counter.

When Rylee began to close her eyes, Andie carried her slowly and attempted to put her in her crib, but Rylee immediately began screaming. Back in the living room, Andie let her fall asleep in her arms. She could not imagine what had caused the knocking in Rylee's room. The room was bordered on one side by her own bedroom and on the other by a bathroom. The sound had seemed to come from the side of the room that was closest to her own room, but it was difficult to be certain now.

She looked down at Rylee's peaceful face and wondered what her young mind had experienced. The noise must have frightened her badly. She was growing up so quickly, her first birthday only weeks away. Andie finally laid her in her crib, and she was so sound asleep after all of the crying that she did not stir.

The weeks passed by quickly as Andie's days were filled with endless details and constant demands for her attention. Steve had tried numerous times to convince her to try and repair their relationship. He used Rylee as the reason, saying that she deserved to have two parents raising her together. Andie decided it was time to file for a divorce. She found a relatively inexpensive lawyer and paid him five hundred dollars to draw up a simple dissolution agreement. She presented it to Steve when he returned with Rylee.

"I can't believe you want to divorce me!" he shouted, flinging the diaper bag to the ground.

"It really shouldn't be a surprise. Did you think I was just playing a game when I went off on my own?"

"Rylee's going to be one of those kids with a broken home and end up insecure all her life."

"She'll be just fine. I'll make sure of it. You need to forget about any chance of us being together, because I could never trust you again. I'll be going next week for an AIDS test and I suggest you do the same," Andie stated.

He tossed the papers toward her and they fluttered to the ground, landing next to the diaper bag. "I'm not going to agree to any divorce! If you try to do this, I'll take Rylee from you!"

"I can divorce you on the grounds of adultery. No judge is going to take a baby girl away from a mother who can support her completely and stay home with her full time. Try to top that one, Steve. I have excellent references. You'll be wasting your time."

"Andie, I made a big mistake and I'm very sorry. I love you guys. Please don't do this! Give me one more chance and I'll prove it to you!" he pleaded.

"What you did was not just cheat on me. What you did was put a gun to my head that might have been loaded, and then you pulled the trigger. That shot was also aimed at Rylee. You know that AIDS is out there, yet for a quick thrill, you were willing to sacrifice my life. You gave me a disease that has probably taken away my ability to have more children. If I have AIDS, then Rylee will too because I was breast feeding. I really don't even want to look at you again, let alone be married to you." Andie felt her emotions harden as she looked at his scowling face. She picked up the papers and handed them to him.

"Just read it and sign it. We'll have joint custody. You can see her as often as you want. I suppose I could ask for alimony, since I wasn't working while we were together, but if you sign this I won't bring it up. I'll take you to court over it if I need to, but it would be easier and less expensive for both of us if we could work it out," Andie said.

"You're as cold as ice, you know that? You can just turn into a robot whenever you decide to. You're so screwed up from your past that you can't trust anybody! I would've been a good husband, but you'll never know. Your loss, Andie!" he said bitterly, turning to leave.

Andie was encouraged that he had taken the papers. If he would sign them, she would finally have this problem behind her.

* * *

Rylee was taking wobbly steps. Andie had to follow her around the house because she would weave and waver as she tried to direct her little body across the room to explore. She had fallen a few times, smacking her head hard on the tile floor. Andie bought corner guards for all of the tables and tried to keep the toys out of her way. Rylee would just plow through rooms without noticing anything under her feet, stumbling and making Andie hold her breath each time she saw her lose her balance. Danger seemed to be a moment away all of the time.

The AIDS test was negative. Andie thanked God that she and Rylee were safe, and vowed never to date a man unless he could prove that he was HIV negative. But she had no time for meeting men, even though she sometimes yearned for male companionship.

Mostly, she looked forward to the evenings when she could finally rest and not hear the sound of crying and loud voices, or be on constant alert for disaster. Three kids were still in diapers, since Stuart was slow at potty training. When Rylee was down for the night, Andie would usually smoke a whole joint by herself and often had a glass of wine with it. Emily would show up at some point and they would smoke more together.

While they were sitting in the kitchen, Andie heard the knocking again. Emily was up and walking with her to Rylee's room when they heard Rylee begin screaming. Andie quickly opened the door and turned on the light, but the knocking continued. She picked Rylee up and felt a stab of fear shoot through her belly as she realized that the knocking was coming from under the crib. Rylee was hysterical, so Andie took her out of the room and Emily followed.

"Heat a bottle of milk, will you please?" Andie said, trying to soothe Rylee.

Emily hurriedly got the bottle ready. "What is it, Andie? Is that what you heard before?" she asked. They listened to the repetitive loud knocks.

Rylee eagerly sucked on the nipple, and Andie motioned for them to go into the living room.

"It's the same, except last time it stopped when I opened her door," Andie replied, her eyes glancing toward the hallway that led to the bedrooms.

"Let's go over to my house. I've got a really bad feeling about this," Emily said anxiously.

"No. Come on, let's go in there for a minute and see if we can figure it out," Andie said, starting toward Rylee's room.

"No! Don't go in there, Andie! Let's go to my house!" Emily was desperate to leave as the knocking grew louder.

Andie walked into the room holding tightly to Rylee, who was intently working on her bottle. She paused, then pushed the crib away from the wall and out of the way. The knocking seemed louder. Andie stared at the wooden floor and thought she could see it vibrating with each beat. Emily watched as Andie took a step, standing directly over the area from where the sound emanated.

"What are you doing?" Emily asked incredulously.

"Come here," Andie said. Her feet felt the shock of each blow, and she bounced slightly in place. She knew it would take a sledge hammer from down below to be slammed upward with immense force to create this kind of impact. "Quick, Emily, come here!"

Emily was wide-eyed as she walked slowly forward and joined her. Another set of knocks jarred them both, and Emily turned to Andie, her face pale and frozen with fear. "Oh, no," she whispered.

The knocking continued as they stood silently, too stunned to move. The pattern of the knocking suddenly changed from single, equally spaced beats, to random quick beats of different strengths.

Andie was terrified. Like most homes in Arizona, there was no basement in the house. Her mind had been able to accept the knocks, when they had happened before, as a rumbling from the bathroom pipes in the wall. Whatever this was, it seemed to be determined to break through the floor. Her mind felt as if it stretched and snapped. It was apparent that this was a spiritual matter. The air in the room was heavier somehow, pressing against her, trying to keep her from moving. Some presence was making itself known, and it was messing with the most precious part of her life, her daughter.

This was war.

The corners of Emily's mouth stretched downward in a taut grimace. Andie saw that Rylee was nearing the halfway point of her bottle and knew that she would not be content when it was gone. Andie lifted up her bare foot and smacked it down on the floor as hard as she could. Emily's mouth dropped open. Rylee looked around worriedly and sucked harder.

She hoped to scare it off, and when it stopped for a moment, she thought that she had. A rapid series of knocks began. Andie tried to return them in the same pattern, wanting to drown it out and show her own strength. Then she stopped mimicking the knocks, but instead made up her own pattern of beats. Terror cut through her as she heard her knocks precisely echoed back to her, but more loudly. Emily's face appeared to have drained of blood, looking ghostly white under the light. Her eyes were transfixed on Andie's face.

Andie began doing a mindless tap shoe motion with one foot, no longer hitting the floor, the energy drained from her by thoughts of what could happen next. The presence was evil and she could feel it. Something might appear and attack them at any moment. The strength and persistence of the pounding had increased. She was acutely aware of her fear, although a buzzing numbness had settled in as she tried to grasp the reality of the situation.

As the knocking continued, it seemed mocking and gleeful, more frenzied. A thread of anger began to grow in Andie. This presence was like a bully going after someone smaller than it. Rylee had been in here, in her room alone with it, while it lurked and plotted. Andie's mind was a jumble of confused thoughts and crazed emotions, but a part of her was keenly strengthening, drawing itself up to the surface of her consciousness. She began singing quietly at first. After a few words, the song boomed out of her. She had not planned to sing, or even knew how this particular song from her childhood had gotten into her mind.

"Knock three times on the ceiling if you wa-annt me," Andie sang. "Rr-rap on the pipe, if the answer is no-oo."

Emily's face flinched, as if preparing for a blow, when Andie started singing.

"Oh, my darling!" Andie stomped three times on the floor. "…means you'll meet me in the ha-aallway. Twice on the pipe," stomp, stomp, "if the answer is no!"

After Andie had sung the verses two more times, she felt something lighten inside of her. She started laughing and continued her song. "Everybody sing!" she cried. "Knock three times on the ceiling if you wa-aant me!"

Emily's voice was delicate at first, then she began singing with gusto.

"Twice on the pipe," two stomps from both of them followed, "…if the answer is no-oo!" Their voices were loud, and their laughter swelled up and spilled out in bursts.

They sang the song over and over, rolling into fits of laughter. Rylee had stopped drinking her bottle and was looking happily at them as they sang. When they finally stopped, they realized that the knocking had ceased some time ago during their singing. They had to actually catch their breath afterwards and were still laughing as they looked at one another.

"Oh, Andie…what just happened?" Emily asked, her eyes searching the room.

"Well, ah, I guess he didn't like our singing," Andie replied, which cracked them up again. They walked from the room and closed the door behind them.

Emily grew serious as they stood in the living room. "I really think you should pack up and come over. How're you going to be able to stay here?"

"I can't leave. I just got here a few months ago, and this is my place of employment, you know? I'm not going to let anything stop me from surviving. If I run off tonight, I'm not going to want to ever come back."

"But aren't you scared?" Emily whispered.

"Yeah, I'm scared. But I've got to deal with it. Rylee's going to sleep in my room from now on. I have a feeling that her room is the one that the guy died in. I'll just move her stuff and close it off."

"I don't want to leave you, but I told Jay that I'd be home early tonight to spend some time with him. Are you sure you don't want to come over?" Emily asked, walking to the door.

"Positive. I'll be fine." Andie held the door open.

"Well," Emily said, looking around outside, "just call me if you need anything, or just come over. And would you watch me until I get in my house?"

"Sure. I'll talk to you tomorrow," Andie said. She watched Emily jog to her yard and into her house.

Closing the door and looking around the living room, she did not feel as confident as she had while Emily was in the house. She quickly went through the house, turning on all of the lights. She stayed in the living room watching TV, trying to block out any thoughts of the strange occurrence. She was terrified, but made herself go from one moment to the next, determined to remain calm, hugging Rylee to her. If the knocking started again, she was not sure if she could stay in the house that night to sleep. She waited hours to hear another round of pounding on the floor, but it did not happen.

Rylee slept in Andie's bed that night. Andie had pulled the mattress off of the box spring and laid the sleeping baby next to her, not wanting Rylee to wake up and fall from the bed. She stayed awake through the night reading a book, jumping whenever she heard a sound. The lights stayed on in every room.

Emily called in the morning to see if anything else had happened. She said that she was too worried to bring her kids over, and so, was going to stay in her own house. Andie held the cordless phone in the crook of her neck, chasing Stuart through the house, trying to get him to lie down for a diaper change while leading Rylee and Kara along to keep an eye on them. She closed them all in her bedroom and grabbed him, quickly laying him on his back as she said good-bye to Emily and tossed the phone aside.

Andie had been looking forward to talking to Emily about what had happened and wanted everything to go on as usual, but now she would have to deal with it alone. Emily had sounded distant on the phone, yet Andie could not blame her for being frightened. She would rather be out of the house herself.

She had the older boys help her watch the girls while she put her mattress back onto the box spring and moved Rylee's crib into her bedroom. She took everything out of Rylee's bedroom and moved it into the spare bedroom, which doubled as a play and nap room.

During the next week, Andie tried to smother her intense fear by drinking more wine when she smoked a joint. She would finally be able to fall asleep once she got tired enough from the wine. Emily still had not come over, but had offered to have Andie over to her house in the evening. Rylee could not fall asleep well anywhere else but in her own crib, so Andie could never stay at Emily's very long. Emily's husband, Jay, had not believed them when he heard their story. He teased them, and asked if they had seen any more "Avon lady" ghosts.

Andie believed that the knocking had probably been caused by the spirit of the dead man, or else by some other menacing spirit that was in the house. Even to think in terms of "spirits" disturbed her deeply. When she was a child, Andie had played "seance" with other kids. They would light a candle in the dark and try to conjure up dead people. They did not personally know of any dead people, so they would try for anyone listening. Sometimes they would try to pick up one of the smaller kids by using only their fingertips and asking for the help of a spirit. Andie had a Ouija board that she and her friends would use to test the spirits. If the plastic piece moved slowly across the board to the letters, it was supposed to spell out answers to questions which were asked by the people resting their fingers lightly on the piece. Back then, it had been an exciting pastime to ponder the possibility of the spiritual realm. Now, it was a horrifying reality as Andie once again faced a battle with something beyond her comprehension.

While Rylee was with Steve one Saturday, Andie walked through the house and said a prayer in each room. She was not sure what might be required to make the spirit go away, so she said her own prayer, asking God to make anything evil leave the house. She carried the Bible that Sarah had given to her when she was in Orlando, feeling reassured by its weight. In Rylee's old room, she spent a longer time, adding the Lord's Prayer. Andie's only knowledge of casting out evil was from seeing the movie "The Exorcist" and other movies from her childhood where vampires fled at the sight of a crucifix, and at the end of the show had stakes driven through their hearts while they screamed in agony.

Andie did not want to think about Farley and all that she had been through, but this current problem seemed connected to her previous trial with evil. Could something be following her? In the spiritual realm, did Satan plot to go after certain people? She was a Christian now, so how could all of this be happening? Andie pondered the situation, even leafing through her Bible for some sign of what to think and do next.

As the days passed with no other occurrences, Andie thought that she must have gotten rid of the problem. She was finally sleeping without all of the lights on in the house, though it would often take too long to fall asleep.

One night, soon after Rylee fell asleep, Andie had a panic attack. It came on suddenly and surprised her with its staying power. She paced the floors, breathing heavily and perspiring. Her heart pounded too hard, and she thought that she could have a heart attack; there was a sharp stitch of pain on the left side of her chest that would not go away. She felt claustrophobic, but did not want to go outside and leave Rylee alone in the house. It felt as if she might die. She held onto the phone as she walked, trying to feel reassured by its three number link to help.

She went into the kitchen and grabbed the bottle of Burgundy wine from the cupboard, taking large swigs, gulping them down. She soon felt the effects of the alcohol and proceeded to guzzle some more. Her heart was still racing, but her fear had subsided to a more manageable degree. Finally, she was intoxicated and able to sit down without the panic rising up again. An hour later, she stumbled into her bedroom and fell asleep. Her dreams were full of evil. Dark figures chased her through narrowing passageways, but she did not remember the dreams in the morning when she awoke with a pounding headache, nausea rolling through her abdomen.

The day was difficult as she attempted to keep the children safe and happy while she trudged along in pain and regret. Only later that night, when she smoked some marijuana, did she begin to feel better. She was so consumed with trying to make it through the day that she did not dwell on the events of the night. She was tired and irritable.

When Emily called to invite her over, Andie told her what had happened and said that she was going to try to go to bed early. Emily insisted that she needed to move out of the house with Rylee, but Andie disagreed again and told her that she wanted to get off the phone.

A dismal gloom weighed her down. She did not even want to talk to Emily. Sleep was the only place that she wanted to go.

Chapter 28

Steve returned the signed divorce papers, and Andie gave them to her lawyer, who had them processed and filed in the court. She was now Andrea Reeves again. Andie celebrated alone in the evening with a bottle of wine and a new bag of pot that she had bought from Emily's brother, Carl.

She ended up crying most of the night. She thought about sad things that had happened in her life, and became overwhelmed with grief and loneliness. The only reason for happiness was Rylee. She needed to get a hold of herself so she could take care of Rylee. With this thought in her blurry mind, she crawled into bed, setting the alarm for the next morning.

One night a few days later, Andie awoke hearing the sound of knocking in the other room. She thought that she was dreaming, until she came to her senses and then sat up in utter terror as it continued. She jumped out of bed and flipped the light switch on, then got back into bed and stared at Rylee's sleeping form in the crib, hoping she would not be awakened.

The knocking soon took on different patterns of beats. Andie felt herself beginning to panic. She thought about calling Emily, but did not want to go out of her room to get to the phone. She tried to say a prayer, but gave up because her throat was tightening in fear. She felt like she was being mocked. She had thought that she had gotten rid of it and had let her guard down. Now it came when she was the most vulnerable, in the middle of the night.

Then it stopped. She waited to hear it again, but it was apparently done. She tried to read her book, but her eyes traveled over the words without interpreting them. She got up and went to the side of Rylee's crib, watching her sleep. She would have killed anything that tried to harm her girl, but this was something that she could not get her hands on. She sat back down on the bed, looking through the open door of the bedroom into the dark hallway.

An evil shriek filled the house and seemed to rush through it and into Andie's bedroom. It sounded like many voices, some deep, some high-pitched like a child, joining together and shrieking, "Eee-yaaa, ee-yaaaa, ee-yaaaaa!"

Andie froze. The cry was so evil and menacing that she was prepared to see something appear in her doorway, ready to kill her. Rylee woke up screaming, bringing Andie out of her state of terror for a moment as she ran to the crib and snatched her up, walking backward to the farthest corner of the bed, away from the dark hall. Rylee was frantically climbing on Andie as if she could not get high enough on her shoulder.

This was more frightening than anything so far. The shriek replayed through her mind, and Andie knew that if she heard it again, it would drive her insane. No movie or sound effect could have captured the horrific evil contained in the mocking squeal. It had seemed to fly through the house, gaining speed, and then blasted into her bedroom loud enough to hurt her ears, as if something had run straight for her from across the house and found her in her bedroom.

Where was it now?

Andie wished that she could escape this paralyzing fear as she sat on the corner of the bed trying to soothe Rylee. This seemed the beginning of a terrible end. She wondered if someone would find them in the morning, dead, maybe torn apart. Her thoughts were getting out of control, her body trembled uncontrollably. The motion of rocking Rylee helped her through each minute. Andie rocked her and held her close to her chest, drawing comfort from her neediness. Rylee finally calmed down, her eyelids drifting slowly shut. When it seemed as if hours had passed and her back was aching, Andie slowly laid Rylee down in the middle of the bed. She wanted to turn on all of the lights in the house, but she could not summon the courage to go into the dark hallway.

She sat next to Rylee and watched her sleep. She made sure that she could see the doorway in her peripheral vision in case something came into the room suddenly. She would leave immediately if she heard the sound again.

But it did not happen.

Her mind strived to classify the cry as something explainable and ordinary. Her thoughts went around every aspect of the incident, looking for a loophole. But there was no escape from the truth. She was finally able to block it out if she thought about Rylee. Her baby's needs were her priority, so she could not let anything push her over the edge. Morning could not come soon enough.

The children were a good distraction for her troubled mind. She did not have time to contemplate anything too deeply while she was busy overseeing their activities. She did not sleep well anymore, but spent most nights in the brightly lit house listening and waiting, drinking and smoking enough to sleep a few hours.

She had grown close to all of the kids, and they vied for her attention each day. When their mother came to pick them up, the older two were often difficult, trying to linger in the house. Kara and Stuart would cry and try to stay with Andie until their mother lost her patience and grabbed them, leading them to her van. Andie thought that it was sad how children yearned for affection and love, but were often neglected. These children had parents who cared and tried to tend to their needs, but fell short because of the work schedules that kept them away for long hours. Andie thought about her own mother, who had been home all day with her when she was very young. She had the time to interact and bond with Andie, but she just never chose to do it. Andie wondered how her mom would have been if she had given birth to her own children. Would she have loved them more?

Andie loved Rylee so much that she would easily choose to be tortured and die for her. Her instinct to protect Rylee was stirred up by the bizarre events in the house. Nothing else had happened since the night of the shrieking, but Andie knew that something was waiting for the next opportunity to show itself.

She was at Emily's on Saturday morning when Steve showed up early for his visit with Rylee. Jay let him into their house and told him that the women were in the kitchen discussing Andie's ghost. Steve walked in and heard Andie say that she had prayed again in each room.

"Hi," Steve said as he leaned against the kitchen doorway. "So, what's with the ghost in your house, Andie?"

Andie had stopped talking when Steve appeared. "Nothing you need to know, Steve."

"Sounds like you're probably having your nightmares again, is that it?"

"I really don't feel like discussing this with you. Mind your own business."

"I'd say it was my business if there are ghosts in my daughter's house," Steve replied.

"I heard it, too." Emily stared at Steve. "Andie is very brave to be able to stay in that house after all that's happened."

"They drink a little wine and end up hearing things is all, Steve. Your daughter's perfectly safe. They just need to find more to occupy their time." Jay laughed loudly.

"Shut up, Jay," Emily replied angrily. "You weren't there. It was definitely something that was pounding on the floor."

Andie wished that everyone would drop the issue. Steve had a smug look on his face, and she was worried that he might reveal something about her run-in with Farley.

"Let's just forget it, okay?" Andie said firmly.

"Gee, Andie, this has always been one of your favorite subjects. Did you tell them about the demons you saw where we were living before? You know, the ones that were chasing you?" Steve said.

Emily and Jay looked at her as she frowned at Steve. "Come on! I'm going to get Rylee's bag and then you need to get out of here," Andie said angrily, getting up to leave.

"Fine. Just point out the ghosts to me while we're over there. Nice seeing you Jay, Emily. Hey, what's that doctor's name again who owns that house?" Steve asked.

"Steve," Andie said impatiently.

"Dr. Morgan, Andrew Morgan," Jay replied.

"Thanks," Steve said, turning to walk out of the house.

Andie spent the day worrying. When she called Emily, Emily said that they were leaving soon, so she could not talk. Andie did not see them leave their house all afternoon. She was afraid that Emily and Jay thought she was crazy. Emily had heard the knocking, but she did not know about Farley. Maybe Emily would think that she should not associate with her now. Seeing demons was a little more extreme than hearing them.

Andie was so angry at Steve that she had not wanted to let him leave with Rylee. He threatened to take her to court, so she had given in. She felt like packing up and driving as far away as she could with Rylee. This was no way to live. But right now, she really did not have a choice.

Dr. Morgan called her the next day and asked if he could come over to talk to her. Andie was expecting Steve to interfere, but not so soon.

They sat in the living room while Rylee walked around the coffee table, slapping it and trying to get their attention.

"Andrea, your ex-husband called me this morning, and we talked for quite a while," Dr. Morgan began. "I don't know how to say this...my wife and I, well, we've decided to put the children in preschool and day-care. We'll find somewhere this week, so I'm afraid that I must give you notice," he said.

"Oh please, Dr. Morgan! I don't know exactly what he told you, but I can explain everything," Andie said emphatically.

"There's no need to explain. We weren't aware of your problem and hospitalization, and we're not completely comfortable with this. You've done an excellent job with the children and we appreciate all of your care. My wife...she's wanted to put the older boys in preschool anyway, since they'll be going to regular school soon. And we'll probably be selling the house," he said.

"But you see, I'm not crazy. That was all a mistake, please listen! There was this high priest in the Mormon church who tried to control me and I nearly died," Andie began, but Dr. Morgan interrupted.

"Andrea, I'm a Mormon," he said. "I don't believe for a moment that any Mormon would do that. We're a good group of people who live for our families. I can't believe that you would say this...or that you think you've seen demons and heard ghosts. Especially in my house. I'm afraid that I'm going to have to end this discussion now, before I get too upset."

"Well, this priest must've been an extremist or something. He knew just what he was doing to me and he was very good at it," Andie said desperately as she watched Dr. Morgan stand up. "Emily next door also heard the knocking, you can ask her! Please, Dr. Morgan, I don't think that all Mormons are like that man, but in some religions there are probably those who are...different. I really need this job, and I love your kids!"

"It's already decided, Andrea. I'm sorry, mostly for Rylee. You should seek counseling. I heard that you were ordered to do it by a doctor, but you never complied. I need to go. You won't be watching the kids anymore, so you can spend this week looking for a new place to live. Your ex-husband sounds like a nice man. Rylee could use a strong father figure in her life. It's too bad that you didn't stay with him," Dr. Morgan said as he opened the front door. "We'll give you two weeks to find a place and also pay you for the rest of the month. Good-bye. I'll be in touch."

Andie felt the gloom that surrounded her deepen to utter despair. She looked around the house and knew that she would never have this kind of life and security again. Rylee was noisily making her way through the rooms that she had gotten used to, so Andie followed her around, trying to think of what to do next. She dismissed calling Steve and yelling at him. It would not do any good, and she had no energy for it. The depression weighed her down so heavily that she could not even smile at Rylee when Rylee tried to engage her in play.

Her mind ticked through her financial status. She had saved a few hundred dollars, but she had spent most of her earnings easily, thinking that more would be coming in. She had spent a good amount on repairing her old car: a tune-up, new tires, brakes, CV joints, alignment, and new belts. At least it should run for a while, she hoped. She pictured them living out of it on the side of a deserted street and began crying. Rylee looked at her, frowning, and then began crying as well. Andie picked her up and took her to the kitchen to get lunch, trying to suppress her emotions. She could not let anything stop her from taking care of her daughter.

Chapter 29

Andie found two places which rented by the month that she could afford. One was bigger than the other, but located in a bad part of town on the outskirts of a business district. The other one was very small, but clean and in a nice neighborhood. Andie paid the deposit and one month of rent on the smaller apartment, leaving her with two hundred dollars. Steve's child support for Rylee would pay three quarters of the rent, but there would be no extra money for food or anything else until she found work. Andie knew that she was going to have to put Rylee in daycare if she was going to work.

Emily helped her move her belongings in their van. She told Andie that Steve had talked to Jay and told him about her past, and that he did not want her to talk to her anymore. Emily quickly said that she did not feel this way herself, but that they had been fighting about it. Andie figured that Emily's too cheerful demeanor meant that she probably would not be seeing her again. After one week, Emily had not called, so Andie knew that she was right in thinking that their friendship was over. Andie called Karin and told her what had happened. Karin came to her new apartment and tried to be upbeat about the tiny studio and its sparse furnishings.

"Just say it, Karin. This place stinks," Andie said tiredly.

"No...no, Andie. It's temporary while you get back on your feet. You're one of the strongest people I've ever known, and Greg and I will help you out in any way that we can. Steve is an absolute loser and you can do better than him. Look at your beautiful daughter! She's a great little girl, only because you're such a wonderful mother," Karin said.

They had a snack and then chatted until Karin had to leave for work. Andie felt a little better; Karin had always been able to raise her spirits. She wished that she could see her more often.

Friday night Andie watched Rylee sleeping, then she went into the bathroom and lit one of her last joints, relishing the smoke as it filled her lungs. When she went back out to the small square of a living room, she decided to call Emily's brother, who would be expecting her to buy a bag of pot from him. He always set one aside for her every other week.

She told him that she would not be able to afford it until she found a job and admitted that she might not be able to afford it even then. He was his usual jovial self, perpetually stoned and wanting others to be. He had always flirted with Andie when she and Emily stopped by his house. He told her that he was looking for someone to hire, but he could not trust too many people. He needed someone to run a few errands for him.

Andie listened as he described the details. She ruled out the possibility of working for him immediately. There was no way that she would jeopardize Rylee's life, and her own, by delivering pot. When he told her what he would pay her, and that it would not take more than ten hours a week, Andie still declined.

She was anxious the next week, frustrated that she had not found a job yet. She had filled out at least thirty applications and learned that most jobs paid five dollars an hour for unskilled work. She would not be able to live on that amount and afford daycare. She was back in the same situation as when she had split from Steve. Her money was running out and rent would soon be due. She called Emily's brother, Carl.

Steve began watching Rylee every other afternoon for two to three hours, since he still got off work at three o'clock. Andie had humbled herself and did not mention that he had been the one to cause her to lose her job. She brought up the idea of watching Rylee as an opportunity for him to bond with Rylee while she did some chores. Andie began her new job.

The people she went to see had all been clients of Carl's for a long time. He was moving up in the dealer world by charging more for a safe and convenient delivery, rather than having various people streaming in and out of his house at odd hours. It was safer and more low profile for him and the customers. So, she went to a gas station, a clothes store at the mall, a law office where two of the lawyers bought bags, people's houses, and various other places. Her conservative appearance allowed her to go unquestioned. She was paid enough each week to live and also got a bag of pot out of the deal. Carl continued to flirt with her, but Andie politely refused his offers to go out.

After she picked Rylee up from Steve's, she smoked out of her new pipe and drank wine. She often woke up with a deep cough that seemed to get worse as the weeks went by. She became chronically depressed, so she would smoke more pot to try to alleviate her sorrow. She never smoked before her deliveries, but saved it for afterwards when Rylee was home safely and resting.

Rylee was beginning to talk and mimic words. She understood commands, but could not always verbalize what she wanted. Andie grew more in love with her all of the time. She still talked to her sisters and Sarah periodically, and they wrote letters and sent cards to one another. But she felt like a failure, knowing they would be shocked at the life she led. Andie's parents in Iowa still expected her to call them at least every other week. Her mom continued to make her feel guilty if she forgot to call.

Andie would sometimes find herself dwelling on Scott and her upbringing, and she was filled with anger. She wondered what she would be doing right then if she had been raised by Sarah. She would probably be a successful, happy person. How had her life come to this? She had vowed to find a different job right away, but the easy money from Carl prevented her from feeling compelled to change her life. She knew that she could not do it forever. She was essentially a drug dealer, and she was not proud of it. She often envied the lives of others as she carried out her business.

As the weeks passed by, she became tired of living on the small amount of money, with the threat of being caught always nagging at her. Each small chore and task seemed overwhelming and drained away her energy. Everything in the past couple of years, ever since she had left Iowa, had snowballed, and she had landed in a place that was hopeless and shameful. Rylee would never have a whole family, and she would not have the life she had hoped to have. She stopped calling Karin, who was finishing the first half-year of her marriage and was back in school. When she looked in the mirror, Andie saw a mother that she would have scorned. She was despicable. She lost herself in drugs and alcohol every night until she passed out.

CHAPTER 30

Months later, Andie was so despondent that she began thinking that Rylee would be better off without her. Maybe Steve was right—he could take better care of her. Who would want a drug dealer for a mother? The mental pain that she felt was constant. It was an accumulation of all of the negative things that had happened throughout her entire life. She mourned the child that she had been, full of hope for the future and trust in people. It was all lost. She was a failure. What could she offer Rylee? Nothing was good anymore, except for being with Rylee, and even then she felt guilty for the way that they lived.

She had been depressed before, but this night it was unbearable. She could not remember the last time that she had been truly happy. She had stopped praying, but she made herself say a brief prayer asking for help. She felt as if God had abandoned her, but she had no where else to turn, so she prayed with every bit of hope that she had left. When she finished, she knew that she was being foolish. When had God come to her rescue in the past? She had stumbled from one situation to the next, always looking for a home. God was supposed to protect her, if no one else would. She had only wanted someone to love her and to be a part of a family.

Was God really there?

She began to cry harder than she had in a long time, the kind of cries that racked her whole body. She went into the bathroom so that she would not awaken Rylee. The pain was enormous, and Andie did not know if she could bear living with it. She could not stop crying. She was so tired of getting up in the morning to face each day. It would be much easier to just sleep forever. She hated living and moving through the days without end.

What would it be like to be dead, she wondered. Free from pain. Nothing to take care of or worry about.

It began to seem like a good idea to end her life. She pictured what everyone would do when they found out that she was dead. Maybe it would finally occur to her parents that they had screwed up her life. Andie longed for the peace that she could have in permanent sleep. She wanted to rest. She already felt that she was dying inside every moment, so she might as well be dead and rid of all of life's burdens.

She had to find a way to do it quickly. A rush of relief came to her as she realized that in a moment the pain would be gone. She looked in the medicine cabinet and sifted through the bottles. As she held a bottle of sleeping pills in her hand, the ones that she had resorted to taking recently, an image of Rylee's face flashed through her mind—how she would reach out whenever she was hurt or frightened, knowing for certain that Andie would protect her and make her feel better.

She was suddenly shocked by her thoughts and terrified of her mind and its ability to lead her to self-destruction. She had been close to taking the pills, and she still felt an edgy desire to do it. Setting the pills down, she gazed in the mirror and then pulled her eyes away. A swell of intense self-loathing for her blotchy, grim face caused her to reach for the bottle again, just to hold it and see how many pills were left. When she pried off the top, wedging her thumb below the arrow of the child-proof cap and flipping it abruptly open, the bottle jerked and pills went scattering across the bathroom floor, some into the bath tub.

"Darn it!" She crawled desperately around on the floor, picking up pills and throwing them into the toilet. "She can't get these, she can't get these." Crying, Andie had to clear the tears from her eyes so that she could see well enough to locate the small white tablets. Rylee could find a pill and eat it. She still put everything into her mouth. When she had searched the entire bathroom two times without finding any more pills, she sat down on the toilet. Her hands were shaking and she felt sick. Life should not have to be like this, she thought.

She needed help.

Andie got down on her knees and began praying. She did not know what to pray for at first, because she thought that she would be repeating herself by just asking for help. Then she remembered the information that Sarah had sent, and it occurred to her that she had not been able to receive God's help because she was not right with God yet.

She prayed aloud, admitting that she believed Jesus was the Son of God and had died for everyone's sins, pleading for Him take over her life and guide her. She asked to be forgiven for her sins and admitted them all. She prayed that He would lift her up out of her situation so that she could be a good mother to Rylee. She cried and cried, releasing all of the pain that had eaten away at her soul for years. She asked God to make His way clear to her, so that she would not make the wrong choices. She thanked Him for sending His Son to die on the cross for her sins, knowing what a sacrifice it would be to give up a child, especially to a painful death. Realizing that she had to forgive everyone for their sins against her, she prayed that she could find the way to true forgiveness, and that the Holy Spirit would live in her heart. She prayed for a long time, letting every fear and care and regret be known. The words flowed more easily and with greater conviction as she continued.

She began to feel a sense of calm easing her body and mind unlike anything she had felt before. She almost expected it to leave; it felt so amazingly peaceful and refreshing. Was it possible that she could always feel this way? But she had lived in such sin, how could she expect to have her prayers answered? She began crying again, feeling guilty and unworthy. She had known that she was sinning before, but she had not wanted to admit it to herself or stop at the time. That made her more guilty than most people because she had considered herself a Christian.

"I'm so sorry, so very sorry." Andie squeezed her folded hands tightly together in despair. She was still kneeling on the tile floor. "Please forgive me."

A stronger sense of reassurance and peace completely filled her and took the place of her doubts. She was unable to have another bad thought remain in her mind. For the moment, it was blocked from anything negative. A feeling of certainty and hope lifted her beyond the grip of her past, because she knew that her prayers were being heard. It was as if the very air in the room had changed, becoming nourishing to her soul, each breath filling her more fully with love. She knew that God was with her, following every one of her thoughts. He was here and alive. Andie was awed by the power of this love, even the word itself did not convey the absolute purity in the gift she was being given, because she had only known earthly love before. A thought came to her clearly: she had no need to feel guilty, because Jesus had already paid for her sins. She was humbled in the face of this incredible sacrifice.

Then she knew that God had been watching over her all of her life. How ignorant of her to not have known that she had made it through all of her trials only because God had intended for her to live. He had a plan for her, but she had been busy making her own decisions and following her own rules. Scott could have killed her, but she had remained alive. Farley could have killed her, or she could have gotten lost in the Superstition Mountains, or hit by a car, or died from dehydration, or even gonorrhea, or any number of other things that she was not even aware of. All of the times that she had felt betrayed and lost, she had been able to keep going.

Now she had the greatest reason to continue on and she had nearly convinced herself to end it all. She would not allow Satan to break her spirit. She was God's creation and deserved to live the life He had chosen for her. She just needed to find the right path and stay on it. She realized that she had to change her ways. While the thought of going without a joint had disturbed her before, she now felt confident that she could overcome it. She would stop smoking and drinking. She needed to do this first; she knew it now.

A sense of purpose filled her. There was a lot to do. No wonder God had not been able to help her; she was living in complete sin, contaminating her body. She lowered her head and thanked Jesus for His guidance and mercy. Before, she had merely prayed without feeling any response, now she did not actually hear anything, but felt a strong conviction and a drive to follow through like never before. She had always wondered what people meant when they said that God was speaking to them.

She wiped her tears and went back into the other room. Standing by Rylee's crib, she placed a hand gently on Rylee's small chest. She said a prayer for protection and asked Rylee to forgive her, as the baby slept on peacefully. Andie vowed to raise her daughter the way God intended. The strength she felt behind this promise and the resolve that she knew would remain, with God's help, allowed her to forgive herself for not being a good mother.

Andie got out the rest of her wine and pot and dumped everything down the toilet. She searched the bathroom again for pills and found three more. She had smoked a joint earlier, but somehow it was not affecting her now. She felt a clarity to her thinking that she had not experienced in a long time.

The ringing phone interrupted her.

"Hi, Andie!" Laura said. "How are you doing?"

"Well, it's a long story actually." Andie smiled, rubbing a hand across her forehead.

"You've been on my mind so much tonight. I had this feeling that I needed to make sure that you're all right. Is everything okay?"

Andie explained to her what had happened.

"You were just saved!" Laura exclaimed. "That's what it's called, you know. Congratulations! How do you feel right now?"

"Well, I've never felt like this before in my life. I can't explain it. I don't want this to end."

"That's just it! It will never end. You'll live forever. Eternal life is now yours."

Andie had not liked hearing expressions like this before; they had sounded lame and unreal. But she knew that it was true; she was saved from a lifetime of misery and a permanent death.

Andie shared everything with Laura: Farley, her addiction to marijuana, the ghosts, her hopeless financial situation.

"Why in the world didn't you ever tell me about this?" Laura asked.

"I guess I was too embarrassed. And it sounded hard to believe."

"What do you think family's for?" Laura replied. "I'm glad you made it through all of that. Thanks for trusting me enough to tell me."

"I just don't know what to do to get on my feet again, Laura," Andie admitted. "I'll pray about it, but I have no job, no income, and soon, no place to live."

"Tell you what, we're going to get everything squared away. I have an idea. Let me call you right back, okay?" Laura asked.

Andie waited fifteen minutes for the phone to ring again.

"Andie, how would you like to get back into school? Remember how you said that you used to want to be a nurse? There's an LPN school here in Orlando that only takes a year. I just talked to Mom, and she said that you and Rylee were welcome to live with her and Dad until you finish school of some kind. What do you think? They've got an extra room that you guys could stay in. It's not much, but it would be free," Laura said excitedly.

Andie started crying, unable to help herself when she heard the generous offer.

"Hey!" Laura exclaimed. "This was supposed to make you happy!"

"Oh, I am! I can't believe that you called me tonight in the first place. And then you go offering to help me, it's just so nice," Andie replied through her tears.

"Well, God does work in mysterious ways. It's not a cliche. His timing is always perfect. You just have to learn to trust Him with everything. Mom's going to call you in a little bit, so think about it," Laura said.

"I'd love to get out of Arizona, there's nothing to keep me here. Steve might not like the idea. I'll have to go to court, I suppose. Thank you so much for doing this, Laura. You know, I'd given up all my old dreams," Andie said.

"Well, it's time to dream again! You have your whole life ahead of you. I'd love to have you here. Tell me you'll come," Laura said.

"Yes," Andie replied. "Yes, I'm coming." She felt certain that she needed to leave Phoenix. "I'll get everything in order and be there as soon as I can!"

"We'll work out all the details when you get here. Just get here!" Laura demanded in a stern voice before she began laughing.

"Thank you so much, Laura. I'll talk to you soon." Andie hung up the phone and then danced through the small room, wanting to wake up Rylee and hug her. She stopped and leaned down close to her daughter, studying her face. The face of an angel, she thought.

When Sarah called, Andie began crying as she told her what she had become in her life.

"Everything's going to be all right, sweetheart," Sarah said. "You're forgiven. You only need to look ahead now at the new life you're beginning. I hope you'll come here."

"I will. I'll be there as soon as I can get everything arranged." The plans were made for her to leave as soon as possible and make her way to Florida.

* * *

The court gave Andie permission to move out of state based on the fact that she would be attending school in Florida, and Steve did not show up to contest the motion. Andie once again sold most of her possessions and packed her bags. This time she knew that she would not be turned away. She was glad that she had spent extra money on the car so that it would make it across the country.

Steve was angry, but calmed down when Andie suggested that he move to Florida. She apologized for all of their past disagreements and asked him to forgive her for anything she had done to him. He had not known how to respond. He watched Rylee while Andie prepared to move.

Karin promised to visit and told her that she would miss her. Andie thanked her for all of her help, wishing that they did not have to be so far from one another. They both said that they would keep in close touch. It was the most difficult to leave Karin, who had only been busy in her new life—not ignoring her as Andie had thought. She had started to believe that no one wanted to be with her, convincing herself that she was worthless. There were so many things to put in order, but she was looking forward to it.

As Andie crossed the line into New Mexico, she wanted to drive as fast as she could to Florida. Her new life was ahead of her and she could not be out of the desert soon enough. She thought about the possibility of going to nursing school. When she was a child, she had proudly told people that she was going to be a nurse when she grew up. There would always be the need for nurses in the world. Andie hoped that the school would not be too expensive.

The only problem was a big one; what to tell her parents in Iowa. She would call from Orlando and break the news to them. She did not want to lie about anything. In the past, she had found it easy to tell "white" lies if it saved her from being in trouble. She was not sure what to do. She only knew that it would devastate her parents, her mom especially, to learn that she was living in Orlando with her real mother. She decided to pray about it.

Texas seemed to go on forever. Rylee was getting irritable sitting in her car seat, so Andie drove through the night, not wanting to stop until she saw the green fertile land of Florida.

CHAPTER 31

Andie contemplated her life as she drove across the panhandle of Florida. The air outside the half-opened window seemed so heavy and moist compared to the scorched atmosphere of Phoenix. She still had hours until she would reach Orlando. The bright sunlight helped her to stay awake after the long night of driving, but it caused a dull ache behind her eyes. She took another sip of lukewarm coffee from the Styrofoam cup, grimacing as she swallowed. The extra sugar had not been enough to take away the bitter taste.

She had thought that she was a Christian before, because she believed in Jesus and occasionally prayed, but she had not lived in a way that was acceptable to God. It had just been easier to get high and watch the world go by. She had convinced herself that she deserved to feel the least amount of pain, because she had endured so much of it when she was young. She knew that children of alcoholics were more inclined to be drug abusers, whether from genetic predisposition, or just having observed alcohol being chronically used to cope with life. This fact had actually given her an excuse to smoke pot; she was not as guilty if she could not help it. She knew that she had become weak and pitiful, looking forward to getting high each night as if it were a tremendous reward. Andie was disgusted to realize how far she had fallen. She had also allowed herself to believe that drugs helped to keep the memory of Farley, and the more recent knocking and shrieking, away from the forefront of her mind. The lurking horrors were always trying to keep her from being at peace, so she had created a mindless cocoon of safety, though she could not see clearly through the haze of her protection. It had all been a waste of her time and life.

Her old nature was tugging at her to feel the depression from these realizations and the guilt that followed. She attempted to stay in a positive frame of mind, but it was difficult because she was tired from the drive. What if Sarah ended up thinking she was a failure, like she was? She had wanted Sarah to think highly of her, though now it might never happen. She was grateful to be offered a place to live, but would it work out? What would her parents say if they found out?

Anxiety and depression scratched into Andie's spirit, waiting for acceptance. She steered the car into the next rest stop and looked back at Rylee, who had fallen asleep, her head leaning on the side of her car seat, favorite pink bear tucked under her arm. It was hard to believe that she would be two years old soon. It seemed as if she had just been a tiny baby not so long ago.

She began praying, asking God to lift away the depression and anxiety. She prayed that she could make the right choices and asked for protection over the rest of the drive. When she finished, she got out of the car and stretched her stiff muscles. Travelers walked in and out of the rest room area. Three children wearing rumpled clothing were trailing their parents, asking "How much longer until Disney World? How long is three hours? Can we go right away to Cinderella's castle?" The parents were wearily walking from their car, which bore a New Jersey license plate, with a dazed look on their faces. Andie laughed for a moment, thinking how excited Colin, Sam and Stuart would be if they were going to Disney World. She missed them, especially Kara. It was difficult to think about the fact that she had not been able to tell them good-bye or explain why they would never see her again. She had done the best that she could with them, and hoped that she had added to their lives.

Back on the interstate, she felt more refreshed and realized that she was not going to suddenly have everything in perfect order and then go on to live happily ever after. This was going to take some effort. During the night, she had felt herself reverting to her previous way of thinking. She had been fondly recalling her drive from Iowa to Arizona and all the excitement of striking out alone, then caught herself wishing she had a joint. It surprised her that this could still happen now that she was saved. She had to make her thoughts turn against this easy, familiar way of being.

It was going to be hard to shrug off her old nature because she had gotten used to it over the years. The sinful nature was like a bunch of weeds, Andie thought. She pictured a flower garden with weeds surrounding and strangling the flowers. The roots and vines of the weeds were thick and tenacious, so the lives of the flowers were nearly extinguished by the weeds' rapid growth. The flowers endured, but had not bloomed and were slowly dying. When a weed was pulled out, sunshine could reach some of the flowers more easily and they were able to grow. If all of the weeds were completely uprooted, the flowers could thrive and bloom, although there was always the possibility that a weed would begin to grow again, maybe not in the same area, but winding its way into an unprotected patch. Each negative thought she could hold at bay, and every sinful desire that she could turn away from, kept her from slowly dying without having flourished in this life. She had failed to remain strong on her own. She had been overlooking the ready assistance that was promised to all who believed. Now she was truly ready to submit herself to the will of God, allowing Him to guide and strengthen her.

She had been fearful to search out anything in the spiritual world because of Farley, but he had just been one more obstacle to overcome. The frightening experiences had shown her that there definitely was a spiritual realm. She absolutely wanted to be on the good side, because she knew that the bad side was more than a little bad. If the bad side had intended to ruin her, which she was sure of, then it had ended up the loser. Instead, the experiences helped her to seek God by proving that the spiritual realm existed. Satan had once again lost.

This thought made her happy, to have subverted an evil plot to keep her from seeking God. Evil had come from the depths to get her, using different tactics and weapons, but she had prevailed. With God's help, she had prevailed.

Andie finally got off of the Florida Turnpike and entered the streets of Orlando. Billboards were everywhere, advertising all kinds of vacation amusements. She followed the directions that Sarah had given her to find their house, pulling into the driveway in the late afternoon, relieved to finally stop driving. The front door opened, and Sarah and John came out to greet her.

"Welcome! Boy, you sure made it in good time. Did you rest at all?" Sarah smiled as she came toward Andie, then hugged her tightly as they stood by the car.

"As little as possible. Rylee probably won't want to sit again for a few days," Andie replied, looking again with amazement at Sarah's familiar face. Rylee screamed in frustration to be in the car when her mother was not, so Andie reached in and lifted her out of the car seat. Sarah held her arms out to Rylee, who looked at her for a moment, then leaned eagerly toward her.

"If you aren't absolutely precious!" Sarah said, with obvious delight to have her first grandchild in her arms. "Oh, such a sweet baby."

John gave Andie a hug. "It's great to see you again. We're awfully glad you're here." Then he looked at her car, slowly walking around it and bending down to look under it.

"You must be exhausted, Andie. Come on in, and I'll get you something to eat," Sarah said.

Andie walked into the house and felt like she was supposed to be moving as fast as her car still. The long drive had made her feel discombobulated. She gratefully sat down at the kitchen table, while Sarah talked to Rylee, carrying her on her hip. Sarah brought crackers and cheese and iced tea to the table in two trips. She did not want to put Rylee down. Andie was surprised that Rylee was allowing Sarah to hold her for so long. Rylee was contentedly looking around the house and then back at Sarah's face.

"I'll go out and bring your boxes in for you," John offered.

"Well, thanks. I have more in the trunk. Here, I'll go out and help," Andie replied, getting up from her chair.

"No, ma'am. You're going to sit right there and relax. I've got it all handled," John said. He picked up her car keys from the table and went outside. Andie hesitated as she stood awkwardly by the table, not wanting to inconvenience anyone. She was not used to such help.

"Come on and sit down, Andie. You'll have plenty of unpacking to do soon. I've cleared out the closet and a desk in your room. Tim and Eric are in the other room together again. They're used to it, actually. Not until the girls left did they have their own rooms. But they're really looking forward to having you here. They should be home soon. I hope you don't mind that I borrowed a crib from a woman at church."

Rylee suddenly clapped her hands. "Mama, look! See it!" she exclaimed happily, pointing toward a shelf on the wall that displayed an array of bells.

"I think Rylee likes it here!" Sarah laughed. Rylee wiggled down from her arms and began to explore the living room.

"Thanks for doing all that," Andie said. She was glad to be with them, but she was uncomfortable for having created so much extra work. The cheese and crackers tasted wonderful. Anything would have after the fast food meals she had stopped for on the way. Sarah and Andie sipped raspberry iced tea and watched John bring the boxes into the house.

"Don't worry if you don't get the boxes unpacked for a while. I can see that you've got your hands full with the little sweetie," Sarah said. Rylee was trying to climb onto the sofa and finally succeeded. Andie made a frantic dash before Rylee stood on the edge of the cushion and fell backwards.

"One is enough to wear a person out. I don't know how you did it with two twice!" Andie exclaimed as she directed Rylee back toward the kitchen table.

"A lot of patience and a good sense of humor," Sarah replied, pouring more tea for Andie.

"And don't forget the hard-working, supportive husband," John added, smiling as he stacked two boxes against the wall.

Sarah and Andie laughed. Andie thought about how it would be to have a caring husband. She wished that Rylee could have lived with a father—if only Steve had been a good man. She probably should have known when she was with him that he was not right for her, but she had been stoned for most of their relationship. She could not regret knowing him, because she had gotten Rylee out of the deal. God had given her a priceless gift when she had not deserved it. Maybe He knew that Rylee would help her get on the right course.

"Not to overwhelm you right away, but Laura dropped off this information for you about the nursing school. I thought you might be eager to have a look at it in the next few days since a class will begin soon."

Andie was glad to have something to occupy her for a moment. She was suddenly shy and embarrassed for being in her bereft state. The course description sounded interesting, then she turned the page. "Wow, it's pretty expensive," she said. The cost for the program was two thousand dollars, not including lab fees or books. Then she felt bad for mentioning money. Here she was getting a free place to live, yet complaining. Feeling tired and sensitive due to her lack of sleep, she began to worry that she might not live up to their expectations.

That evening she learned exactly what their expectations were. John sat across from her in the living room after she had gotten Rylee to sleep, and told her that they had a few conditions for her to live there. She must try to attend church, any one of her choice, which she had hoped to do anyway. They expected her to attempt to further her education. She could not stay out all night or drink alcohol in the house. Andie assured him that she had given up any kind of drug use. He said that they did not want any payment for rent or groceries because they wanted her to channel all of her resources for school. However long it took for her to complete her classes, they would support her.

Andie thought how kind John was to be helping her. She was his wife's child from another relationship, and she had never been their responsibility. Even so, he was opening his home to her and taking on two more mouths to feed. They were not wealthy, so Andie knew that it was quite an endeavor for them.

Sarah came into the room and told John that Andie would probably like to go to bed. He had finished his discussion and was talking about the merits of a good education, not noticing Andie's eyes fluttering closed. Andie hugged them and thanked them for having her there. Sarah gave her an extra squeeze and told her that it was good to have her home. Once in the comfortable bed, between the soft clean sheets, Andie said a quick prayer and was out for the night.

* * *

Andie called the nursing school and learned that they had a waiting list for not only the next session, but the following two sessions. She was dismayed and did not know what to do. She could not wait ten months before she began the program; that would make it almost two years before she graduated. She had already gotten the financial aid forms from John and was prepared to take on another student loan. There were more stringent guidelines for being granted a loan, and she was worried that she would not receive one because she had defaulted on the one for broadcasting school.

At least everything was working out well at home. Sarah and John were caring and fun to be with. Andie loved John's southern accent. He was from Mississippi, which explained why Andie had received her first letter from Sarah with a Mississippi postmark. She and John had moved to Biloxi for two years to be near his family, but ended up returning Florida.

After two weeks Rylee had managed to stake out the entire house and would squeal in excitement when Sarah came home from work and the boys or John from school. John taught history at the private Christian school that Tim and Eric attended. The boys enjoyed playing with Rylee, and they often followed Andie around the house, chatting almost non-stop.

Andie helped Sarah in the kitchen with dinner and noticed how the two of them moved in the same way. She even hummed and whistled like Andie did when she was stirring something or chopping vegetables. Andie still felt shy. She had watched how Lisa and Laura interacted with Sarah when they came over and envied their easy, more outspoken way of relating. They were immediately captivated by Rylee, who also took to them right away. Andie wondered if Rylee would even mistake one of them for her. It seemed like her dream had come true: she was living with her mother, and she had two great sisters and brothers. At night Andie prayed, thanking God for allowing her to be where she was now. She remembered how her original birth certificate had seemed to have "fallen" into her lap. She thought that it might have had some help. It was incredible to be spending time with her real mother and doing everyday things with her. They laughed together as they watched Rylee and listened to her budding vocabulary. Sarah told Andie to pray about school and the right "door" would be opened if it was meant to be.

But it appeared that the door was closed and locked, since there was such a long waiting list, and the student loan representative had told her on the phone that she would not be eligible for a loan due to her non-payment for six months. Andie had nearly given up when Sarah suggested that she mail a letter to the secretary at the nursing school. Andie had gone to see the school and had talked to the secretary about the program. Mrs. Bosen had been friendly and patient as Andie attempted to keep Rylee in one place while they spoke.

Andie wrote the letter to thank Mrs. Bosen, but left it sitting for a day. She knew it would be futile to continue dreaming of nursing school. It had been exciting to think about becoming a nurse and being a professional. Now she would have to devise an alternative plan. She needed to pray for God to give her direction and guide her.

The next day Andie had the urge to drive the letter to the school instead of mailing it. She had laundry to do, so she tried to ignore the urge, not wanting to procrastinate fiinishing her chores. But it seemed important that she go to the school. She kept seeing an image of herself handing the letter to the secretary. A few minutes later, she set the basket of dirty clothes next to her bed and gathered up Rylee and the diaper bag.

Andie walked off of the elevator on the fifth floor of the school and went into the office. Mrs. Bosen was on the phone, so Andie waited, instead of putting the letter on her desk and leaving. Mrs. Bosen was engrossed in her conversation, yet still typed on her computer keyboard.

Another student came in and sat down on a chair in the waiting area. An instructor walked by and placed a document in front of the secretary. Andie really did not want to disrupt Mrs. Bosen, who had a few other stacks of papers and folders on her desk, so she thought that maybe she had better leave after all. Just then the secretary hung up the phone.

"Well, hello again!" Mrs. Bosen said as she shuffled some paperwork.

"Hi! Sorry to bother you, Mrs. Bosen. I just wanted to give you this letter. I want to thank you for being so kind the other day when I came in," Andie said as Rylee began squirming to get down.

"You're welcome! I don't get much gratitude around here from the students, I'm afraid. Usually, it's only complaining that I hear."

Andie grabbed Rylee's hands as she began trying to pull papers out of the waste basket. "Draw! Want to draw!" she demanded.

"Well, I guess I'd better be going. She's about to take your office apart," Andie said.

"Wait. Are you still interested in coming to school here?" Mrs. Bosen asked, peering over the tops of her bifocals.

"Oh, yes," Andie replied, looking up at her from where she was gathering her belongings.

"I just got a phone call from a woman who can't start in January because her family is moving out of state, so I have an opening in the next class. Would you like to fill it?" Mrs. Bosen asked.

Andie stood up from her crouched position next to Rylee. "You mean there's no one else on the waiting list?"

"Oh, we have a huge waiting list. But you're here right now, and you seem to be very eager to start. So, I'll offer it to you first."

"I want it more than ever!" she said. "Oh, but I'll have to figure out how to pay for it first." She was excited until she remembered that she had no money to pay the tuition. The school had a payment plan for the year, but she did not even have enough to pay the first installment, let alone the cost of the books.

"Are you a single parent?" Mrs. Bosen asked.

"Yes, I am."

"Have you checked out the single parent program yet? They have funding and even offer help with childcare."

"Really?"

"Yes. Here, go down to the third floor, room three twenty-four, and ask for Mrs. Harris. Take this note and she'll help you. Then come back up here and we'll see what we need to do, okay?" Mrs. Bosen smiled as she handed Andie a slip of paper.

"Oh, thank you so much!" Andie exclaimed.

"You're welcome, dear."

Andie hurried out of the office and stood waiting for the elevator. Rylee was looking at a group of nursing students gathered in the corridor. They had apparently just taken a test and were worriedly discussing the answers that they had given for certain questions. They wore nursing uniforms, even the men wore a version of the white uniform.

Andie was filled with anticipation and hope as she sat down to talk with Mrs. Harris. She learned that if her income was below a certain level, the single parent program completely paid for the entire cost of nursing school: tuition, lab fees, books, uniforms, childcare, and even alloted twenty-five dollars a week for gas money and lunch. It was privately funded, separate from the school or the government programs. She filled out the paperwork and was told that she was eligible for the program. She signed up for the required five-day class for single parents that began the next week. She also had to take a two month prerequisite health course in order to be admitted to the January nursing class. Mrs. Harris had to make some phone calls to see if the class was still open, and luckily, she was able to get Andie into a class that had been full, but the instructor decided to allow one more person. The course would begin in two weeks and end just before Christmas. Andie would then have two weeks off until the nursing program began.

Mrs. Bosen gave her more forms to fill out and told her that she would receive confirmation in the mail of her final acceptance from the director of nursing when her background check was complete. Andie thanked her again and left the office smiling at everyone. She wanted to run up and tell someone of her good fortune, but the nursing students had tired, grim faces. Andie hoped that she would be able to make some friends in the program. These people looked like they were stressed out and exhausted. They could not lessen her excitement though, because she was going to be a nurse!

Chapter 32

Andie finished the single parent class, and just before she was halfway done with the prerequisite course she received her letter of acceptance from the director of nursing. Sarah and John celebrated the news by taking her out to eat. John told her that he would be glad to have a nurse in the family, so someone would take care of him in his old age. Andie felt that she was with family, but she had not known them for long, so there was a difference. She knew that it could never be the same as if she had grown up with them, but this was more than she ever imagined.

Sarah was friends with a neighbor who offered childcare in her home. They had gone to see her after Andie had found out that she would be going to school. Andie had liked her immediately. She was a cheerful widow with grown children who lived in another state. She had two kids whom she cared for full-time and a spacious, clean house. Her price was below that of any daycare, and she was registered with the Department of Children and Family Services, which was a requirement to receive assistance with childcare expenses. Rylee had wanted to stay and play with the two other little girls.

Early each morning Andie would pack her book bag and then walk Rylee to Mrs. Calloway's. Rylee had only cried on the first morning and then eagerly went into the house each day to find the other girls. Andie never thought that she would have been comfortable leaving Rylee with a sitter, but Rylee seemed happy to be around other children again. She had gotten used to spending her days with kids in Phoenix, and she was old enough to express her needs to a caregiver. It was a great relief to see Rylee scrambling from her arms to go into Mrs. Calloway's house, but Andie missed her while she was at school.

Andie would have to call her parents again. She had called them when she had first arrived in Orlando, though they had not known that she was not in Phoenix, and told them that she needed to move because her job was ending due to the children starting school. That was supposed to have prepared them for her next phone call. They would not believe that she had moved out of state, all the way to Florida. Andie had prayed about what to tell them. She decided to just omit the fact of who she lived with, by saying that she was living for free with a family in exchange for help around the house. It was somewhat true, without being a lie. Andie simply did not want to hurt them.

They were surprised and critical at first, but she described the nursing school and her chance for a free education. They were pleased that she had taken such measures to move to a place where this kind of opportunity was available. She promised to call more often. They wanted to hear all about nursing school and especially the clinicals that she would be doing in the hospital. When she got off the phone, she felt shifty and nervous, but glad that it was over. She thought that she had made the right choice because they might never talk to her again if they knew the truth. They worked so hard seven days a week, and they were getting older. It did not seem right to upset them.

Andie called Karin to let her know what she was doing. Karin was happy for her and the new life she had begun, but said that she missed her. Steve had called a few times to check on Rylee. He was apparently not going to be moving anytime soon. Andie had heard a female in the background during two phone calls and figured that he had another girlfriend. He said that he could not afford to move, but would try to save some money. Rylee always chattered happily to him on the phone before he hung up.

The holiday season was rapidly approaching. Andie passed all of her tests in the prerequisite class, enjoying the fulfillment of succeeding. There were general courses on CPR and first aid, as well as infection prevention and control. Only a few of the tests were difficult, but Andie had studied diligently each night after Rylee was in bed.

For Rylee's second birthday party, they decorated Sarah's house with pink and white streamers and balloons. Lisa made a chocolate cake and a smaller, bear-shaped cake just for Rylee. Rylee patted it softly, noticed everyone watching her, then dug into it with glee. They clapped and sang to her as she mashed the cake, smearing some of it into her mouth.

Rylee was tall for her age, but no longer chubby. She had developed an impressive vocabulary for a two-year-old. Her brown hair had grown long, falling below her shoulders in soft ringlets. Her bright blue eyes were accentuated now that her eyebrows had filled in and darkened. She was quick to try to help everyone in the house with their chores and would mimic Andie as she sat reading a medical book. Rylee would look at one of her books, slowly turning each page after studying the pictures, a look of concentration on her face. Andie could not have imagined such a beautiful girl. She was going to have to watch her closely as she got older, so no one would steal her. The least likely person could be dangerous—Andie knew that too well. She prayed over her nightly and each morning whispered a quick prayer for protection on her way to class.

Christmas was especially meaningful that year. Andie went to the same church that Sarah and John attended, but to a different service to take advantage of the nursery. She liked sitting alone and being able to unselfconsciously flip through the Bible during the choir songs. She tithed part of her child support and a portion of her twenty-five dollar single parent allowance. She knew it was not much, but she wanted to give something to the church that she had grown to love. Everyone was genuine and friendly, laughing at the pastor's jokes during the service. Many people wore casual clothing, so Andie felt at home in her simple attire.

She watched couples sitting together, noticing how they behaved. Most men seemed to be very caring toward their wives, putting their arms around them, whispering and smiling at them, holding the door for them when they left. It was nice to see couples bowing their heads together and worshipping God. If only she had a Christian husband. A man who put God first would not cheat on his wife. He would be more likely to think of his family before himself. Andie found herself longing for a man who would be true to her. She tried to stop thinking about it, because she knew that she had enough to contend with for the moment. The young families with children who left the church together made her wish that Rylee had a father to dote on her. So many times she had wanted to share Rylee's achievements with a partner who was as involved in her care as she was.

The new year began and Andie was busy getting the supplies that she would need for nursing school. It was amazing that all of it was free. God had not just opened the door for her—He had made it impossible for her to not walk through it. Now she just had to do her part and pass all of the tests. When the year was over, she would have to take the State Board of Nursing licensure exam, which she heard was grueling.

Class began at eight o'clock and ended at three o'clock. After the first week, Andie thought that she had landed in army boot camp by mistake. The two instructors were older RNs and let everyone know the rules on the first day: If you failed two tests, you were out of the program. You could only miss nine days out of the year, no matter the reason, or you were out of the program. Each minute after eight o'clock that you were late would be counted as an hour missed. There would be no gum chewing, drinking, talking, or interrupting during class. You could not wear more jewelry than a wedding ring and a simple necklace. Hair was to be up off the collar at all times, and if your uniform was not clean and neat, you were sent home. No nail polish was allowed. Nursing shoes had to be clean and white at all times. On average, twenty-eight out of the fifty students would end up conpleting the program.

The amount of homework was staggering. Students were called on during class without having raised their hands to answer questions. If she had not read the assignment, she would look like a moron. There would be an average of two tests each week, with some weeks having as many as five. That did not include pop quizzes, which could occur at any time. During clinicals, the instructor would evaluate the students performance and skills and give a pass or fail grade.

After talking to some of the other students, Andie learned that many of them had returned after flunking out. A student was allowed one time to "recycle" or try again, but the rules were more stringent then: only five days in the year could be missed and no tests could be failed. One woman told Andie that she had passed every test, but her son had gotten sick a number of times and she had missed too many days staying home with him. No daycare would take a child with a fever.

Andie hoped that the year would go quickly and without problems. Before each test she would try to calm herself down, praying for recall and wisdom. Once she started in on the questions, she methodically thought out the answers, and so far, had passed every test. Three people in the class had already quit and seven more had failed two tests, so they were already down to forty students. She felt like she did nothing else but sit in class or study at home. For six and a half hours each day, she listened to lectures and took notes, trying to keep up with the instructor's rapid speech. One notebook was nearly full and covered with yellow highlight marks over the key points. The information was interesting, except they went so quickly from one subject to the next that Andie felt there was no time to absorb it thoroughly.

Clinicals were to begin the next day. The students would be going to a nursing home for three weeks and then to the first hospital. They would rotate through the specialties: pediatrics, obstetrics, geriatrics, and work in different areas, such as the emergency room, cardiac care, the med/surg floor, and the burn unit in four different hospitals. They would observe various surgeries, do treatments, and pass medications, which of course included injections.

Andie still became uncomfortable at the sight of a needle and hoped that she would be able to give injections without panicking. They practiced drawing up sterile water and injecting it into oranges, but doing it to a person would be different.

Maureen, a friendly student who sat next to her, had trouble drawing up the water into the syringe to the correct level. She would inject the necessary amount of air into the vial, then hold the vial upside down to withdraw the fluid, but she could not manage to do it without fumbling. The instructor was walking around and checking everyone's syringe, so Andie whispered to Maureen to help her before the instructor approached them. They were about to be tested individually at a special station in the room and this was their last chance to practice.

The instructor rushed over and said, "Don't help her, Andrea! She's not going to have anyone help her when she's out in the real world. You ought to have this down by now, Maureen! Everybody! Get in line for testing!"

Andie stood in line and listened as each student went behind the partition with the instructor. Maureen's turn came. "Here are the orders for your diabetic patient, Maureen. Her blood glucose was two fifteen at six a.m. Draw up the correct amount of insulin and give it to the patient."

Andie listened and imagined Maureen getting the syringe ready and injecting the orange. She said a silent prayer for her.

Maureen exclaimed, "I did it right! It's perfect!"

"Wait, Maureen. Give me that syringe," demanded the instructor. "Look at this—there's only air in here! You could kill someone! How could you screw this up? You're incompetent!" the instructor shouted.

Maureen hurried out from behind the partition and ran out of the room crying. Andie stared at the door until the instructor called out, "Next!"

Andie had no trouble with her syringe, but it would have been easier without the instructor hovering over her. Clinicals were going to be very challenging. For each treatment or medication given to the patients, the instructor would be observing them and asking questions about the medications, such as action, side effects, and interactions with other medications or food. The instructors were always quick to humiliate anyone who hesitated or made mistakes.

The nursing home was a depressing place. The students gave bed baths, dressed wounds, cleaned bed pans, gave tube feedings through nasogastric and G-tubes, and changed soiled sheets on many beds. They were all looking forward to getting to the hospital and having more diverse patients.

Andie noticed how the CNAs, certified nurse assistants, who did most of the hands-on care, treated the patients. They were brisk and often robotic as they hurried to complete their huge amount of work. A licensed or registered nurse passed the medications and then spent a lot of time at the nurses' station writing in the patients' charts. There seemed to be a pecking order, with the RNs at the top, LPNs in the middle, and CNAs at the bottom. Andie knew that she would never want to work in a nursing home.

The first day at the hospital, one of Andie's patients was a twenty-eight-year-old male with a gunshot wound to the chest, which had paralyzed his lower body. He had been in the hospital for two weeks and was known to be difficult.

The students were on the "indigent" floor that week, where the patients had no insurance and challenging social situations. There were two prostitutes and various homeless people on the floor that day. It was well-known that the nurses offered up the worst patients to the nursing students. It was a break for them to have a lighter patient load, so they tolerated the students, as long as it meant that they had no extra work.

Andie was supposed to assess her patients first thing each morning after a brief report from the night nurse. The paralyzed man greeted her listlessly as he stared at the TV and told her that he was not hungry. Andie moved his breakfast tray out of the way and stood by the bed, fingering her stethoscope, which was draped around her neck. This was much different than dealing with the sleeping nursing home patients, who hardly heard her moving around them as she took their vital signs and checked them over.

"That's a great tattoo," Andie said as she looked at the lion that covered his entire chest. There was a bandage over the lion's mouth. The bullet had entered his chest going through the lion's mouth.

"Gee, thanks," he replied sarcastically.

"Do you mind if I take your vital signs now?"

"Why ask? No one else does."

"All right then." She palpated his wrist and took his pulse.

"Good thing they didn't get you a little more to the left with that bullet," Andie said as she looked at the amount of drainage that had seeped through the gauze pad. "It would've been close to your heart."

Andie finished assessing him and checked to see if he needed any help catheterizing himself. He insisted that he was fine, so Andie went out to the nursing station to find his chart. She read over his history and learned that he had tried to commit suicide. He was the one who had aimed the gun into the lion's mouth. She did not have long to think about it because she still had two more patients to assess and get ready for the day.

She became more comfortable as she took care of each new patient. As long as she had a confident air about her, most patients responded with respect. Many were kind and tried to talk to her about their problems. The students had fewer patients than the RNs, so spent more time listening to and getting to know their patients. Andie began to enjoy the feeling she received from helping someone feel better. She was proficient at assessing patients and had passed medications, but she had not given an injection yet. One of the students related her first attempt at giving a shot. She had hesitated so long that the instructor had finally taken her wrist and pushed it down to the patient, shoving the needle into his arm.

The day came when Andie was assigned to a patient who needed daily insulin shots. Andie took his bottle of insulin from the refrigerator and prepared the syringe in the medication room while the instructor intently watched.

Andie knocked on the patient's door and went in with her tray. "Hi, I've got your insulin ready," she said, trying to appear relaxed. Her heart was pounding furiously, and she was afraid that her hands would shake.

"I hope you're good at giving shots. The last nurse said she was and then it hurt more than ever," the thin, middle-aged man whined.

Andie peeled open the square foil packet and wiped the alcohol pad over a spot on the back of his upper arm.

"Have you given a lot of shots?" he asked apprehensively.

Andie opened her mouth, prepared to tell him the truth.

"Oh, she's given many shots!" the instructor interjected.

Andie looked over at her, and at the brisk nod of the instructor's head, went on to pick up the syringe. She took a deep breath then poked the short needle into his flesh, feeling the soft resistance and quickly pushing the plunger. When she finished, she needed to recover her thoughts. It had been so dramatic in her mind while she was doing it, that she had to stop and think to complete the rest of the requirements. "Never recap needles to avoid finger sticks and contracting AIDS," echoed through her mind. In her haste to be thorough, she had nearly done just that. She dropped the uncapped needle in a special red box on the wall that all sharp objects went into, then thanked the man and picked up her tray.

Her instructor told her that she should never admit doing anything for the first time to a patient, and that her patient was known to be a big cry-baby. Also, technically speaking, she had given many shots—to oranges.

That week Andie gave six more injections and did her first catheter-ization. She was beginning to feel like a real nurse, instead of just a student. Some patients told her that she was friendlier and more gentle than other nurses. Andie grew confident as she continued passing her tests and doing well in clinicals.

A difficult part of clinicals was being assigned to a patient who was dying. Other students had spoken of it, but Andie had never seen a dead person.

Until Mrs. Kincaid.

Andie took report from the night nurse. "Room four twenty-five is comfort measures only. She's eighty-seven, been going down for days and is probably about gone. Check the 02 flow rate and that's about it for her. Four twenty-six is a post-op mastectomy..." the exhausted nurse droned on with the rest of the report.

Andie went into room four twenty-five first. The patient was lying on her back with a nasal cannula delivering oxygen into her nose. She had a head of messy white hair and her skin was pale yellow. She was taking sporadic slow breaths while her eyes were closed. Andie stood next to her and looked around the room. There was a small vase of wilted flowers on the windowsill. Her personal toiletries were on the bedside table, a bottle of perfume, a blue hairbrush, a pastel flowered scarf, and some hair pins. A business card with the name of a pastor from a Presbyterian church lay next to the hair pins. A romance novel, book mark barely in place, was lying on the floor. Andie picked it up and put it on the table.

She did her assessment and learned that the woman did not respond to any kind of stimulation. Her feet and lower legs had mottled purple marks and the bag of urine attached to the side of the bed held a small amount of dark brown urine.

Rebecca, a student who had had Mrs. Kincaid three days before, came into the room and told Andie that the woman had been alert and able to talk when she had cared for her. Andie asked if any relatives had come to visit, but Rebecca had never seen anyone but staff in the room.

Andie read the chart and saw that a daughter lived in Orlando and a grandson lived in a nearby town. This was no way for someone to die, she thought. Their last days and moments spent in a hospital room with strangers. Mrs. Kincaid should have a room filled with the smell of beautiful flowers and have someone in her family next to her. Her three other patients were low maintenance, so she spent most of the morning in the room with Mrs. Kincaid. After lunch, which was offered to her patient anyway, some students had come in to observe the special type of breathing that Mrs. Kincaid was doing. Shallow, rapid respirations were followed by deeper, longer breaths, then no breathing for a few moments. Cheyne-Stokes respirations were a certain sign of a person being close to death.

Andie wanted the other students to leave because they talked about Mrs. Kincaid as if she were not even there. Rebecca pulled the covers back and showed everyone the purple marks on Mrs. Kincaid's thin legs. It was similar to a crowd gathering on the side of a road to stare at an accident.

"Okay, everybody. That's enough gaping for now. I'd like a little privacy for my patient, if you don't mind," Andie said firmly.

"You aren't in charge around here, Andrea," Rebecca said, not wanting to give up the limelight of sharing her knowledge of the dying woman.

"I am today in this room, so get out right now!"

As they left, Rebecca glared at her. Andie shook her head and looked away. This was Rebecca's second time in the program, and she plainly irritated the instructors. Mrs. Kincaid deserved to have peace in her room. During the process of dying, the sense of hearing was known to be the last to go. Andie did not want the elderly woman to hear her body being talked about like a piece of meat.

Andie cut her half-hour lunch break short and hurried back upstairs to Mrs. Kincaid. Her breathing now seemed to be more like brief gasping, so Andie went quickly over to her. She leaned close to her and saw her eyes moving beneath her eyelids. Andie felt a sense of urgency and heightened emotion as she watched the frail woman cling to life, fighting for each breath. She stroked her soft white hair. "I'm right here.

Everything's going to be all right. I'm going to hold your hand, so you'll know that I'm here." The pauses between breaths increased. Andie hummed a nameless soothing tune as she continued stroking the woman's hair. She held her hand, noticing how only the very middle of the palm had any warmth.

Then Mrs. Kincaid's head turned purposefully toward her, and her eyes opened and looked directly into Andie's eyes. Andie stopped humming and gazed into the light blue eyes, which were alert and searching. Andie smiled, and just as she was about to speak to Mrs. Kincaid, the woman took a deep breath and then let it out slowly, still gazing into Andie's eyes. As she exhaled, the look in her eyes became vacant. Andie tensely waited for her next breath, but instinctively knew that she would not be taking one.

"Oh, no. Oh, dear God. Be with her Lord, take care of her now," Andie whispered, beginning to cry. She turned her eyes away from the blank eyes of Mrs. Kincaid and bent her head forward, overcome with sadness.

"Go on, Mrs. Kincaid, go with Him," she said mournfully. She looked back at the eyes that were still aimed at her and reached up to close them. She gently moved Mrs. Kincaid's head into alignment with her motionless body. Andie was quivering, uncertain of what to do next.

Rebecca walked into the room. She looked at Mrs. Kincaid and then at Andie. "Oh my gosh, she's dead? Wow! Let me see." She walked over and pulled the covers off of Mrs. Kincaid's body.

"Stop it! What's wrong with you?" Andie cried.

Another student had taken a few tentative steps into the room, then stepped back into the hall and made a motion for someone to come. Andie grabbed the blanket and pulled it up to cover Mrs. Kincaid.

"What's wrong with you? This is a good learning experience!" Rebecca replied haughtily. Three students came into the room and hurried to the foot of the bed.

"Don't touch her!" Andie insisted, looking at their eager faces. "I'm going to get Mrs. Sullivan." But the instructor was already walking into the room. "Back up," she said as she bent over and listened with her stethoscope for a heartbeat, then reached over and turned off the oxygen. "Andrea, get ready to clean her up. I'll go get you the kit, and you can do the post-mortem care. Everyone else out of the room." Mrs. Sullivan walked briskly from the room and the students filed out, throwing backward glances at Andie and the bed.

Andie filled a basin with warm water, wondering what she would have to do to Mrs. Kincaid's body. She did not recall learning anything about post-mortem care, and she hoped it would not be too difficult.

The instructor strode into the room with a doctor, who listened for a heartbeat. He nodded at Andie and left the room. "Here's the post-mortem kit," Mrs. Sullivan said. "Finish cleaning her, check for stool, then follow the instructions. When you get her in the bag, come and find me." She looked at Andie for an extra moment before turning and leaving the room.

As Andie cleaned Mrs. Kincaid, she thought about how the woman's body had once been young. The frail, wrinkled legs had been plump baby legs that had taken her exploring. They had walked her through being a young woman, perhaps dancing with a sweetheart or running on a beach with salty waves slapping at them. Pregnancy had created the indented silvery lines across her abdomen. So many meals had passed through her lips and into her body, nourishing it. A mother had cleaned her bottom countless times, probably taking extra care to pin her diaper on just right. Andie hoped that Mrs. Kincaid had been immediately comforted when she had stopped breathing. The way that she had suddenly looked into her eyes would stay with her forever.

She opened the plastic bag and removed a small sheet of instructions, various straps, a toe tag, and a zippered plastic body bag. She carefully applied all of the straps, which would hold the body in an aligned position as rigor mortis set in. The chin strap was the most difficult to arrange, because her mouth would not stay completely closed even when the strap was tightened.

Andie wondered what Mrs. Kincaid's life had been like recently and hoped that she had not suffered physically or emotionally. By the looks of the stark room and absence of visitors, it was apparent that she could have had better moments during her last days. So this was death, Andie thought as she slipped the toe tag around the big toe. It could come quickly with no warning, allowing no time for introspection or evaluation, or it could slowly weaken someone, causing the person to linger, with the constant knowledge and certainty of approaching death. But to die alone, no one would want that. Andie felt that God had put her there for Mrs. Kincaid and believed the woman had known that someone was with her at the end.

She checked all of the straps, then took out the long bag and unfolded it halfway. She rolled Mrs. Kincaid to her side and slipped the folded half under her as far as she could, then went around to the other side of the bed and rolled her the other way, unfolding the bag from that side. She fit the body inside the bag and then hesitated before she zipped it up.

"I know you're somewhere much finer than this," Andie whispered. She felt that there should be some ceremony or acknowledgement of the life that was about to be covered and closed away. She slowly zipped up the bag and then went to find Mrs. Sullivan.

After the instructor had unzipped the bag and checked the body, they transferred Mrs. Kincaid to a special metal gurney and covered her with a thick black hood. Andie was told to deliver it to the morgue in the basement. She wheeled the gurney awkwardly down the hallway. It kept swinging out at the end until she figured out how to guide it along as she walked beside it. She waited for an empty elevator and then rode to the basement where a man had her sign a sheet to check the body into the morgue. He told her to park the gurney next to a door that led to a refrigerated area.

Andie looked back at Mrs. Kincaid's covered body and wished that she had gotten to know her. She was reluctant to leave her in such a strange place. It was so final and lonely. Though Andie tried to keep in mind where Mrs. Kincaid was now, she was profoundly shaken by the whole experience.

The instructor showed a sign of softness when Andie returned to the floor. "Andrea, you did a fine job. That was your first one, wasn't it?" Mrs. Sullivan asked.

"Yes, ma'am, it was," Andie replied quietly.

"You go ahead and take a fifteen-minute break. Have something to drink. I'll check on your other patients until you return."

Andie went outside and sat down on a bench in front of the hospital, watching the endless stream of cars stop and go at the light. People believed that they were infallible, Andie thought. They rushed around in life, tending to duties and worrying about what had not been accomplished, hurrying toward an unreachable goal of completion and contendedness. Then they either suddenly died or drifted into illness and pain, possibly lying in a hospital room all alone as their life burned out.

How many people were satisfied with the way that they had lived their lives, she wondered. How frightening it would be to die slowly, but not believe in God. What would the purpose of life mean at the end for an atheist? To rush and acquire things, but be forever extinguished when it was all over. Without the belief in God and heaven, there would be no peace in dying. Even people who believed in God were probably a bit reluctant, because they had to leave behind family and friends. It was hard to imagine how it would really be at the moment of death, but Andie knew that everyone was going to experience it.

Andie did not doubt for a moment that heaven and hell existed; she had seen obvious signs of both on earth. She was grateful that she had been led to find the way to eternal life. Sarah's daily prayers for her had probably kept her safe during the many trials in her life. Who else had been praying for her? Sarah was the one who had faithfully looked out for her, without even knowing who or where she was all of those years, with her prayers to God for protection for the child that she had relinquished. Those prayers had very likely saved her life numerous times.

Andie had to get back upstairs to see her other patients. She said a quick prayer for strength and thanked God for allowing her to be with Mrs. Kincaid.

Chapter 33

After she had gotten Rylee to sleep, Andie was studying at the small wooden desk in her bedroom. Sarah knocked quietly on her door and motioned for her to take the phone. Andie went out to the living room so Rylee, curled around a blanket on the slightly sagging mattress, would not awaken at the sound of her voice.

"Hey, Andie! Let me guess...you're studying!" Laura said.

"As usual," Andie laughed.

"Do you know that it's Saturday night?"

"I know, I know. But, I've got a huge test on Tuesday and I'm way behind."

"Every time I ask you to do something, you always have a huge test and you're way behind. We're going over to a friend's house for a little get-together, and I'm going to make you come with us."

"Make me? Really? Well, if you can drill the entire endocrine system into my mind and make it stick, I'll go," Andie replied.

"I know all about the endocrine system. There are these hormones and they make your body do different things. So now it's covered. We'll be over in half an hour to pick you up."

"Really, Laura, I have so much reading, and I haven't even gone over the notes yet."

"Mom said that she'd be home to watch Rylee, and we won't be out that late. I want you to meet some friends of ours."

"Great, it's a couples' party, right? I'll be the only single person there, so I can pine away as I sit alone and stress out because I'll flunk out of school and end up homeless and then Rylee will never—"

"Andie!" Laura shouted. "We're coming over, so be ready. Bring your doggone book if you want, but you need to get out of the house! It'll do you good, I promise."

"You know what?" Andie sighed. "I do need to get out. Your persistence has finally won me over. But I am going to bring my notebook, so I can at least review the notes if no one talks to me. That's the only way I'll go."

"Excellent! See you in a little while."

Laura and Tom picked her up, and Laura filled her in on who would be at the party. Mike Tanner, the man having the party, was divorced and had two kids who lived with his ex-wife. He would be the only other single person at the party. Laura's husband, Tom, was the manager for his band. Mike was the leader of a Christian rock band and wrote all of the songs as well as sang and played the guitar. Andie had never heard Christian rock music.

She was pleasantly surprised when she saw the handsome man who greeted them at the door. Mike was about two inches taller than she was and had an easy-going, genuine manner that was apparent right away. His blue eyes were set off by thick, dark eyebrows that contrasted with his light blond hair. He had filled his kitchen table with snacks and soft drinks. Three other couples were in the living room, chatting and laughing. Andie was introduced to everyone and felt relieved that she was included in the conversation. The other men were all members of the band and had their wives with them.

They played a board game around the long coffee table and listened to music. Mike and Tom were good friends and laughed together wildly during the game. They all took turns creating crazy definitions for the words that they were supposed to trick others into choosing as the correct meaning.

Andie watched him, wondering if he had a girlfriend. Someone as handsome and friendly as he was, and in a band, would have women flocking to him. She was curious about his divorce and thought of asking Laura if she knew what had happened to their relationship.

Looking around the house, she saw papers taped to the walls showing crayon doodles and stick figures. A few of the drawings were more advanced with assymmetrical animals and houses, a smiling yellow sun at the top. One wall was covered with framed photographs of a boy and girl in various stages of growth. Healthy plants hung from the ceiling in pots, and a perky cockatiel sat in his cage next to a huge fish tank that contained one large fish, which swam slowly back and forth.

When she went into the bathroom, Andie saw that it was clean and decorated in a colorful ocean theme. A container of bath toys was next to the tub, and bottles of bubble bath and tear-free shampoo sat on a shelf. She could see into one bedroom as she came out of the bathroom, getting a glimpse of bunkbeds, a doll house, two big toy boxes, a poster of Beauty and the Beast, and a small blue table and chairs.

As the evening progressed, Andie became even more interested in Mike. He kept choosing her definitions for the words that were to be defined, without knowing that she was the one who had created them. Each time the true definition was revealed, he would look at her and laugh as he realized that he had chosen hers again.

She tried to stop herself from thinking about him, because it would certainly end in disappointment. He would still be in love with his ex-wife, or have a girlfriend, or not want to date anyone. Andie told herself that she had too much going on, adding a boyfriend would just complicate matters. He was probably not interested in her anyway. She was wearing old jeans and a plain looking shirt, and she had cut her hair short so that it was easier for school.

The board game ended, and everyone continued talking and eating the cookies that Mike had brought out to the living room. He asked if anyone wanted coffee or espresso. Andie and he were the only ones who wanted espresso, so Andie offered to help him.

He was quiet in the small kitchen, and she began to feel nervous and shy as she watched his strong hands get the tiny cups out of the cupboard.

"Your house is very nice," she said.

"Thanks. I've lived here for about eight years now. I had it built back when this area was out in the boondocks. It's changed a lot," he replied.

Andie could not look directly at him, for fear that he would see her interest. "How old are your kids? They're very cute."

"Michelle is seven, and Elijah's four," he said as they watched the steam rising from the espresso machine.

"My daughter, Rylee, is two years old. I can't believe how fast she's grown."

"Just when you get used to them at one age, they go and change on you." He smiled and took a sugar bowl out of the cupboard, setting it by the cups.

Laura mentioned that you go to Pine Castle," he said. "Which service do you go to?"

"I always go to the nine o'clock, so Rylee can go to the nursery. Do you go there?"

"I do. My family has been going there since I was fourteen, when we moved to this side of town. I usually go to the early service, because I try to get to the beach on Sunday. My schedule's crazy with work and the band, but I like to go surfing whenever I can."

"I've always wanted to try surfing. Is it difficult to learn?"

"Actually, it is. Well, it was for me. I weigh a lot compared to some of the little surfer boys out there. You'd probably be good, though. You're thin and you look strong."

Andie was startled for a moment when he mentioned her body—he had noticed her body. She looked down at the floor. She wanted to impress him and seem friendly, but her shy side was taking over.

He held up a spoon. "How much sugar would you like?"

"Uh...two teaspoons, please," Andie replied, about to reach for the spoon, but he turned and scooped up the sugar, mixing it in for her.

"Let's see what they're doing out there." Mike let Andie walk ahead of him into the living room while he carried the coffee cups, setting her cup down on the table in front of where she had been sitting.

Andie could have kicked herself for clamming up in the kitchen. He was just making conversation, and she was playing out this drama in her mind. She had to stop before she got herself too distraught. He was a stable, responsible man with a busy life. She was trying to get her own screwed-up life in order and could offer nothing to a man like him. She did not want to think about him any further, because she did not want to be disappointed.

Everyone talked about the upcoming show at a college the following weekend. Andie sat and listened to them as she sipped her espresso. She would glance at Mike, and a few times their eyes met, but they both quickly looked away. She wondered what, if anything, he thought of her.

In the past when men were interested in her, they usually came on too strong by pursuing a physical relationship right away. Andie even expected men to act that way; her father had set a pattern of behavior she saw in every man. Steve had failed to be faithful, even after she had devoted her life to him. Could it be that some men were truly decent?

At parties in her old life, there would often be a couple who got drunk and ended up having a loud fight. They would break up, but usually be back together by the next party. People would become so stoned or drunk by the end of the evening that someone would almost always pass out.

This peaceful gathering had been more enjoyable than any she had ever attended. They joked and kidded one another—some jokes were inside jokes that she did not understand. They had intelligent conversations and even talked about certain problems in their families. Someone would tell the person with the problem that they would pray for them and everyone else would agree. It was nice to see genuine caring and friendship.

Andie decided that she would try to go to the concert on Friday night, regardless of her homework. Sarah had told her that they were concerned because she was not having enough recreational time in her life since school began, and she offered to watch Rylee anytime Andie wanted to go out.

Laura went into the kitchen at the end of the night to help Mike clean up, then it was time to go. On the drive home, Laura anwered Andie's questions about Mike. He had married his high school sweetheart the summer after high school graduation. He had been a wild kid, experimenting with drugs, lying to his parents, going to school stoned nearly every day. A few years into their marriage, after Michelle was born, he became a Christian. His wife, Marsha, had not joined him in his beliefs and scorned his new ways.

She left him a few years later, three weeks after their son, Elijah, was born. She took three-year-old Michelle, baby Elijah, and moved in with her boyfriend. She came back for most of the household items. Mike had stood by watching as she and her boyfriend loaded his truck with the washer and dryer and other belongings. Apparently, he was in such a state of shock that he could not react or believe what was happening.

Mike was a devoted father and spent the next few years taking on most of the responsibility and care of the children, though his ex-wife received full child support. He arranged his entire life around the children, even turning down a golden opportunity to travel with a popular band and be the opening act. Marsha continued to make his life miserable. She played games with the visitation arrangements, sometimes leaving them overnight with him when it had not been planned and not calling to tell him where she was, sometimes denying visits if she wanted to punish him for no apparent reason.

Mike waited two years before signing the divorce papers. He had made every attempt to get back with her, overlooking all of her cruelty and continuing to be at her beck and call. He just wanted to be with his children. Finally, he had realized that there was no hope.

Laura said that women were always trying to get his attention. They would often come up to him after a concert and shove phone numbers into his hand. Some even offered to take him to their house that evening for a rendezvous, but he had never accepted. He had dated one woman, a model, for a month, but she had been seen kissing a man on a dance floor one night by a wife of another band member.

Mike, at twenty-six, three years older than Andie, was carrying on alone. There was currently a woman who called him and would sometimes show up at his house in the middle of the night, but Laura did not think that he liked her.

"You and Mike would make a great couple," Laura said.

"Sure, Laura. I'll get in line behind the others," Andie said tiredly. She had been staying up late all week to study and was now ready for bed, disheartened by the information about Mike. He had an ex-wife that he had wanted back. He had dated a woman, someone undoubtedly gorgeous, and might still desire her. Another woman was after him, and he had women throwing phone numbers at him. It sounded like heartbreak waiting to happen.

Andie decided to forget about the idea of dating. But his light blue eyes, and how they crinkled at the corners when he laughed, kept showing up in her mind. He had such a contagious laugh.

Chapter 34

The endocrine system test, known to be one of the most difficult in that part of the program, had caused five people to flunk out and seven more to live in fear of failing their next test. Andie had passed the test, but it was her lowest score yet. Everyone in the class was looking tired and stressed out. Andie remembered the nursing students she had seen months before and now understood what they had been going through.

The instructors had told them at the beginning of the program that many relationships were tested by nursing school. In every class, a divorce or two occurred among the students. One girl in the last class had committed suicide. Only the strong would survive the constant demands and rigorous requirements.

Andie prayed that nothing would happen to keep her from finishing. Rylee had been healthy, and she herself had gone to school a few times when she was feeling ill, but if a major flu broke out, she could be facing problems. Rylee would have to be well enough to go to the sitter's house. No child with a fever, diarhhea, chicken pox, or chest cold was allowed. Her car had been making a strange sound recently, so she hoped that it would make it through the year. Too many obstacles could be thought of if she let herself dwell on the "what ifs."

Her parents had been pleased to hear about her experiences and said that they were proud of her. Andie felt guilty for living with Sarah, but they would never find out if she was careful. They had talked about coming to visit, but Andie told them to wait until school was over so she could spend more time with them. It bothered her to feel as if she were lying when they asked about the people she was living with. Andie described them truthfully, but left out the part about who they actually were to her. She would be tense as they spoke, wanting to hurry and get off the phone.

On Friday evening Andie got ready to go out with Laura and Lisa, who would be picking her up and then meeting Laura's husband, Tom, at the concert. He would have to remain backstage with the band, overseeing the show. Andie wore jeans and a white T-shirt, feeling glad to be out of her nursing uniform.

They arrived and walked into the crowded auditorium. Three bands would be playing, with Mike's being the only Christian group. Laura said that they tried to play for secular audiences because they were the ones who needed to hear the messages.

When the first band was done, Mike's group began to set up. The crowd had grown, and a line of young women could be seen up along the front of the stage. Laura pulled Andie and Lisa toward the front, and they wove their way to the stage. The lights dimmed as a guitar began playing softly. Then a blast of light came on and the entire band came to life. Mike, as lead singer, walked up to the microphone and grabbed it just in time to begin singing with the music. Andie watched in amazement as he sang and moved. He did not dance, but strode around the stage with an intensity that held everyone's attention, his voice deep and melodious. Young women were yelling, jumping up and down, and Andie looked over and saw that they were watching Mike. She felt a tug in her chest as they clapped and danced.

Andie was impressed with the band. The music was good. She had imagined that Christian rock music would be fluffy and wimpy, yet their songs varied from fast, driving songs to softer love songs. The music was about the love of God and struggles in the world. Mike came over near where they stood and smiled down at them.

By the time their set was over, Andie was fascinated by Mike. She did not want to tell Laura and Lisa because she was embarrassed, feeling that she was too new a Christian, and that she could not measure up to all of them. She really did not know much about the Bible, and she had so recently been living in total sin. Mike was obviously a very devoted Christian.

They stayed for part of the last band while Mike's group packed up. Laura said that they usually went out to eat afterward to talk, so the three of them went ahead, planning to meet everyone else at a the restaurant.

Andie kept looking at the door of the restaurant until Mike finally walked in with Tom and the others. They sat down and ordered sodas and coffee. Andie said hello to him and told him that she thought the show was excellent. He thanked her politely. Everyone was talking at once, and she and Mike were sitting across the table from one another, so she could not speak with him as easily as she had wanted.

Mike did not behave as if he were impressed with himself or his performance. He was the quietest male at the table, while the drummer was a chatterbox. Andie could tell that Mike was a good listener because everyone kept vying for his attention, and he calmly gave it to them. She had reached a point where she knew that she had to find out more about him to know if she should put any more energy into hoping for the possibility of dating him. If he had any qualities that were obviously negative, she would stop all of the daydreaming that she was doing. She had no extra time to devote to extraneous pursuits.

As they walked out to the parking lot afterward, she wished that she could say something clever to Mike, but Tom was talking to him and everyone was about to get into their cars. Then he walked over to her and thanked her again for coming to his show.

"I'll go to another one if I can," Andie said, noticing Laura and Lisa exchanging a look.

"I was wondering if I could call you sometime. Maybe to see a movie or have coffee. Would that be all right?" Mike asked, looking very serious.

"Yes, I'd like that," she replied. "Here, I'll write my number down for you."

"I already have it. I mean, your parents, if you call them your parents, are in the church directory," he said, looking mildly embarrassed.

"Oh, okay, great! Then I'll look forward to hearing from you." Andie smiled, realizing that he was also shy.

Laura smacked Andie on the shoulder and laughed loudly when they were in the car. "I'd say you've got someone very interested in you, Andie!"

"I don't know about that," Andie replied.

"He's never asked anyone for a phone number. All the girls have always gone after him. You are the only one."

"Well, maybe he just feels sorry for me." Andie laughed as Laura poked her again.

In bed that night, Andie stared at the ceiling, watching the slices of light as they filtered through the mini blinds from the headlights of passing cars. All she could think about was Mike. He was unlike any man she had ever met. Laura had told her that he also taught a Bible study every Tuesday night to a group of adults, and he regularly visited two elderly friends, who were bedridden in a nursing home. Andie prayed that if she was supposed to know him, that it would be apparent to her if she should become involved with him. She fell asleep and dreamed of the beach.

Mike called Thursday evening and asked her to go to a movie with him on Saturday. She accepted, and they spoke for a short time. Rylee was fussing loudly because she was tired.

"I'm sorry. Rylee needs to go to bed soon and she still needs a bath," Andie said.

Mike laughed, "That's all right. It's nothing new to me. I'll pick you up at six, so we have time for a cup of coffee before the show, if that's okay with you."

Andie picked up Rylee and tried to calm her, but she only screamed louder, right into the phone. "That sounds good, I'll see you then." Andie hoped he heard her say good-bye because she was unable to hear anything else he might have said.

She tried to get extra studying in before Saturday night. Three major tests were coming up the following week, and she had caught herself daydreaming in class. This was not the time to be distracted, she knew; there was too much at stake.

Mike arrived Saturday in his old truck and apologized for her having to get in on his side, since the passenger door was broken and could not open. Andie laughed about it and told him that at least she could see the floor in his truck, her own was full of papers and toys. He admitted that he had cleaned it for the evening and that it had been a terrible mess. They laughed and their eyes met, neither of them looking away when their laughter faded. Something passed between them, an understanding that they were both vulnerable.

Their conversation was comfortable on the drive. Mike was easy to be with and seemed familiar to her, as if she had known him before. As they walked around outside after their cup of coffee, she realized that he seemed familiar because he had a lot of the same qualities that she had. He was sensitive, honest, and kind. She found herself relaxing and opening up to him, because he was a very good listener. She told him how she had become a Christian, and then she went on to relate the entire experience about Farley to him. When she finished, she was agitated, worried that he would think that she was strange, but it had all just poured out of her.

"I've read about the Mormons. They're like a cult. They try to base their religion on Christ, but their founder was a man who was wanted for a number of crimes in different states," Mike said. "I know an ex-Mormon, and you should hear some of the stories he can tell. Did you know that they only recently allowed African-Americans as members because they had viewed them as an inferior, tainted race? Some still practice polygamy, even though they were forced to give it up. That's a terrible thing to have gone through. You must be a very strong person to have handled it so well." He patted her arm and tilted his head to try to meet her downturned eyes.

"I didn't handle it well. I made some of the worst choices after it happened. If it weren't for my family here, I'd probably be lost," Andie replied, relieved that he did not seem disturbed by what she had confided, but feeling tense from having recalled it.

"Laura told me about how you found them. That must be something to have discovered your blood family. What was it like?"

Andie began telling him about it, but then looked at her watch. "The movie starts in five minutes. I guess we'd better start walking over there," she said.

As they neared the front of the theatre, Andie was disappointed that they would not be able to talk until after the movie. "How would you feel about not going to the movie? I'd really like to talk to you more," she suggested.

"Really, you too? I didn't feel like going either, but I didn't want to say anything," Mike answered, smiling. "I have an idea. I want to show you one of my favorite places." They headed toward the parking lot.

As they drove on the interstate, Andie noticed that the silences were comfortable. She decided that, if nothing else, he could be a good friend. He took her to downtown Orlando, and they walked around Lake Eola. The fountain in the middle of the lake had lights that changed the color of the water as it sprayed outward in a huge umbrella. People peddled boats shaped like giant swans around the fountain. At an outdoor theatre, a Shakesperian play was being performed. The actors boisterous voices carried across the lake, fading in and out with the breeze.

Mike told her about how he had started the band three years before. Their purpose was to help non-Christian young people find out about Christ. He said that he dressed the way he did while onstage to fit the persona that was expected and accepted by the youth of today. People could listen to the music and enjoy it, while hearing a message about God.

They leaned against a railing, looking out at the lake. She gazed at his profile, studying his square jaw line and the shape of his mouth. Andie felt her stomach flutter as a physical desire for him occurred. She felt guilty and pulled her mind away from the thought. He was a gentleman. He had not even attempted to hold her hand. She asked for forgiveness in her mind and vowed to remain pure.

It was midnight, but Andie was not tired. She did not know when she would be able to see him again since they were both so busy. They walked to his truck, and she laughed as she crawled in on his side because he was apologizing again.

Once seated, he turned to her. "You know, I haven't enjoyed myself this much in a long time, if ever. I know it's late, but I don't want the night to end. Would you like to come over for a little while? I don't mean to make it sound like I want to throw you down on my couch." They both laughed. "I just want to spend some more time together."

"I'd love to," she replied. "I don't want the night to end either."

They stared at each other. Then they both smiled. "Come on, let's go," he said.

He showed her the "band room" in his garage, and they goofed around with the equipment. He played the guitar and she sang into the microphone, listening to her voice booming out of the large speakers. She was not even embarrassed to sing in front of him. He took her home just before two o'clock.

"Can I see you again?" he asked quietly as they sat in his truck.

"Yes, I'd really like that."

"I'll call you soon. I had such a great time. Thank you. I'd come around and open your door, but I can't." They laughed again, and she followed him out from his side.

"Goodnight," he said as they stood next to the front door. Sarah had left the light on, and Andie hoped that she would not wake them up when she went inside. She felt like a teenager again.

"Goodnight, Mike. Thanks for listening to me."

"Anytime, Andie. Anytime."

When the truck pulled out of sight, Andie felt a longing to hear his voice again and to have him look at her with his sincere expression. This man was too good to be real and he was interested in her, not for her body, but as a person. Andie allowed the hope for true love that she had suppressed for so long to be released. She hugged herself and smiled.

Chapter 35

Mike and Andie established a ritual of meeting twice a week at a park with their children. She would pick up Rylee after school, and he would get his kids after work, which ended at the same time as her classes.

The first day that they had met at the park, Andie had been impressed with how well-mannered his children were and how much he interacted with them. Rylee followed Michelle and Elijah around and started calling out to Mike in the same way that they did.

"Look! Look at me!" Rylee would cry, waving her little arm at Mike as she went down the slide.

Michelle had been shy at first, but when she saw how Andie joined in playing and was tireless at hide-and-seek and tag, she asked her to meet them there again. Elijah was easy-going like his father, taking Rylee's hand while they played hide-and seek, helping her hide.

Andie was surprised when she had first seen Mike wearing a tank top. He had muscular arms and shoulders, but he seemed completely oblivious to his attractiveness and never showed the slightest bit of vanity.

He invited them over to dinner often and served spaghetti each time. On the phone one night, he apologized for the lack of variety to the meals, admitting that he did not have much money left after paying all of his bills and child support. Andie reassured him that she did not care what they ate because the company was what mattered. She began to pick up little extra things at the grocery store—pizza kits for the kids to prepare, ingredients for Alfredo sauce, a loaf of French bread.

He gave her a key to his house during the third week that they were together. Andie often studied in the evening at his house, while Rylee dozed in the bottom bunkbed in the childrens' bedroom. Mike had band practice twice a week, and Andie learned to study while the house vibrated from the music in the garage. Rylee could even fall asleep with the music booming, and she had taken a keen interest in Mike, expecting to see him daily after being picked up from the sitter's house.

Sarah and John kidded Andie because she was only home to sleep, but they liked Mike and approved of their relationship. Laura was taking the credit for being the matchmaker. She told Andie that she expected to be the maid-of-honor in the wedding.

Andie knew that Mike was someone whom she could implicitly trust. So far, they had not touched one another except for an occasional pat on the arm. Andie knew that she needed to tell him that she would not have sex unless she was married. She had decided this when she became a Christian, although she did not believe there would be a man who could accept it. Even on television people were portrayed as having casual sexual relationships—it was assumed they would. Sex was everywhere: commercials, sitcoms, soap operas, movies, billboards, books, radio, music. Andie thought that the day would soon come when AIDS would affect nearly every family, and the media would finally back off because it would be dangerous and in bad taste to encourage casual sex.

She was not sure what Mike would think. Did Christian young people wait to have sex until they were married? Faithful ones would. She wanted to start out right in a relationship. She knew that God required this, and that if everyone subscribed to this rule, AIDS would not be rampantly growing.

Mike asked her if she wanted to go on another date. They had only been out alone together once because they were always so busy with the children. He picked her up Saturday evening and they drove the hour of highway to the beach.

There was so much she wanted to know. Did he feel what she did? They had been cordial and friendly, with the occasional long stares into one another's eyes. The children had a great time together and when they were at the park or at his house, it felt like they were one big family. Was this just a friendship to him? Did he ever want to get married again?

They found a place to walk on the beach where there were no other people in sight. It was windy and the damp ocean air chilled her. Mike had a coat in his truck, so he ran to get it after he noticed Andie shivering and talking through clenched teeth. He came back and put it around her, buttoning it up to her neck. When he reached the last button, he lifted his hand and smoothed the hair away from her forehead.

"Shall we walk?" he asked, taking her hand for the first time.

The sudden intimacy in the warmth and strength of his hand made Andie forget the cold. The waves rolled and hissed along the sand. They both started speaking at the same time and laughed.

"You go first," he said.

"I was just going to say that I never thought I'd meet someone like you."

"I've thought that same thing about you many times already."

They had to move up higher on the beach when the water lapped at their shoes. "Here, I'll walk on this side, so you won't get wet," he said as they traded places. The wind seemed to steal the words as they came out of their mouths, making them speak louder than usual.

"I didn't think that I would ever trust a man again. I'd given up hope in men."

"I'd done the same thing, for women though, of course," he laughed.

"It looks like God brought us together before we abandoned all hope in humankind."

Mike stopped and reached for her other hand. She could see the moon over his shoulder as it made its slow trek above the ocean, and she wished that she could see his face as well as he was probably able to see hers in the moonlight.

"There's something I have to tell you," he began.

Andie immediately knew that he was going to tell her that he could not become involved with her. She set her mind as firmly as she could for the news to be delivered, but felt sadness filling her up.

"Don't look so sad! Please, Andie, just listen. I have to let you know…if we're going to have a relationship, I won't have sex outside of marriage."

"What?"

"Didn't you hear me?"

"I thought you said that you wouldn't have sex outside of marriage."

"That's right. I hope this isn't a problem."

The implication of his words sank into her mind. He was thinking of her romantically and wanting a relationship, or he would not be telling her this. She had never met one man in her life who felt this way about sex; the way that she knew was right.

She let go of his hands and put her arms around his neck, hugging him. He returned the embrace, then he drew back and looked at her. "Is this good news?" he asked.

"Mike, you have no idea how much I've been worrying about this. I didn't think there was a man on the planet who would want to wait for marriage."

"Honestly, I didn't think I'd find someone either. You really feel this way?"

"Yes! This is perfect. Can you believe that we found each other?"

Placing his hands on the sides of her face, he said, "Andie, I love you."

She felt his warm hands on her skin and moved closer to see his eyes, the clear eyes that held the promise of all that she hoped to know. God had shown her the man that He intended for her. Mike was more than she could have ever asked for.

"I didn't actually plan on saying that so soon. I wanted to—" Mike began awkwardly when Andie had not responded.

"Mike, I love you too!" Andie said, reaching out to hug him again, but more tightly this time. She noticed how their bodies fit perfectly together as they embraced, feeling safe in his arms and comforted by his gentleness.

"This is incredible," Mike said. "I've known from the first time that I watched you talking that you were someone special. I didn't think a woman like you existed."

They stood looking at each other, letting their eyes drink in the depth of feeling that had been restrained before this night. Mike took her hand and softly kissed the back of it. "I promise that I'll never hurt you. I want you to be happy, Andie. You deserve so much," he said.

She was speechless, wanting to laugh and cry at the same time. God had put everything in her life that she had ever wanted in just a few months. It was as if He were reassuring her of His care for her, knowing that she had not intended to be given anything in return for her devotion and faith.

"You are so wonderful," she said.

"You're pretty great yourself, kiddo."

They laughed and he took her hand as they began walking along the shore, leaning against one another, impenetrable to the cold wind.

Chapter 36

The next few weeks were blissful, but always too busy. The second phase of the nursing program began, and she was under intense pressure as the tests became more difficult. She was not getting much sleep because she was either at Mike's house late in the evening or on the phone with him after she had finished studying. She tried to cover the material as best she could, even though her mind wandered off into thoughts of Mike during lectures, and while she was studying she would often drift into a daydream.

They spent every relatively free moment together. While Rylee slept in the bunkbed, Andie would study and Mike would read or take care of chores. She would look up from her book and see him watching her. He had told her to not mind his staring. When she took a break, he would often massage her tired neck and shoulders and bring a cup of coffee to her. They talked about everything, sharing their pasts and their dreams for the future.

He had his children every afternoon, and they would sleep there one night on the weekend. His ex-wife had heard about Andie and had called to threaten him. Mike said she was accusing him of allowing the kids to see immoral behavior and that they were upset. Apparently, she often came up with ludicrous ideas and threats, but this time she had done something to the kids.

They were sullen when they were first picked up, then would finally cheer up and play good-naturedly, but by that time it would be nearing the end of the visit. Mike had tried to talk to them, but they would not disclose anything. Michelle would start crying if Mike tried to find out why she was acting aloof, so he decided to just let time take care of it. He and Andie knew that they were not in the wrong; Marsha simply did not want to see him happy. It was sad to know that she would go as far as involving and harming the children in the process.

Andie told her friend at school about Mike. Maria was a single parent whose two-year-old boy had undergone open heart surgery when he was a baby. Maria had decided to become a nurse after going through the experience. She and Andie sat next to one another during lecture and would meet for lunch at the hospital during clinicals. Maria was looking forward to moving out of her parents' house, where she was living with her son and two daughters.

"My parents won't stop trying to run my life," Maria said, her dark eyes squinting in anger. "It drives me crazy! They contradict me in front of the kids when I'm trying to discipline them. I wish I could meet someone and get away. You're so lucky to find a good man. Maybe you'll get married!"

Andie smiled. "That would be something. But I'm not sure how he feels about marriage now. His ex-wife really did a number on him. I do know that God has been putting everything in order for me ever since I became a Christian, so if it's meant to be, then it will happen. I could see myself being really happy with him."

A strong feeling to be understood came over Andie. "Listen to this, Maria, you won't believe what I've seen." She shared the story of how she became a Christian. When she described the strange occurences in the house where she had lived, Maria listened intently.

"I've seen that kind of thing," Maria said as they finished their lunch in the crowded hospital cafeteria.

"Really?"

"I'm very worried." Maria leaned toward Andie. "I've got to get my kids out of my parents' house. It's the only way I can go to school, so I'm stuck right now. There are some really weird things going on."

"What do you mean?"

Maria looked around the room and then whispered. "Have you heard of Santeria?"

Andie shook her head.

"My parents and sisters are really into it. They've been trying to get me involved, but I don't want my kids to be around it. I've seen ghosts, or spirits, whatever they are, and so have my kids. My eleven-year-old is terrified every night, so she locks her door. I put the other two in bed with me."

"What do people do who are into this?"

"Well, my dad and mom have these ceremonies where he talks to the spirits and gets help from the…the other world. One night I caught him using my son. I walked into the living room to find him. I was studying and my mom was supposed to be watching him for me. Then I heard my dad doing his chants and all, so I went out and he had put these necklaces made of some kind of bone around David's neck, and he and my mom were praying over him."

"Oh my gosh, what did you do?"

"Well, I grabbed David and threw the necklace down, then I told them that they needed to leave the kids alone. I can't really upset them too much because I need a place to live."

"Maria, that's awful! And the kids have seen ghosts?"

"Oh, yeah. David will point them out sometimes if we go out of our rooms. I've seen people, or what look like see-through people, walking through the hall or up on the ceiling. My parents just say that they're the spirits that have been sent to help us. Look at this," Maria said, opening her purse and taking out a a small pouch.

Andie looked at the transparent plastic packets that Maria held. There was a strange coin inside of each one, surrounded by liquid. Dark flecks of something floated around the coin in the fluid. "My dad made these for me. He calls it "preparing" them. They're supposed to be for different things, like luck or wisdom or protection. I've got a special necklace of beads that he put in my car. He told me not to take it out." Maria held out the packets for Andie to take.

"No, thanks. I really don't want to touch them."

Maria put them back into her purse. "I know it sounds strange, so I don't tell anyone about it. You won't tell anyone, will you?" she asked anxiously.

"The only person I'd tell is Mike, so he could pray for you. Would you mind?"

"No, I don't mind. I mean the people in school. I don't want them to know," Maria replied. "I'd appreciate it if you'd pray for me."

"You should get rid of anything your dad gives you and make sure the kids stay away from those ceremonies. We don't have that much longer in school, so you'll be out on your own with a good job soon."

"You know, I do believe in Jesus. But they say that they do, too. My family is so intent on cramming this stuff down my throat. The thing is, it works. I mean, the stuff that they pray for, they usually end up getting. But I know it's not right. Sometimes they use it to hurt people they don't like."

"I'd like to talk to you again about this, okay? We'd better get back up to the floor. I'll be praying for you and your kids." Andie wished that they had longer to talk, but they would be sent home for the day if they were late returning to the floor. She believed what Maria had said and knew exactly how it felt to tell someone about a spirititual encounter, hoping they would not think you were crazy.

Mike had heard of Santeria. He explained to Andie that it was a bizarre combination of Catholicism and African religion. African slaves in Cuba had incorporated their own religion long ago with that of their owners. To avoid beatings for practicing their religion, they had outwardly worshipped the Catholic saints that they were supposed to worship, combining their own spirit guides into the ceremonies. Animal sacrifices were often performed, and spirits were called on to help in daily life. Millions of Hispanic people practiced Santeria, along with many others worldwide. Mike and Andie prayed for Maria and her children. He always led the prayers because Andie was still shy about praying aloud in front of others.

Andie began going to the Bible study that Mike taught. She admired his way with people, especially the elderly women. He would give each one a kiss on the cheek and usually make a humorous comment, which always drew a smile. With his accoustic guitar, he led them in song before they prayed, then he would present the lesson that he had planned. Andie met Mike's mother, Beth, at the Bible study and was immediately drawn to her kindness. Mike and his mother had a close relationship that Andie knew played a major role in forming Mike's generous nature. Her eyes were the same light blue as Mike's, and she radiated kindness, always with a positive word for everyone.

Beth invited her over for dinner, so Mike and Andie began taking the kids over for Saturday dinner every other week. Andie felt comfortable around his parents, and she was pleased that they took such a great interest in Rylee. Beth even bought toys for Rylee to keep at her house and call her own. Andie often found herself imagining how it would be if she were a member of the family.

It had been a difficult night of reviewing for the next day's test, but before she went home Andie realized that she needed to tell Mike that she could probably not have children. They were sitting on the couch talking about their kids, and Mike brought up what he thought a child of theirs might look like. His kids both had dark hair and brown eyes like their mother.

"He'd have blond hair, blue eyes and be tall. Hopefully, he'd get your nose," Mike said.

"Mike, I've got to tell you something."

"What?" He became serious when he noticed her discomfort.

"This is hard for me to say. You know that Steve was unfaithful. Well, the way that I found out was...he gave me a disease. Gonorhhea." Andie looked away from him.

"Oh, no."

"It's very embarrassing," she said quietly. "I had such a bad case that the doctor said my Fallopian tubes were severely scarred. I've looked up information in medical books, and gonorhhea almost always results in sterility for females. Given my advanced case of it, I believe that it's definite that I can't have children now."

Mike watched her as she stared at her hands in her lap. "Hey, Andie?"

She looked up at him with tears in her eyes.

"I'd say that with three kids, we have our hands full anyway. I love you, okay? Please don't worry about this. I'm just sorry that you had to go through it."

"I know you'd like another child. I would, too. I'm sorry."

Mike reached over and hugged her. "Don't say another word about it, because it's all right. If I could have you in my life...I'd give up just about anything."

"I love you so much, Mike."

"I love you, too. We're meant to be together, you know. If God wanted us to have more children, then it would happen. But if this is how it is, then I know that it wasn't meant to be. Imagine the cost of college for four children!" He laughed.

She was relieved to have finally told him. His children would replace the ones that she could not have. Rylee would have siblings if they ever married. Mike and Andie had alluded to their future so many times, without actually speaking of marriage, but they both knew that they had found their mate for life.

CHAPTER 37

When Andie arrived home from school, there was a phone message from her dad to return his call. She reached him and learned that the following morning her mother would have a cyst removed from her neck. The lump had grown from the size of a pea to the size of golf ball in one month. He asked Andie to call back the next afternoon.

She prayed for her mom that night, but was worried during class the next day. At break time, she decided to call Grandma Reeves, her dad's mother, to see if she had heard anything because her parents had not answered their phone.

"Grandma, it's Andie. Have you heard from Dad yet?" she asked.

"Oh, Andie. Don't you know? It's terrible! They found cancer!"

"No!" she exclaimed.

"I'm afraid so. The doctor took out as much as he could, but they had to stop. She's got to have chemotherapy next week in Iowa City."

"Oh, Grandma, this is awful." She imagined how frightened her mom would be in the hospital and how dreadful it must have been to hear the news when she awoke after the surgery.

"Andie, I'm so sorry, honey. Your dad is just beside himself over this. You can call her room at the hospital. She'll be there until tomorrow morning."

Andie went back upstairs to return to class. She tried to keep herself from crying, but the tears came and she could not stop. The instructor was on her way into the classroom when she saw Andie outside in the hallway.

"What's the trouble, Andrea?" Mrs. Sullivan asked.

"My mom," she cried. "I just found out that my mom has cancer."

"Oh, dear. I'm very sorry. Maybe you should take the rest of the day off, if you don't have too many absences."

"Yes, that's what I'll do," Andie said.

Mrs. Sullivan put her arm around her shoulder and hugged her. "We'll see you tomorrow."

Andie glanced at all of the eyes staring at her as she picked up her book bag and left the quiet room. She went to Sarah's house to change her clothes and call the hospital.

"Hello," her mom said softly, sounding like a child.

"Mom, it's me. How are you doing?"

"Andie," her mom cried out. "It's cancer!"

"I know, I know, Mom! I talked to Grandma Reeves. Everything's going to be fine, okay? Iowa City has some of the best doctors in the country." Andie tried to make herself sound positive, but she ached with sadness for her mother, and the desperation that she heard in her mom's voice ripped her up inside.

Andie heard loud sobbing and then a muffled sound as her father took the phone. "Andrea, your mom can't talk right now. We're going to go home tomorrow, and then in four days we'll go to Iowa City for the treatment. Call me tonight at home. I've got to go."

Andie hung up and cried into her hands, feeling guilt and grief and fear. She did not want to be home when everyone returned from school and work, so she packed her books and some snacks for Rylee, then went to pick her up from the sitter's house. She wanted to hold Rylee and feel her strong little body in her arms.

She drove to Mike's house and chose a few toys for Rylee to play with. She tried to study for the test that was scheduled for the following day, but her mind was so stricken that she could not concentrate or retain anything that she was reading. She kept hearing her mom's voice and the anguish that it held. Rylee came over to her and patted her leg. "Mama is sad?" she asked.

"Honey...Mama has a little owwie that's hurting her right now," Andie whispered as she wiped the tears from her cheeks. She had been trying not to cry.

"I give you a kiss," Rylee said, and she leaned up and kissed Andie on the cheek. "Better, Mama? You feel better?"

"Yes, sweetie. Your kiss made me feel much, much better." Andie lifted Rylee up and hugged her tightly. "Come on, Rylee, I'll play with you," she said, carrying her over to the toys.

When Mike walked in with his kids and saw Andie's puffy eyes, he said to the children, "Hey guys, in a little while, maybe we'll go outside and play hide-and-seek. Right now, I'm going to talk to Andie in my room while you have a snack." He quickly served crackers and juice at the table, then he walked Andie into his bedroom and closed the door.

"What is it?" he asked worriedly.

Andie told him everything, and he held her as she cried.

"Maybe the treatment will cure her. Some cancer is curable," he said.

"She's done so much damage to her body through the years, drinking and smoking. I just can't stand to hear her so upset. I know she's terrified, and I'm afraid my dad won't comfort her. He's not good at that kind of thing."

"Should you go up there?" Mike asked.

"No. Not now, anyway. I mean, unless she's going to die or something soon," she replied, and began crying harder.

Andie stayed for the spaghetti dinner that she could not eat, and after Mike had taken his kids to their mom's house, he played with Rylee so that she could study for her test. Andie tried to study, but knew that she was not going to be able to finish what she needed to do. She was exhausted and overwhelmed.

After Rylee had fallen asleep, they had a chance to talk. They prayed for her mom and dad, and Mike said a prayer for Andie to have strength and be able to pass her test the next morning. Andie called her dad, who wearily told her that the surgeon had found a mass of squamous cell cancer just below her mother's jaw. The cancer had spread into surrounding tissue, so the surgeon had removed what he could and then closed her up. They were going to run tests to see if the cancer was anywhere else in her body. Her dad told her to call her mom at least every other day. Andie could tell that he was frightened, but was trying to lessen her worry.

"You just concentrate on school, Andrea. Mom wants to see you become a nurse more than anything. She's asleep right now. I don't want to wake her up."

"No, don't. I'll call tomorrow and talk to her. I'm so sorry, Dad." She said good-bye, hearing her father's voice break. She needed to go home and sleep. Mike scooped Rylee up from the bed and put her in her car seat. He told Andie to call him anytime, even at work if she needed him.

The next day, her mind was bleary as she took the test. She prayed just before the test, but as she took it she knew that she had not covered all of the material well enough. She had to guess on many of the questions. The students would find out their grades after lunch.

When the instructor returned them, Andie flipped hers over to see the score; a ninety-two. Somehow, she had made a high grade without studying sufficiently. She nearly started crying from relief. Her emotions were on the verge of being out of control at any moment, and she knew that she would need to get a hold of herself if she was going to be able to function.

Sarah and John said that they would be praying for her mom. Mike had the Bible study praying for her and had put in a prayer request to the church. She told Mike that her parents were not really Christians. They did not disbelieve that Jesus was the Son of God, but they were not spiritually active in any way. He was concerned and told her to try to reach out to them and see if they would accept Christ into their lives, to pray the prayer of salvation. She knew her dad believed that you could get into heaven by "just being a good person." Andie and Mike prayed that there would be others in her parents' lives who would lead them to the light of God.

Her father called her the next week and told her that more cancer was found on her mom's lung. When they biopsied it, they discovered that it was another kind of cancer, small oat cell. Andie asked her dad what the doctor's prognosis was, but he said that one had not been made. They were going to do both chemotherapy and radiation therapy for her neck and lung. The rest of her body appeared clear of cancer.

Her mom always attempted to be stoic whenever she spoke with Andie. She continued working at the cafe every morning and did not sound drunk on the phone. Andie knew that she was probably still drinking, or she would have gone into delirium tremens. She knew, too, that this serious symptom of alcohol withdrawal could result in death for some people if it was left unchecked. At this point, it probably did not matter if her mom drank, unless it interfered with the treatments. The newer anti-nausea drugs had prevented her from experiencing terrible side-effects. She was scheduled to have five more treatments during the next few months.

Andie spent many lunch breaks in the school library researching cancer. What she learned painted a grim future for her mother. Small oat cell lung cancer was incurable and metastasized rapidly, especially to the brain and bone. The squamous cell mass in her neck was near lymph nodes and might have already spread to them, which was like jumping on a super highway to the rest of her body. Andie never told her dad, who seemed to not want to know any more details than necessary. The doctors still had not given her mom a time frame or told her parents about the cure rate. Andie thought it was best to keep their hopes up.

She tried to focus on school, but fear and sadness were always swirling in the back of her mind. She had never given up on the hope that she and her mom could be close, waiting for the day when her mom would somehow become sober, so that she could see all that she was missing. Though there had been many problems and a lack of compassion, Andie still cared about her mother and did not want her to suffer. Her mom had done the best that she could at the time.

A crucial, but difficult, part of becoming a Christian had been forgiving everyone who had hurt her, even Scott, though no one had asked to be forgiven. This freed her from the bitterness that had caused her to relive the bad experiences in her life over and over again, blaming everyone else for her pain. She knew that if God could forgive her for her sins, no matter what they were, then she would have to completely forgive others for hurting her, regardless of their crimes. Now, she was able to think about her parents as people with their own problems due to their own childhoods.

Her mom's mother was a stern, cold woman. Andie had never seen them hug or touch one another, and her mom seemed afraid and subservient around her. Andie knew that her mom had failed to learn how to be a mother because she had never had a good role model, and she had not been able to naturally develop the maternal instinct because her body had not produced children. Andie felt sorry for her mom and wanted to comfort her. She wanted to make up for all that they had missed out on. Alcohol had stolen her mother from her and now this disease was about to take away any hope of having her mom in her life.

Her dad's father was a womanizing alcoholic who had abused his wife. Being an only child, her dad did not have anyone to learn how to communicate with during difficult times. His father had ended up marrying three other women before he had died of a heart attack. Her dad had grown up in the depression era, so he took pride in being able to provide for his family.

When she told them about becoming a Christian, she knew that her father's silence meant that he was not comfortable with what she was telling them. Her mom listened and said "Thank you" when Andie told her that she was praying for her every day. Andie was glad that she had made the decision not to tell her parents who she was really living with. If her mom was dying now, it would have haunted Andie forever to have hurt her with this revelation.

Chapter 38

Sarah watched Rylee on Friday evening, so that Mike could take Andie out to dinner. Andie was surprised when he drove into the parking lot of an expensive French restaurant and parked his truck between a Jaguar and a Mercedes.

"I thought you might like a change from spaghetti and sandwiches," he said.

She was reluctant to order, because the cost for two meals could buy a week of groceries.

"Come on, Andie. Order whatever you'd like. I see you sitting there worrying about the price. But don't, order anything that looks good."

They had a wonderful meal with creme brulee for dessert, which Mike had ordered for her, knowing that she had a sweet tooth. Afterward, they went downtown to walk around Lake Eola. Seagulls were standing on a small beach on one side of the lake, their chests puffed out and beaks resting on the bulge of their craw. The lights of the tall buildings nearby were reflected on the lake's surface. They held hands as they slowly walked around the glassy lake.

"Come over here a minute," Mike said, leading her to a piece of land that jutted out into the lake. Two enormous palm trees stood in the middle of the grassy area. Andie felt the warm night air on her skin and noticed that Mike was staring at her. "You've made my life so complete," he began. "There's nothing that I wouldn't do for you." He knelt down on the grass near her feet, surprising her. It crossed her mind that he had dropped something.

"I can't imagine life without you. I'd be honored if you would share your life with me forever, Andie. Will you marry me?"

She knelt down on the grass with him and put her face close to his, searching his eyes as he smiled. "It would be the best thing in the world to be with you forever. I'd love to marry you." He kissed her and they embraced. They got up from the ground and stood looking at one another. "Oh, one more thing." He reached into his pocket and retrieved a small box. He opened it and took out a ring. Picking up her left hand, he slipped the delicate gold and diamond ring around her finger.

"Oh, Mike, it's so beautiful! I've never seen one like this. How did you…?"

"Leave the details to me, sweetie pie!

She kissed his cheek and hugged him tightly, then they began walking with their arms around one another. Andie kept looking at the ring on her finger. "Did Sarah know about this?" she asked.

"Yes. And I told her that you'd probably be late getting home." He stopped and twirled her around to face him, laughing. "This is it! The rest of our life is now beginning. I promise that I'll be the best husband to you. Things might be a little tricky at first with the finances, but it'll all work out."

"I'm not worried about money. We'll make it. In half a year, I'll be done with school and then I'll be able to get a good job.

"You're going to be the finest nurse in the country."

"I just need to make it through the rest of the year. When should we get married?" Even as she said it, she was amazed that it had actually happened. He wanted to marry her.

"As soon as you'd like. How about tonight?" he asked, smiling broadly and raising his eyebrows up and down mischeviously.

"I'd do it, you know, so you'd better not try too hard to talk me into it."

They stayed out late, discussing their life ahead and wedding plans. They were not sure when to have it, but they wanted a small wedding and decided to ask his parents if they could have the ceremony in their backyard next to the pool. Mike and his ex-wife had been married at the church they attended, so they did not want to have the ceremony there.

When he dropped her off, he gave her a lingering kiss that sent chills through her body.

"Maybe we should get married tonight," Andie said, smiling.

"Patience, my dear, patience. We've made it this far."

That night, she slept better than she had in weeks.

She called her parents and told them that she was getting married. They were surprised and concerned that she was rushing into things. She had never been so sure in all of her life about anything and said that they would see why when they met Mike. Her mom apologized because there would be no way for them to go to her wedding. They were having a hard time covering the shifts at the cafe during her treatment days and did not have the money to fly to Orlando. Her dad said it would be best for her mom to stay close to home, and that they would try to visit as soon as she was better. Andie did not want to seem too excited on the phone because she felt it was unfair to be so happy while her mom was going through such a trial.

Their wedding took place three weeks later in his parents' backyard. Beth had placed red rose petals in the pool, and they floated slowly around in a wide circle. An arched trellis covered with flowers was set up for them to stand under as they said their vows. Laura and Lisa were the joint maids-of-honor, and Michelle and Rylee were the flower girls. Elijah, in his little black suit and tie, was the ring bearer, walking bashfully across the grass toward the family and a group of friends.

Tim and Eric walked Andie down to where Mike waited. He had not seen her outfit before this day and was thrilled to see her in the simple ivory dress with eyeclasp hooks from the waist up, accentuating her slender body. She had rarely worn make-up around him, but that day she took time to get ready and even put on lipstick. She saw the surprised, pleased look on his face and smiled at him.

The children were included in the ceremony, the girls looking like angels in puff-sleeved, white dresses. After they had said their vows, Andie turned to the children, who stood next to them, and promised that she would devote her life to their care. Mike knelt down and held Rylee's small hand, "I would be honored to be your father," he said. "You are so special to me. I love you."

Sarah and Beth began crying as Rylee clapped and said loudly, "I get to stay with you, Mike! At your house!"

They were pronounced husband and wife. Andie and Mike hugged the children to them and then the two of them embraced and kissed. Mike prolonged the kiss and dipped her backwards as everyone clapped and congratulated the exuberant couple. After hors d'oeuvres and cake, they said good-bye to all of the guests. Beth was going to keep the kids until the following evening when they returned from their one night honeymoon.

They spent the night at a fancy hotel on the beach, using money that had been a wedding gift. They were both nervous when they finally settled into the room, glancing at the king-size bed. Mike had not been with a woman in over four years. They stayed up until three in the morning, and the next day they walked on the beach and had a picnic lunch. Joyful and tired, they drove back to their house, where John and Sarah had moved all of Andie and Rylee's belongings that morning.

"Welcome home, my love," Mike said, laughing as he picked her up and carried her across the threshhold. Andie hugged his neck and smiled as she went into her new home. The next day they had to go back to work and school, but they still stayed up again until three a.m.

And every night for weeks they stayed up late, talking and enjoying one another. Unlike most newly married couples, their only time together was after the kids were taken care of and in bed. Andie dozed off a few times during lecture and had to pinch herself awake. She somehow managed to pass her tests with minimal studying. She was doing well in clinicals and looked forward to pediatrics and obstetrics, the next rotation.

She sent pictures of her new family to her parents and continued calling her mom every other day. They were pleased to hear how she was progressing in school, and her mom told her that they wanted to come to her graduation in January. Andie prayed that it would be possible.

Her mom was still managing to go to work each day. She said that she had back pain, but she was taking both the radiation and chemotherapy treatments with no other side-effects besides fatigue and hair loss. Her parents fortieth wedding anniversary was in October and they were hoping to have a big party. It was only a little over three months away, so Andie believed that her mom would be able to celebrate.

* * *

Andie's first pediatric patient was a five-year-old boy named Zacharey. He had AIDS, which he had gotten from his mother while she was pregnant with him. Her husband had committed adultery and contracted AIDS, infecting her and their unborn son. Andie recalled how frightened she had been when she thought that Steve could had given her AIDS. She had been spared this horrible fate.

Entering the room, Andie observed the sandy-haired boy playing with a toy mailbox. Zach was what was referred to as a "frequent flyer." He had spent so much of his young life in and out of the hospital that the staff had watched him grow up.

"See, Mommy. I'm mailing my letter to you. Here it comes!" Zach said, carefully putting the plastic piece into the mail slot, his thin arm moving slowly.

His mother, looking pale and tired, lay on his bed. Andie had heard that she had discontinued her own medications recently, so she would not have the assistance of the drugs to bolster her immune system.

Andie took his vital signs then told his mother that they would be ready in a few minutes to take him to the treatment room. Zach needed a new nasogastric tube put in so he could get nourishment and medication into his emaciated body. His other tube had clogged up from so much medication being put through it without flushing it thoroughly enough afterward.

In the treatment room, the nurse's aid asked Andie to help hold Zach down when the time came to insert the tube. The nurse who was going to insert it was reading over the instructions that came with the tube.

"It's been a while since I've done this kind," the nurse said, mumbling. She looked like she had just gotten out of bed, brown hair disheveled and dark circles under her eyes. She had been called in to substitute for a regular pediatric nurse.

Zach's head was held tightly as the thin tube was inserted through his nose and down into his stomach. He gagged and coughed, trying to hold still. "Is it done?" he said, crying. "Done?!"

The nurse could not hear the sounds in his stomach with her stethoscope when air was introduced through the tubing. If a "whoosh" was heard, the tube was in place. She drew it out of his nose and tried to re-insert it. Zach was arching his back and crying, but Andie could tell that he was trying to control himself. He had been through many procedures.

Again, the nurse did not hear the sounds that were necessary to leave the tubing in place, so she withdrew it.

"Why is this so difficult? Nobody ever had problems before," Zach's mother said angrily. Her skin was an unnatural yellow, and the bright light from above created smudges of shadow below her protruding cheekbones. The nurse seemed agitated and ignored the question as she checked the tubing and came toward Zacharey again.

The thin boy trembled as the tube was introduced into his other nostril. He yelled instead of swallowing when the time came for him to help the tube down through his esophagus by swallowing juice through a straw that his mother offered to him. Andie tried to hold Zach's arms down, feeling as if she were helping to torture him. The nurse leaned over to listen to his stomach. "All right, you're done," she said, looking away from Zach, whose face was beaded with perspiration. After his cheek was dried with a towel and the tubing taped to the side of his nose, the nurse instructed the nurse's aid to clean up and then she left the room.

Andie could not eat her lunch that day. She thought about how Zach had never had a chance to live a normal life, and he never would. Then Andie thought about her mother and how she had wasted so much of her life by drinking. Some people had the chance to live a good life, and others seemed born to suffer. God had given people free will, so their actions affected their lives and the lives of others. Zacharey's father had made a fatal mistake that would kill his entire family. Zach was innocent, so it did not seem fair that he had to suffer. His future had been altered permanently by an act of free will, but Andie knew that God would take care of him in the end.

She felt that she was moving on into a new life with both joy and sorrow. She was grateful for her devoted husband and fine children, and it was still incredible to her that she had found Mike, but her mother in Iowa was not sounding as strong on the phone as she had at the beginning of her illness. Her father complained about the exorbitant medical costs and how tired her mom was becoming from the treatments. He called Andie when he could talk to her without her mother listening. He said that the doctor was going to do a full set of body scans after the treatments were over to see if there was any other cancer in her body. Andie told him that she would be praying.

Mike and Andie's days were full with work, school, and the children and their needs. Marsha had been furious when she learned that he had remarried. She called and told him that if he could afford a wife who did not work and another child, then he should be paying more in child support. Mike was frustrated and hurt when she changed the kids' visitation schedule, taking away the overnight stays and three of the afternoons a week. Michelle and Elijah had seemed to be doing better lately, but after the schedule change they were often withdrawn and anxious.

Andie found Michelle crying one day on the top bunkbed. "Are you all right, sweetie?" she asked. Michelle seemed reluctant at first, but after Andie had rubbed her back and stood by quietly for a few minutes, Michelle sat up.

"I try to make my mom and dad happy, both of them, but it never works. I just don't know what to do. They always fight about us. They never get along!" Michelle cried, her face pink and streaked with tears.

Andie climbed up higher on the bed and hugged her. "It's not your job to make them get along. They're both happy with you, honey, and they both love you. I know you hear them disagree sometimes, and I'm sure it must be upsetting. You and Elijah are so precious to them, and they both want to be with you, so they sometimes argue because you can't be in two places at once."

"I always feel like I did something wrong. They should be happy. I wish they'd never gotten divorced," Michelle replied, new tears forming and threatening to spill over.

"I know what you mean. You're such a sweet girl, Michelle. I want you to be happy, too. Just remember that it's not your responsibility to make anyone happy. I'm here to listen whenever you need."

As the weeks went by, there were more and more days that the kids had something supposedly going on that prevented them from coming on their scheduled days. Rylee even cried about missing them. She loved her new sister and brother and did not understand why they were not able to stay with them all of the time.

Mike and Andie had to keep a tight rein on their budget. They lived from week to week, just making their bills. Amazingly, the single parent program continued to pay for the school's expenses. Andie could have hidden the fact from them that she had gotten married, not knowing how it would affect her grant, but she informed the counselor and was told that she fell under what they referred to as the "grandfather" clause. She was still eligible, so she would continue to receive childcare expenses for Rylee and the twenty-five dollar a week check for gas and lunch. Andie thanked God for putting everything into place once again. She and Mike were prepared to have to manage if she had to pay for childcare and the rest of the tuition, and so they were greatly relieved to not have to take on the burden of somehow coming up with money that was not there.

Andie longed for the time when she would not have the pressures of school and she could get a job to help Mike with the expenses. There was so much that she wanted to buy and do for the children. Rylee had been living with second-hand clothes and toys from garage sales and thrift stores most of her life, and Andie wished that she could go out to a store and buy her something brand new. One day soon, she thought, I'll be able to buy everyone something new and we won't have to worry so much about how to pay the bills.

Mike never complained, but she knew that he was concerned. Their old cars kept needing to have work done, and so he had to repair them himself. He would spend hours trying to replace a part, scanning the instruction manual and becoming frustrated because he did not have all of the right tools. He would come inside afterward, various parts of him covered in grease, shaking his head and hoping he had done everything correctly. But they had each other, and their love had deepened as they became partners in raising their children and taking care of everyday things together. Though life was hurried and often stressful, they were not facing the challenges alone. Mike's calm confidence that God would provide helped Andie to realize that she had to let go of her worries and allow God to take over. He had done wonders in her life already, so she knew that He had her in His care.

Chapter 39

In early September, Andie's father called to tell her that the results from the scans showed a few spots of cancer in her mother's brain. Just weeks before, they were relieved to have found out that the chemotherapy had reduced the size of the cancer in her lung. Now they would need to treat her brain with radiation.

Andie tried to find out what "a few spots" meant, but her dad said that this was all that they were told before the nurse had rushed her mother to the radiation department to start treatment immediately. Andie got the name of her physician in Iowa City and the number for the oncology center at the hospital. Her dad sounded tired and depressed. She told him that she wanted to visit over Christmas, just before graduation in early January. Her dad said that it was a good idea, because there would be no way for her mom to get there for her graduation.

Andie called the hospital and was surprised when she was able to track down the doctor who oversaw her mom's case. Andie told her that she was a nursing student in Florida and wanted to know the facts of her mother's condition.

The young doctor was frank. "We've found eleven tumors in her brain," she said. "One of them is on the brain stem. I'm so sorry to have to tell you this, but as a nurse, you must know what this means. We'll do all we can to prolong her life and make her comfortable."

"What kind of time frame would you expect in a case like this?" Andie asked, trying to sound calm.

"If I had to say...she has maybe three to six months left, if that. These tumors, especially on the brain stem, could cause any number of problems at any time. I'm afraid that she could even have only weeks left, but I'm trying to be optimistic and give you the best case scenario."

Andie thanked her for her time and the information. She hung up the phone and felt a heavy weight pulling her spirit down. Her mom had happily told her the last time they had spoken that she believed she would be cured soon, since the tumor in her lung was responding so well to the treatment. She had related to Andie how she had met a man who had come into their cafe. He had been cured of his cancer and had given her mom even more hope. Now, Andie knew that there would not be much time left. Her parents' wedding anniversary was the following month.

Mike tried to console her, and she attempted to be cheerful, but it was difficult to be light-hearted knowing that her mom would be dying soon and probably dying painfully. She had trouble studying, but continued to pass her tests.

In clinicals one morning, Andie got her assignment amidst the rush of the morning change-over of nurses. She saw that one of her patients was a female, exactly her mother's age, who had cancer. Andie chose to go into her room last for the assessment.

Mrs. Lane was lying in bed looking out her window at the passing clouds. Her short white hair was only an inch long, giving her a look not unlike a newborn baby bird. She had wide cheek bones and deep set blue eyes. Andie guessed that she was Scandinavian.

"Good morning, Mrs. Lane. My name is Andrea. I'm a student nurse who will be helping your nurse care for you today."

"Hello, Andrea. I'm afraid my mouth hurts too much to speak well. Radiation has done this to me." The woman's mouth had ulcers around the lips, and Andie knew there would be more in her mouth and throat.

As Andie assessed her, Mrs. Lane tried to smile as she whispered, "I don't always look like this, you know. I used to take such time with my appearance."

"Your face has such a beautiful bone structure," Andie said.

"You're very kind. The nurses here all run around the room, hardly ever looking at me. This is all so frightening, but no one has time to care."

"Do you have family here?" Andie asked.

"My husband is ill and is at home. He cannot make it out of the house. He also has cancer. My daughter is supposed to be flying down from New York tomorrow."

"I'm very sorry to hear about your husband." Andie reached out to rub Mrs. Lane's shoulder.

"I think I have to go to the bathroom again," Mrs. Lane said suddenly, grimacing. Andie helped her onto the bedside commode, as diarhhea shuddered through the woman's weakened body. "I'm sorry you have to see this," Mrs. Lane gasped, trying to reach around to wipe herself. She could not manage to turn sideways well, so Andie assisted.

"That's what I'm here for, no need to apologize." Andie helped her back into bed, being careful not to let her fall because her legs could not bear any weight without buckling.

Andie checked on her throughout the day, and after lunch she sat down on the side of Mrs. Lane's bed. Though Mrs. Lane was very ill and weak, a glimmer of her gregarious personality was evident. They began talking about dying, because Mrs. Lane had confided that she thought she would not live much longer.

"Do you believe in heaven?" Mrs. Lane asked.

"Absolutely," Andie replied. "It will be paradise."

"I thought I believed at one time, but we have had so much tragedy that I just don't know anymore." Andie sat quietly as she watched Mrs. Lane gather her thoughts.

"The other night I was watching the sunset, and I wanted to fly away into it...and never return to the pain. Then I wondered if I will just cease to exist," Mrs. Lane said quietly.

"If you believe in Jesus Christ, then you have a great adventure ahead of you. It will be better than anything we can ever imagine."

"How do you know for sure?"

"God promises to everyone who's faithful and believes, that they'll have eternal life. I've seen miracles in my own life. It's real, Mrs. Lane. Don't doubt for a moment that your life will be over."

"You are such a nice girl. I've enjoyed this day so much because of knowing that there are still kind people. Thank you."

"Mrs. Lane, do you believe that Jesus is the Son of God?"

"I've always professed to be a Christian, but there have been many things I did not do right."

"Can I pray with you?" Andie asked.

"All right."

Andie reached for her hand and prayed aloud with someone for the first time. She prayed that God would give Mrs. Lane assurance of His love for her and ease her pain. She asked that He heal her body and help her husband during his illness. Mrs. Lane had tears in her eyes when she thanked her. The school day was over, and Andie would have to leave after she caught up on her charting. The students would be returning to the hospital only one more day.

The following day, Andie asked to have Mrs. Lane as her patient. Mrs. Lane's smile, though painful for her to make, welcomed Andie into the room. She spent all of her extra time with Mrs. Lane, who told her that she had been a highly-sought-after graphic artist during her professional life. She said that her eyes and hands were not steady now, so she could not demonstrate her skill.

A knock on the door stopped their conversation, and a young woman came into the room. She looked just like her mother, but with long blond hair and an unlined face. Mrs. Lane introduced her daughter, Yvonne, and then Andie left so they could have privacy.

She went in later to give Mrs. Lane her medication and picked up on the gist of their conversation. Yvonne was trying to convince her mother that she could not be that sick. They had just been shopping only three weeks before when she was visiting. Mrs. Lane was upset and tried to defend herself.

When Andie went in to check on her again, the daughter was not in the room. Mrs. Lane motioned for her to come closer. "My daughter is not used to me being weak. I was a very strong woman, and it terrifies her to see me this way. My husband is her stepfather, so I am all that she has of family. This is making me so tired."

"Try to rest a while. Can I get you anything?" Andie asked.

"No, thank you. Unless you have a spare body for me."

Andie had just walked into the hallway when the daughter approached her. "You're my mom's nurse, aren't you?"

"Yes, I'm a student nurse and I've been caring for her yesterday and today."

"She's really sick, isn't she?"

"Cancer is a serious illness."

Yvonne sagged against the wall, her face crumpling as she began crying. "I don't know what to do. I'm so scared!"

Andie reached out and touched her arm, and Yvonne extended her arms to Andie. Andie stood hugging this woman that she did not know, while the woman sobbed into her hair. When Yvonne had calmed down, Andie told her that she understood her feelings because of her own mother's condition.

"I would make the most of your time together," Andie said gently. "Because you might one day wish that you had enjoyed every moment while you could."

Yvonne nodded at Andie through her tears. "This is so hard," she whispered.

Andie heard a softer tone to Yvonne's voice when she went into the room later. It was nice to hear them laughing together.

At the end of the day, Andie told Mrs. Lane that she would not be caring for her again because the students were moving on to a different hospital, but that she would try to visit her soon. Mrs. Lane smiled sadly and waved at her as she left the room, too tired to speak.

That evening Andie, Mike, and Rylee went to the hospital. Yvonne had gone to her hotel for the night, and so Mrs. Lane was alone when they entered the room. Andie introduced everyone as Mrs. Lane's eyes lit up with happiness.

"I didn't think you were serious when you said that you'd visit," Mrs. Lane whispered.

They spent nearly an hour with her, until Andie saw that she was tired.

"Your daughter is so beautiful. I wish I could draw her." Mrs. Lane tried to push herself up. "Do you have a picture of her?"

Mike opened his wallet and took out a photo of Rylee.

"Could I keep this for a while? Write your address on the back of it lightly, and I will mail you a drawing of her. Yes!" she said excitedly. She struggled, but managed to sit upright. "I'll have my daughter go to the art store tomorrow and buy some good pencils and paper."

"That would be wonderful, Mrs. Lane," Andie said.

"It might not be as good as usual because my hand is shaky. I'll need a lot of light."

Andie could see how much energy Mrs. Lane was getting from her idea. "I would love to see how you draw! We'll be looking forward to it."

Mike asked if they could pray for her, and Mrs. Lane agreed. They stood next to her bed and held hands with her. Rylee put her hand on top of Andie's.

Mrs. Lane was tired, but smiling as she said, "Thank you so much for coming to see me. You don't know what this means to me."

"You're very welcome, and it was our pleasure. We'll talk to you again soon. Have a good night's rest," Andie replied, reaching down and carefully hugging her.

The following week, Andie received a short letter from Mrs. Lane. It was not easy to read because of the nearly illegible words. She wrote that even though she and her husband were not doing well, she was feeling at peace and praying regularly. She apologized for not having started the drawing of Rylee, and said that she would try to as soon as she was able.

Andie showed the letter to Mike, and they talked about how it would be if nurses could all pray for their patients. Andie wanted to write a letter back to Mrs. Lane, but she had three important tests coming up, so she would wait and write the letter as soon as she could.

She was still worried after she spoke to her parents. They were unaware of the seriousness of the brain tumors and believed that they would shrink, just as the spot in her lung had. Andie did not tell them otherwise; she prayed that it could be true. Her mom tried to joke about her hair loss. She had gotten two wigs that she wore, but they were too warm when she stood over the grill at the cafe cooking food. Andie suggested that she take a few days off work to rest.

"Oh, no!" her mom exclaimed. "I've got to work. I'll be fine. I've got a little stool up front now, so I can sit down when I need to. When the radiation is over, I'll have more energy. They said it might take a year for my hair to grow back, though."

Andie knew that her mom would equate quitting work with giving up to the disease to die. She did not want to take away her hope, but it was troubling to hear her sounding so confident when her chances were not very good. Andie prayed that her mom would be cured if it was God's will.

The three nursing exams were supposed to be difficult ones, so Andie stayed up late for almost a week. After passing all of them, she began the reading for the next test. She was counting the days until graduation, and she had saved enough for part of one plane ticket for Christmas vacation. Mike would have to work, so he would not be able to go. Andie made the reservations and planned to stay for ten days. When she returned, she would only have two weeks of class left.

Her mom continued talking about how excited she was to have her home at Christmas. "You haven't been home in years for Christmas!" her mom said. "I have this red coat that's too long for me. It's new and very nice, so you can wear it while you're here. I'll find some warm clothes for Rylee. She's in a size three now, isn't she? And I've got a lot of sweaters you can wear, so don't worry about buying any."

Her dad told her that her mom's face had recently "fallen." Half of her face was slack and her mouth did not move on one side, but hung open. She had trouble keeping herself from drooling, and one eye was drooping and tearing up, interfering with her vision.

Andie opened a letter from her mom. Inside were two photographs of her parents that they had taken for their anniversary. She was saddened by the sight of her mom's puffy wig, and the drooping face and bulging eye made her look terrible. She cried when she read the letter her mother had written in her neat handwriting. "Dear Andrea, Mike, and family: Well, these pictures of me will certainly keep your bugs and mice away. Every one of Dad was so good. I'm sorry I didn't know this was going to happen to my face because we could have had them taken in August. Wish you could be here for our party, but I want you to get your schooling done. I did send a small picture for Rylee's baby book so that someday she'll have one! Hope things are going great for all of you. We love you! Love, Mom and Dad."

The letter reminded Andie that she had never written back to Mrs. Lane. She felt guilty that it had taken so long to remember to reply. She sat down and wrote the letter, telling Mrs. Lane how glad she was to have met her, and that she would still be praying for her and her husband.

The late nights with Mike and the constant studying had taken a toll on Andie. She always felt tired. She would think about her mom and Mrs. Lane battling their illnesses, and she would shrug off her fatigue as best she could. Mike began taking the kids out in the afternoon, so that she could study during the day.

The next week, a large cardboard envelope came in the mail from New York. She opened it and read, "Dear Andrea, I'm sorry to inform you that my mother died last week in her home. This is a very difficult time for me. I was in Orlando all week, and I have just returned to New York. While going through her things, I came across this. I knew my mom really liked you, even though she did not know you long. She would want you to have this.

I want to thank you for being so good to her and for helping me that day in the hospital. My mom said that you were the best nurse she ever had. I hope your mother is doing well. Take care and please know that I am very grateful for your kindness. Sincerely, Yvonne."

Andie opened another large envelope and took out a thick white paper. It was an exquisite drawing of Rylee in colored pencil. Mrs. Lane had drawn an exact likeness of Rylee's face and added a body. She sat in front of a giant doll house, surrounded by toys and animals. The beautiful drawing was without any indication that the person drawing it had a problem with steadiness or vision. It must have taken her days of painstaking concentration to complete it, for it was done and even signed at the bottom "C. Lane."

Andie closed her eyes and tried to fight off the pain. Mrs. Lane had probably not received the letter that she had waited so long to write. She had put off writing it, and now Mrs. Lane was dead. Such care and time had gone into doing the drawing, but she had not taken the time to reply right away to her letter. She had allowed her busy life to keep her from making time for someone.

Andie was depressed all week. She could not forgive herself for taking so long to write the letter. She wondered if Mrs. Lane had even received it. It had probably arrived right around the day that she had died. Andie framed the drawing and hung it in Rylee's room.

The highlight of the week was when she spoke to her parents on their anniversary and heard how happy they sounded. Her mom had made it to celebrate.

Chapter 40

In mid-October, Andie calculated that she had fifty-two days of class left. She wondered what it would feel like to not have to study or have the threat of failure looming daily. There were only twenty-eight people left in her class.

She had told her parents months before that she would be willing to drive up to Iowa and help out at the cafe, but they were always adamant that she needed to finish school. Mike told her that if she wanted to go and stay with them that he could handle things at home. Andie knew that, financially, she needed to start working as soon as possible. She had often thought of getting a job while she was in school, but Mike insisted that they would make it until she graduated.

Grandma Reeves called often. They had developed a closer relationship during the past year than they had ever had. Her grandma lived in town near her parents, but was quite independent, volunteering weekly at a hospital and a high school.

Andie called her grandmother back after she heard her message on the answering machine.

"Andie, I stopped down to the cafe and your mom looks like she's in a lot of pain. She moves around so slowly and just looks exhausted."

"Is it worse than two weeks ago?" Andie asked.

"It's much worse. I want to tell your dad to have her take some time off, but the last time I did, he got upset. I know she wants to keep working, but it's getting ridiculous."

"Oh, Grandma. They never tell me what's going on. She always says that she's feeling fine."

"I know. She doesn't want you to worry. She's really looking forward to seeing you and Rylee at Christmas. I can't wait either! I just hope that she makes it until then."

"Me, too. But I feel like I should be up there doing something right now."

"No. They want to see you stay in school and graduate. Christmas is only a little over two months away and then you'll be here. Just keep praying, sweetie."

"I will. Listen, Grandma, I've got to go. I'll call you soon."

Andie felt she was on the verge of falling apart. She continued to keep moving through the days, tending to the kids, chores, and school. Each time that the phone rang, her heart rate sped up and her mouth would get dry as she answered. She felt like she was going through the motions, biding her time until disaster struck. It was inevitable that she would get a phone call informing her that her mom was in the hospital, or that she had died.

When she was younger, she had been torn by conflicting emotions regarding her mother. There were times when her mom had been so cruel that Andie had pondered how it would be if her mother was gone. It might be easier to have no mother than one who made her desperately lonely and sad from rejection and scorn. Yet when she saw her mom in a situation that made her feel sorry for her, it would cause her chest to ache with pity. What she had really wanted to have die was her mom's alcoholism and lack of compassion for her. She had never stopped wishing that her mom would be pleased with her and love her.

Mike tried to boost her spirits, but there was still an undercurrent of anxiety and fear just below her determined facade. The pressures of school and the financial strain that was a daily reality left her in a troubled state of mind. She was nearly done with a one-hundred-page report, which she would be presenting to the class at the end of the week. She had been up all night two days in a row. There just seemed never to be enough time in one day to take care of everything.

When she managed to sleep a few hours, she often had dreams about her mom. In one dream, Andie was talking to her when her mom suddenly paused and would not move. Andie tried to wake her up, becoming more frantic, and then her mom disappeared. In another dream, she was pushing her mom, who was sitting in a wheelchair, through a set of wide metal doors. Andie would wake up exhausted, with her eyes burning and feeling as if they were full of sand.

The day before her report was due, her father called in the middle of the night. She was finally about to have a good night's sleep, after having finished typing her report just before midnight.

"Andie, I really don't want to call the doctor, but I don't know what to do. Your mom's throwing up in the bathroom and it looks like...well, it looks like feces that's coming out."

"Oh, no! Her intestinal system might be backing up from a blockage or something. Call her doctor and see what she says to do. If it's really bad, maybe you'd better take her to the emergency room."

"Andie, it's not good," her dad said slowly. "I didn't want you to worry, but two days ago they found cancer in her bones—her back and upper legs."

"Dad, you've got to tell me these things! I'm not a child!"

"I know, I know. Mom really wants to see you graduate, and we don't want you to worry."

"I'm coming up there."

"No! You've got to stay in school and take care of your family."

Andie detected the slight note of weakness in his wavering voice. "I'll be there tomorrow night. There's nothing you can say to make me change my mind. Now, go see how she's doing and call the doctor," Andie insisted. She got out of bed and turned on the light.

Mike watched her pack. "When do you think you'll be back?" he asked.

"I'd like to stay until I'm no longer needed. Until it's over."

"How will you get there by tomorrow night?"

"I'll find a way," Andie replied. "She's throwing up feces. I have to go! She's probably not going to make it much longer." She was tossing clothes into a suitcase that she had pulled out from under the bed.

"But it could be months," he said.

She stopped and looked up at him. "It could be. I'll be lucky to have that long with her."

"I'm sorry. I know you need to go. It's just that I'll miss you and I don't know when I'll see you again."

"I've got to go. I may never see her again if I don't. I'll need to get Rylee's things ready and call the school and Mrs. Calloway tomorrow. I should be able to find a flight by…wait a minute. The airlines are probably open now."

Andie let the details of planning push back the sadness and trepidation from the forefront of her mind. She was driven by the conviction that she would not allow anything to prevent her from being with her mother during her final days.

By mid-morning she had called her grandmother, gotten her credit card number, reserved two seats on a noon flight, notified her school, informed Rylee's sitter, and completed packing.

Mike was quiet as he drove them to the airport.

"Call me when you get there," he said as they stood in line to board the plane. "I'll miss you so much."

"Me, too. I really love you," Andie replied. "Thanks for understanding. Pray for us all, okay?"

"Of course I will. I love you guys." Mike kissed Rylee and then Andie.

"Bye-bye, Mike. Here we go, way up high!" Rylee said excitedly. She held her yellow backpack against her chest, eyes glowing at the prospect of flying in an airplane.

He watched them board the plane and then waited for it to leave the gate and taxi onto the runway, leaving his sight.

Once they reached cruising altitude, Andie set Rylee up with crayons, paper, and snacks. She pushed the metal button on the armrest and leaned back in her seat. Her head felt like it weighed fifty pounds. She had told Rylee earlier that morning that they would be visiting the grandma and grandpa she had never met. She explained that her new grandma was very sick, so because she was almost a nurse, Andie would take care of her for a while. Rylee had nodded happily, saying that she wanted to help and would pack her doctor's kit.

Andie thought about school and how it felt as if she were abandoning all hope of securing their livelihood. Mrs. Bosen had to get the director of the nursing program when Andie had called. The director told her that regardless of the reason, even though she had completed most of the program, she would have to "recycle," or start over. There would be a waiting list for the next two classes, so they could not guarantee a position for her. Mrs. Bosen had tried to be reassuring when she told her not to worry.

She knew that her decision would put Mike and their family in a terrible financial situation. The flight alone would set them back nearly a thousand dollars that she would have to reimburse her grandmother. She would have to find money to pay for tuition and childcare if she was going to get back into school. She was so used to living and breathing school that she felt out of sorts to be without the goal of graduating. She had been so close.

Mike had not mentioned anything about money while she was getting ready to leave. She knew he was distressed, but for different reasons. He had told her that he was worried that she would never return if she left.

She insisted that nothing would keep her from coming back, but the strained look had not left his face.

Her father picked them up at the small airport. Andie noticed how much he had aged since she had last seen him. He had a grim look about his weathered face, even when he smiled and greeted them. He seemed more awkward, less sure of himself than she remembered. He tried to hug Rylee, talking loudly to her, demanding a hug and kiss in a playful way, but Rylee grabbed onto Andie and hid behind her.

Andie's mom was waiting at home. The doctor had said to call again if she kept vomiting, but to stay at home and rest if it subsided. She would be quitting work, her dad informed her, though her mom also said that she would go back to work after their visit.

"Your mother's upset that you quit school, but I can tell that she's glad you're here. I'm glad you're here too, Andrea." Her father's hands gripped the steering wheel tightly. They drove through the icy streets.

Dirty strips of snow lined the curbs, and crushed brown and yellow grass was matted down in all of the front yards. Small blobs of snow, like mounds of half-melted marshmallows, dotted the vast fields. Andie thought how fitting the weather was for the occasion. There was no way to tell where the sun was in the sky. It radiated a weak light behind a dense layer of grey haze that encapsulated the world, lowering the ceiling of space.

People appeared pale and wore thick, bulky clothing. They were rushing to and from their destinations with their heads down to ensure safe footing across the patches of ice. An Iowa day in early winter, Andie thought. She had been in places of continuous summer for years and had forgotten the often dismal netherworld of the north during its state of hibernation. She wished that it was a blue sky, sunny winter day with a fresh coat of snow on the land and trees.

They reached her parents apartment building. Her dad said that he would bring her bags in for her, so Andie picked up Rylee and began to walk up the two flights of steps that led to their door. Before she got to the top, the apartment door opened and her mom came into view, smiling. "Andie! Oh, Andie!" she cried.

"Hi, Mom!" Andie said as she hurried up the steps and hugged her with one arm. Rylee sat on Andie's hip, staring at her new grandmother. She was gaunt and her skin color was ashen. She had a thin, cotton turban on her head instead of a wig. The slack side of her face made Andie want to look away, but she continued to smile.

"And this must be my little Rylee. Hi, sweetheart! Grandma has some things for you inside. Come in!" She held the door open and walked in. As they went inside, Andie noticed that her mom was limping, but trying to hide it.

"Here, Rylee!" her mom said. The living room was full of all kinds of toys. It looked like someone had robbed a toy department and started their own store.

"Ohhh," Rylee said in awe.

The two sofas were covered with every sort of stuffed animal, sitting upright on the cushions as if they were going to watch a television show together. There were various colors and sizes of teddy bears, bunnies, jungle animals, and dogs and cats. On the floor were coloring books, crayons, puzzles, a Playdough kit, Barbie dolls, a Lego set, dress-up play clothes, videos, and even more toys hidden underneath the packages in view.

"Mom, you went crazy!"

"I had Dad take me out when I heard you were coming. Go ahead, Rylee! It's all for you, honey." Her mom gestured around the room, moving her torso slowly.

Rylee glanced at Andie, and Andie nodded and put her down on the floor. Rylee walked forward, unsure of where to begin.

"My granddaughter deserves to have fun while she's on vacation!" her mom exclaimed.

Andie's dad was bringing in their bags. "Someone's going to be up late tonight!" he said.

"Would you like something to drink?" her mom asked, reaching out to hold onto the back of the reclining chair.

"Oh, no thanks. We had enough on the plane. I don't even think candy would stop her from the mission she's on." Andie watched Rylee run her hand over the stuffed animals, picking them up and then putting them back into their previous positions.

Her mom sat down on the recliner. "I'm so glad you're here. But I sure wish that you hadn't left school. You could've just come at Christmas."

"It's okay. I can jump back into the program again. I was almost done anyway."

"Well, how long do you plan to stay?" her mom asked.

"I don't know," Andie replied carefully. "I can't start school again until January at the earliest, so we'll just have an extended vacation until you throw us out of here."

"Mama, look! It's a skydancer!" Rylee said, running over and holding up a box that contained a sparkly doll with wings.

"Wow, sweetie! It looks like Grandma is spoiling you from the start. I think you should go give her a big hug and kiss and tell her thank you," she said, hoping Rylee would not balk at the suggestion.

Rylee hurried over to where her grandmother sat and threw her arms across her lap, leaning her head down for a moment. "Thank you, Grandma, thank you!"

Her mom's eyes brightened. "You're welcome! I also bought you some warm clothes and a sled in case we get more snow. That would be nice if she could see snow while you're here," her mom said, turning to look at her.

"I'd like to see some, too. We could build a snowman," Andie said.

"We're going to build a snowman?" Rylee asked eagerly.

"If it snows, we will," Andie replied. "And maybe even snow angels."

"Snow angels? Wow! Can they fly?" Rylee was torn between continuing the conversation and searching through the treasure on the sofas. She looked back and forth at Andie as the adults in the room laughed.

"I'll have to show you sometime, sweetie. You can look at your new toys now."

She and her parents made idle conversation that evening, steering clear of any talk of cancer or doctors. Rylee was a good distraction for everyone. It was a relief to go to bed that night. Her mom had started to look tired soon after they ate their sandwiches, so Andie excused herself and took Rylee to their bedroom.

Andie lay next to Rylee in the big bed, and Rylee put her arm around her neck. "Your mama is nice. Why does she wear that funny hat?"

"Remember that she's sick? The medicine that she takes made her lose her hair."

"And her face is kinda scary. Her eye pokes out, and her mouth moves funny."

"That's all from being sick, Rylee. She used to be very pretty. Never say anything to her about looking funny, okay? That would make her sad and we don't want her to feel bad. She can't help looking different."

"Okay, Mama. I'm really tired. I like sleeping with you."

"Goodnight, sweetpea." Andie kissed her forehead, marveling at how grown up Rylee seemed for an almost three-year-old. She sighed deeply, longing for sleep and a chance for pleasant dreams.

Andie looked over her mother's medications the next day and sorted out the bottles. She wrote down the different times and amounts to take. Her mom had said that she was having trouble keeping up with the right dosages. There were twenty-eight pills to take in a twenty-four hour period. Her mom told her that she had a doctor's appointment the following week in Iowa City concerning the possible radiation treatment for her back.

"Now I know why my back and legs were hurting. I guess the radiation will be like what they did for my lung. It cleared it up pretty good, you know," her mom said.

"I know. That's great. There's so much that can be done these days for cancer, Mom," Andie replied, hoping her enthusiasm was not too transparent.

Her mom maintained a cheerful front for the first three days. She moved slowly, but was able to manage most tasks. It seemed possible that she would be able to continue functioning for months. Then one evening, as her mom was walking out of the kitchen, she suddenly collapsed. Her legs gave out, and she fell against the side of the buffet table, breaking a vase that toppled off and to the floor. She was hunched down and awkwardly straddled over a large ceramic duck, which stood next to the table. Her face was smashed against the side of the table, making her lips pucker obscenely. She was not moving or making a sound. The head of the duck jutted out from between her legs, and Andie wanted to pick it up and throw it against the wall.

She lifted her mom and pulled her up off the duck, but then she silently admonished herself for having moved her without checking for injuries first. Some kind of nurse, she thought to herself. She winced at the startled, frightened look on her mom's face.

"I'm…okay, I'm okay," her mom gasped, blinking slowly and trying to stand. She began dropping to the floor again, but Andie reached out to stop her.

Her dad stood helplessly watching them. He had made a move to assist Andie, but then backed up. He looked like someone who had just seen a body cut wide open, horrified and disgusted.

When her mom was seated in the chair that she had helped her into, Andie told her that she would get her a cane the next day.

"That's what we'll do, Joan," her dad said, sounding relieved to have heard a potential solution.

"I didn't even know it was going to happen," her mom said in a monotone voice. "One minute I was walking, and the next, I just couldn't control my legs."

The cane was only used for two days. Her mom took sliding steps and stayed next to the walls, bracing herself with one hand on the wall and one on the cane. It was still too much of an effort, and Andie could see that she was still at risk of falling. She struggled to get around the furniture, which prevented her from leaning against portions of the walls.

"It's just too heavy a cane. Maybe a lighter one would be better," her mom said, panting from the effort of getting into her chair.

Andie wanted to put off making the phone call, because it would clearly signify that the end was on its way, but she went ahead and called the local Hospice organization and asked for whatever services they would provide for her mother. A nurse was scheduled to come over the next day to assess her needs. She told her mom that she wanted to get the benefits of using the equipment that Hospice offered. Andie worried that her mom was upset because she had called, but she only nodded her head and looked away.

Sally came the next morning, a large, cheerful woman bustling with competency. She filled out paperwork and examined Andie's mother. "Let's get you some other things to make your life easier. You look like you're in more pain than the Tylenol is taking care of. I'll call your doctor and get a prescription for something stronger. Since you have your own fine nurse here, I'll just check in periodically to see if you need anything."

Andie walked the nurse outside after the visit. "How do you handle the payment for everything?" she asked.

"Oh, it's free. You don't need to worry about bills at a time like this," Sally replied, reaching out to touch Andie's shoulder.

Four hours later, a wheel chair, morphine pills, waterproof bed pads, and a pill dispenser were delivered in a van by an efficient young man.

Her mom sat down in the wheel chair, but it hurt her legs, so Andie put a pillow on it for extra padding. Everywhere her mom wanted to go, Andie wheeled her. They rarely tried to leave the apartment, but strolled around through the rooms, leaving long trails of lines in the carpet like spiderwebs.

Soon, her mom could no longer manage to lower herself onto the toilet, so Andie lifted her down and up from the toilet seat, pulling her mom's pants up for her and helping her wash her hands. She was still smoking non-filter cigarettes and usually requested one as she sat in the bathroom. Andie knew that there was no reason to quit now; the damage had already been done.

Rylee played well alone and busied herself with all of the toys and the children's shows on cable TV. Andie's dad had wordlessly delegated all of the household chores—cooking, cleaning, laundry, and care of her mom and Rylee, to Andie. He would go to work and then stay down at the Elk's Club until the late afternoon when he would come home and enjoy the meals that Andie had prepared. Andie knew that he did not want to face the situation, and he had never taken care of a home in any domestic way.

Andie tried to find appealing soft foods that her mom could eat. She complained of not being able to swallow and having lost her appetite, so Andie went to a health food store and bought a large container of protein powder to mix into the puddings and milk shakes that she served. She called Mike each night, and they whispered on the phone. When he said that he could not wait to see her again, it seemed that he wanted her mom to hurry up and die. She knew that he had not meant it that way, but she felt so emotionally worn out that she was irritable. She continued to reassure him that she would be back one day and asked him to rephrase his words. She missed him, but she was totally engrossed in the urgency and critical nature of her mother's health.

While Andie drove her mom to Iowa City for her doctor's appointment, Rylee stayed with Grandmother Reeves for the afternoon. It was too quiet on the hour drive. Andie wanted to talk to her mom, but did not know what else to say. Her mom looked out the window at the farms and withered cornfields that stretched for miles.

In front of the entrance to the oncology department building, Andie realized that her mom would not be able to walk all the way to the door. She left her in the car and went to find a wheelchair. They waited twenty minutes for the doctor to come into the small exam room. Finally, she entered and introduced herself and the older doctor with her, who was involved in the radiology department. Her mom sat facing them in the wheel chair, holding tightly to the purse on her lap.

The man slapped X-rays of her mom's back and legs onto the viewer and pointed out the "hot spots." He appeared to be in a hurry and had a familiar, condescending manner that Andie recognized from a few other doctors she had had to deal with during her clinicals.

"Get up on the table," he said, nodding his head toward the high exam table.

Her mom looked up at him from the wheel chair and then awkwardly searched for a place to put her purse.

"Here, Mom," Andie said as she took the purse, helping her up onto the table.

The doctor held each of her mother's limbs and briskly moved them, manipulating them through their range of motion, asking, "Does this hurt? Does this?"

Her mom gazed at him quizzically, wide-eyed and waiting, answering, "No. A little…yes! That hurts!"

Andie wanted to slap his hands away from her mom and yell, "Of course it hurts, you idiot! She has bone cancer!" Instead, she waited tensely until he finished. Then he told her mom to sit back down in her chair, so Andie helped her and was disturbed to see the trusting, hopeful look her mom placed on the doctors. The doctors were discussing when and how to do the radiation treatment on the bone tumors. They paused for a moment and then her mom said, "Well, I'd really like to—"

But the male doctor ignored her, turning away and talking to the other doctor again. Her mom stared at them, her eyes tearing up and the slack side of her mouth pulled down even more.

"We'll need to make a decision," the woman said finally, looking at Andie's mother, who had turned to look at Andie.

Andie glared at the man and said loudly, with exaggerated enunciation, "What was it that you were trying to say, Mom?"

Her mom glanced at the doctors. "Well, I'd just like to think about it for a little while."

"Fine, fine," the male doctor said. "You just call us when you make up your mind. But you don't want to wait too long." He turned and left the room with the other doctor right behind him.

Andie told her mom that she would be right back. She went out of the room and caught up with the female doctor, asking her questions about the side effects of the radiation. Five minutes later, Andie wheeled her mother through the wide automatic doors of the hospital, out into the cold afternoon.

"Let's stop and get some kind of dessert and a coffee before we go home," her mom suggested.

Her mother wanted to walk into the restaurant, so Andie took tiny steps next to her as they shuffled along. She had her arm around her mom's waist and was practically lifting her for each step. There was an open booth in the front of the dining room near the revolving cake and pie case, so Andie took her right over to it without waiting to be seated by the hostess.

They each ordered a piece of pie and coffee. Andie thought how enjoyable it usually was to sit in a restaurant, but right now she could not relax.

"Andie, what do you think I should do about the treatment?"

Andie poked holes in the top of the pie crust with her fork. "Well, how do you feel about it?"

"I don't know. These trips down here are just getting to be too much."

"The doctor did mention that you could go to the clinic near home for treatment."

Her mom ate one bite of pie, then pushed her plate away. Her coffee cup shook as she raised it to her lips. Some coffee dribbled out of the slack side of her mouth, and she hastily tried to blot it.

"Just think about it for a while. There's no rush," Andie said.

They ordered blueberry muffins to take home to her dad. Her mom opened her purse and took out her wallet, putting a twenty-dollar bill on the table and sliding it toward Andie. She took her driver's license out and stared at it, running her thumb across it. "That's when my face was normal." She continued looking at it for a moment and then handed it to Andie. "Look at me." It had been issued just before she had been diagnosed with cancer. She was smiling and her hair was her own.

"They gave me a choice to renew it for one, two, or four years. I paid for four years…I guess I was being too hopeful. I didn't know." Her mom attempted to wipe up the spilled coffee in front of her. "I just didn't know."

"Oh, Mom," Andie replied, feeling inadequate for her lack of words.

"I'd like to go home now," her mom said, trying to make her way to the edge of the seat. Andie helped her up, and they paid and left with their bag of muffins.

It took her almost ten minutes to get her mom up the two flights of steps and then into their apartment. She kept remembering what the doctor had told her, "She needs to be very careful. The tumors have weakened her bones, and if she falls or twists the wrong way she could cause a stress fracture to her spine or legs." Andie understood that the bones would eventually deteriorate, but she did not want to think about what that would mean. She knew that her mom feared going into the hospital because she was afraid that she would die there.

By early November, Andie was taking care of everyone as they all became needier. Rylee wanted her to play and no longer wanted to take a daily nap. Her dad was leaving dishes around the house and asking for drinks whenever Andie was near the kitchen. Her mom had become restless at night. Andie would hear her call out to her, so she would go into her parents' bedroom and get her out of bed. She would wheel her through the apartment in her chair, transferring her back and forth to different chairs in the living room to find the most comfortable position. Nothing seemed to ease her ever-increasing pain.

The Hospice nurse called to check in with Andie, and it was decided that another step needed to be taken. A hospital bed was delivered and set up the next day. Andie found a spare set of sheets with red roses on them and a matching comforter for the stark looking bed. Bringing in the hospital bed seemed a drastic step to Andie, but her mom did not question or complain about the decision.

"This might sound bad," her father said to her in the kitchen. "But, I've been worried about waking up and finding her dead next to me. It's really been worrying me." He was relieved that her mom would be sleeping in the living room. Andie put a bell next to the hospital bed for her mom to ring at night and summon her. The distant ringing would pull her out of a deep sleep, and she would rush into the living room trying to clear the need for rest out of her head.

Scott had come over twice. He was still loud when he spoke, as if all that he said was very important and needed to be broadcast to everyone. He made superficial comments to her mom about getting better and needing to eat more. He did not stay long either time, but was civil to Andie as he had always been in front of her parents. His arrogant manner was so irritating that Andie had to leave the room for a while. Rylee hid behind Andie when Scott had tried to talk to her; she was a good judge of character. They were both glad when he left.

The doctor's office called and asked if they should schedule the radiation treatment. Andie, indecisive, stood holding the phone and looking over at Rylee, who was watching TV. Her mother was in the bedroom, lying down for a nap. It was difficult to keep Rylee content now unless she was playing in front of the TV, but the hospital bed was in the living room, so her mom often went into the bedroom during the afternoon to rest.

Andie asked the receptionist to wait, then she walked to the door of her parents' bedroom. Her mom lay on her back, breathing heavily in the slow, stertorous way that indicated she was asleep. Andie walked over to her and stood looking down at her thin body. Her turban had slipped off one side of her head, revealing her dry, gray scalp, which had sparse wiry hairs flattened onto it, and she had taken her false teeth out. There was spittle shining in the corner of the slack side of her mouth. She could easily be mistaken for an eighty-year-old, Andie thought. An ashtray full of cigarette butts was on the night stand.

She imagined trying to take her mom down the two flights of steps. Her mom had not been out since her last doctor's visit. The treatment was supposed to help slow the tumors' growth, but was likely to damage her bladder and intestines. The doctor had said that there was a chance that the radiation would not impede the growth of the tumors much, but it was all that they could offer her as palliation. The risk of falling while going out for the treatments seemed worse than the potential benefits. If her mom broke a bone, it would be devastating.

Andie walked out of the bedroom and picked up the phone in the living room. "No, we don't want to schedule any treatments, thank you."

She told her parents that evening that she thought her mom should wait to have more treatments. Her mom was watching her, but did not comment. Andie had trouble meeting her eyes.

"I think it's best to wait," her father said.

"When you feel a little stronger, we can call back and schedule something here in town." Andie said. "Then you won't have to sit in the car so long, Mom."

Her mom turned away and looked at the sliding glass door that led to the back porch, but only a reflection of herself in the wheelchair filled her vision. She reached up to adjust her turban.

Chapter 41

Andie's birthday was the next day, and Rylee was very excited. She had hidden a stack of papers that she had been working on for her mom. She had ripped her favorite pictures out of a coloring book after carefully filling the images with pretty colors. She tried to draw a red heart at the top of each page, but she was not happy with how they had turned out. Rylee imagined her mom's face when she would surprise her tomorrow. She had told her mom that she was going to give her a big birthday party, but she was worried because nothing had been planned, except for the pictures that she had colored.

Her mom seemed sad lately and did not really play with her anymore. She was always busy with her grandma, who could no longer walk. She had walked when they first got there and even laughed, but now she never laughed or smiled.

Rylee had heard her mom crying in their bed a few times at night and it frightened her. She stayed still in the bed and just listened to her because she was afraid that her mom would be even more upset if she asked her why she was crying. She knew that it had to do with her grandma being sick.

Her grandma did not talk to her much anymore either. She would just sit in different chairs and in the big bed that was in the living room. She would look like she was sleeping with her eyes closed, but then she would ask her mom to get something for her or help her move to another chair. When she ate, food dribbled out of her mouth. Rylee thought she needed a bib.

She did not like to see her mom's face all worried and tired. She used to smile and joke around, though she would still try, but Rylee could tell that she was making herself act happy because her eyes were still sad and her voice sounded different. She wanted to make sure that her mom had a good birthday and that there would be cake and ice cream and balloons. She imagined a table full of brightly wrapped presents and games to play. Her mom would be so excited to see all of the pictures that she had made. She had even managed to stay inside the lines on most of them, which would make her proud.

She fell asleep that night, hoping that she would not hear her mom crying so close to her birthday.

* * *

Andie was up all night with her mom. The liquid morphine that was to be given every four hours for pain seemed to offer no relief. Sally had been over again and told Andie that it was time to make her mother as comfortable as possible.

When her mom coughed, she would have trouble catching her breath. Her lungs sounded congested and full of phlegm, but nothing would come up. In the corner of the living room sat the oxygen machine, which she used mostly at night, but she was needing it more often. Once, Andie had left the room and come back in to see her mom with the nasal cannula in, the loud chug of the oxygen machine going, and she was lighting a cigarette. Andie had yelled "No!" and run over to flip the switch off. She had previously instructed her mother to never smoke with the oxygen going because it could ignite, but she had apparently forgotten. She did not leave her mother alone after that, because she still insisted on having her cigarettes handy.

Andie watched the sun come up and remembered some of her other birthdays when she was a child. Her mom always had presents on the kitchen table waiting for her when she came downstairs. She was allowed to have a birthday party that all of her friends looked forward to. They would go to places like the pizza restaurant, which had giant ice cream sundaes for dessert, or swimming at the recreation center that had an indoor pool. Her mom always ordered a chocolate cake with white buttercream frosting, decorated elaborately.

Andie looked at her mom, who had finally fallen asleep in the hospital bed with the oxygen flowing into her nose. Rylee would be up soon, and Andie knew that her daughter was expecting a birthday celebration. Grandma Reeves, Scott, and his girlfriend were supposed to come over later for dinner, but nothing else was planned. Andie would have preferred to not even look at Scott on her birthday, but she knew it was important for her parents to feel that they were a happy family. For her mother's sake, Andie would not complain or insist on her own way. She knew that this would be the last birthday that she would be sharing with her mom.

Her mom awoke, so Andie got her out of bed and into the bathroom. She would have to mention using adult diapers soon. Andie had been able to lift her, because her mom had used some of her own strength to raise herself up, but now she was unable to help. Both of their bodies shook as Andie lowered her onto the toilet seat. Andie had bought some baby wipes for her mom to use, because she was no longer able to get into the shower or bathtub. Andie had given her bed baths with soapy water, but her mom would not let her clean her completely, out of modesty.

They were in the kitchen, her mom's wheelchair pulled up to the table. Andie was trying to help her eat some yogurt with protein powder, but her mom had trouble swallowing. She only spoke now when it was absolutely necessary because it took too much energy.

Rylee trotted into the kitchen and ran over to Andie. "Happy birthday, Mama!" she exclaimed.

"Thank you, sweetie," Andie replied, hugging her and then looking over at her mom.

Her mom frowned, "Oh no, it's your birthday today! I forgot."

"That's okay. Don't worry about it."

Her mom pushed herself away from the table and tried to wheel backward in the chair. "No, it isn't. Take me to my room. Please." Andie got up and wheeled her down the hallway into her bedroom.

"Just put me over there." She pointed to a spot next to her dresser. "Could you open that drawer for me? I'll call you when I'm ready."

Andie waited in the hallway for a few minutes. She could hear the drawer closing and the sound of paper being handled.

"All right!" her mom called out.

Andie pushed her back into the kitchen. Rylee had followed Andie and stood by quietly watching them. Her mom handed her the puffed out envelope that she had on her lap. "Happy birthday," she said.

Andie opened the envelope, which was not sealed, and read the card. Her mom had written "I love you very much, Mom" in terribly scrawled handwriting. Inside the envelope was her mother's diamond pendant necklace that Andie's father had given to her on their wedding day. Andie felt all the air leave her chest. She burst into tears. Her mom had turned her face away while Andie opened the card, but her body shook as she tried to hold back from sobbing. Her face looked even more disfigured as tears wet her strained cheeks.

"Thank you, Mom," Andie whispered as she bent down to hug her mom's quivering body. She wanted to tell her that she could not take the necklace, but knew she would insult her if she did. It was her mom's favorite and one that Andie had admired all of her life. Her mom just kept shaking her head and then lowered her face toward her lap again, overcome with emotion.

"Mama, that's a pretty necklace." Rylee looked at Andie, her forehead wrinkled in concern. She wanted to cheer her up, because her mother was much too sad for having just gotten a nice gift. She could not understand why they were crying.

"Yes, it's the most beautiful necklace," Andie said quietly.

Andie's mom was trying to stop crying. "Could I have a tissue?"

She looked at her mother blowing her nose and sniffling, wanting to say something, but not knowing how to begin. "Are you hungry, Mom? I'll make some pancakes, or there's that new kind of yogurt I bought for you."

"No. I couldn't eat a thing." She gazed vacantly at the window, her jaw clenched.

Andie went to the counter to start a pot of coffee, and then Rylee wanted breakfast, so Andie poured a bowl of cereal for her. Andie knew that her mom would not be comfortable talking about anything at the moment, and Rylee was looking perplexed and anxious as she chewed her Cheerios.

That evening Scott was late. Andie had spent a long day trying to keep her mom comfortable. She had to give her extra liquid morphine throughout the entire day. No one had gotten a cake, and there were no decorations. Andie knew that if her mom realized that no one had gotten a cake for her birthday, she would be upset.

Her mom was in the hospital bed in the living room. She was sitting up and trying to see out the window. "Where is he?" she asked irritably.

"I don't know, Mom," Andie replied, setting the dining room table for dinner.

"Well, he'd better get here soon. I'm sick and tired of waiting!"

She had never heard her mom speak negatively of Scott. Andie went into the kitchen and unwrapped an old loaf of pound cake, setting it next to a bowl. She got out a bag of powdered sugar, milk, butter, and vanilla and began to mix up frosting. She tried to spread it over the pound cake, but the cake crumbled and fell apart. When it became apparent that the cake was hopeless, Andie started crying. She chided herself for being a baby. So what if there was no birthday cake, she told herself. But her mom already felt bad enough about forgetting her birthday, and she wanted to keep her from becoming more upset. Rylee would also be expecting a cake.

"Darnit! Where is he?" her mom said angrily.

"I'll call his apartment, Mom." Andie cleaned up the mess of crumbs and frosting.

"No, no, no. He's always late. He can never, ever be on time. I'm so sick of his crap!"

Grandma Reeves was trying to appease her. "Joan, I'm sure he'll be here shortly."

"I doubt it. You can't count on him for anything!" her mom argued.

Andie's dad stood in the hallway with his hands in his pockets, listening and shaking his head.

"He's so selfish. I'd like to tell him to not even bother coming over. I'm sick of this!" she said.

Andie knew that Scott would be walking in the door any moment. She had always wished that her mom had seen him for what he was and confronted him, but it should not be done on this night. If her mom died soon, the last time that Scott would have with his mother would be negative. More than anything, Andie did not want her mom to regret the way she had behaved. She took the liquid morphine and told her mom that she was due for her medication. She squeezed extra into her mouth. Soon her mom lay back on her pillow, mumbling still, but subdued.

Scott came in with his girlfriend, a petite blond woman with a shy smile, and he carried on in a flamboyant manner. Andie watched her mom, who greeted him calmly and was fighting to keep her eyes open. The birthday party had started. Rylee cried when she found out that there was no cake, so Scott's girlfriend drove to the grocery store and bought one. She seemed like a nice young woman, Andie thought, a little subservient, but one would have to be to stay involved with him.

When the lasagna was eaten, Andie cleared the table and brought her birthday cake out to the dining room table. She let Rylee put as many candles as she wanted on it and told her how nicely she had arranged them. Her mom had not eaten dinner, and she looked nearly asleep. Andie was about to light the candles on the cake.

"Wait!" her mom said. "Bring me over to the table."

Andie helped her into the wheelchair and parked her at the table next to everyone. Rylee started the singing, and Andie had to keep herself from crying when she heard her mom's croaking voice joining in. When the song was over, Andie looked at her mom, who smiled at her and tried to pat her hand, whispering "Happy birthday." She was bent forward in the chair, as if her body could not support itself any longer. She asked for a piece of cake, but took one bite and then put her fork down. She was trying to adjust her body's position in the wheelchair.

"Would you like to lie back down, Mom?" Andie asked.

Her mother hesitated a moment and then sighed. "I'm sorry, but it really would feel better."

Scott and his girlfriend left soon after the cake and ice cream. Grandma Reeves offered to come over and help anytime. Her dad went to watch TV in his bedroom, and her mom feel asleep with the oxygen machine pumping steadily next to her.

Rylee had quietly followed everyone around until they left, then she hurried to the bedroom and returned with the stack of papers held to her chest. "Mama, I have a surprise for you!" She proudly offered the papers to Andie, who was sitting on the floor, leaning against the sofa.

"Oh, my goodness!" Andie exclaimed. "Did you make all these for me?"

"Yes! They're for your birthday! Happy birthday, Mama!"

"You made such beautiful pictures! Do I really get to keep these?" Andie asked, looking carefully at each one.

"Oh, yes! And I can make you more! A whole lot more!" Rylee said, jumping up and down in little hops, just as she always did when she was excited.

"Thank you so much! These are the most wonderful presents I've ever gotten. You are some kind of artist, Rylee."

Rylee put her arm around her mother's neck and slipped onto her lap. She smelled her mom's familiar scent and nestled closer to her warmth. I made her happy, Rylee thought, her smile is a real, happy smile. She let out a deep breath, feeling a great sense of accomplishment. She believed that mamas were the best thing in the world. Rylee looked up at her mom's face and knew that she was safe.

CHAPTER 42

"Why hasn't Grandma Crouse come again to see Mom?" Andie asked her dad. She had visited one time since Andie had been there, but only lived thirty miles away.

Her dad restrained his anger as he replied, "She says that she has bridge club and church functions, so she'll come when she can. Last time she was here, she only stayed half an hour."

"Mom must wonder where her mother is, don't you think?"

"I called her and told her that Joan's not doing well and might not make it much longer. She just listened and said she'd be in touch. It really burns me up! I'd like to tell her where to go!" he exclaimed.

"Shh, Dad! Mom might hear you. I'll call her later tonight and talk to her. Maybe she'll come soon."

"Better you than me, because I'd probably end up biting her head off. This just stinks!"

"I don't understand it either. But then, they've never been close."

"Well, I'll never understand it. The woman is heartless!" her dad said angrily. "I've got to go down and close up the restaurant." He stepped into his shoes by the door and shoved his arms through the sleeves of his jacket. The apartment wall shuddered from the force of the door closing.

Andie was bleary with fatigue after another night of no sleep. Her father had already left for work again, and Rylee was still asleep. She sat next to her mother in the morning light. A morning news show was on TV, the announcer talking about where the best vacation spots were to escape from winter.

"Andie," her mom said. "I need to make a list. A Christmas list, so I can go out and get everyone their gifts."

On a small notepad, Andie wrote down her relatives' names. Her mom told her what to write for each person.

"I'd like to go to the mall, maybe later today or tomorrow and get this done." Her mom pushed the button to sit herself upright in the hospital bed. Andie had not seen her this energetic for days.

"Well, Mom. I don't think it's a good idea for you to go out yet." Andie watched her mom's face sadden. She looked as if she might cry.

"You don't think I can?" her mom asked.

"I mean, you could, but it would be easier if I did the shopping for you. The front walk is still icy and the stairs are a little tricky. As soon as you have a bit more strength, we'll go out." Andie felt terrible for having to take away one of her mother's greatest pleasures—buying gifts for others, especially at Christmas.

"Oh." Her mom looked away from her, turning toward the wall.

"Just tell me the colors and sizes for everyone, and I'll bring some things back here. If you don't like them, I'll return them and try again, okay?" Andie would have done anything to take away the grief that her mom held so tightly inside.

"I'm tired. I'm going to rest now," she muttered.

"I'm sorry, Mom."

Andie went down to the storage room in the basement of the apartment building. Before turning on the light, she stood still in the cold darkness and tried to regain her composure. It was getting more difficult to remain strong. She prayed as she walked forward to the side where her parents stored their belongings. It was nice to have a moment to herself during the day, though it seemed wrong to think of herself at all.

Andie wanted to find a few old photos for Rylee. She located a big box full of loose family photographs that had never made it into a photo album. While digging through the box, she saw a shoebox wrapped in frayed twine. Inside were two stacks of greeting cards. Sifting through them, she found that they were all to her mom. She saw her own scribbled handwriting inside a slightly yellowed Mother's Day card. Andie's penmanship had improved with each year. Her mom had saved all of them. Every single card that Andie had ever given to her was in the box.

The Christmas shopping list was finished. Andie drove to the mall alone, while her dad took care of her mom and Rylee. She parked in the crowded mall parking lot and went into her mom's favorite department store. Her mother had instructed her to buy quality gifts and told her to take the envelope of money that she had hidden in her sock drawer.

Andie made the selections and felt almost dizzy from the rushing crowds and the loud, colorful environment. There was no sickness here, no sadness or pain. Everyone had Christmas on their minds, oblivious to the life-threatening dilemmas that some people faced. Andie felt out of place and knew that her mom would have been overwhelmed by her inability to function here in the busy store. It may have made her more aware of her decline into helplessness. Still, Andie could not forget the look on her mom's face when she had told her that she should not go out.

She found some warm socks that had skidproof rubber lines on the soles and bought two pairs for her mom. They would help in the linoleum-floored bathroom when she was getting in and out of her wheelchair. She also bought a Christmas card for her parents and a container of hot chocolate mix. Andie remembered a winter when she was young. After they had all shovelled the driveway, her mom had made hot chocolate for everyone. She could not decide what to get her mom for Christmas, so she would wait for another day to buy it. There was exactly one month until Christmas. She hoped her mom would make it that long.

At night, Andie prayed and read the Bible. Certain passages seemed to reach out and give her extra comfort. She now prayed that God would not let her mother suffer. She needed to talk to her mom about God and offer to pray with her. She was waiting for the right time, but knew that it had to be soon.

Her mom had liked the gifts that she had chosen and asked her to wrap them. Andie's father said that they should wait to put up the Christmas tree, but she went to the storage room anyway and found the big artificial tree jammed in its bulging box, dragging it upstairs. She set it up in the living room by the picture window, right across from the hospital bed. Her mom slept while Andie assembled the tree. When her mom woke up, Andie had Christmas music playing and the tree lights on.

"Oh, how pretty! It's beautiful." Her mom struggled to get a better look.

"Rylee helped decorate. She did a good job," Andie said, patting Rylee on the head.

"Very nice, Rylee," her mom said. "Can you sit me up more?" She had forgotten that she could use the button to raise the head of the bed. Andie walked over and pushed the button for her. Her mom drifted in and out of sleep. She would only eat a few bites of pudding laced with protein powder and had more trouble swallowing the Pedialyte that Andie had mixed with crushed vitamins.

That evening Andie took her Bible out to the living room and tried to wake her mom up. "Mom? Can I talk to you a minute?" she asked loudly, over the drone of the oxygen machine.

"Yeah, okay, I'll get it," her mom replied sleepily.

Andie raised the head of her bed all the way up and then shook her mom's shoulder lightly. "Mom, listen! This is important!" Andie said urgently.

Her mom opened her eyes and looked at her. "Oh. Okay."

"How do you feel about God?"

"What? What do you mean?"

"Do you believe that Jesus is the Son of God and died on the cross for our sins?" Andie asked, trying to fit everything in before her mom fell asleep again.

"Well, yes. I do." Her mom blinked and frowned, attempting to focus.

"Good. And you know that He offers eternal life to those who believe and are faithful?"

Her mom nodded.

"Since you don't go to church, I thought I'd see if you wanted to pray with me."

Her mom was staring at her intently. "All right."

"There's a prayer that people can say if they're ready to turn their lives over to Jesus. But first you have to make the decision, and then you should ask for forgiveness for your sins. You also need to forgive others for their sins against you. How do you feel about this?" Andie asked.

Her mom's lower lip began trembling. She started to cry, but her eyes remained on Andie. Andie leaned over and hugged her thin body. Her mom sobbed and coughed, her body shaking with grief. "I've been so weak!" she cried. "I was so stupid!"

"No, Mom! You did all that you could in everything. Nobody is ever perfect!" Andie said. "Only Jesus was. Now, listen to this prayer when I read it and see if it's something you believe and want to say."

Andie read a prayer of salvation. When she finished, her mom said that she wanted to say the prayer. Andie read the lines, and her mom repeated them. She placed her hand softly on her mom's head and silently thanked God for the chance to be with her and help her. They prayed the Lord's Prayer together, which her mom knew by heart.

Andie knelt on the floor next to her, holding her hand as they looked at the Christmas tree. "You know what? I'm going to make some hot chocolate for us," she said.

"Oh, good!" her mom replied. Her smile was lop-sided, but she looked beautiful to Andie. "Don't make mine too hot."

"I won't."

They sipped their hot chocolate, Andie helping lift the cup to her mom's mouth, and listened to the Christmas music that played on the portable cassette player.

Outside, snow began to fall.

Grandma Crouse came the next afternoon to visit. Andie's prompting on the phone did not cease until her grandma had promised to come. Andie sat with them in the living room, amazed at the lack of real conversation during the short visit.

"Wilma Nelson had hip replacement surgery last week," Grandma Crouse said. "She'd been having such trouble for years. She should've had that surgery long ago."

"Really?" Andie's mom replied.

"Oh, yes. She was barely able to get down the stairs of the church for quilting group."

"That's too bad."

Grandma Crouse looked at her watch. "Seems that most folks get right back on their feet afterwards."

Her grandmother, a wealthy widow who lived in a small town, continued to talk about herself and her friends. Andie's mom sat in the hospital bed, looking like a child poised to receive any stray bit of attention. She nodded eagerly at her mother across the room.

"Well, I guess I'd better be going. The snow has started up again, and I don't want to get stuck." Grandma Crouse had been there under an hour.

"Okay. If you really have to," Andie's mom said sadly.

Grandma Crouse walked into the kitchen following Andie and made her departing statements. "Good to see you, Andrea. Such a cute little girl you have. Let me know if there's anything I can do." She began to walk out of the kitchen.

Andie grabbed her shoulder and waited for her to turn around. "There is something you can do," she said.

"Oh? What?"

Andie leaned forward and whispered vehemently, "Go give your daughter a hug." She boldly met the eyes of her grandmother, who had a startled expression that quickly turned to one of disdain.

"Well," her grandma said, turning to go into the living room on her way out.

Andie rinsed a cup at the sink and then followed Grandma Crouse.

"All right then, I'll be going," her grandma said loudly. She stood beside the hospital bed. Slowly, she reached her hand out to touch her daughter's frail shoulder. Andie watched her grandma bend down to hug her mom. Her mom lifted her arm up and put it around Grandma Crouse's neck in an awkward half embrace.

"Thanks for coming," Andie's mom said too happily, drawing back to look at her mother, who only nodded curtly and then walked to the front door.

"Uh-huh. We'll talk to you later, Joan," she said, walking out the door.

It was the last time that she would see her daughter alive.

Chapter 43

Andie had to call Grandma Reeves and ask for help, because she was beginning to feel sick from the lack of sleep. It seemed that her mom had no trouble sleeping on and off throughout the day, but in the night she would be awake and full of pain. She planned to pick her grandma up after dinner, so she could stay during the night while Andie tried to sleep.

Some old friends of her parents were planning to come over and visit. Sandy, always cheerful and energetic, said that she was bringing a casserole for dinner. Andie gave her mom a bed bath, then chose a comfortable cotton sweatsuit that went well with her mauve turban.

"Do you want to wear earrings?" Andie asked.

Her mom paused. "Well, why not!" she said enthusiastically.

"Okay, here you go. How about this necklace and these earrings? And here's a pin that goes with them." Andie put the jewelry on her mom and then wheeled her out of her bedroom.

Her mom turned to look into the long oval mirror hanging on the wall. Smoothing the front of her shirt down, she said, "Okay! Looks fine!" Her face had become more pulled down on the one side and her eyes were sunken in. Her gray skin color was not completely hidden under the make-up that Andie had carefully applied.

Her mom sat in the hospital bed, trying to follow the conversation. The morphine had affected her reaction time to everything, but Sandy filled in the awkward pauses with her kind laughter. The couple did not stay long. They wanted to visit, but Sandy said that they had brought the casserole over for everyone else to eat. "It's the first time I've ever made it. I hope it's good," she said.

After they left, Andie set the table and served the ground beef and cheese casserole, which was encased in a gooey dinner roll shell. Andie was hungry and began to eat, relieved to have dinner prepared for her. She looked over at her mom, who was frowning and slowly chewing. Her dad looked at her with wide eyes and then shoved his plate away. Rylee had not wanted any casserole, so she was having a peanut butter and jelly sandwich.

"This has got to be the worst thing I've ever eaten!" her mom said.

"It's like meaty glue!" her father exclaimed, a revolted look on his face.

"I was too hungry to notice on the first bite, but now that you mention it..." Andie said, beginning to laugh.

They all looked at the large pan of casserole still sitting in the middle of the table.

"We'd better not give the pan back to her for a few days, or she'll know that we didn't like it," her dad said, starting to chuckle.

"Yeah, but one day soon, she'll make this for her family and find out what she put us through!" Andie said, laughing harder.

Her mom started giggling, then laughing and patting the table.

"Poor Sandy, she never was much of a cook!" her dad roared.

"Poor us!" Andie's mom said, gasping for breath as she brayed laughter.

They laughed for minutes. When they would stop, one of them would snicker, and then they would all begin again. Rylee laughed along with them, pleased that they were having so much fun for once. "Meaty glue, meaty glue," she sang, enjoying the laughter that followed.

Andie heated left-overs for them and then made hot chocolate for everyone. They sat in the living room around the Christmas tree, listening to music as the snow fell heavier and faster outside.

"Mama, when will the snow angels get here?" Rylee asked from where she stood by the window, watching the cascade of drifting white.

"Probably soon," Andie said, sharing a smile with her parents.

Later that evening, her dad went into his bedroom to watch TV. Andie put Rylee to bed early, next to a pile of books that she told her she could look at before she fell asleep. She picked up Grandma Reeves, and when they walked back into the apartment, her mom was having more difficulty breathing. Andie hurried over to her and put the head of her bed in a more upright position. She turned up the flow of oxygen slightly and gave her more liquid morphine.

"Joan, are you all right?" Grandma Reeves worriedly asked.

Her mom shook her head, darting her eyes around, panting for air. The breath sounds she made were gurgling, desperate gasps. They sat by her side and watched helplessly as she struggled. Andie tried to give her a morphine tablet crushed in pudding, but her mom was unable to swallow it. Her dad came out and stood looking at her mom, a pained expression on his face.

Suddenly her mom gagged and a gush of frothy, yellow-white liquid spewed out of her mouth. She sat forward and coughed as more thick fluid poured from her. She looked frantically at Andie as she choked, seeming to plead for help. Andie could see the terror in her wild eyes.

"Hold on, Mom," she said. "Dad, go get some towels. Grandma, help her with this." Andie gave her grandma a wad of tissue that her mom was reaching for to wipe her face. Andie helped her mom lean forward so that she would not fall sideways as she retched.

She had the morphine bottle ready and when her mom finished, she gave her a triple dose on the inside pocket of her cheek. She did not know how much morphine she could safely give, but at this point, she knew that her mom should have every chance for comfort.

Her mom sat back, exhausted and terrified. She tried to speak, but it sounded like gargling.

"Just lie back and try to relax, Mom."

Her mom tried to get out of the bed by rolling sideways. Andie held her arm gently, but firmly. "I'll help you get up in just a minute, okay?" She hoped the morphine would kick in soon so that her mother could relax.

When her mom closed her eyes, Andie picked up the sodden towels and then cleaned up the area. Her mother continued to rest. If she appeared to begin struggling to get out of bed, Andie would give her a small amount of morphine. Finally, she remained still for hours, occasionally opening her eyes and trying to talk.

Her dad said that he had to get some sleep. They had all sat by the hospital bed for over three hours. Grandma Reeves told her to go to bed.

"You've got to come and get me if she vomits again or even wakes up, all right?" Andie said.

"I will, honey. You need to rest so you've got some strength. You look so tired. Go on, I'll be fine."

Andie checked the oxygen machine and put the bottle of morphine in the kitchen cupboard. She got into bed next to Rylee and turned toward her, studying her face. Her creamy smooth skin and easy breathing were a welcome sight. She lay as close to her daughter as she could without waking her, kissing her cheek softly before closing her eyes.

Andie awoke with a start. The clock showed two-thirty in the morning. She sat up, feeling distressed until she remembered that her grandma was with her mom. The oxygen machine was humming in the living room, so she figured that her mother was fine or her grandma would have awakened her. She lay back down, telling herself that she must get some sleep so she could function the next day. Her body felt heavy and weary, but her mind was troubled. She closed her eyes, ready to let herself relax into slumber.

A moment later, Andie sat up, certain that she had to go into the living room. Hurrying around the corner, she saw her grandmother on the sofa, sleeping. Andie looked at her mom, who was taking deep gulping breaths in a slow, familiar manner. She remembered Mrs. Kincaid and the way that she had breathed just before she died. Her mom was about to die.

Panic held her still for a moment. She looked at her grandma sleeping, but quickly decided not to wake her up. Her mom had been lying there for hours and might have awakened to realize that she was alone. She knelt down by the bed and took her mom's swollen hand. Her rings were embedded in the puffy, purple flesh of her fingers. She whispered close to her mother's ear. "Mom, I'm right here. I'm not going to leave you, okay? You just relax, because I'll stay here next to you."

Her mother's eyes remained closed, but Andie thought that she had felt her hand move. She adjusted the nasal cannula, which had slipped out of one nostril, and then straightened her mom's necklace. She held her hand again. "Mom, I know you can hear me. You need to know something. I've always loved you and I always will. You've worked so hard your whole life and it might not seem fair that you can't stay here much longer, but God must need you in heaven." Andie tried not to cry. Her mom's mouth was straining upward with each labored draw of breath.

"You know what? I found the box that you kept. The one with all of the cards that you saved. I didn't know you saved all of the cards I gave you, Mom. That was so nice." Andie began crying and turned her face away, pressing her mouth against her shoulder to stifle the sound. She turned back, glancing at her grandma, who was still in the same position on the sofa.

"Mom, I'm going to say a prayer for you. God is right here with us and He'll take care of you, I promise." Andie put both of her hands on her mom's hand. "Dear Lord, my mother needs you so much now. She's prayed and offered her life to you. Please, dear Jesus, be close to her and fill her with your peace and love. She's a wonderful person. Thank you for allowing her to be my mother. Your Father created her, and now she needs you to take care of her completely. I pray that you ease her pain and comfort her spirit. Please put angels around her, Lord, and let her know that you're here for her. Thank you for your promise of eternal life. In Jesus Christ's name I pray, amen."

Andie put her hand on her mom's forehead and stroked her warm skin, watching her struggle for each breath. The pauses between respirations were becoming longer. "Mom, you've been a great mother. I want you to believe that. Thank you for taking care of me. I really love you. I promise that I'll make sure Dad is all right." Andie felt as if she were babbling, but the words were spilling out faster. "If you see angels and a light or something, don't be afraid to go. It's time for you to go. Don't worry, you'll never be alone. I'll stay right here until you go, but I want you to go when it's time. And you won't be alone in heaven. Your life is just starting the best part, okay? I love you and I want you to be happy." Andie stopped and put her face in her hands. She was tensing up and taking deeper breaths, as if she could assist her mother's effort.

"I'll never forget you, none of us will. You'll always be in our thoughts. I love you so much. You're a wonderful woman. You...you have no more work to do here. You've done everything you need to, so you can go. God will take you home, to your real home. Just let go. Your body has worked hard, and it's time to let it rest now. I love you." Her mom appeared to be rousing as her head shifted slightly, eyes fluttering open for a moment.

"Mom? I'm here. Everything will be all right."

Andie was overwhelmed with grief as she watched her mom fighting to stay alive. She began to say the Lord's Prayer, and then her dad came rushing around the corner, looking alarmed but half asleep.

"What, what?" he said urgently, looking at Andie and then back at his wife. "Oh, no."

Andie finished the prayer, crying without trying to stop now.

"I love you, Mom! Dad and I are both here. We'll be fine, I promise. We love you and want you to go now. We're going to miss you, but we'll see you again, okay?"

Her mom took in a breath and held it, never taking another. Her mouth was open and her eyes were closed.

The oxygen machine seemed too loud.

"Oh, Mom!" Andie cried. She put her arm across her mother's body and held onto her. She could hear her dad crying behind her as she squeezed her eyes closed. For minutes she remained sobbing, her stomach aching from the convulsions.

Still crying, Andie sat up and gently took the cannula out of her mom's nose. She stood and her dad leaned on her as they both cried, looking down at her mom's body. Andie slowly walked over and turned the oxygen machine off.

"She's gone…she's gone!" her dad exclaimed, crying harder.

Grandma Reeves woke up and said, "Is she…?" Then she took in the scene and hung her head. "I'm so sorry I feel asleep!"

"It's okay, Grandma." Andie said as she hugged her.

Her dad stood looking at her mom. He began to reach his hand out to touch her, but withdrew it. "I'm sorry, Joan," he whispered.

Andie walked back over to him. "Do you realize that God made sure we were here with her when she died?" Her voice was strained as she tried to speak through her tears. "I know she wouldn't have wanted to die alone. We were both woken up to be with her."

Her dad gazed at her from red, watery eyes, "I don't know why I got out of bed like that…maybe you're right." He wandered into the kitchen and sat down at the table. Grandma Reeves followed him.

Andie reclined the hospital bed to a flat position. She held her mom's hand, noticing the absence of its previous warmth. This emaciated woman, who had endured so much strife and discontent in her life, had been braver than she herself could have been facing death, she thought. Looking at the familiar face that she had always longed to have adore her, Andie realized that Joan was meant to be her mother. She was the only one who could ever be thought of as her mother.

She was her real mother.

Andie sat by the bed for half an hour in the dimly lit room. She looked out the window and could see the snow falling so heavily that the apartments across from their building, lit by the street lights, could no longer be seen through the blur of white. She wondered what her mother was experiencing at that moment. Her mom had joined the ranks of a mysterious membership; she knew exactly what lay beyond life in this world.

She looked back at her mom's lifeless body, still expecting to see her chest rise and fall. Leaning closer, she saw that her mother's face appeared to have changed. Where the lines of age had become deepened and accentuated by pain, and her drooping cheek and eye so pronounced before, all was erased and now replaced by a smooth complexion and graceful bone structure. Andie called to her dad, who was still sitting in the kitchen with his mother.

"Look at her, Dad. She looks...beautiful."

Her dad came over and stopped at the bedside. He turned on another light and then stared in amazement. "She hasn't looked like that for years. How can it be?"

Andie remembered how elegant her mom had seemed to her when she was a child. "She's at peace. She's in heaven and has no more pain." Andie reached out to her father, who had started crying again.

"So many years, so many years," he said, mournfully. "She was a good woman. She meant to do well."

Andie walked with him into the kitchen. Next to the sink were the mugs that they had used earlier that evening to drink hot chocolate. Andie picked up the white one that her mom had used. It was still half full and the impression of the shape of her mouth could be seen on one side, outlined in dried chocolate. Andie rinsed out the other mugs, but carefully put her mom's in the refrigerator with the chocolate milk untouched.

Three hours later, a hearse parked out front and two men came into the apartment. Andie's dad tried to talk to them in his friendly way, as if nothing unusual was happening, but he began crying, making a whining noise in his throat when they put her mom's body on the stretcher and covered her up.

Andie felt as if her chest was on fire from crying so much. Now, as she watched her mom being wheeled out, covered up and on the stretcher, she felt that her chest might burst apart. She had painstakingly tended to her mom's body for so many hours, that it seemed as if someone had stolen her baby from her and she needed to get her back to make certain that she was all right. She knew that she was not thinking clearly. She had not slept a full night for weeks, and grief had locked her into a whirling mass of extreme emotions. She was relieved that Rylee had not seen her new grandmother lifeless in her bed or being taken away on the stretcher.

Standing by the empty hospital bed, she ran her hand over the sheet. The depression of her mother's body was still there. Andie wished that she could talk to her just one more time. She remembered how they had all laughed about the casserole and how her mom had tried so hard to drink the hot chocolate, even though she had choked on each sip. She pictured her mom sitting in her wheelchair, enduring the pain as she sang the birthday song. Her mom was gone, and it was much too final.

On her mom's bedside table were a vase of yellow roses that Andie had given her and a photograph of herself and Scott together when they were toddlers. Andie was glad that she had put up the Christmas tree when she did. Maybe her mom had thought that they had been together for Christmas after all. She broke down crying again and had to sit on the couch. She was light-headed and felt as if the passage of time had taken on a randomly changing pace.

She had known that her mother was going to die, but the reality of it happening was abrupt and shocking. This biting grief could never have been imagined. Andie had watched her mother's rapid decline and valiant fight to live, then witnessed her last breath. She could not fathom how it would be to know that she herself was slowly dying, while her body broke down and betrayed her with its course into terminal illness.

Her mom had been so concerned about making sure that everyone had a nice Christmas present under the tree. Andie was upset with herself for not coming home at Christmas time during the last few years. In the hall closet, she brushed her hand along the red coat that her mom had wanted her to borrow. She had not worn it because she did not like it, and she had found a warmer, full-length men's coat to wear, which had been packed away in the storage room. Now she wished that she had worn the red coat. Her mom had been so excited for her to borrow something. She should have seen that it was important to her mom and worn it to satisfy her.

All of the chances to please her mother were forever gone. There was a finite number of beats for a heart, and her mom's had completed its mission of moving her body through its journey of life.

Her mother was gone.

CHAPTER 44

Andie called Mike that morning and told him of her mom's death. He cried with her on the phone when she described the details of her last moments. "I'm so sorry that I never got to meet her!" he said sadly. "Thank God you were there for her. She accepted the Lord just in time."

"I know she's in heaven, but this is killing me. I had no idea how it would feel," Andie said. She could only feel alternating waves of pain and numbness. There seemed to be no even ground for her emotions.

"I'm so, so sorry, honey. I know it doesn't help, but try to remember that she now has no more sickness, only peace and joy. I'll be there on the earliest flight available, which looks like dinner time. I love you."

"I love you, too. Be careful, okay?" Andie said worriedly. More heavy snow was expected. She tried not to imagine his plane crashing, but anything seemed possible. Life was so fragile and fleeting.

"Don't worry, I'll be fine. Just take care of yourself. I'll call you back soon with the exact time and flight number, all right? I really miss you." When Andie hung up, she prayed that he would arrive safely.

Early that afternoon, Andie, her dad, and Scott went to the funeral home to make arrangements, while Rylee stayed with Grandma Reeves. Andie handed over the grocery bag, which contained the clothes that she had chosen for her mother to wear. She did not want to see her in a dressy outfit, with some high lacy collar. Her mom had preferred stylish, comfortable clothing and pant suit outfits. Andie ended up choosing a white, heavy cotton sweater that had recently been given to her mother, and a pair of comfortable slacks. On the sweater was a beautifully embroidered picture of a boy and girl kneeling in prayer by a Christmas tree. A bright star could be seen outside the window, and its light shone onto the children. The words below them said "Just believe."

Andie also gave the man the gold cross necklace that Sarah had given to her on her last birthday. She wanted her mom to be buried with it. She felt that she should be tending to her mom's body, not some strangers. The two men were gracious and had a soothing manner that Andie knew was necessary to have when dealing with grieving families. Still, it was difficult to flip through the pages of the catalogue to choose the flower arrangement to be placed on the coffin, and to write down the format of the funeral service and which songs they wanted played.

She had been the one to make the decisions, because her dad and Scott seemed unable to make choices. Their discomfort was obvious as their eyes darted around the dark-panelled room where they sat around the table. There was nowhere safe to look, because the room contained every reminder of the reason for being there, so her dad finally stared at his hands and Scott gazed at the ceiling.

They were led into a huge room filled with coffins and told to look around and take their time. Andie wanted to stop this morbid shopping spree; no one had told her that she would be subjected, so soon after the blow of her mother's death, to making these kinds of decisions. She wanted to tell the men to just give them standard everything, so that she could return home to hold onto the shreds of memory.

After her dad had gone off down an aisle of coffins, which were fully equiped with colored satin linings and matching pillows, he came back over to Andie. "Your mom deserves the best. Which one do you like?"

"I don't know, Dad. How do you decide to buy a coffin that's going to be buried?" Andie was tired. She had not eaten since the the little bit at lunch the day before.

"Well, Scott's looking at that one over there, the white one," her dad said.

Scott was standing by a gaudy, expensive coffin. It had gold trim, bright red lining, and a frilly red pillow. Andie walked over to him. "Mom wouldn't like that one," she said.

"I was just looking at it. These guys must make a fortune off these boxes! Four thousand bucks for this sucker!" Scott said loudly.

One of the men had stayed in the room with them and now looked over their way.

"Could you show some respect, Scott? Or are you incapable of having any kind of consideration?" Andie said sharply, walking away. She heard his quick intake of breath and shook her head as she continued walking. She approached a simple looking cherry wood coffin that was in the relatively moderate price range. She called her dad over and it was decided that the cherry coffin would be the one for her mom.

When they left the funeral home, it was still snowing and the roads were fast becoming treacherous. Andie hoped that Mike's flight would not be delayed or cancelled. She prayed again for his safety, hoping to soon feel his arms around her and be comforted.

Andie and her father warmed the food that people had dropped off, and they tried to eat. Mike's flight had been delayed, so she made coffee to help her stay awake for his arrival at midnight, pending the weather. Her dad offered to pick him up, telling her to go to bed, but Andie insisted that she wanted to do it.

Her fatigue almost made it easier to handle the grief, because she was so numb that she would stare for minutes at nothing, her mind a hazy blank. She took care of Rylee and had explained to her, in general terms, what had happened to her grandmother. Rylee did not ask any questions. She had her mom giving her attention, and they would be going back to Florida in a few days. Plus, Mike was coming! They would get to go home on the airplane together.

The airline confirmed that the flight would arrive at midnight. The snow had abated early enough for the flight to leave Orlando, and the plows were already out clearing paths and sanding the roads. Andie watched Mike's plane land on the runway. It seemed to take forever for him to walk down the steps. He ran to her when he saw her standing by the gate.

"I'm so glad to see you," Andie whispered as he put his arms around her.

"You don't know how much I've missed you," Mike said. He looked closely at her. "You look like you've lost ten pounds! Are you all right? Hasn't anyone taken care of you?"

"I've just been busy. This is really hard for me right now."

Mike led her toward the baggage claim area, "I'm going to do whatever I can to help you, okay? As much as I'd like to stay up talking tonight, I'm going to put you right to bed when we get there." They picked up his small suitcase and went out to the parking lot. "Now this is cold!" he exclaimed.

On the drive home, Andie stopped on the side of the road by a field. "Come on, I know you want to feel this," she said. He had grown up in Orlando and had only traveled as far north as Tennessee. This was his first time to see snow. Mike bent down and picked some up, then he ate a bite of it. He kicked his tennis shoe toe into a mound, then made a snowball and threw it across the dark field.

"I should take you sledding before we go. Mom bought Rylee a sled." Andie hung her head.

"I'm sorry. I can't imagine how hard this must be. I wish there was some way I could ease your pain."

"You already have."

They drove on through the white land in the quiet night.

*　　*　　*

Just before the funeral was to begin, the family had a "private viewing." Andie walked up to the coffin and saw her mom lying in it with her hands folded across her midsection. Scott was behind Andie and Mike. Her mom's turban was tucked behind each ear in the way that she had not liked, so she reached into the coffin and pulled the material over the tops of her ears. Her skin felt like cold wax.

"What are you doing?" Scott demanded.

"Just what she'd want me to do, Scott," Andie replied.

"But, you can't— " he began.

"I'm not afraid to touch her." Andie put her hand on her mother's and again felt its stony coldness. This was only her shell. "It's the last time that people will get to see her. She wouldn't want to look goofy." Andie put her finger on the cross of the necklace to straighten it.

During the ceremony, she cried a little. She had already cried countless tears in the last two days. They did not have refreshments afterward, so people mingled for a few minutes before they drove off to the cemetery for the burial.

The ground was too frozen to dig down far enough, so there was a time of prayer under the black vinyl canopy next to the grave site. The wind chill was close to zero and everyone was cold, crossing their arms and leaning forward. The coffin would be buried when the earth warmed up, but for now it would remain above the ground. Andie placed a long stemmed rose on top of the coffin, then took off her glove and pressed her hand against the cold, lacquered wood.

"Good-bye, Mom. I'll be seeing you."

Chapter 45

In Orlando, Andie finished loading the dishwasher and wiping the counter. She had been back for two weeks and was recovering from a terrible bout of stomach flu that had hit all three of them only days after they had returned. Rylee had been sick on her third birthday, so they had given her a late, small party a few days before.

Andie felt as if she were on auto pilot. She was going along taking care of things, but feeling detached and sad. Christmas was in ten days, and she was not prepared for it in any way. She still felt sick from the nasty flu bug, and she had no energy.

She often sat looking through the boxes of her mother's belongings that she had packed and brought home. Her mom's old photo album, which Andie had never seen before until she found it at the bottom of a box, showed black and white photos of a teenaged Joan. She had been homecoming queen of her high school, and was surrounded by smiling friends in all of the pictures. It gave Andie bittersweet comfort to know that her mom had experienced some kind of happiness in her life.

She kept one of her mom's turbans and the socks that she had bought for her. She was given her mother's jewelry, but did not know what to do with most of it because she never wore large, flashy jewelry. Other bits of memorabilia were more important: the old fashioned measuring spoons, a recipe box with years of recipes collected inside, her perfume bottles, her sewing kit, her mom's Bible from her childhood with her name printed carefully inside.

When Andie had gone through a bureau drawer to help her dad sort out her mother's things, she found three items in an envelope hidden under a jewelry box. One of the items was a newspaper clipping of a dark-haired, stocky boy who had Scott's face. He looked about eight years old and was riding his bicycle through a puddle of water. The caption read "Spring is finally here!" and gave the boy's name. Her mom had written on the side "Scott's son."

Another piece of paper had a note from her dad to her mom that said "I won't be home until later. Don't wait up." On it her mom had written "The first night Richard cheated on me." The last piece of paper had only a date written on it. Her mom had written next to it, "When Andie found her real mother." The date marked the day she had told her mom about finding Sarah and had shown her the letter that Sarah had written.

Her mom had stored these hurtful pieces of everyone's transgressions. She had tucked them away to remind herself of how she had been wronged by those in her family. Just as these cruel facts had physically remained in her possession, they had never left her mind. She had never released the pain or found a way to forgive, so she had carried on stoically, knowing that everyone could be proven guilty. But she had paid a high price for it. The anger and sadness had eaten away at her spirit and closed off her heart from receiving love. Andie had thrown all of the papers away.

She wished that she could shake off the weariness and find a way to return to her life, but nothing seemed very important anymore. She looked at the calender that she had written school assignments on and noticed how she had marked down the last ten days of class in January. She would be graduating in only weeks if she had stayed in school.

She did not regret quitting school to be with her mom; she would do it all over again. She had gotten closer to her mother than she had ever been in her entire life, and her mom had accepted Christ. Nothing was more important. It was the bleak outlook on their financial future that was worrisome. They were behind on bills, since Mike had taken a week off of work to go to Iowa and then they had gotten sick with the flu, so he had stayed home until she was feeling well enough to function. Her grandma and his parents had both said that they did not expect to be repaid for the cost of their flights, but Mike told them that he would begin making payments after Christmas. There would not be presents for the children, unless Andie found some inexpensive ones at a thrift store. She had not called the school yet to check her status on the waiting list. She knew that there was no point in thinking about going back to school. There was no extra money.

For the kids and Mike, she tried to have a cheerful demeanor, but she would hear someone calling to her and realize that she had been lost in thought and did not know what was being said. She continued to feel sick, even though Mike and Rylee were over their flu symptoms completely. She did not feel like eating and was tired all day long. Mike had told her that she should go to the doctor, but she knew that they had to save any money they had for Christmas. The kids should at least have a full stocking and one gift. Steve had stopped sending child support while she was in Iowa. He had changed jobs and had not reported to the courthouse in Phoenix. It seemed that they were sliding down a hill of mud into a deep pit. Andie could not remember when she had last smiled a real smile.

On Saturday, one week before Christmas, a letter came for Andie from her nursing instructor. It read: "Dear Andrea, I am writing you to offer my condolences for your mother. I know that you will not be reading this until you return to Florida, and that will not be until your mother has passed away.

What you have just done is a most noble act of love. It is a rare thing these days for someone to sacrifice their time and future for someone else. Your mother was blessed to have a daughter like you. I know that it was not an easy decision to drop out of the program when you did, but I understand why you had to go.

You have what it takes to be an excellent nurse. Not many really do; I know this too well. I have nominated you to be a member of the National Honor Society and to receive recognition at our graduation in January. I also took the liberty of petitioning the school board to allow an exception in your case. As far as I'm concerned, you have just completed the most grueling type of clinicals any nurse could ever be asked to perform.

The board has okayed the petition and you are going to be offered a place in the next class which begins mid-January. You will not be required to retake any tests that you have already passed, so you will be able to graduate in March. If you have not returned by this first entry time, you will be allowed into the next class, no matter how long it takes.

Grief is a lonely, difficult thing, but time will lessen your pain. It really will. Let go and let God.

Andrea, I hope if I'm ever in the hospital, that I have as fine a person as you to care for me. God bless you, Mrs. Sullivan."

After she stopped crying, she showed Mike the letter. He could not understand why she was so unhappy.

"Even if there's a place for me, we have no money," she said.

"Andie, there can always be a way. Before you give up, let's just check everything out and see if we can get you back in, okay? You read what she said…you're going to be an excellent nurse. I'm proud of you, no matter what."

Andie called the school and reached an operator who forwarded her call to another office because classes were out for the Christmas break. She was transferred to the voice mail number for the single parent program representative. She briefly explained her situation and asked if there were any other places to get a loan or grant for school. She left her number, but figured that she would not hear back from the woman until after the holidays, if at all.

Mike spoke to her early that evening about her grief. "I've never been through what you have, so I can't say that I know how you feel. Have you been praying about it?"

"Not really. I don't know. I don't even feel like praying. I mean, I say a prayer for the kids to be safe, but I'm so worn out that I haven't tried much else."

"I've been praying for you, and I'd like to pray with you now, if you don't mind."

She agreed, so Mike prayed for her to be released from the hold of grief and to be at peace. He read some passages in the Bible that he had looked up about mourning. Andie listened and then pleaded to God to help her with her life. She asked that He become her strength and guide her through each day, because she had nothing left to go on by herself.

Mike made her a late dinner and talked about trying to go to the beach again soon. He gave her a back massage just before bed. She slept well that night and in the morning felt a freshness to the day that had not been there for months.

Rylee held her hand as they walked outside, and she noticed how everything kept on going after someone had died. She had almost stopped living along with her mother, but it was not her time to die. There was still pain from the grief, but it was not as overpowering every moment. Andie knew that her mom would want her to take care of her life. There were people who needed her here right now.

"Guess what, Mama?" Rylee asked.

"What, sweetie?"

"We never saw any snow angels in Iowa, but I think there're sun angels, too." Rylee had taken off her hat and was filling it with stray wildflowers and grass from their overgrown yard. "You just have to look at the right time to see them."

"Guess what, Rylee?"

"What?"

"You're my angel."

Andie prayed whenever she felt the gloom of sadness coming on too strong. She still felt weak and not fully recovered from the flu, but her spirit was lightened and she began to feel hope for the future. At the thrift store she found some decent toys and wrapped them in bright paper, taping small candy bars on them instead of bows. She let the kids bake sugar cookies and decorate them, dropping bits of sprinkles and dough all around the kitchen as they laughed and deliberated over the cookie cutters.

Christmas Eve Day, Andie vomited twice in the morning and again in the early afternoon. She had lost fifteen pounds since leaving for Iowa and was increasingly more fatigued. Mike insisted on dropping Rylee off at his parents' house and taking her to the emergency room.

The grim, tired looking doctor told Mike to wait in the crowded reception area. Twenty-five minutes later Andie came back into the room.

"What did he say? Are you all right?" Mike asked worriedly.

Andie was pale under the flourescent lights. "I'll be fine. Now I know why I've felt so sick."

"Why?"

"I'm pregnant." A smile spread across her face.

Mike gazed at her. "You're...pregnant?"

She nodded her head. "Now we're really in trouble."

He grabbed her and hugged her tightly to him.

"Merry Christmas, sweetheart," she whispered.

Chapter 46

The call came the week after Christmas. The single parent program representative had received Andie's message and wanted to inform her that the committee had decided to allow her to continue on in the program with full benefits, including childcare. The woman had asked members of the committee to decide right away, since Andie would be needing the assistance immediately. So, Andie finished nursing school, never failing a test, and graduated in March with honors.

All of her children attended the graduation ceremony. They sat near the front of the auditorium with Mike. Next to them, his mother and father were leaning over talking to the kids, who fidgeted in their seats as they glanced around at the crowd. Behind them were Sarah and John, with Tim and Eric, who were looking more like young men now. Lisa and Laura arrived and took the two saved seats next to Sarah.

When Andie's name was called to walk up front and receive her diploma, there was a burst of applause and various whistles and yells from her family. Andie blushed as she looked out at all of them, then put her hand on her small belly. She had felt the baby moving a few times during the last week and now it stirred and fluttered, as if it, too, was acknowledging her achievement.

Her father had called to congratulate her earlier that day. He apologized for not being at the ceremony, but told her how proud he was, and that he knew her mother would be watching her from heaven that night.

At the reception afterward, Sarah gave Andie a new gold cross necklace.

"How did you know that I…?" Andie began, uncertain how to tell Sarah that she had given the other necklace from her to her mom.

"When I noticed that you no longer wore it, I had a feeling that you might've found someone who needed it," Sarah replied.

"I hope you don't mind, but I gave it to my mom. She was buried with it."

"Of course I don't mind, honey. You know, we're all family. Everyone is a child of God. Some people just decide to dismiss that fact, or have forgotten that the greatest power is love. Although I didn't know her, your mother was dear to me, like family. I'm honored to know that you gave her something from me, because I was never able to thank her for taking care of you. I wish I could have given her more."

Andie saw her own smile in Sarah's face and felt a deep, secure peace. Sarah was her…Godmother. That seemed right. Sarah had been able to protect her by praying for God to watch over her all of her life.

Lisa and Laura gave her a gift certificate to a uniform store. "You may need some maternity nursing uniforms. This store carries some. We checked it out," Lisa said.

"I can see you now, Andie. Nurse! Nurse! Will you please stop eating the desserts off my tray before I even get it!" Laura smiled.

Andie laughed along, feeling pampered.

"We thought you'd enjoy these," Lisa said, handing her a bag full of chocolates.

"Wow, guys! They'll never have a big enough uniform for me!"

Mike's mother took Andie aside just before she had to leave. "I am so proud of you! You are such a blessing to us, Andie. Anytime you need anything at all, you just call me, okay?" She handed Andie an envelope.

Andie opened it and read the card. Inside was a check folded in half.

"You can't say no, do you hear?" Beth insisted.

Andie opened the check. It was for one thousand dollars. "What…?" she said, her mouth open in surprise.

"We don't want you to worry about working until after the baby is born, so you can study and pass the State Board exam without stress. It's from all of us in the Bible study group. We all prayed about it and want you to have it."

"Oh, this is just too much," Andie said.

"Please, Andie. Do it for all of you. My little grandbaby needs a relaxed mommy. Now, I've got to go. I'll talk to you soon!" Beth kissed Andie's cheek and squeezed her hand, hurrying away before Andie could protest further.

"Hey there! I'm looking for a nurse who can help me out in the evenings." Mike tried to disguise his voice as he approached her from behind.

Andie turned and hugged him. "For you, I'm available twenty-four hours a day." Over his shoulder, she could see Michelle, Rylee, and Elijah standing by the cake table, angling for another piece. "We'd better get the wild ones before their blood sugar peaks out."

Before they left, Andie spoke with her instructor, Mrs. Sullivan. "Thank you so much for all that you've done for me," she said.

"You're the one who did it, Andrea. I only made sure that you were given what you deserved. You take care of those beautiful children. Keep in touch. Let me know when you get your first job."

"I will," Andie said. "God bless you."

"And God bless you, dear," Mrs. Sullivan replied.

EPILOGUE

Andie and Mike sat in their living room watching the kids play. She would go to work later that evening, doing private-duty home care for a young quadriplegic woman. She worked three nights a week, which was just enough for now. Childhood was too short, Andie knew, and she did not want to miss any more of her childrens' early days than she must.

Eight-month-old Noah sat on his dad's lap, kicking his chubby legs as he watched his older brother and sisters move around the room. Their son was a small version of his father, blond hair, blue eyes, and a captivating, dimpled smile. Mike held him carefully, talking to him about what he was seeing.

"See Michelle? She's about to get in trouble for standing on the chair."

Michelle smiled bashfully, and quickly got down. The kids were planning to put on a play for their parents; one of many that Andie and Mike had to sit through.

"Now look at Rylee trying to put socks on her hands," Mike said.

Noah giggled and waved his arms. Andie leaned back against the sofa and sighed contentedly.

"Okay, we're ready!" Elijah shouted. The kids disappeared around the corner into the hallway.

Michelle marched out and loudly announced, "The Wedding Day!"

Elijah and Rylee walked slowly into the room, suppressing laughter as they strode purposefully, arms linked together.

"Dearly beloved!" Michelle said, her voice as loud and low as she could make it. "We are gathered here together on this day—"

Rylee started snickering, and then Elijah screamed and began jumping up and down.

"Stop it! Come on!" Michelle said, stamping her foot in frustration.

Rylee and Elijah had completely lost their actors' composure and were laughing crazily, knowing that they should not, which made it even funnier to them.

"Cut it out!" Michelle yelled. "Now, where were we?"

Noah was scrambling to get down on the floor. Mike lowered him and patted his diapered behind as he crawled away.

"I think you should just get to the part where they all live happily ever after," he said.

Andie leaned over against Mike. He put his arm around her, and they watched Noah crawl onto the designated stage.

"The baby's not supposed to come until later!" Elijah yelled, laughing hysterically.

Rylee had fallen dramatically onto the floor and was now crawling after Noah and giggling.

Andie smiled. It was good to be home.

About the Author

Julie A. Barnes is a nurse who lives in Tennessee. She is currently at work on her next book.

0-595-12225-6

Printed in the United States
817100002B